Praise for the novels of "master storyteller"* Patricia Rice

Much Ado About Magic

"The magical Rice takes Trev and Lucinda, along with her readers, on a passionate, sensual, and romantic adventure in this fast-paced, witty, poignant, and magical tale of love." —*Romantic Times* (Top Pick, 4½ stars)

This Magic Moment

"This charming and immensely entertaining tale . . . takes a smart, determined heroine who will accept nothing less than true love and an honorable hero who eventually realizes what love is and sets them on course to solve a mystery, save an entire estate, and find the magic of love." —*Library Journal*

"Rice has a magical touch for creating fascinating plots, delicious romance, and delightful characters both flesh-and-blood and ectoplasmic. Readers new to her Magic series will be overjoyed to learn that she has told the stories of other Malcolm women and their loves in previous books." —*Booklist*

"Extremely capable storyteller Rice bewitches, beguiles, and tickles your fancy as Harry and Christina discover that love is truly a magic moment in this fast-paced, sensual romance." —*Romantic Times* (Top Pick, 4½ stars)

"Another delightful, magical story brought to us by this talented author. It's a fun read, romantic and sexy with enchanting characters." —*Rendezvous*

*Teresa Medeiros

continued . . .

"Very sensual."   *—The Romance Reader*

"I love an impeccably researched, well-written tale, and *Must Be Magic*, which continues the saga of the Iveses and Malcolms, is about as good as it gets. I'm very pleased to give it A Perfect Ten, and I encourage everyone to pick up this terrific book. It will brighten your summer."   —Romance Reviews Today

Merely Magic

"Simply enchanting! Patricia Rice, a master storyteller, weaves a spellbinding tale that's passionate and powerful."   —Teresa Medeiros

"Like Julie Garwood, Patricia Rice employs wicked wit and sizzling sensuality to turn the battle of the sexes into a magical romp."   —Mary Jo Putney

"*Merely Magic* is one of those tales that you pick up and can't put down. . . . She is a gifted master storyteller: with *Merely Magic* she doesn't disappoint. Brava!"   *—Midwest Book Review*

Other Signet Romances by
Patricia Rice

The "Magic" Series

Merely Magic
Must Be Magic
The Trouble with Magic
This Magic Moment
Much Ado About Magic

Other Titles

All a Woman Wants

Magic Man

Patricia Rice

A SIGNET ECLIPSE BOOK

SIGNET ECLIPSE
Published by New American Library, a division of
Penguin Group (USA) Inc., 375 Hudson Street,
New York, New York 10014, USA
Penguin Group (Canada), 90 Eglinton Avenue East, Suite 700, Toronto,
Ontario M4P 2Y3, Canada (a division of Pearson Penguin Canada Inc.)
Penguin Books Ltd., 80 Strand, London WC2R 0RL, England
Penguin Ireland, 25 St. Stephen's Green, Dublin 2,
Ireland (a division of Penguin Books Ltd.)
Penguin Group (Australia), 250 Camberwell Road, Camberwell, Victoria 3124,
Australia (a division of Pearson Australia Group Pty. Ltd.)
Penguin Books India Pvt. Ltd., 11 Community Centre, Panchsheel Park,
New Delhi - 110 017, India
Penguin Group (NZ), cnr Airborne and Rosedale Roads, Albany,
Auckland 1310, New Zealand (a division of Pearson New Zealand Ltd.)
Penguin Books (South Africa) (Pty.) Ltd., 24 Sturdee Avenue,
Rosebank, Johannesburg 2196, South Africa

Penguin Books Ltd., Registered Offices:
80 Strand, London WC2R 0RL, England

First published by Signet Eclipse, an imprint of New American Library,
a division of Penguin Group (USA) Inc.

First Printing, July 2006
10 9 8 7 6 5 4 3 2 1

This book is dedicated to my loyal readers
who have waited patiently for Aidan's story.
Please let me know if he is as satisfying as you hoped!

Prologue

Outside Edinburgh, Scotland, 1734

"It isn't fair!" Fourteen-year-old Aodhagán Dougal's shout rattled the ancient timbers of the great hall of his home. His wide shoulders and long legs displayed the promise of the man he would become, as he paced restlessly before the meager coal fire in the enormous fireplace.

Mairead Dougal, his mother, looked up from the book she was poring over and shook her head in disapproval. "Learn to control your ill humors, if you please. The rafters cannot tolerate your temper tantrums, my boy."

Disgruntled, the tall, black-haired lad gazed at the dust sifting from the distant ceiling, but he visibly relaxed taut shoulders and took a breath before speaking again, this time more calmly, in the deep voice he'd so recently grown into. "If I cannot go to school with the other boys, then I want to go to India."

"You are too young to go to India," she said in the same even tone. "You have books here to study. The vicar will help you with your Latin."

"My knowing Latin will not repair the roof!" he shouted. This time, the coal in the bucket vibrated. Glaring, he returned to pacing the hearth, and the rattling halted. "Go to India with me. The doctor said warmth is better for your lungs."

She smiled benignly. "My place is here, and so is yours. The hills provide the coal we need for warmth and the food we need for the table. If you would learn to harness your passion toward more productive purposes, the roof would not crumble so quickly."

"I do not cause the roof to crumble!" He shook his fist at the ancient timbers. "It is old and decrepit, and the stones need mortar. I cannot dig enough coal to heat this place. I read that in India there are rubies and emeralds to be found for the looking. I can find them, just like I find the coal. There is an East India ship in port this week. I could book passage with them."

Mairead's broad forehead developed a small line of worry. "Your place is here, my son, on this land where your grandmother's grandmother grew up. It is your heritage. I wish that your grandmother had lived to share her knowledge with you, but I am trying to learn enough to control your gift. Give me time. Learn from my mistakes. You cannot run away from what you are."

"I am a great clumsy ox with a *gift* for breaking things," he cried, storming off toward the door. "I am not fit for civilized society," he added, repeating what his teacher had said after he'd broken a valuable lamp with his temper. "I am man enough to make my own way in the world."

He slammed out the timbered door, and the wind sighed down the chimney, shaking the hall's old stones.

A moment later, the door opened again. "I am sorry, Mama. I will fetch some more coal." With the calm assurance he'd been taught from a very early age, Aodhagán closed the door more gently this time.

"How can I teach him what he won't believe?" Mairead muttered to the wind whispering through the tapestries.

A tear of frustration and despair hit the book Mairead was studying. It would do no good to teach her son of his heritage until she could find the woman with whom he needed to share it.

Somerset, England, 1737

"No one else wanted the child, Martha. I believe she was sent to us by God in answer to our prayers."

Morwenna Morgan ducked her nine-year-old head and clutched the book in her arms. She couldn't expect strangers to love her when she was so unlovable that even her own father wouldn't claim her. The only person who had ever loved her had died so horribly, so suddenly, that she still could not allow her mind to dwell on it. She sniffed back a tear, refusing to let it fall.

"She's such a lovely child, John!" The plump woman standing in the dark vicarage parlor touched a hand to the wild auburn frizz of Morwenna's hair. "If we brush out all these curls and braid them, she'll look like a proper little princess. May we call you Mora, dear?"

Your name is Morwenna. Never forget it. I am here if you need me.

"Mama?" Morwenna lifted her head and looked around, hope and love filling her eyes. "Where are you, Mama?"

The plump woman looked doubtfully at the gray-haired man who'd rescued the orphan in Wales and brought her all the way back to Somerset with him.

The vicar shook his head. "It was a very rural, superstitious community. They thought her mother was a witch. The fire that killed her may have affected the child's mind a little, but she'll be fine once she's been here a while."

"I suppose, if Mora resembles her mother . . ."

The vicar finished the thought for her. "She was beautiful, and made herbal remedies, yes. It's an old and sorry tale of jealousy and superstition. Mora will be better off here with us, where we can give her a good education and upbringing."

The vicar's wife nodded in firm agreement and asked sympathetically, "Would you like a big glass of milk and some biscuits, dear?"

"I want my mama," Morwenna replied, tears finally spilling down her cheeks. "She's here. I heard her."

The woman smiled and patted her shoulder. "That's just your imagination you hear, darling, but your mama will always be in your heart."

Her mama wasn't in her heart; she was in her head.

Clutching her mother's most precious book, Morwenna didn't want the voice she'd heard to be her imagination. The voice was all she had of her mother besides the book, and she meant to keep it.

One

Mora Abbott shoved a lock of crinkly auburn hair beneath the plain rim of her cap and fought off tears by defiantly opening her beloved book, looking for guidance. The page fell open on *A Spelle for Trubble.* She already had plenty of trouble. Why would she need more?

She longed for just a whiff of the vicar's pipe smoke, or the scent of cinnamon drifting in from her foster mother's apple tart. She'd often internally rebelled against their narrow strictures, but they'd offered her a home when she'd had none, and over the years, they'd made a family together. And now she was without either again.

Both her adopted parents had died in the ague epidemic last month.

Orphaned twice and still unmarried at nearly thirty, she was free to do anything she liked now. Instead of letting the freedom intimidate her, she ought to find some positive use for it.

Why not start by trying the spells she'd been forbidden to use? She could think of no better way of deciding what to do next. Reading the receipt her hand had fallen on, she learned it was to be used to call for help in times of trouble. She didn't know what constituted trouble, but homelessness ought to count. She couldn't keep living in the village's only vicarage.

Perusing the page of required ingredients, she realized she had goose fat left from Christmas, and salt and thyme, and no one to object should she accidentally burn the pot. *Spirits* were a trifle difficult to obtain, since the vicar hadn't approved of alcohol. Perhaps the fermented cider from last fall.

It seemed exceedingly odd to have no one to question her actions, but she supposed she would eventually learn to enjoy living alone.

Puttering around the kitchen kept her from having to think too much about her lack of family. The duke who owned the vicarage was a kind man and would never throw her out, but she couldn't deny the village a new vicar by usurping the only house available for his use. She simply needed to find a new place to live. Somehow. Without family who must take her in, she didn't precisely fit in easily elsewhere.

She smoothed the page of recipes and mixed the fat and other ingredients in a pot over the fire, flinging salt on the flames as instructed. She couldn't imagine that such humble ingredients could produce anything except the smelly smoke that was traveling up the chimney now. Very possibly her mother had burned up in a fire caused by such foolishness. Mora had spent twenty years harboring an insane hope that the haunting voice in her head meant her mother was still alive and would one day come for her. But she knew it was past time to let go of that false belief.

Still, she murmured the incantation with a whisper of prayer. She knew she didn't belong in Sommersville. No matter how hard she'd tried to blend in, she'd never been as honest and good as her adopted parents, or as humble and accepting as the villagers. Always there was a little voice in the back of her head urging her to do things differently than she'd been told, telling her there was more to the world than her limited view suggested. If only the spell could tell her where she *belonged*.

In her youth, she had thought being good would make her loved, but no matter how hard she tried, even her adopted parents had come to accept that she would never be the proper little princess they wanted. That failure had hurt most of all.

At nearly thirty, Mora had to accept that she was cold and unlovable. Most days, it didn't bother her greatly. Practically speaking, though, the loss of her only family meant she had no one who wanted her.

The grease in the pot popped and bubbled, then caught fire. Feeling foolish at the dreadful stench from the burning grease smoking up the kitchen, Mora doused the fire with flour, and opened the window to dump the pot's contents on the garden. So much for witchery. The least the stink could have done was arouse her mother's voice to scold her for playing with fire. But Mora had ignored the voice for so long that it had taken to hiding.

A brightly garbed, slender woman stepped briskly through the fog outside the window, and Mora hastily attempted to blow the lingering smell away with a towel.

Since the first time they'd met, Mora had felt a connection with the wealthy young woman who had married the duke. She supposed it was because the duchess had book learning to match Mora's, even if Christina tended to be more athletic than intellectual. Mora counted Christina Malcolm Winchester, Duchess of Sommersville, as her only friend. An eccentric one, perhaps, but one who did not question Mora's unmarried status or odd notions as every other person in the village was inclined to do.

Mora opened the door to the damp spring air before Christina had time to knock. "You really must learn to use the front door or scandalize Mrs. Flanagan with your lack of ceremony," Mora warned her.

Christina breezed in, unfastening her rich cloak with a dramatic sweep that scattered droplets in her wake. "I have already scandalized her. I do not know how you hold your tongue so politely in her presence. It is more than I can do."

Taking the duchess's cloak, Mora ignored the old complaint. As the daughter of the vicar, she'd never had any choice except to be polite. Holding her tongue so often had fed her hidden mutinous nature—not to mention raising calluses on her tongue.

"The grocer just brought me a tin of his new tea shipment." Hanging up the cloak, Mora took the faded teapot down from its shelf. "Have some before you tell me who needs aid now."

"Tea would be lovely. Douglas refused to eat his porridge this morning, and it is now decorating the nursery ceiling. I could not abide his nanny's scolding any longer." Christina roamed the kitchen rather than settle in a chair.

"Are the maids blaming ghosts or Dougie's unnatural abilities today?" Mora asked in amusement. A one-year-old who flung porridge onto a twenty-foot-high ceiling made for much speculation.

"Both. You do not want to hear what admirable diaper habits he's developed lately." Christina came to an abrupt halt.

Her unusual stillness alerted Mora. Cursing herself for not hiding her mother's peculiar book, Mora set down the tea tin, but it was too late. Christina had already opened the cover. "Let me put that old thing away." Feeling oddly protective of the ancient tome, Mora reached to take it from the counter.

Christina caught her hand. "No, wait. This is fascinating. My family keeps journals just like this one." She flipped the old vellum to the title page. "*A Journal of Lessons*, by Morwenna Gabriel. *Wherever* did you find this?"

Mora attempted to wrestle the tome from the duchess's grasp, but Christina pressed her hand against Mora's, preventing her from closing the book. "It belonged to my mother," Mora admitted reluctantly. "Her name was Brighid Morgan, so I do not know who owned it originally. I had hoped Morwenna might be a distant relative." As a child, she had dreamed of having a real family, and Morwenna Gabriel had often played the role of fairy godmother in her imaginings. But she wasn't a child any longer. "It's mostly foolishness, but there are some excellent recipes—"

"But wait! There is something appearing beneath our hands. Lift your thumb. Look."

Mora removed her palm from the page. In the weak light from the window, she could see nothing unusual. "It's stained, that's all. It's a very old book."

Christina lifted the page closer to the window. "No, there—it's writing, just where our hands met. I'm sure of it."

Mora strained to see. She wasn't short, but Christina was taller than most women, and Mora had to stand on her toes to get closer to a page she had seen a thousand times over the years. "It's impossible."

"Heat," Christina replied abruptly, bringing the book back to the sink. "The heat from our hands brought out the letters. Hold the teakettle behind the page."

"That will ruin it!" But Christina was a duchess, and years of serving the church and her adopted family had taught the efficacy of obedience. Mora brought the steaming kettle to the sink.

"Gently, now. I'll hold the page. You hold the spout behind it." Christina lifted the book.

Trying not to harm the brittle pages, Mora swung the steam back and forth. At Christina's cry of triumph, she set the kettle down and peered over her shoulder.

An aging brownish yellow script appeared right beneath the author's name.

"It's an old trick," Christina explained. "My sisters and I learned it from one of our mother's books when we were little. You write with lemon juice and it is impossible to read. Add heat, and the writing appears."

It hadn't appeared in all the years that Mora had perused the book, but she refrained from saying that aloud, or from mentioning that her mother had been too poor to buy lemons. The duchess talked with ghosts. Perhaps she could read ghost writing as well.

Years of upbringing in the Church of England had failed to dispel Mora's fascination with supernatural subjects. Her mother's voice had faded over time, perhaps because Mora had been forced so often to deny its existence. Her adopted parents had disapproved of the spell book, but they had not objected to her experimenting with the book's herbal recipes. By selling possets and potions, Mora had helped keep the table full in times of scarcity. Making scented lotions wasn't the same as performing magic, her parents had reasoned.

Hoping the faded words would provide the answer to her prayers, and afraid that they wouldn't, Mora left the book in Christina's hands. "What does it say?"

"It's an inscription. 'To Brighid Gabriel upon the birth of our daughter, Morwenna, named after our common ancestor. With love and adoration, your husband, Gilbert.' Is Gabriel your real name? If so, your father may have given this to your mother as a christening present."

Struck dumb by the suggestion, Mora stumbled to a kitchen chair and sat down with a thump. The chair skidded a little, but she failed to notice.

She had never known the name of her father, had never been certain that her mother was married. Could she possibly have had a real father all these years?

If this inscription was meant for her mother, she'd been named after a *common ancestor*. She might have a family. The world as she knew it had just turned upside down. She was so shaken that she didn't think she could stand again.

Mighty heavens, was this the answer to the spell she'd conjured? Had she performed magic and found a solution to her problem?

Christina laid the book in front of her. The magical writing was still there. Her name might be Gabriel. Her brain froze.

"Gilbert Gabriel, isn't that the name of the viscount who lives in the north?" Christina asked.

"I don't know," Mora whispered, staring at the yellowed ink. "We seldom had newssheets." She caressed the page her real *father* may have held. "I had no idea—"

"You said Brighid was your mother's name, didn't you?" Christina asked blithely, settling on a chair with her tea as if prepared for a cozy gossip.

"Her name was Brighid Morgan, or so I thought."

Mora had used *Abbott*, the surname of her adopted parents, all these years, but she'd always thought her real name was *Morgan*, a common name in Wales. She'd thought her given name had come from the author of the book. Her mother was eccentric enough

to name a child after an author she admired. But to
change her last name from *Gabriel* to *Morgan*? Why?
None of the possible reasons were good ones, and
Mora shivered even while staring at the writing with
rapt interest.

She was aware her past was mysterious, that her
foster parents often whispered about her origins when
she was particularly defiant in those early years. But
she remembered her real mother as having loving
arms and laughing eyes and a carefree acceptance of
her childish foibles. That was the last time she'd felt
truly loved for who she was, and why she so desperately wanted to find her family now. The book had to
be an answer to her prayers. Or to her spell.

"*Brighid* and *Morwenna* are unusual names. Surely
it refers to my mother and me," she murmured.

Christina raised her golden brown eyebrows. "I've
always thought of *Gabriel* as a Scots name. I thought
the vicar adopted you in Wales."

"He did," Mora murmured, still dizzy with new
knowledge. "I'm Welsh. *Morwenna* is Welsh, isn't it?"

"Not necessarily. *Morgan* is certainly Welsh. *Gabriel* is biblical, so it could be also." She frowned at
the inscription. "Didn't you say the book was saved
from a fire? I wonder why the writing did not appear then."

"The book was kept in an iron box in the vegetable
cellar," Mora said, her mind racing. "The heat never
reached it." Perhaps if it had, her life might have
turned out differently. Instead of being the adopted
daughter of a village vicar and his wife, trying desperately to fit her wayward nature into their unassuming
lives, she might have lived with her real family—if
they could be located.

Christina looked at her with curiosity. "Mora? What
is wrong? Your aura is quivering."

That bit of nonsense brought a smile to Mora's lips. "I never thought I had a legal father. How would I find out if this Gilbert Gabriel is still alive?" She didn't dare express all her hopes aloud.

But the duchess understood. Her eyes widened. "If your father is still alive, you may have family to go to!" Her expression changed to one of dismay. "Surely you would not desert Sommersville? How would we get along without you?"

This was the only home Mora had really known. She had spent a lifetime watching the children of the village grow up, marry, and have children of their own. She had nursed the elderly and babies alike, laughed with their joy, and wept with their sadness.

Yet, she had never, ever been one of them.

Such aching longing ballooned inside her that it was all Mora could do to hold back tears. "A real family might accept me as I am, wouldn't they?"

Christina chuckled. "Families don't necessarily accept one's faults, but I cannot imagine any family not welcoming a calm, prudent, orderly woman of rare practicality such as yourself."

In her heart of hearts, Mora knew that wasn't who she really was. That was who the Abbotts had wanted her to be, and she had tried very hard not to disappoint them. In the eyes of the world, she was a staid old maid. In her heart—she was a terrible, wicked person who wanted to fling off her cap and dance beneath the stars with her hair blowing unbound. To sing with joy without people staring. To practice magic, experiment with herbs, think odd thoughts. In her very deepest, darkest soul, she longed to *live*.

Fingering the starched linen covering the tight plaits that held her unruly hair, Mora dared open her mind to the immensity of the world beyond the village.

"The village," she said, abruptly brought back to

earth. "There is none left to help. And I have no means to go looking for a family that may not exist."

The duchess waved her hand as if it contained a magic wand. "Nonsense. You've devoted your life to Sommersville. If this is what you wish to do, we owe you the opportunity to seek your family. Now that the weather is improving, Harry and I must go to London to round up my nieces and nephews and take them to Wystan. That is very near Scotland and the home of the only Gilbert Gabriel I'm aware of. You shall go with us!"

The tiny spark that was Mora's inner self flared and spoke in her mother's voice. *You must go, my love. Without you, he may die.*

"Who will die?" she protested aloud, startled by the sudden clarity of the voice. Had she really just heard her mother speaking to her after all these years of silence? Was her mother telling her that someone was in danger? Who?

Her father?

Instead of looking shocked, the duchess grinned. "The children are going to love you. Just think, your father could be a wealthy viscount. You could be a long-lost daughter whom he has mourned for years."

Which would mean that Mora's mother had run away from him, for a reason or reasons unknown. That was not necessarily a possibility she wished to explore.

Scotland, Valentine's Day 1757

Aodhagán—familiarly known as Aidan—swung his sledgehammer like a golf stick at the parapet of his castle home. A fifty-pound stone flew from the loosened mortar with the speed and accuracy of a ball, flying through the air, and hitting the pyramidal stack of previously smashed stones in the kitchen garden three stories below.

A shattering blast in the hills beyond echoed the stone's landing.

"It's a crumbling pile of rock, by damn!" he shouted into the growing force of the wind. "What care I if the old witch turns the cellar into a coal shaft and tumbles the eyesore into the ground?" The question was rhetorical since no one was present to answer. Winter-brown hills sprawled empty as far as the eye could see—except for a lone figure in the distance riding this way.

Aidan knew the folds and creases of the hills surrounding his home like a lover knows the face of his beloved. He had a sense for the way different layers of rock formed angles, which ones were under pressure from the earth's weight. He'd used that talent to uncover riches in exotic lands.

It was a fairly useless talent here, where the hills hid only a seam of coal—and the cottages of people who kept their small herds on the nearly barren land, the people who called him laird even though he was nothing of the sort.

Another blast of black powder in the distance shook the old stones, sending trickles of ancient mortar from between the blocks. With the fury of frustration, he swung at a loosened stone, one large enough to bend the backs of two brawny men. The stone shot straight toward the pile below, and the parapet shivered with the force of his blow—or with the force of his fury, as his mother would have had it. But his mother was dead, and he needn't heed her foolish superstition any longer.

Mairead Dougal had been a fiery redhead with the fierceness of a soldier and the imagination of a poet. Her tenants barely supported themselves, so his mother had never charged them rents, leaving her nearly penniless.

With the wanderlust and idealism of youth, Aidan had marched off into the world to seek his fortune. His instinct for locating precious stones had found fertile grounds in the mines of India. Over time, he'd sent home wealth enough to turn the keep into a palace. Instead it remained a drafty pile of rock.

He hadn't expected his mother to use the money to build palaces, but he had expected her to improve the lot of their tenants, and still have enough to keep from freezing.

When his mother's health had worsened, he'd sent more than enough money home for her to hire the finest physicians. Instead, Mairead had thrown his money away on moldering books and manuscripts that had done nothing to save her. She had died before he'd arrived home.

When he'd returned to learn of her death, he had wallowed in grief and nearly burned the books she had collected, until he had used one of the papers to scratch his itchy nose. Discovering the name of his father on the paper had been all that had kept him sane. He hadn't been much interested in knowing he was the by-blow of an English earl, but he'd been fascinated by the collection of half brothers he'd acquired with the knowledge.

Not that he'd informed any of them of his connection. He'd been almost thirty by then, a trifle old to romp with younger brothers. But they'd accepted him as a friend, and their Malcolm wives had been thrilled to learn that the moldering old books Mairead had gathered were part of their long-lost library.

Now, at thirty-seven, Aidan had harbored hopes of developing a deeper relationship with his Ives family—until the letter in his vest pocket had arrived. It might as well have been a sword point.

In the letter, his haughty neighbor maintained that she was the legal heir to his land. It seemed the viscountess was his mother's closest living relative, the only *legitimate* offspring who could claim the title. And she wanted to mine the coal seam that ran through the hills between their properties.

His mother's paper gathering had taken on an ominous new meaning. She'd known of this threat, and had been searching for a *legitimate* heir. Why hadn't she *told* him? Even though he had scorned the family stone pile that had brought such grief, it was home. He had no desire to sacrifice it to a rich woman's greed.

Attacked by a sudden itch, Aidan rubbed his nose with the back of his coat sleeve and cursed the untimely interruption. His nose never failed to tell him when one of his family was about, and they were never about unless there was trouble. "Go away, divil blame ye!" he shouted at the heavens before aiming another blow at the wall.

"If you insist," a polite masculine voice replied from the tower doorway.

His focus shattered, Aidan hit the stone off center, rocketing two blocks to the yard, missing the pile, and striking his cook's turnip bed.

"Aye, and apologize to Margaret on the way doon or I'll be havin' stale oatcakes and raw tatties for me supper," he grumbled in response. Aidan leaned on his hammer and glared at Drogo, fifth Earl of Ives and Wystan, his half brother—although Drogo was unaware of this blood connection.

"I don't suppose you've come to bring me a valentine. The only reason you'd leave your toasty hearth in London to visit these icy climes is the women."

Aidan dropped the hammer and brushed off his callused hand on his leather breeches. "Which of them is in the family way this time?"

Once Drogo had married a Malcolm female, the Ives family had been overrun with his wife's many relations—most of them blond, blue-eyed temptresses. His brothers had fallen like toy soldiers, one by one marrying into the eccentric family. And the Malcolm women refused to bring forth their babes anywhere but at their ancestral home in Wystan, a little over a day's journey south of here.

The silver accents in the thick black hair at Drogo's temples gave the earl the air of an aristocratic gentleman. Although Aidan sported the same black hair, large nose, and brown complexion of his father's younger offspring, he towered head and shoulders over most of his half siblings. Possessed with the build of an ox, he was impatient with the small rooms, elegant manners, and delicate ladies of English society. Scotland was his home by choice as well as birth.

Drogo held his reply until Aidan gestured for him to return to the tower stairs, and both men stepped out of the frigid wind.

"Both Felicity and Leila are with child," Drogo acknowledged, "and Ninian will not hear of them staying in Wystan without her. They've even charmed the vicar's daughter into accompanying them."

"The vicar's daughter?"

"From Somerset, a friend of Christina's. If Christina's complaints are of any validity, you managed to avoid Mora as well as all her other acquaintances when you were there."

Aidan grunted. "Christina's friends are too likely to be flibbertigibbets just like her. You are a glutton for punishment."

Drogo shrugged. "Mora seems sensible enough. I had to go to Edinburgh on some legal matters, so I thought to stop here on my way back to enlist you in my defense. Ewen and Dunstan insist I must stay to keep them company. I would prefer a more sensible head to balance their addled ones."

Aidan snorted and descended the worn steps with the ease of familiarity. "Do not ask me to play to the whims of your Malcolm wives. They are the most illogical, interfering lot of females placed upon this earth. They'd have my hair shorn, my clothes darned, and my manners polished before I slept a night under your roof."

To Drogo's credit, he did not mention that Aidan's shaggy mane resembled that of a Shetland pony, his clothes had too many holes to hold a darn, and he had no manners to polish.

"Actually, it's my stepsister, Sarah, who is more inclined to those pursuits, and I left her in London," the earl corrected. "The women are all nesting, which means they've turned every room inside out and upside down until I fear I'll be set upon the library mantel as an adornment should I fall asleep in the wrong chair."

Aidan snickered. "And you expect me to act as beast of burden for them? Does my home look as if I know anything of refurbishing?"

In truth, the old castle had undergone extensive improvements, thanks to Aidan's inventive half brother Ewen. Although Aidan hadn't repaired the ancient parapet or the crumbling tower, the keep now had a sound roof as well as the heat and running water he'd wanted his mother to have. He had briefly entertained the fancy of finding some good, fearless, *normal* woman to feather his nest, but he'd not discovered such a rational creature among the assorted friends and siblings of his half brothers' eccentric wives, or anywhere else for that matter.

"The women claim you are sulking up here because Lucinda painted a black cloud over your keep," Drogo offered casually as they descended the last of the stairs and emerged in the great hall. He acted as if he didn't realize he was throwing fuel on smoldering fires by mentioning the eccentric Malcolm who was said to predict the future with her paintings.

"I don't believe in foolish superstition and I am not sulking!" With outraged strides, Aidan crossed the echoing stone hall to a table near the fire where a tray of whisky waited.

Pouring a stiff drink for his guest and another for himself, Aidan was painfully aware of the letter crackling in his pocket that had driven him to vent his rage on the parapet. Perhaps he ought to leave his home, if only to avoid the black cloud approaching in the form of a neighboring viscountess.

Too late. The old church bell rigged to resound throughout the castle clattered the ancient rafters.

Aidan ignored the peal. Drogo raised a black eyebrow in inquiry.

Margaret, his maid of all work, hurried to the door. Seeing her employer standing idly by the fire, she shot him a glare that no well-trained servant ought. She dragged open the heavy oak portal and fell into a curtsy. "Lady Gabriel."

The crone swept past Margaret into the great hall and found Aidan at once. The viscountess had two daughters of marriageable age, but her blond hair bore no hint of gray, and her complacent features showed no lines. Aidan assumed the lady never laughed or frowned for fear of wrinkling.

She gave the elegant Earl of Ives little notice, pre-

ferring to turn up her haughty nose so she might look
down it on a man who stood a full foot and a half
taller than she. "I have not had your reply, sir."

As if the pressure of his temper strained the air, the
stones of the old keep shook, and the tapestries bil-
lowed. The lady nervously crushed her gown with her
hands, but she refused to be the first to look away
from their glaring contest.

"You'll have my reply in court, madam," Aidan responded, curbing his temper with enormous restraint.

When the candlesticks no longer rocked, and the
castle didn't fall upon her head, she straightened her
gray-cloaked shoulders to reply. "So be it, then. I had
hoped we could achieve an amicable settlement, but
you have inherited your mother's obstinacy."

"You thought I would simply hand over my mother's home because you have some idiot need to turn
it into a muddy quarry?" All on its own, the library
door swung open and slammed against a wall.

Focused on his nemesis, Aidan didn't even look up,
but Drogo and the viscountess jumped in startlement.
Obviously rattled, the lady recovered through sheer
strength of will.

"We are not asking you to move, although the land
is clearly mine," she continued with arrogant presumption. "You may live here as before. It's not as if you
do anything with the land."

"It's my home!" Aidan roared. "You would mine
the foundation right out from under it, poison the
water that feeds my tenants, bring down the barns and
homes their forefathers built, then let the whole of it
sink into the great pits you create with your blasting!
I'll see ye in court, my lady, and not afore!"

Even Drogo glanced up at the ceiling as dust filtered
from the trembling rafters.

The viscountess fearfully followed his gaze, then

jumped as a pewter pitcher tumbled from the shaky mantel. The cobweb-infested iron chandelier swayed over their heads. The crash of an ancient suit of armor was the final blow. Wide-eyed, the viscountess picked up her satin skirts and raced for the door, shrieking, "I refuse to let you frighten me! You'll hear from my attorneys!" The wind slammed the door closed behind her.

"Diplomacy is not your strong point," Drogo observed wryly. With interest he examined the solid— no longer shaking—rafters overhead. "Has the mining damaged the foundations perchance?"

"The place is falling down around my ears. She simply hastens it." Unable to fight the inevitable any longer, Aidan jerked the letter from his vest. "The harridan claims she is a second or third cousin. She was a thorn in my mother's paw for as long as I can remember. It seems the lady has been searching the Land Register and has found a codicil in some ancient document giving her claim to my home and lands. The estate is entailed through the female line. I am allowed to hold it for any daughters I might have. But with the codicil, it seems only *legitimate*"—he emphasized the word sarcastically—"heirs of the female line are allowed to inherit, and she claims to be the last of the same."

Drogo frowned as he scanned the solicitor's letter. "I am sorry. I have never questioned—"

Aidan didn't want him to question. He didn't even want to ask for the favor, except Drogo was an earl and knew more men of authority than he did. "I am willing to give it all up to any legal candidate who promises not to destroy the lands or the homes of my tenants."

Drogo tucked the letter into his inside pocket. "The viscountess . . . ?"

"Is mining her side of the mountain and wants to tunnel through mine," Aidan admitted grimly.

"I'll have my attorney look into the legitimacy of the codicil. Perhaps a bill can be passed to override it." Drogo gave Aidan a considering look. "Should I have the attorneys search your family tree for a legal heir as well?"

Aidan shuddered at the notion of Drogo discovering that they shared a father. What man would wish to know that his father had played loosely with another man's mother? "No, that I'll be doing myself. I thank you for anything you might find on the other, though."

"You will go to Wystan to see to the ladies?"

Knowing he was trapped by obligation, Aidan grudgingly nodded acquiescence to being beset upon by a tribe of meddlesome females.

Only after Drogo had departed did Aidan ponder the oddity of his itching nose when no trouble was about. The earl had not mentioned any urgent difficulty in the family that required his attention. It seemed the women were quietly breeding, with the vicar's daughter and Lady Ninian to attend them.

Idly, he scratched his nose and said thanks that he was not the vicar's daughter. Her life would never be the same after the Malcolms finished refurbishing it.

Two

"Imbecile." Aidan walked his limping stallion across an icy burn, stroking the animal's sleek neck to calm it. "Dolt. Oaf. Sapskull."

He couldn't think of enough names to call himself for abandoning his search of Edinburgh for information on his ancestry for a wild-goose chase to Wystan. Despite his promise to Drogo, he knew the ladies would do fine without him. They always did. He'd ignored his itchy nose while he'd torn the library apart and hired an attorney to search court records, but in the end, he'd talked himself into following his nose, even though the roads were still a misery. He'd nearly maimed Gallant by riding him through the icy *glaur*.

"Knobhead. Lackwit." He rubbed his nose with the back of his coat sleeve and proceeded down the forest path. Melting snow dripped from the evergreens over his head. "Idiot!" he roared at the bleak March sun peering through the fog. And he wasn't certain if he was speaking of himself or of his mother for leaving him caught between a rock and a hard place. He'd finally discerned the direction of her search and *that* had been enough to drive him into Bedlam. "She thinks we're bloody *Malcolms!*" That was the worst epithet of all.

Not until he'd started searching the library and seen

her notes had he understood that his mother had sacri-
ficed her health to research her family tree.

Didn't she realize he would have preferred to have
her and not the land?

Although why she'd thought she could find an heir
on the gnarled Malcolm family oak was a mystery.
Half Scotland could be related to them, he supposed,
and they were certainly a family inclined to protect
the land. Even he would gladly hand his home over
to any one of the Malcolm ladies if it meant keeping
it out of the hands of the woman his mother had called
"the Traitor," for reasons beyond his fathoming.

Rather than make sense of her senseless actions, he
had no choice but to accept she knew what she was
about and continue her search of Malcolm records.
The Wystan library held more recent volumes than his
own did. Traveling to Wystan to research the library
there would be more constructive than venting his
frustration on crumbling parapets.

He considered the height of the sun and the remaining distance to the manor. He had more than
enough time to reach Wystan before nightfall, devil
take it. He would have preferred a solitary night under
the stars to the suffocating proximity of a bevy of
Malcolm women.

Gallant neighed, alerting Aidan to his surroundings. His hand froze as he realized he was scratching
his nose . . . again. Cursing under his breath, he
halted, resigned to searching the area for one of his
Ives half brothers, or their women, knee-deep in
trouble. He could never be so fortunate as to have
a nose that itched simply because he had an intoler-
ance of trees.

"What are they doing out here in this damp cold?"
he muttered, sensing the air and the wind and waiting

for direction. "Shouldn't they all be by warm fires, heating water, and waiting for the babes to come?"

The stallion nudged his shoulder. They'd been together for seven years, since his return from India. Gallant knew his moods better than any human.

"I don't know how the lot of them find so much trouble to get into," he complained, following his nose down a side path. "Yes, I do," he countered his own argument. "They're forever running away. The unmarried ones, at least. Maybe once they're all wedded and bedded, I will have some peace."

A woman's cry of alarm rang out over the rat-a-tat-tat of a woodpecker. A crow squawked and flew off. Aidan increased his pace in answer to the loud altercation that erupted.

"Just come along, lidy," a rough voice wheedled from the other side of a copse of evergreen saplings nearly obscured by the swirling fog. "Herself's just been after sending you to a better place."

"Desist, or I will part the hair from your head," a woman's melodic contralto retaliated with regal—and ludicrous—authority.

Aidan had to grin at her fearless retort. He thought he'd met all the Ives ladies, but he didn't recognize the voice. Perhaps she spoke differently when not terrorized by a lawless knave.

"I've got a knife and ye don't," the male voice warned. "It'll go a lot easier if ye come quietly."

"Do you think me deranged?" she replied. "Who is Herself and why would she wish to send me anywhere?"

That certainly sounded like a lunatic Malcolm argument. Aidan eased into the copse to better study the situation. He hoped one of his half brothers was about, but their women tended to stray with some frequency.

"Come near me," the woman warned, "and I'll scream the trees down. My friends will be here in an instant. They will not look kindly on your threats."

She said it bravely enough to discourage the most intrepid of thieves, but this rascal seemed determined. Aidan could hear the hard crack of a stick, and he shoved hurriedly through the underbrush, leaving Gallant with his reins untied.

He reached the edge of the clearing in time to glimpse a hulking brute dodge a stout oak branch wielded by a curvaceous woman in a faded riding costume. Her hat had fallen in the scuffle, and her thick auburn braids gleamed in a bit of sun breaking through the gloom.

Auburn? Malcolms and Ives were all blond or black-haired.

Had he followed his itchy nose down the wrong path? Was there some part of his family in trouble, and he'd taken the wrong turn? He hoped not, because he didn't have time to look. This woman needed help now.

The brute grabbed the brave lady's stick and ripped it from her gloved hand. Flinging the staff into the bushes, he seized her wrist.

The woman's amazing blue green eyes widened in such terror that Aidan reacted without thought.

The skies thundered, and a giant strode out of the mist.

Both Mora and the thug manhandling her turned to stare in awe.

The newcomer stood so broad against the fog-shrouded evergreens that he could have been part of the forest come to life. Thick hair the color of coal fell in a queue over his caped cloak. The anger tightening his carved lips would cause a saint to tremble.

The square, solid bones of his features spoke of a character as strong as his brawny size and clenched fists. The narrowing of his dark eyes threatened menacingly. Mora should have been frightened, but his very stillness when all around him trembled conveyed an odd note of safety.

She could have studied the colossus forever, but she had only this one moment to save herself. With her attacker distracted, Mora formed a fist with her free hand and swung it as hard as she could at the thug's nose.

Her attacker squawked in surprise, but nose apparently undamaged, he recovered without releasing his hold. Focusing on the true danger, he brandished his blade in the giant's direction. "This ain't none of your business. Come no closer or I'll lob off that great beak of yor'n."

Mora had scarcely noticed the giant's nose. Strongly carved, with an intriguing hook at the end, his nose was that of an angel if he would free her from this embarrassing predicament. "This fool apparently believes I am someone I am not," she informed the giant, who was cannily sizing up the knife and its wielder. "If you would be so good as to inform the inhabitants of Wystan Manor of where I am, I would be most appreciative."

She was shaking in her shoes, but she'd learned to face her fears with scorn. In response, both men glared at her as if she were insane. Growing angrier by the minute, she brought her bootheel down on the thief's instep to show she wasn't about to keel over in a faint.

The thief howled and tightened his grip, even as his knife hand faltered.

Using her diversion to advantage, the colossus took one enormous step into the clearing, reached out his muscular arm, and grabbed her captor's coat by its front placket. "Aye, and I assume you've already sent bats to alert the witches at the manor?" he inquired, effortlessly raising the thief off the ground.

The action released Mora's arm, enabling the giant to shake her molester into dropping his knife while she was still attempting to translate his question. With the same ease with which a normal man would fling a hammer, he heaved the disarmed bundle of squalling rags into the bushes.

Dazed by her abrupt release, Mora struggled to catch her balance. The stranger caught her elbow to steady her, and for a moment, she thought the sun had broken through the mist; so warm was his touch.

In that instant, Mora could have sworn he was a gallant knight stepped directly from King Arthur's tales.

"Bats?" she murmured, basking in the heat of his gaze. Avoiding the mysterious depths of the stranger's eyes, Mora shook him off to balance against a tree so she might untangle her shabby riding skirt from her ankles and recover her senses.

"Or is it pigeons they use?" he asked inexplicably, looking down at her from his great height.

Having been saved from the hands of a thief only to land in the presence of a madman, Mora was slow to respond to the rustle of leaves that indicated another approaching danger. She nodded at the mist around them. "Beware, sir," she whispered.

Before he could spin around, a band of brigands burst from the undergrowth. Two leaped on the giant's back and clung like ticks on a dog, holding him captive so the third could seize Mora. She screamed and lashed out with both feet when he hauled her off the ground.

Despite her struggles, her captor lugged her through the clearing as if she weighed no more than a sack of feed. She grabbed a slender tree branch and hung on in hopes that her shaggy knight might fight off his attackers to save her again.

She watched the colossus abruptly bend forward. The two ticks on his back tumbled over his head and hit the hard ground, losing their weapons. Before they dared clamber to their feet, the giant swept up a dropped cudgel. He roared and swung it in a broad arc as if it were a claymore, causing them to fall back or risk losing their heads.

Cursing, her captor pried Mora's hand from the branch, but she kicked and fought, foiling his efforts to heave her over his shoulder. She screamed her fury when he was reduced to dragging her every inch of the way out of the clearing.

At her screams, the giant's black gaze left his attackers. Unchecked rage at her predicament burned in his eyes, and he swung his weapon recklessly to beat back two more brigands who were running to join their fallen comrades.

Five against one was more than any normal man could keep down. Mora could swear the ground trembled beneath the force of the knight's wrath as he wrapped an arm around the neck of a man who was daring to grab his coat. With a swift downward movement, he tossed the villain over his head with enough strength to crack his spine—leaving his own back exposed.

Mora watched in horror as a blade caught her gallant's shoulder, ripping open his cloak and drawing blood. Weeping in rage as her savior staggered and the thieves swarmed over him, Mora snagged a dead tree branch from the ground. With effort, she shoved the rotten stick between the boots of the man dragging her away. He tripped and swore, slowing down but not releasing her.

The rumbling thunder increased. Trees swayed as if

whipped by a violent wind, yet the dew-laden air remained undisturbed by a single breeze. The brigands glanced upward in surprise. Using the distraction, the giant blocked a punch aimed at him. With his hand wrapped around his foe's wrist, he swung his heavy load like a pike into a second villain wielding a knife. The two collided and fell unconscious.

Seeing his comrades fall, the rogue holding Mora aimed his fist in her direction. Before he could connect, Mora let her weight go limp. His blow flew over her head.

The giant twisted a cudgel from the last brigand in such a manner that a bone snapped.

With their attackers almost defeated, Mora sank her teeth into her captor's hand, foiling his attempt to seek a new purchase in her loosened braids. Screaming in pain, he staggered and dropped her.

Spitting his filthy fingers from her mouth, she jumped up and swung a foot at his kneecaps. He grabbed her arm and tugged, almost toppling her. Skirts flying, revealing her plain muslin petticoats, Mora aimed her mended boot at his knee again, but he jerked her off-balance before she could do damage.

She screamed her frustration. Seemingly in response, the ground heaved in fury, frightening her even more. All around the clearing, trees swayed.

Finally free of his attackers, her gallant knight raced across the surging, rolling ground to wrap his massive fist around her captor's throat.

A swaying pine crashed across the clearing.

"Drop her gently," the giant roared over the din.

Wide-eyed and pale with terror, the thief obliged. Mora nearly crumpled trying to stand upright on the lurching ground.

With a roar, the giant chased the last rogue away and caught her before she fell.

As his strong arms clutched her protectively, Mora felt cherished and safe against a chest broader than her view of the sky. She leaned her head against his shoulder and tried to stop trembling. Perhaps it had just been her own terror that had shaken her. In the moment he caught her, the sun emerged through the fog to smile on them.

She didn't have time to appreciate the welcoming strength of her savior cradling her head with a gentle hand, or the frantic beat of his heart beneath her own. A loud, unearthly groan broke the silence.

Mora glanced up in horror to see an enormous oak tree tilting toward them, its massive roots rising from the shuddering mud.

The giant shoved her into the bushes, covering her with his great bulk as the tree toppled. Branches crashed past evergreens to sweep them into their powerful embrace long before the trunk hit the ground with a thud that shook the entire forest.

Wincing at a stick poking her in the back, Mora woke in a thicket of oak leaves with what surely must be the entire tree trunk crushing her into a nest of bushes. Not until she'd brushed her hair out of her eyes did she realize she was buried beneath an unconscious giant.

She'd never had this much contact with a man, much less one as large and . . . imposing . . . as this one. The circumstances didn't allow her to contemplate the various sensations engulfing her. First, she had to determine that he lived.

He groaned as she pushed down a branch and inched out from under him. Thank the heavens, he was alive!

She knew enough of nursing to understand she should not move him until she looked for broken bones. She knew enough of weather to realize the freezing breeze out of the north, and the black clouds forming on the horizon, meant trouble.

She would concentrate on her immense stores of knowledge and try very hard not to think about lurching ground and trees that swayed without wind. She very much wanted to help this wonderful knight who had saved her, and not run screaming from his presence like a frightened child.

Three

Aidan groaned and squeezed his eyes shut against the thudding in his skull. He'd never been laid low in his life and had no experience with pain.

Cool fingers caressed his brow, and the scent of rosemary intrigued him enough to battle the black cloud over his wits, but pain prevented words.

"If you'll lift your great shoulders and sit up so I might put this behind your back, I've a posset for you to drink that will soothe the ache. Or I could spoon it into you, if you wish."

The pleasing contralto contrasted with the bluntness of her words.

"It's your choice," she insisted. "The pain of sitting up or the ignominy of a strapping man like yourself being spoon-fed."

Discovering that he lay on his side, Aidan grunted and shoved his elbow against the hard pallet to pry himself half upward. His other shoulder felt as if it would rip in two at the action. He opened his eyes, but the woman wasn't where he'd placed her voice.

Swift hands slid a lumpy, wool-covered object behind him. Head spinning, he sat back against it, wiggling his aching shoulder over what was definitely not a pillow. Eyes still open, he sought his mysterious nurse from this new angle. "What in hell is this?" he grumbled, unable to find a comfortable position.

"I have no pillows. I thought your saddle might work."

This time, he moved his throbbing head in the right direction.

She stood near a wall lined with books and jars of dried herbs. The light of a small peat fire flickered over her faded gray riding skirt. With some difficulty, he lifted his eyes to examine a tightly corseted waist and a high, firm bosom. The prim linen bodice and neckcloth weren't quite so pleasing, but he forgot their modesty when his gaze reached her face.

He remembered that face. Had it haunted his dreams? In the shadow of a velvet fringe of lashes, her eyes were a changing mixture of rich blue and green. Firelight caught on luxuriant shades of copper, gold, and wine in the wiry plaits of hair crowning her head. Tendrils fell loose and curled rebelliously at her nape and ears. She was a faerie come to life in full, glorious size and color. She was the most beautiful, intriguing creature he'd ever seen.

And she was staring at him with the same fascination with which he studied her. His heart almost pounded through his chest. Paired with his sudden memory of the courageous way she had fought her assailants, her beauty swept his mind clear.

Once he'd seen her from a distance with his brothers' wives, and like the smart man he was, he'd avoided any woman in their meddling company. Why hadn't he noticed her beauty before?

"The posset?" he demanded, eyeing the cup in her hands.

"I think I should have made twice as much." She stepped forward and held the mug to his lips. "Are you by any chance a boxer, sir?"

He snorted at that inane reference to his physique. And probably his garb, since only common men fought in the ring. If she'd seen him in Sommersville as he'd seen her, she hadn't asked about him. That made them equal in their oblivion.

Propping himself up again, using the shoulder that didn't hurt, he grabbed the mug and swallowed the honeyed concoction in a few gulps. The heat of it woke him to the cold of the drafty room.

Leaning back on the hard lump of his saddle, he closed his eyes again. Other than an erratic heartbeat from the shock of her unusual beauty, his head pounded, and his shoulder throbbed, but the rest of him seemed whole. Something warm covered him, and he could feel the fire near his toes. The room was little more than a gardener's shed, with the icy chill of winter seeping through the cracks.

The impossibly lovely woman wore no jacket or cloak—because one was under his head and the other over his lazy self.

"Unless you're the Witch of the North, put the cloak on. You're likely to freeze before I do." The posset must be working. He'd found his tongue.

"We'll both freeze unless I find dry kindling or bring your great beast inside. We need to reach the manor where your wound can be better tended. I was hoping you might recover faster if I warmed you."

There were many ways a man could be warmed, but life had taught him not to expect what he wanted. She did not strike him as the type to be amused by the prurient drift of his addled mind. "How did I get here?"

She laughed, a silvery chime that ran up and down his spine and heated the family jewels in ways she didn't intend. He'd have to make her laugh again sometime when he was in a better position to act on the sensation she produced.

Which made him wonder who she was and how he

could hold on to her. "How did I get here?" he repeated.

"Magic," she declared with a careless wave.

"Magic?" he roared, nearly splitting his head in two.

She looked a little startled at his sudden fury. The roar of wind outside the window distracted her long enough for him to temper his distaste for the mystical. "I am twice your size," he insisted. "You could not possibly lift me into a saddle."

"I daresay you're twice the size of most of the world's population," she replied. "I had to tie branches and your cloak to the reins to create a sled. It wasn't so very far, and your horse is well trained. The manor is some distance away, and I did not wish to risk either of you by dragging you too far."

It hurt too much to figure out how she had done that. He could not think of any woman he knew who could have accomplished such a Herculean task, but he preferred the prosaic explanation to the mystical one. He searched the murky cloud of his memory. "What hit me?"

"An oak tree." For the first time, he heard a note of uncertainty in her voice. "The earth moved, and the tree toppled."

Aidan cursed inwardly. "Earthquake," he muttered aloud. "The area is prone to earthquakes."

"Is it?" She sounded relieved. "I've never been this far from home. I wonder that no one mentioned such a phenomenon. Does it happen often?"

"No. There'll not be another." If he held his temper—if he believed his mother's superstitions. Which he didn't. Catastrophe just happened around him. There was no such thing as magic.

The return of his memory forced him upright again. This time he didn't wince from the pain. "Did you fetch the weapons in case those brigands return?"

Her hand slid over the bench behind her and lifted a knife. "I used it to cut branches, so it is somewhat dull. But you injured too many of them. I cannot think they will be back soon. I have you to thank for my life."

"I could have cost it just as easily." He shrugged off her gratitude. "Clever of you to use the knife. Have you a name?"

Oddly, she hesitated before saying, "Mora. Mora . . . Abbott. And you?"

He grunted and threw back the cloak she'd covered him in. "They call me Aidan." Since he didn't pass out from pain, he swung his boots off the straw-filled pallet and sat up. It felt as if she'd padded his shoulder wound and bound it as professionally as any medicine man. He studied his open shirt and tried to imagine her soft hands on his weathered skin, but his head wasn't up to the task, any more than it could imagine how she'd lifted him.

"Aidan!" she replied in evident relief. "Oh, you must be the gentleman from Scotland the ladies are waiting for. I remember you now—you were a guest of Christina's. They say you may know Lord Gabriel."

"Gabriel?" Was it his imagination, or did his head start pounding harder? "I don't know the bastard, but I'd like to kill him."

He ignored her squeak of dismay and rose to stagger to the room's one window. The sight beyond had him cursing under his breath. "We'd best leave for Wystan or we'll be spending the night here. There's a blizzard on the way."

Besides, the cabin was feeling alarmingly cozy, and he couldn't allow that, not while brigands roamed the woods and this fearless woman set his head spinning. That was asking for trouble, and he didn't need any more than he already had.

*   *   *

"Over there! It's either a monumental snow beast or Aidan."

Aching in so many places he'd lost count, Aidan readjusted his grip on the woman he'd set in the saddle before him. He'd wrapped both of them in his cloak when the blizzard struck, but her teeth had started chattering so badly he feared he'd made the wrong decision by insisting they venture into the storm.

He'd done it to protect her reputation and safety, or so he had told himself. They could have been snowed in for days without wood for fire and only each other for heat.

"Tell the women to stir the coals and fix hot whisky," he yelled over the howling wind at the men stomping toward them through the drifts. "We're near-frozen."

"You found Mora, then?" a deep voice called.

The earl. Relieved that Drogo was still here, Aidan squeezed his companion's waist a little tighter, hoping to stir her from her lethargy. "She was attacked by thieves," he called. "When the weather clears, we need to scour the woods for them."

He ignored the exclamations of male outrage that followed. He knew his reserve of strength was too low to track the scoundrels until after he had rested. He fretted over the intrepid woman in his arms, but he trusted she had enough backbone not to succumb to cold, if only so she could murder the miscreants when they found them.

His frozen lips formed the ghost of a smile at the thought.

With a hail to his brothers, the earl trod through the drifts toward the well-lit manor house to alert the household. Aidan slid off his horse, but before he

could persuade his sore arm to reach for his frozen
companion, she toppled from the saddle in a faint.
Terrified, Aidan caught her before she hit the snow.

Ice coated the lashes clinging to her pale cheeks,
and she seemed so still, he feared the worst. Not until
he held her tight against his chest and felt her heart
beat did he breathe freely.

"Take her in. I'll see to the horse," Dunstan said
gruffly. The earl's next-eldest brother took Gallant's
reins.

"Here, old boy. Let me have her. You look done
in." Ewen, a ladies' man and the youngest of the earl's
legitimate brothers, held out his arms to take Miss
Abbott. Aidan resisted, but she stirred in his arms,
and he feared the wound in his shoulder would cause
him to drop her. Reluctantly, he surrendered the frozen bundle that had become so precious to him during
these last hours.

"I'll walk," she whispered as the transfer was made.

"Then we'd have to drag you like a Yule log when
you fall again," Aidan told her, hiding his relief that
she was still alive and undaunted. "It's only a few
yards more."

He suspected her lack of argument reflected the
level of her exhaustion. He stumbled alongside, shel-
tering her from the wind as they climbed the manor
stairs.

"Why the devil did you allow her to roam free?"
he grumbled to Ewen under his breath while opening
the door.

"And when have we mere men been able to stop
our women? Mora makes soaps, and the scents are too
noxious for Cook. Ninian told her of the woodsman's
cottage, so she goes there to indulge her craft."

"I'm right here," a faint voice reminded them as

they entered the drafty great hall. "Lye has a strong odor."

"The thieves smelled it and decided they had need of a bath?" Aidan hid his amusement at her combative attitude. Here was a woman after his own heart.

The silks and scents and chatter of a butterfly swarm of ladies instantly raised his desire for flight. He wanted to crawl into a quiet cave to lick his wounds, but he had to know he'd caused no permanent damage by dragging Miss Abbott into the storm.

Following the women upstairs, he saw her settled into her own room before the door was shut in his face. Defeated by the ladies, who both fascinated and repelled him with their lunacies, Aidan followed a servant and his saddlebags to a guest room. He would check on his valiant warrior later, after he had shed his wet clothes and replaced his sodden bandage.

"There, she's coming around. You needn't hover so, Aidan. She'll be fine. Go to the library and help yourself to the brandy."

Floating in a pleasant haze, Mora recognized the gentle scold of Ninian, Lady Ives, and knew all was well with the world.

A distinctly masculine grumble followed Ninian's words. Mora struggled to translate it, but the deep bass notes were too soft and distant. She sensed the departure of a welcome presence, and a protest deep inside woke her more fully.

Ninian returned to press a warm cloth across her brow. "By the goddess, you'd think the man owned you," she said as if she knew her patient had wakened. "We should all try fainting in his presence to see if he would notice us as well. He doesn't, usually. You must sit up and take some broth. You're quite safe."

Safe. She might never feel safe again.

She could feel the bruises up and down her arms. Her ribs ached. Even her toes hurt where they'd connected repeatedly with shinbones. She hoped the villains ached as much as she. Never in all her days had she feared for her life as she had during those minutes that had seemed like hours. Recalling the injuries the massive black-haired warrior had sustained, she shuddered.

She had told herself that bandaging his muscled shoulder was no different from tending the wounds of the villagers, but she hadn't dared undress him as she would another. Torn between lascivious thoughts and her desire to help, she'd compromised and tied the dressing only to his shoulder instead of around his chest. She'd been taught that lusting thoughts were the work of the devil, and she had no interest in losing her immortal soul.

Although if she must lose it, her valiant knight was the man who might have it.

Needing to see that her savior was well, Mora allowed Ninian to plump up the pillows. At first she had feared the man called Aidan meant to murder her, so great was the fury upon his face when he'd entered the clearing. Instead, not even knowing who she was, he had leaped to her defense with naught but his bare hands.

He had held her against his great body through the snowstorm, warming her better than a blazing fire. Not since infancy had she been held so close, sheltered as if she was of great value. The experience had been so disconcerting that she'd given into numbness just for relief from the overwhelming sensations.

But now curiosity opened her eyes to the old-fashioned boudoir with its curtain-draped bed where she lay. She sought Lady Ives for reassurance that she was not dreaming. The ladies had insisted on the informality of first names. The wild part of her accepted the lack of ceremony without argument, but as the vicar's daughter, she had occasional difficulty remembering the command.

A pleasingly rounded woman with tangled blond ringlets, Ninian held up a mug of steaming liquid. "There you are. How do you feel?"

"Fine," Mora replied honestly, accepting the cup and sipping while she organized her questions. Why would anyone attack her? She had no money. She didn't dress as if she had any. Who in the name of all that was holy could be the lady the brigands had spoken of and why would she wish to kidnap a nobody? Or had they mistaken her for someone else?

"What happened?" Mora finally asked when her memory didn't explain enough.

"We had hoped you could tell us. Aidan is being his usual surly self and saying nothing. Finish the toddy. The warmth is soothing."

"Is she awake?" A tall, dark-haired woman heavy with child appeared in the doorway. Lady Leila, the only brunet Malcolm, glowed with the elegance of a Renaissance Madonna. "How are you feeling, dear?" she asked with genuine concern. She carried the scent of summer roses into the room.

"A little bruised, but fine," Mora assured her.

The ladies had welcomed her into their family home like one of their own. She didn't understand why, and she was still a little in awe of their sophistication. It had been a long time since she'd stood in awe of anyone.

Christina was young and something of a hoyden, so Mora had accepted the friendship of the duchess without too much question. She had no such excuse for the regal Leila's concern or the motherly Ninian's kindness. Perhaps she might understand Felicity's amity, since the younger woman was so unassuming that she couldn't intimidate, but even she possessed an air of quiet intelligence beyond her age.

"I don't know how Aidan can be an Ives," Leila declared as she swept through the room. "He shivers the air with his wrath, and brings tears to the eyes with his concern. Ives men are usually stone walls."

"Nonsense," Ninian replied. "Aidan is much like your husband, only Dunstan is more successful at hiding his feelings."

"That's just it. Ives men are all stone walls concealing volcanic passions," Leila retaliated. "Aidan conceals nothing, even when he tries."

In these past weeks, Mora had grown accustomed to these weird and wonderful discussions among the sisters and cousin. The women seemed to possess an extra sense or insight, which she secretly envied. But she'd learned to hold herself aloof and had not yet grasped the full extent of their knowledge.

"Christina claims Aidan has a hint of Malcolm aura, but she says the same of Mora. Perhaps we are contagious," Ninian said with a chuckle.

Settling into a chair to ease the bulk of her heavy belly, Leila dismissed the jest with an impatient wave. "Aidan claims you were set upon by thieves," she said to Mora. "We'll send men out in the morning to look for them. We've not heard of highwaymen so far out in this wilderness."

"They didn't ask for my money," Mora replied. As her brain cleared, she'd come to at least one conclusion. "They wanted me to go with them."

Both women nodded knowingly and looked worried.

"We'd better not let the maids go to the village without an escort," Ninian said. "I cannot believe it of any of our people. Where do you think they came from?"

"Criminals escaped from prison, perhaps?" Leila suggested. "It is a good thing Aidan finally joined us. They'll not come near while he's about."

"Thieves would have to be moon mad to come near the manor at all," Ninian said dryly. "Ewen would try out experimental rockets on them, and Dunstan would plant them like rutabagas."

Mora almost laughed at that wise perception. From what little she had seen of the earl's brothers, Lady Ives wasn't exaggerating. "That makes me feel much safer," she admitted, surprising herself by the comment. She wasn't the type who teased or joked, especially with lofty aristocrats who held the lives of common folk in the palm of their hands.

"We just heard what happened!" Christina raced into the room with a fair-haired toddler in her arms. "Mora, are you all right? I will never forgive myself for bringing you here if anything should harm you."

"But it would be all right if something harmed others?" Lady Felicity asked in amusement, entering the room at a more sedate pace as befitted her petite size and immense belly.

"Mora is fine, but she should have quiet," Ninian admonished. "The two of you are of more use in the nursery. What is Dougie doing up at this hour?" She reached for the boy in Christina's arms. "Come here, you naughty child, and let your mama rest."

Mora finished the warming drink and, as promised, felt much better for it. She needed to thank the man who had saved her life. She had never seen anything quite so incredible. He had tossed aside grown men with less effort than another man would take to throw wood on a fire. He had the longest lashes and darkest eyes—like deep wells of compassion hiding depths of pain. A woman could fall and get lost in those eyes, if she could get past his nose.

She almost giggled at that rude thought. He wasn't a truly handsome man. No man of such size and harsh features could be called handsome. It would be like calling the sea pretty. He was as dark and rugged as the hills of Scotland were purported to be. He possessed the beauty of the earth's craggy terrain—and its elemental violence and gentleness as well, if today's episode was any example.

"Just who is this Aidan?" she finally gained courage to ask. "Have I not seen him in the village?"

"Aodhagán Dougal," Christina replied promptly, frowning as her son reached for Ninian's box of herbs on the bedside stand. "You would have met him at my house if he didn't avoid women so deliberately."

"We don't really know who he is," Felicity explained. "He looks like an Ives, but no one knows the connection. We've adopted him because he seems to have no family of his own."

A kindred soul, Mora mused, or as much as a man could be, she amended. Most of her knowledge of men was based on the gentle vicar and the farmers of Sommersville. None of them compared to a force of nature like Mr. Dougal. But she could sympathize with anyone who had no family.

"He first appeared at my wedding to Drogo," Ninian explained, "when all our families were a little . . . unsettled by our marriage."

"And then he found Dunstan's son when the boy wandered off," Leila continued.

"He let Ewen work on his castle while I was looking for a book I desperately needed," Felicity said quietly.

"He always appears when one of our family is in trouble," Ninian added.

Four pairs of Malcolm blue eyes suddenly focused on Mora.

Unnerved by their stares, Mora reached for the active child who was trying to climb from his aunt's lap. "Ann-teee!" he cried in delight, diving forward, trusting that Mora would catch him.

After Dougie's cry, silence filled the room.

Mora prayed that the ladies did not think she had brought trouble among them. Despite Christina's reference to the color of her *aura*, she was not family.

Four

*T*he *vicar's daughter. She had to be.*

Aidan threw back a hearty swallow of good malt whisky. It was only midafternoon, the day after his arrival, and the ladies already had him diving into the bottle.

One lady in particular. If Mora was an example of what the clergy was raising these days, perhaps he should attend church more often.

He could bathe a thousand days in hot springs or icy snow and never scrub away the sensation of her bounteous curves pressed against his chest or her firm weight in his arms. His head was still filled with her scent of rosemary. No sweet flowery fragrances for his brave beauty.

His. Idiot thought. He knew nothing about her save her name and her courage. She had not come down for breakfast, although he'd been assured she was doing well.

"You can't arrive quietly like a normal guest, can you?" a male voice asked from the library door. "You must rescue damsels in distress and turn the entire household out in the snow to hunt for brigands who can't be found."

Without waiting for a reply, Ewen Ives entered, flinging off his cloak and scrubbing melting snowflakes from his hair. The morning's hunt for the thieves had been abandoned when it started snowing again, but Ewen had stopped to work on a frozen pump and hadn't come in with the others.

He eyed the whisky bottle Aidan had left open on the table. "It takes only a drop of that stuff to warm the bones. I wouldn't touch any more if I were you. I think it was made by faeries."

Aidan nearly choked on his last swallow. Coughing, he wiped his mouth on his coat sleeve and glared at the most handsome of his half siblings. "Faeries? It's good Scots whisky."

"It's not brewed on this earth," Ewen said in a tone of agreement, leaving the whisky alone but circling the table where a metal contraption that appeared to be half bird, half dragon, rested. "I'm saving the stuff for the night Felicity gives birth. One glass, and the world goes away."

"Aye, and you wake up wearing an ass's head." Aidan slammed the glass down and glanced around for something else to distract him.

"He knows Shakespeare!" Ewen crowed mockingly, examining his strange contraption.

"We read him off stone tablets in school." Restlessly, Aidan paced to the fire and watched as Ewen adjusted a wing on the dragon-bird. "What the devil is that?"

Ewen stepped back to eye the device critically. "Either a flying machine or a dangerous toy for Jamie's second birthday. I'll have to take the wings off to carry it up to the roof and find out."

Aidan rolled his eyes and wished for more whisky. Or half a stag. He was fair famished. And trying hard not to think of the woman abovestairs. "And what will you have accomplished if the contraption flies over the trees, never to be seen again?"

"Success!" Ewen flashed the devastating grin that

had had ladies falling at his feet before he'd discovered Felicity. "A pity we couldn't fly on it to find those brigands of yours. They appear to have fled north."

"The rogues had the accents of the north. I should have stomped them while I had the chance."

"Six of them? All by yourself? With Mora in your arms? Now, there's a fine conceit." Ewen shoved his coattail back and rummaged in his breeches pocket as a maid arrived bearing coffee and pastries.

"How have I missed that one?" Relieved to have something to occupy his hands, Aidan snatched a sugar cake before the tray reached the table.

"She's from Sommersville. You must have seen her when you were there chasing the duke's ghosts." Ewen produced a small tool and began adjusting a piece on his flying machine. "Of course, you so assiduously avoid women that you might easily miss a mousy one like that."

Mousy! Aidan wanted to roar in protest, but Ewen was a clever brat. He could be trying to get a rise out of him. He could play ignorant, too. "Ah, she's one of the older, married sisters, then. I've not met them."

"Sisters?" Ewen looked up in obvious confusion. "As far as I'm aware, she has no sisters. The vicar and his wife couldn't have children. They adopted her when she was a child."

"She's not a Malcolm?" he asked in puzzlement. If she wasn't somehow related—why had his nose itched?

"Of course not!" Ewen was indignant. "Didn't you notice her hair? There are no red-haired Malcolms. Do you always close your eyes when the women are in the room?"

He would if he could, but he had to keep his eye on them every minute for fear they'd set his pants on fire or trip him into a lady's bed with their meddling antics. "Lucinda dyed her hair red once," he pointed out, to keep from sounding too simple.

The lady wasn't a Malcolm. That was a great load off his mind. His half brothers had been mad to knowingly marry into the family of would-be witches that called themselves Malcolm.

He supposed he could understand why his mother had wanted to believe she had a distant Malcolm relation whose claim could supersede that of the Gabriels. The daughters of dukes and marquesses could easily defeat the viscountess in court. And he had to admit, they had a generous care for the land. But for all else, a simple vicar's daughter was more to his liking.

At least he hadn't terrified her. That was a promising start.

"Then why is she here?" Aidan asked, too curious to bite back his question. "Is she a nursemaid? You can't have enough of those the way the lot of you breed."

Ewen grinned, taking no offense. "Her adopted parents died. She's looking for her real family, as I understand it. Since she is originally from Wales, I'm not entirely certain why Christina has brought her here, but I imagine there's a reason."

"There you are!" Felicity slipped into the room in a rustle of petticoats. "Mora is in the drawing room. She would like to thank you."

"Thank me?" her husband teased. "I repaired her old tester bed rather well, did I not?"

Felicity snatched a pastry from the tray and glanced sympathetically at Aidan. "If my husband's arrogance swells his head any bigger, you have my permission to puncture it. Just do it outside so the maids needn't clean up afterward . . . after you speak with Mora."

The lady wanted to thank him? Frozen to the spot,

Aidan let the banter pass right by him. What if his forest sprite wasn't the fascinating woman his over-heated brain had conjured? How many times had he sought out women, believing them to be the helpmeet that he'd hoped for, only to discover they were as faint of heart or poor of spirit as any other?

He wanted to settle down to a peaceful, normal sort of life. He'd had quite enough of the restless, troubled kind. A vicar's daughter sounded very promising. Then again, if she was a missish mouse or an addlepate, best to know it now so he could go on as before. He needed a woman who faced falling towers and toppling trees without fear or foolish superstition.

Aidan dusted sugar off his coat. Leaving Felicity to spar with her husband, he crossed the great hall, anxious to see his fantasy again. He'd combed his hair and changed his coat when he'd returned from search-ing the woods. His shoulder ached, but the binding hadn't leaked. He was about as presentable as he knew how to be.

He approached the drawing room with a trepidation he seldom experienced. If this anxious hope was any-thing akin to what his half siblings felt for their wives, it was a miserable way to exist, but curiosity compelled him forward.

It was just his luck that after all these years of searching, he'd find the ideal wife just as he was about to lose his land. He was here to research his fate in the Wystan library. That's what he ought to be doing instead of mooning over a female who could cast a spell with the flash of her extraordinary eyes.

Feminine laughter from the drawing room should have spurred him back to the masculine security of the library. Instead of retreating as all logic dictated, he slowed to enjoy a husky chuckle unlike the higher-pitched chimes of the other woman. He strained to hear the ladies' words but had to step closer before they were audible.

"You are wicked to poke fun at poor Mrs. Flanagan," the melodic contralto was insisting. "She means well, and I cannot give up my concern for my neighbors."

"Writing the old gossip proves you are still the vicar's daughter when you have no need to be," he heard Christina chide. "You should have seen the livid green in her aura when we told her you would be traveling with us."

"That is only because she dreams of traveling to London in an elegant carriage, not because she envies my position as companion and nanny."

Aidan relaxed and smiled at the lady's commonsensical reply to the duchess's delusions. A vicar's daughter and a nanny! He supposed the prim braids and cap suited those positions, but he had seen her courage. She was far more than she appeared or claimed to be.

He could hardly believe his good fortune in finding a rational woman in this household of fey Malcolms. Learning more about her was worth risking the infernal company of the other ladies.

He propped his shoulder against the doorjamb and crossed his arms while admiring the scene in the cozy drawing room. A fire burned merrily in the grate. Lamps had been lit to combat the wintry day beyond the tall mullioned front windows. The velvet curtains should have been drawn to keep out the draft, but the woman at the desk with her back half turned to the door was gazing at the falling snowflakes instead of attending to her letter, although her hand remained poised above the stationery.

She was every bit as striking as he remembered. A little over average height, solidly built and not frail, she sat with back straight, revealing the full glory of her generous curves. The lamplight cast shadows below her slanted cheekbone. He wished she would turn his way so he could admire the contrast of sensual red lips with her prim little nose.

To his delight, she looked up to meet his gaze. Aidan felt a jolt much like recognition, as if he'd finally found the treasure he'd misplaced. He'd had that feeling in India, just before he uncovered his fortune—after which thieves had attacked him. His resultant fury had been followed by an earthquake that had nearly destroyed a village. It remained to be seen if this treasure meant equal disaster.

It almost had yesterday, he acknowledged soberly, straightening from his lounging position.

Her hand continued to guide the quill across the page as if it had no need of her attention while their gazes locked. He thought he'd imagined the luminous quality of her turquoise eyes, but the vivid contrast with her dark lashes held him entranced.

At her companion's silence, Christina glanced up. "There you are. I don't believe the two of you met in Sommersville when Aidan last visited us, did you?"

Aidan heard the laughter in her query. The she-devil knew he avoided meeting the women her family collected.

"Mora, meet Aidan Dougal," the duchess continued, acknowledging Mora's gender over any rank Aidan might possess, in the usual Malcolm manner. "Aidan, this is Mora Abbott, a friend of ours come to help us in our hour of need."

Nervously, he tugged his neckcloth into place. He hated the things. He didn't know why he pretended to be what he was not.

Yes, he did. As he stepped into the lady's presence,

he was smitten all over again by the wisdom in her eyes.

"I owe you my life, Mr. Dougal," she said, apparently not affected by muteness as he was. "I cannot thank you enough."

"Dinnae fash yerself," he replied, reverting to the accent of his youth.

Christina giggled disrespectfully and settled back in her chair like a good chaperone.

"It is glad I am to see you well." That didn't sound right either. He'd never in his life been knocked spinning off course by a pretty face. Shouldn't he be too old to start now?

"Your shoulder?" the lady asked with a questioning lift of her eyebrow. "How does it fare?"

"His shoulder?" Christina was on her feet in an instant, shooting him an accusing glare. "You were injured? And did not tell Ninian?"

"It is naught but a scratch," he growled.

"Men! You are such babies. I'll be right back." She ran from the room, apparently in search of the Malcolm healer.

"The duchess is a trifle impulsive," the lady agreed, interpreting his scowl correctly. "You needn't wait on me. The ladies are bored and looking for any diversion. Hide before they all descend upon you."

A fellow conspirator in his war against the fey Malcolms! Aidan almost grinned. "Only if I might whisk you away with me. I have never met such a warrior as yourself. Might I call you Athena?"

A flicker of laughter danced in her marvelous eyes, but otherwise, she sat as still and primly as a vicar's daughter should.

"Athena, indeed," she murmured in a voice smoother than the whisky he'd just consumed. "Re-

gardless of how it might have looked, I am no warrior.
I make candles and soaps. Won't you have a seat?"

He knew their proximity without a chaperone was
improper, but if she did not care, neither would he.
He should probably flee before the ladies stripped him
half-naked to mend his wounds, but it would take a
brace of oxen to drag him from this woman's presence
before he had a chance to learn more about her. He'd
thought he'd go mad this past day waiting to see her
again. He took the chair Christina had vacated.

"Not candles scented with sorcery or soaps laced
with magic?" he asked, not entirely jesting, since the
Malcolms claimed to create such things.

She smiled faintly. "I am not so talented as that.
You are the one who made the ground tremble."

A silence rose between them at the memory of the
unnatural shaking of the forest yesterday.

"It was an earth tremor," he repeated, to reassure
her. "I have felt the like before. We have them in my
home north of here."

"An earth tremor? Isn't that what sank Atlantis?"

Her interest seduced him into reeling out his reply
longer than he normally would have. "Atlantis is fic-
tion, but tremors are real. When I was in India, the
waters rose from the riverbanks and the ground
opened into lakes. The tremors here are much
milder."

"Then we should thank God for his timely intervention."

Relieved that she accepted his explanation without
giving it some superstitious, mumbo jumbo twist as his
mother had, Aidan nodded. "But do not tell the others or they'll be crawling aboot, looking for cracks in
the earth or setting up altars to the goddess of nature,
or some such."

A chuckle bubbled up from deep in her throat, and

he had to force his gaze not to drift to the lacy white linen covering the full curves that had left such an impression upon his chest.

Mora thought the floor had trembled with Mr. Dougal's entrance. Somewhere in the back of her mind she was aware of the snow falling outside the luxurious room, the quill in her hand, and the fine paper beneath her fingers, but every other particle of her being was focused upon this man who reeked of the outdoors and appeared as out of place in the delicate floral room as a Greek god.

Aidan Dougal didn't dress like a gentleman. He wore a rough woolen coat of a brown and black herringbone weave that would never be donned in the fashionable south, although its ruggedness suited his broad shoulders. His brown leather vest hung unfastened over a linen neckcloth that appeared to be of good quality, although it had plainly not been starched.

A vision of this giant wearing a colorful plaid over his shoulder, and a kilt around his waist, momentarily obscured the reality of doeskin breeches and knee-high boots. Clubbed in back, his long black hair accented the weathered angles of his cheekbones and the firm jut of his square chin. She could almost swear she heard the haunting sound of a bagpipe in the distance, but she thought it might be his bravery and assurance that conjured the image.

"The ladies are rather unusual in their beliefs, for which I am grateful," Mora observed. "They have not said a word of censure regarding our arrival together last night."

He almost looked alarmed and rose as if to escape the impropriety of their being alone. Mora hastily gestured for him to halt. "No, please, I—"

The letter she'd been writing blew off the desk in the breeze from her movement. It wafted across the room on the currents of drafty windows and the heat roaring in the fireplace.

A man as large as Aidan Dougal shouldn't be able to move so swiftly and gracefully, but he caught the paper with a simple sweep of his arm and clasp of his hand. With a bow, he returned it to her. His nimbleness shouldn't surprise her. She had seen him duck and dodge and swing to great effect just yesterday. He was amazing to watch.

"Thank you, sir." She dipped her head to hide her blush at his closeness. The other gentlemen currently occupying the manor were large, handsome, and much better dressed than this one, but she did not have the same reaction to them as she did to Mr. Dougal. His presence prickled her skin and flushed her with warmth.

"I fear I startled you. I am not accustomed to delicate ladies like yourself."

He spoke with blunt honesty rather than the charming flattery of a more polished gentleman, so his words took her by surprise. Delicate? Even after bearing a child, Christina was more slender than Mora had ever been.

She blushed deeper. For years she'd rebuffed the overtures of farmers and merchants alike. Why did this man's reluctant rumble cause her to tingle as the attentions of others did not?

Trying to regain her normal composure, she used her palm to smooth the paper he'd rescued. She was usually quick with her tongue, but it seemed to be tied in knots while he hovered.

"I am not—" she started to demur when her gaze caught the writing on the paper beneath her hand.

The writing wasn't hers. The words were not English.

She stared at it in puzzlement, wondering if her brain had been damaged by yesterday's incident, and if she should retire to her room and rest. That was precisely the advice she would have given anyone else who had told her that strange writing had appeared where before there had been only her own words.

She was extremely aware of the masculine presence near her, but the writing may as well have been in dancing flame. She could not tear her gaze away. "What does *bagairt* mean?" she murmured, touching the bold, looping characters that did not in any way resemble her own formal copperplate.

"Threat, threatening," he replied promptly. "Are ye being threatened?"

His deep, masculine tone of concern startled her, but not his reply. She had unconsciously known he'd have the translation. "I shouldn't think so," she said with her usual calmness, although the strange words were alarming. "Unless you are in the habit of frightening women."

She was generally a shrewd judge of character. She couldn't imagine this frank man would have switched papers on her, or done it with such sleight of hand that she had not noticed. Yet she could think of no other explanation for the appearance of this odd message.

She had no reason to keep the paper from him when he snatched it from her fingers without hesitation or apology.

"What is the meaning of this?" he demanded as he scanned it, using a tone so belligerent that she was jarred from her trance.

She stared at the paper that he shook beneath her

nose. "I rather thought you could tell me. It does not appear to be in English."

"I should have known!" With a disparaging gesture, he flung the sheet onto the desk. "You are one of *them*," he said in such a tone of disgust that Mora sincerely hoped she wasn't whatever he thought her. "Well, madam, I will not fall for your trickery. Go haunt some other poor fool and make his mind such a muddle that he doesn't know up from down."

He started to walk away, and suddenly afraid, Mora didn't wish to be left alone. Had her hand written that message unbeknownst to her? How was that possible? What could it say? He couldn't leave her with this mystery!

"I am myself and not anyone else," she said sharply to his back. "I have no need of trickery, since men are quite easily muddled without it. But I cannot read this writing, so if you wish to frighten me with the message, you are not succeeding."

Clenching his great hands at his side, he swung around. His dark eyes blazed, and Mora thought she really ought to be more afraid of him than of the letter. But she wasn't. She was very proud when her fingers trembled only slightly as she held out the sheet. "Is this some kind of warning? Do you think Christina has stirred one of her ghosts?"

"I think it's all flimflammery." He snatched the sheet and skimmed it again. "This is your writing, the part telling of your journey from London?"

She nodded, relieved that reluctant curiosity had replaced his abrupt anger. "I've never been anywhere before, so I've been indulging in a daily diary of my travels. I wished to assure my father's parishioners that I'm quite safe, and Mrs. Flanagan is the one who will happily spread the word."

He grunted and relaxed slightly. "Then the women are up to some mischief, no doubt. They've picked up a bit of the Scots language and thought to show off."

Mora could not imagine how. The only hands that letter touched were hers and his. But a man who held the odd talents of the ladies in such disrespect would not like to hear that. Accustomed to hiding her thoughts, she let him think what he would. "Perhaps it is a game," she suggested. "They've been without amusement for weeks and have grown bored."

"A game." His jaw twitched, and his eyes lit with speculation as he translated the foreign words. "Does this sound like a pleasant game to you? *The family is in dire peril unless they find the index the manor conceals.*"

Family? Whose family? As far as she was aware, she had no family—none who acknowledged her, at any rate—and neither did he. If the voice in her head had taken to writing, why would it warn her of peril to a family she didn't know? And if the words were Scots, they could not have come from her mother, could they? Although there was something about the wording . . .

No, that was simply Mr. Dougal's slight burr. In her vague childhood memories of her mother, she remembered an accent of sorts, probably Welsh. His reading simply produced a memory of a safer time.

"How very odd." She hoped she sounded calm. "I thought one word spelled *dream*?"

"In Gaelic, it means folk, family. The translation is loose and open to interpretation, but if it's a game they're playing, then the termagants mean us to play hide-and-seek, I wager."

Mora shivered. She didn't believe that for a minute. She had attempted her mother's spell and ended up here, in the frozen north, looking for her father. And now she was writing words she couldn't pronounce. For a game? She never played games.

But if he thought she believed in the magical gifts of her hostesses, the man before her would walk away from her as fast as he could.

She had never needed a man about. Indeed, heeding inner warnings, she had pushed them away. But for whatever reason, she didn't wish to turn this one away.

Perhaps she had grown as bored as the ladies and simply wished for fresh company.

"It is very bad of you to speak of our hostesses that way," she admonished. "And I hear one coming now. If you value your privacy so much as you seem, you'd best flee."

"You won't run away anytime soon?" he demanded.

"I'll let you know before I do," she promised, although why he should think she'd leave she couldn't fathom.

With her promise, he bowed and escaped, leaving her with the challenging puzzle in her hand.

"Aidan Dougal!" a woman's voice called from the great hall. "I won't help you if you come down with a festering fever."

Mora buried her smile. The image of that great ox of a man fleeing before Ninian's petite form tickled her funny bone. A part of her that she hadn't known existed had come alive the instant the intriguing giant had stormed into her life.

"Oh, yes, you will," Christina was saying as she ushered her shorter cousin into the room. "I've never seen you resist a patient yet, no matter how obstinate."

"Someone must bring the god to earth," Ninian grumbled. "Honestly, I believe he really thinks he is the Adonis he calls himself."

"Adonis?" Mora chuckled, admiring the man's sardonic humor. "With that nose? He is mocking himself, if so."

Both Christina and Ninian stared at her. "An Ives who makes fun of himself? Such a creature doesn't exist," Christina protested. "They are all rational men who take themselves much too seriously, and Aidan is the worst of the lot."

"Adonis wasn't a god. He was a vain mortal with heroic ambitions. He's hiding a wicked sense of humor if that's what he calls himself." Or was she fooling herself into believing what she wanted to believe? Aidan Dougal was so physically intimidating that it would be easy to consider him a supernatural being, but she wanted him to be as human as she was. Elsewise, she'd have to believe him Vulcan, god of fire, who made mountains tremble.

"A challenge!" Christina cried. "We must make the gods laugh. Or the vain mortal, at least. It will give us something much more interesting to think about than whether highwaymen lurk in our woods."

That sounded as if the ladies were as ready for mischief as she'd feared. "I'm not here to play games," Mora reminded them, wary of offering the letter until she made herself clear. "I must make myself useful while I wait for Lord Gabriel's reply."

Christina waved away her protest. "If you are Lord Gabriel's long-lost daughter, he will come racing over the hills to find you once he receives your letter. If you are not his daughter, then we will look for other Gabriels when the weather improves."

Mora did not hold out much expectation that she had any father who had been searching for her all these years, much less a viscount. But Christina's insistence on sending a letter, and the Earl of Ives' agreement to frank it, had encouraged her one forlorn hope.

"I know for a fact that I'm from Wales. I'm more likely to find the right Gabriel there. Until I do, I must earn my keep."

"And so you shall," Ninian said consolingly. "But there is not much entertainment in a wilderness where the snow prevents our venturing far. Waiting for babies wracks the nerves. You will help distract us."

"Especially if she makes Aidan dance to her tune," Christina agreed gleefully. "This will be better than a puppet show."

The lass is plotting, and your magic man is part of it, the voice in Mora's head said with a hint of laughter.

Mora rubbed between her eyes and resisted asking if the voice wrote in Gaelic. She knew from experience that people thought her mad if she argued with thin air. It was the reason she'd taken to ignoring the voice long ago. Besides, the voice never answered.

Magic man indeed. Aidan Dougal was so grounded in this earth that flights of fancy would fly right past him like birds through a tree.

And *she* had voices in her head. That would not go over well with a man who thought fey Malcolms were to be avoided.

With resignation, she held out the letter for the ladies to see. "Mr. Dougal is not much fond of children's games, it seems, so if this is one, please tell me now."

Five

Retreating to the blessedly empty library, Aidan began the tedious task of scanning the shelves for anything resembling a Malcolm genealogy. In his search of his mother's library, he'd discovered her notes in the family Bible. She had been attempting to match names there against the old journals she had collected. A tendency to use the same given names in different generations made dating entries difficult. Given his parentage, it was obvious it was his mother's family who held the grant to his land.

His mother had seldom talked of family, and he'd not grown up on tales of any family legends except his grandfather Dougal's in the Highlands, so he could not believe they had many relations. All he had on which to base his search and his hopes was his mother's notes showing his granny Kate's full name of Katherine Malcolm Macleod Dougal.

He vaguely knew Malcolms played a part in Scots history back to the Dark Ages. Their descendants could inhabit half of Scotland, and his grandmother could be one of them. Women like his brothers' wives who claimed the surname as a given name, however, came of noble families and were likely a different breed. As far as he was aware, his mother had been plain Mairead Dougal, not Mairead Malcolm Dougal.

The thought of asking for help beyond what Drogo

was providing gave him a throbbing headache. He would never hear the end of it if there was even a remote chance his grandmother was some relation to his brothers' wives. He would prefer to keep his secrets to himself. Besides, he had no real idea of what he was looking for until he found it.

He would explore on his own while he waited for Drogo and his legal staff to find a simple solution to the viscountess's threat. So far, Drogo had reported no progress. Aidan had set his own attorney to searching the family papers and Edinburgh registers. Surely among all of them, a solution could be found. That was a much more practical way of spending his time than fretting over strange Gaelic writing in places it had no right to appear.

Dire peril, he snorted. The only dire peril here was to himself.

The tap-tap of light feet on the stone floor of the corridor warned that his privacy wouldn't be long-lived. Sinking into a leather chair, Aidan put his feet up on an ottoman and opened a book as if he were but idling the time away.

To his pleasure, Miss Abbott entered.

"I gave Ninian the letter," she said without preamble. "She is holding a meeting upstairs and wishes us to join them. She assures me she knows nothing of a game."

She stood there steadfastly, not simpering, flinching, teasing, or batting a foolish eyelash. Completely captivated by her casual regard, Aidan resisted arguing. Setting aside his book, he rose and followed her to see what she would do next.

He never chased women. He was a man who chose his own path and always walked alone. His path just happened to go the same way as the Vicar's Daughter this time, that's all. He thought of her that way, in capital letters—the Vicar's Daughter. He liked the sound of it—prim, practical, sedate. Quiet, studious, and sensible.

As her skirts rustled and swung enticingly ahead of him, his thoughts took a less academic direction. She was a good handful of woman, slender in comparison to him, perhaps, but not skinny.

He was searching for more descriptive qualities when she led him into the upstairs nursery.

No matter what he thought of the meddling Malcolm women, he had to admit that they produced admirable offspring. Not namby-pamby aristocrats dressed in velvets and lace but good strong lads and lassies with minds of their own.

Ninian's six-year-old son, Alan, immediately came forward to show him a wooden horse with wheels. Serious, dark-haired as an Ives should be, Alan would make an excellent heir to the earldom one day. Aidan was proud to claim him as family, even if he must keep the relationship to himself.

"I can make him gallop across the nursery," Alan informed him.

"Of course you can," Aidan agreed without much attention, his gaze still following the Vicar's Daughter.

"Hello, Margie." Miss Abbott stooped to sweep up the dirty two-year-old tugging on her skirt. "Have you painted Jamie red again today?"

"He bit her." Ninian retrieved her daughter to dust the red from her hands before the child smeared chalk on the newcomers. "The two of them are like little animals, nipping and chasing each other about."

"Do you think Margie might be seeing auras and is attempting to express them in chalk?" Christina asked from near the basin where a nursemaid washed red chalk off the cheeks of Felicity's squirming two-year-old, Jamie.

"I think she retaliated to his biting in a peaceful and appropriate manner," Miss Abbott said. "If Jamie has to take a bath every time he bites, he'll learn not to bite."

Aidan inwardly cheered. *This* was the kind of sensible woman he wanted.

Felicity appeared from the back room, still studying the stationery that Mora had held earlier. "This is beyond understanding," she said. "I feel no vibrations on this paper other than Mora's."

Aidan backed away as the women gathered to spout similar idiocies. He didn't know why he was needed here at all. Leaning against a wall, he followed the errant path of the horse Alan had sent careening off the other toys. Ewen must have designed the wheels. He'd never seen a toy zigzag in quite such a fashion, almost as if it were deliberately running into blocks and dodging dolls.

Deliberately. Aidan swiveled his gaze to Alan, who was concentrating on the path of his horse, narrowing his eyes and focusing as if he had a bet on the outcome of an important race—as if he could force the horse to win.

Aidan rolled his eyes. The women had him thinking in foolishness. The lad was just a child playing. A child who could concentrate that well would make an excellent earl someday, just like his father. Drogo had a sharp mind that drilled unerringly to the center of any matter. Alan had the same genius. He was *not* moving the toy with his mind.

"You can read this?" Christina asked, waving the letter beneath Aidan's nose, diverting him from his weird notions. "What does it say?"

The attention of all four women abruptly focused on him. With a sigh, he nudged a quacking duck with his boot for Dougie to chase. "The message asks us to find an index in the manor. I assume it means a list and not a mathematical index number or some other definition, but Miss Abbott thought she'd ask your learned opinions." He managed to keep most of the sarcasm from his voice.

Miss Abbott sent him a look that indicated she hadn't missed his intentional editing of the message. He was waiting to see if one of them mentioned that which he had not revealed so he could catch them at their games.

He couldn't imagine what peril they would be in unless it was from him, and even that didn't make sense.

"An index? How odd," Ninian mused. "Have you shown this to Dunstan or Ewen?" She handed her daughter off to a nursemaid and headed for the door. "Let us repair to my parlor so the children may settle down for their naps."

"I don't need a nap!" Alan argued in a tone that indicated this was an old complaint. "I want to see Uncle Ewen's dragon."

"And you shall. You need to finish your schoolwork first. Pick up your toys so Nanny needn't do so. Her back is hurting," his mother admonished.

Lifting his shoulders from the wall, Aidan tried not to notice toys ambling onto the shelf with little aid from childish hands. Alan must be pulling their strings. And in toddling over to the ailing nanny in her rocker to pat her on the back, Dougie was only imitating an action he'd seen before. A child of one year did not know how to heal through touch, especially any child of madcap Christina's.

Thoroughly distracted, Aidan marched out of the nursery and considered continuing straight down the stairs and out the front door. He needed fresh air to clear his head. All the perfume was permeating his brain.

But Miss Abbott fell in beside him as Ninian started down the corridor, and he had a sudden passionate desire to see what happened next.

"Do you think the message means the children are in jeopardy?" the Vicar's Daughter murmured so softly that only he could hear.

He hadn't considered that. Appalled, he ran the single line through his head again before he realized she was serious, and he was not. The message must be a game.

"Of course not," he said curtly, then almost bit his tongue. He didn't know how to talk around women. He'd never had reason to practice being charming.

She didn't seem in the least dismayed by his rudeness. "Thank goodness. I cannot imagine how you would protect all of them at once."

That startled him into barking, *"Me?"*

She nodded, her gaze drifting off in the calculating manner he'd noticed earlier. He hoped it meant she was just thinking and not scheming like a Malcolm.

"It is rather obvious you are the only gentleman prepared on all suits. Dunstan is immersed in his agricultural experiments. The earl is a brilliant man, I'm sure, but a scholar who belongs in libraries. And Ewen . . . well, I fear his head is anywhere but on the here and now. Delightful gentlemen, all of them, but the children need a warrior like you to protect them."

Warrior? Him? He didn't even know how to wield a sword.

She was remembering yesterday. That's all she knew of him.

That was all right, then. Let her think he tossed brigands into bushes all the time. Perhaps she would be less prone to mischief if she thought him fearsome. He'd wanted respect, hadn't he? Aidan generously resisted puffing up at the notion that she considered him stronger and more useful than the responsible earl.

They met Leila coming out of her bedchamber. Caught between her heavily rounded figure and Felicity's, Aidan wished himself a thousand miles away. They ought to be in *bed*, not running around the drafty manor.

"The parlor," Ninian commanded as Felicity led them toward the stairs. "If I find you in the library one more time, Felicity Ives, I shall have Ewen tie you to the bed."

"Oh, he's tried that," the youngest lady acknowledged cheerfully. "It was fun. And if going up and down stairs means I shall deliver this child sooner, then I am quite willing to go up and down all day."

"I don't think I need to hear this," Aidan muttered. "I'll go out and search the snow for tracks of yesterday's villains."

"Nonsense," said the Vicar's Daughter. "The snow fills them too quickly, and I am sure the rogues are long gone. You're the only one who can translate the writing." She appropriated his arm to steer him after the ladies.

The firmness of her hand felt much too right. Despite their petting and pampering, the other ladies instinctively refrained from touching him. Even Ninian had left his shoulder untreated once he'd made it clear he wished to be left alone. Only the Vicar's Daughter had the temerity to invade the wall of aloofness he'd erected.

Well and truly caught, his last hope of making an escape dashed by the insistence of a gentle hand, Aidan followed her rosemary scent without a word of protest.

*   *   *

She had spent years tending fevers and mending bones without regard to whether she touched men or women. Now, however, Mora was exceedingly aware that the arm she held was masculine.

It was also as hard as a rock, if a rock could express tension. Aidan Dougal was so stiff she feared he didn't have enough give to keep from breaking. But she didn't think she could let him go. His breadth and height dwarfed her and made her feel frail and feminine as no man ever had. All of her life, she'd had to be strong for her elderly parents, and for the sick and needy. With a man like this, she instinctively realized she needn't carry all the burden.

At the same time, touching him gave her the oddest sensation. She was almost giddy with it.

She was nearly thirty, an untouched old maid. Until this moment, she had met no man to change her mind. She had no room in her life for obstinate, obtuse men, or for weak-minded flirting. She was convinced that marriage was not for an independent woman like her.

Had Aidan Dougal entered her world earlier, her circumstances might be very different.

Physical desire rippled through her as he led her to a wingback chair in the parlor and offered his arm in seating her. She didn't need a man's aid in sitting, but she clung to his sleeve while she settled her skirts, reluctantly letting him go only when she had no more excuse to touch him. Her hand suffered from his absence.

She ought to be concentrating her superior mental abilities on the oddity of the warning that she—or someone else—had written. But she could not seem to focus on anything but the man lounging slightly behind and to one side of her. He consistently held himself apart from the company, but she was more aware of his presence than of the warmth of the fire.

She thought he might be older than the other gentlemen in the manor, as she was older than all but Lady Leila. There must be a reason a man such as he had never married. Perhaps he was poor and landless. That possibility actually raised her hopes. Perhaps he thought he had nothing to offer a lady. But she was used to having nothing.

What on earth was she thinking? Had she grown so desperate for a home that she looked on marriage as a means of escaping her predicament?

"You say you cannot recall writing these words?" Leila asked, studying the letter that had brought them all to this room.

"I could not have. I do not know Gaelic, and that is not my writing." Mora tried to present her case convincingly, as she knew Aidan's approval rested upon it, and she did not wish him to disdain her as he did the others.

"But the letter never left your hand?" Felicity took the paper from her sister.

"It did, for a moment. A draft carried it off, but Mr. Dougal caught it before it even touched the floor, and immediately returned it to me. That's when I saw the strange handwriting."

Mora watched the sisters and cousin exchanging looks, and the odd feeling in the pit of her stomach returned. They *did* know something. Mr. Dougal was right. They must be playing games.

And to think that, for a tiny moment, her longing to be one of this family had led her to hope she really had done something remarkable. How silly of her.

"Aidan, write something for us." Leila turned the

paper over and produced pen and ink from a writing desk.

"Don't be foolish." He crossed his arms over his massive chest and refused to budge from his corner. "If this is a game, let's be on with it. Otherwise, I have better things to do."

"As I understand it, the writing did not appear until *you* entered the room, and only *you* can speak the language. I don't think we're being foolish," Ninian said sensibly. "None of us has a talent for speaking foreign languages or distance writing. Unless . . ." She turned to Christina. "Do you think your ghosts might have done this? Weren't you in the room?"

"I left before the writing was discovered. Besides, the ghosts here have never done anything like this in the past." Christina ran her hand across the page. "I do not see any aura attached to it." She glanced speculatively at Mora. "We produced handwriting in your book as well. Is that a coincidence?"

"But you said that message was merely lemon juice and heat," Mora protested. "This writing is in no way alike."

She breathed a sigh of relief when they all nodded in agreement and took the subject in a different direction. Given Mr. Dougal's earlier reactions, she did not think he would appreciate her spell book.

"You say the message indicates we must find an index?" Felicity asked. "It does not say what sort of index?"

"Nor why," Aidan added.

He did not snap at the younger woman as he snapped at Christina, Mora noticed. His grumpiness almost sounded affectionate. Felicity was a slight, bookish lady who wore spectacles and looked frail with the burden of her pregnancy. It would take a hard-hearted man to scold her.

Which is why, she supposed, everyone, including Mr. Dougal, listened when Felicity spoke.

"Do you think perhaps it might refer to the index of the Malcolm library?" she asked so softly, the question may well have been directed to herself.

The silence following this question was so immediate that Mora had to turn to Mr. Dougal to confirm she'd heard it right. To her amazement, even he appeared intrigued by the suggestion.

"The library index is missing?" Mora finally had to ask, since all the others apparently knew the answer.

"The entire Malcolm library was sold well over a century ago," Felicity explained. "Recently, we have been trying to rebuild it. Aidan possesses many of the volumes. The index would tell us how many more are missing."

"If the library was sold, wouldn't the index have been sold as well?" Mora didn't understand the importance of a century-old library, but she loved books enough to be interested.

"It is all ancient history," Christina protested. "We have done quite well without ever setting eyes on those volumes."

"I didn't," Felicity replied with a misty look in her eyes. "Who knows what other valuable information may have been lost? Can we afford to ignore a message like this?"

"Surely you would have discovered the thing by now if it was here," Aidan said.

Ninian corrected him gently. "We have only returned to this castle since my marriage, and only then for a month or two of the year. There are entire rooms we have yet to explore. The staff is necessarily limited, and we have no use for the extra space."

"What does an index look like?" Aidan asked with

resignation. "We may as well give the place a thorough going-over until you're satisfied."

Did he really believe someone would be in dire peril if they did not find it? Or did he have some motive of his own for the suggestion? Mora glanced in the gentleman's direction, but he refused to meet her eyes.

Six

"If you wrote the message, you really could be one of us," Christina whispered excitedly to Mora after Aidan left to enlist the other gentlemen in their search.

"What if I don't wish to be one of you?" Mora replied, hiding her passionate desire for just that. Her two natures did not often betray her, except when she was in the presence of these freethinking women.

"Don't be silly. Of course you do. I can see it in your aura. You have a Malcolm rose, and it grew more vibrant when I mentioned the possibility. You have produced two pieces of mysterious writing in a month. Where there's smoke . . ."

"It is just as likely that you and Mr. Dougal produced the writing," Mora argued. "Or that there is a natural explanation for events."

"Will you two quit whispering and join us, please?" Leila demanded from the sofa where she rested with her feet upon a cushion. "I trust Christina is telling you of the Malcolm curse?"

"Malcolm curse?" Mora inquired, although she noticed all the others appeared equally startled.

The elegant woman in burgundy velvet sat on the sofa like a queen on her throne. She smiled now that she had their attention. "Of course. We're cursed to need Ives men to enhance our gifts. If Mora has some latent Malcolm gift, it is evident that Aidan has brought it out."

Stunned, Mora did not join the family laughter at this jest. Latent gifts? As much as she longed to be part of their family, honesty compelled her to repress any such assertion. "If anything, Mr. Dougal is the one with the gift," she insisted, overriding their laughter and boldly contradicting her hostess.

"That's not possible. Ives do not have gifts. They are all stubborn, insensitive men," Christina declared, speaking as the only one who was not married to an Ives. "Even if he does have a touch of Malcolm rose in his aura," she amended, "you are most likely the one who channeled the words."

Mora listened with a sense of wonder. These ladies—Malcolms all—seemed to accept that she might be one of them, as if they had known all along and merely waited for her to admit it. As they waited for Mr. Dougal to declare himself an Ives? How odd.

"This gets us nowhere." Ninian interrupted Mora's reverie. "We are overlooking the most important point. Tell us what was in the message that he is not telling us."

All eyes turned to Mora, and she wished she could sink through the chair. There were times when she was certain the countess could read minds. "He thinks it is a game, and he's testing you," Mora admitted, because the ladies had taken her in and she could do no less than be honest. "I don't think he would appreciate it if I spoiled his fun."

"The message frightened you," Ninian continued, ignoring Mora's objection. "You are trying very hard to suppress your fears, as you suppress your true nature. You are safe with us, you know."

Under Ninian's soothing reassurances, Mora felt her

resistance melting. "No one is ever safe," she protested.

"True," Felicity agreed. "You were attacked by brigands just yesterday, so you have reason to fear. But I lived in fear for most of my life and learned there is freedom in overcoming it. Do you think the message has anything to do with your attack?"

Mora had not given the possibility a single thought. She shook her head in denial. "I cannot see how. I can't believe the message applies to me at all. I have no family."

They waited expectantly at her mention of *family*.

"It really is not a game?" she asked, dismayed as she read the answer in their faces. "If it is not a game, then I fear I am obliged to break Mr. Dougal's confidence because the message must be for you."

Telling herself she owed her loyalty to the ladies and not to the sardonic gentleman who scarcely knew she existed, she sought the right wording. "I believe the exact translation is 'The family is in dire peril unless they find the index the manor conceals.' "

Mora studied the surprise and shock in their faces and could see no falsity in any of their reactions. That left only one explanation—the supernatural.

Christina must have unwittingly stirred a ghost.

A tiny part of Mora delighted in experiencing such a thrilling event. She had an open mind. She was quite willing to accept that ghosts existed.

But if spirits really existed, they wouldn't go to this much trouble to warn them unless it was important. That knowledge restrained her enjoyment.

"I do not wish to imagine what kind of peril we might be in," Felicity said firmly, pressing a hand to her belly.

"Far better that we search for the index than

worry," Ninian agreed. "If the index is in the manor, it shouldn't be difficult to locate."

"Christina, take notes," Leila commanded. "We must map out a strategy for our search."

"Neither you nor Felicity can leave this floor," Ninian insisted. "You cannot be wandering up and down stairs."

"We can divide the manor into segments." Rather than sit at the desk, Christina paced the room. "Leila and Felicity can search this floor. Perhaps I should begin in Drogo's study in the tower. I'm sure there must be ghosts up there who could help us."

"I doubt Drogo will appreciate your intrusion," Aidan said with irritation from the door, "since he cannot be persuaded to join us."

"Oh, good, there you are. Now we can begin." Leila beamed as her husband strode in behind Aidan. Dunstan took a seat on the cushion so he might massage his wife's swollen feet. He merely lifted a dark eyebrow in question at the gathering.

Mora sighed in appreciation of the intimate exchange. It spoke not only of love but also of an earthy relationship whose pleasures she might never know.

Ewen entered and drifted toward Felicity with a charming smile that reflected shared moments. Christina continued her frustrated pacing. Mora rose to appropriate the writing desk. She told herself it was to hasten the proceedings, but mostly, she needed to escape the restlessness aroused within her by the domestic scene. She was glad Christina's duke had business in London and the earl worked in his study, or all the couples together would make her most uncomfortable.

"If we could harness all the energy in this room," Mr. Dougal murmured, leaning his elbow on the top of the secretary and speaking so only Mora could hear, "we could power Ewen's flying machine."

She fully understood his reference to *energy*. The room bristled with primal vibrations that seemed to be affecting her as well. She was amazed that their thoughts took parallel paths. "Flying machine?" she asked faintly, his closeness reducing the room to the two of them.

"I'll show you later. Did they pry the rest of the message from you?"

She nodded. "I'm sorry. If it applies to their family, and there's some real danger, I thought I must."

"Let's make the best of it, then," he said without reproof.

Before she could question him further, he spoke loudly to break the chatter filling the salon. "If we divide up for a search, I recommend the ladies stay in pairs. If Felicity and Leila are confined to this floor, then Ninian should help Christina search the tower, if only to keep Drogo from flinging the duchess out of it. Ewen, you take the public rooms downstairs. Dunstan, the servants' quarters and greenhouse."

"That leaves Mora without a partner," Christina pointed out.

"She and I will search the walls for hiding places," he said with satisfaction.

Dunstan and Ewen hooted and whistled knowingly. The ladies exchanged laughing looks. Aidan disregarded the provocation. He'd accomplished what he wanted. Miss Abbott was looking at him with admiration and a hint of surprise.

He'd never been one to feed on flattery, but her approval seemed worth the teasing he would suffer later.

"Do we have any notion of what an index looks like?" Ewen asked.

"If it is the index to the library, it should be a very large book," Felicity explained. "The original would have been handwritten. It might be bound in leather to protect the contents. But no one has seen it for a century, so it would be best to examine everything."

"The library could take a lifetime to search!" Ewen protested.

"I've spent several winters in that library," Felicity chided. "Unless there are hidden partitions, I would have found something so very obvious."

"Then that is where Miss Abbott and I shall start, hunting for hidden partitions." Aidan straightened and offered his hand to the lady, who was writing down their instructions.

"We'll send a maid to chaperone," Dunstan warned when the Vicar's Daughter dutifully set her pen aside and rose from her chair.

"I'll send the maid to clean out your dirty mind," Aidan retorted, wrapping his big fist around the lady's free hand.

Distracted by her delicate palm in his, impatient to have Miss Abbott to himself, Aidan didn't concern himself with her puzzled frown as she studied the notepaper in her other hand.

Without waiting for Dunstan's reply, he led his treasure out of the family circus. If he was to be the brunt of some practical joke, he would take what enjoyment he could of it, and having the lady to himself was the prize he would claim. The way her slender fingers wrapped obediently around his big palm enchanted him, and he played with different grips, squeezing until she shot him a warning glance.

"This is improper, sir," she warned as the rest of the adventurers followed them into the hall, laughing and arguing. But she did not withdraw her hand.

"I should think we are both old enough to know how to behave, but I will send for a maid if that is your wish." He was a man of his word and would do

as she asked. That didn't mean he wouldn't try to lose
the maid once she was found.

To his delight, she shrugged, reclaimed her hand,
and caught up her skirts to descend the stairs. "I am
perfectly capable of taking care of myself without
need of anyone's aid."

Aidan smiled smugly to himself. That was his intrepid lady. If he was really lucky, she would lead him
a merry chase. He had time enough to decide what to
do with her when he caught her.

Downstairs, she swept across the great hall and into
the library like a woman on a mission. The lamplight
caught a fiery glow in her coronet of auburn braids.
Aidan decided his next goal was to remove the lacy
cap hiding the full glory of her hair.

"Is this the dragon Alan mentioned?" She halted
in front of the colorful apparatus on the table.

"Ewen is building it for his son. It might or might
not fly."

"I see." She studied the winged creature for a moment, then briskly shook off her fascination and
turned to the shelves. "Where is one most likely to
find a priest hole?"

"A priest hole?" That sounded like a capricious
comment the Malcolms would make, and Aidan regarded her with suspicion.

"You know." She gestured impatiently. "Where the
Royalists hid their priests when the Roundheads came.
That was a little over a hundred years ago. The index
might still have been here then, and that would be an
ideal hiding place."

"We are nearly in Scotland," he said dryly, relieved
that she was simply being practical. "Loyalty to any king
was unlikely. The original owners were probably
Roundheads."

She tilted her head in agreement. "Possibly, but as I understand it, the manor is the Malcolm ancestral home. They could have had druidic priests or magicians or any number of oddities they might wish to conceal."

"That I'll believe." He studied the book-lined walls with a frown. "Although now that I consider it, the person hidden would most likely be a Malcolm, and a female at that, and she would want her creature comforts."

She shot him a turquoise glance that reflected neither approval nor disapproval but snagged him with the mystery in its depths.

"Just so," she agreed, her tone not giving away her thoughts. "We should examine the fireplaces first."

He groaned. "Do I look like a chimney sweep?"

He thought an imp of mischief flared as she regarded his vast size, but then she turned away and the moment was lost. To his surprise, he was disappointed. He *hated* it when the women looked at him with mischief in their eyes, didn't he?

"Does Adonis not do chimneys because he is too pretty?" she asked demurely.

He growled, just to see if she flinched. She didn't. "These women corrupt you. You'll be expecting me to perform magic acts next."

"Only if you are the Roman god Vulcan and truly shake the earth." Before he could so much as rattle a window in ire, she continued. "Perhaps we could measure the depth of the fireplaces and the walls in between and see if there is space that is unaccounted for?"

"Very clever," he said with true admiration—for both her wit and dodging his ire. "Since I am not Vulcan, let's avoid sticking our hands in the fire." He picked up an iron poker and ran it past the flaming coals until the iron clanged against the stone wall at the back.

Mora produced a wire from Ewen's oddments on the table, and tied it to the poker where it met the outside of the fireplace. "There, that ought to mark the depth. Now, how do we measure the thickness of the wall?"

With a proprietary gesture, Aidan placed his hand on the small of her back and guided her toward the door. At his touch, she slanted a sideways glance at him that he could swear had a sultry fire to it, but she lowered her lashes before he could see more. The supple sway of her hips as they crossed the room together had him sucking in his breath until he thought his lungs would explode.

How the devil did he go about courting a vicar's daughter? He couldn't keep his hands off her, and he'd known her only a day. *Courting* sounded much too slow when just touching made him think of silken skin and lush flesh. He didn't want to frighten her, but raw need shook him as if he were truly a mythological god instead of a civilized man.

He led her through the ancient first-floor dining hall with its elaborate table designed to seat an army, into the smaller withdrawing room, where he reluctantly released her waist.

"The walls of the old part of the keep and the towers are thick. But this front part of the house was added later, and the fireplaces and inner walls are not deep. If we measure their depth, I'll wager the sum total leaves no room to hide even a very small Malcolm."

The smile of understanding she bestowed upon him could have lit the room without need of candles.

"Then perhaps we ought to stay with the old parts of the keep. If we measure all the walls, surely we will find any priest hole that exists."

"A book does not need an entire room to be hidden," he reminded her.

"But there is most likely a priest hole," she insisted, irrationally in his opinion.

The pounding of a door knocker distracted him before he could disagree. A moment later, Ewen entered the drawing room from the foyer. "You have a visitor, old boy. He says he's your attorney, so I've left him cooling his heels in the great room."

His attorney. Scotland to Northumberland was a harsh journey in this weather. The news must be horrendous to send him here. Aidan clenched his fingers into a fist to contain his rising trepidation. Had Harrowsby come to tell him the court had given his land to the viscountess? Or had he found a ripe genealogical plum on the family tree?

Hoping for the latter, Aidan stalked from the drawing room, leaving the tempting Miss Abbott behind.

Ewen snorted with suppressed laughter as Aidan brushed past him as if his pants were on fire, leaving the vicar's daughter holding a poker and looking bewildered. Mora hid behind a spinster's lowered lashes, but Ewen had seen the spirited light in her eyes. He hoped the lass gave Aidan a run for his money.

"The man never stays in place for more than three minutes," he explained, hoping to assuage any wounded feelings.

"Busy men seldom do," she said without an ounce of rancor. "We have been looking for a priest hole. Do you know if there might be any?"

He cocked his head to listen to the sound of Felicity's peals of merriment above. Reassured that all went well with the upstairs hunt, he considered her question. "Unless one was added with this new part, I doubt it. This is a pretty basic manor house."

"Well, I know naught of looking for partitions so I'll continue as Mr. Dougal instructed. Do you think he will be returning?"

Ewen shrugged. "He could throw his visitor out on his ear and be back in a trice, or mount that black stallion of his and be gone for weeks. He is the mystery among us. Shall I work with you?"

Mora hesitated. She did not wish to pry without the express approval of her hosts, but she had no desire to be hampered by Ewen's distracting charm either. Mostly, she was frustrated by the departure of the one man who was willing to listen and act swiftly. She feared there was a greater danger here than any believed.

"I think I shall simply measure a few more walls as Mr. Dougal taught me and see if he returns. Since you're searching the rooms down here, and I am not one of the family threatened, I'm sure I'll be quite safe."

"That makes sense. Call me if you find anything." Ewen returned to the library.

Mora assumed he would soon be engrossed in improving his dragon and would forget all about the search.

She couldn't forget so easily. The list of instructions she'd written down earlier crackled in her pocket. At the very bottom of that list, in the same hand that had warned of dire peril, she had written, *The priest hole. . . .*

She had written it. No one else had touched the pen or paper. But it had not been her thought, and it was in the same loopy handwriting as the earlier warning.

She did not know whether to be terrified or elated.

Seven

"That's impossible," Mr. Dougal shouted with such stark horror that Mora halted her measuring and froze.

The floor beneath her feet shook, and she glanced hastily at the walls. The gilded frame around the portrait of some ancestor swung back and forth. She clutched her measuring rod nervously.

She'd made quick work of evaluating the fireplace and had started measuring the walls of the new front addition. Mr. Dougal had apparently taken his attorney to the study across the foyer from where she stood.

Behind the partially open paneled door, the visitor tried to sound reassuring. "Remember your history, lad. It was just after the Jacobite uprisings in 1715 and 1719. The English were prowling the Borders, and your mother was none too quiet in her support of her father's Highland countrymen."

"All the more reason for this to be completely impossible!"

Mora knew she ought to leave them to their privacy, but a lifetime of living in a small village had taught her the wisdom of knowing problems in time to solve them. She had frequently used knowledge gained from eavesdropping to advantage—not for herself, but for those affected.

"Your mother was gallivanting aboot with the English earl," the attorney reminded him. "She did not seem so concerned until the English soldiers showed up on her land and threatened to take it away."

"She was no doubt harboring Highland traitors," Aidan growled. "Or all the Pretender's men, for all I know. Playing about with the earl would be her way of hiding her deceit. That, I accept. I do not accept that she married the man."

"I have the soldiers' reports of their marriage, signed and witnessed by her neighbors. Her marriage to an Englishman is the only reason the Crown did not take the land away from her. You have the means to prove your legitimacy, keep your home, and prove you're an earl," the stranger insisted.

Mora did not think Mr. Dougal was a man accustomed to expressing horror, but she could scarcely ignore the bellow that followed, especially since the ancestral painting fell to the floor with a loud bang.

"I cannae do that, mon! Do ye know what ye ask?"

He was slipping into his Scots. That could not be a good sign, she thought.

"You are the earl's legitimate heir," the stranger asserted. "Your mother did not wish the reports released, but under the present circumstances, even she could not argue against their being filed to save her home."

"She would never leave her home for an Englishman," Aidan protested, lowering the volume of his shout by half.

"And she did not, which is why she had her attorney find and hide the reports, and swore her executor to secrecy. They are not legal marriage documents but they would stand up in court as evidentiary material. If you want to keep your home, you must present these to the court."

Aidan was about to lose his home?

Even giants could not fight the law. She'd not considered that Mr. Dougal held himself aloof because he thought he had been born on the wrong side of the blanket.

It was extremely odd that he seemed angry to learn he was not only legitimate, but also the son of an earl. He should be crowing with joy. And defending his home.

The study door behind her swung open with an angry slam, indicating someone's imminent departure. Not wanting to be caught eavesdropping, she darted behind the door of the drawing room.

"Ye have no idea of what ye speak," she heard Aidan mutter furiously in an undertone. "I accept that the Earl of Ives was my father. There's no denying what is plain as the nose on my face. But there's naught *legitimate* aboot my birth. And there's an end on it. Ye'll keep looking for a deserving cousin or two on the family tree, as will I."

"As you say, sir," the attorney replied stiffly, "although it is against all your best interests. You have but a fortnight before the court will hear your neighbor's case and your land will be given over to mining."

"Talk to the lord advocate, have him delay the court. There is bound to be *someone* suitable to inherit."

Mora dropped to a low satin chair and held a hand to her chest as two sets of angry footsteps stomped over the marble foyer in the opposite direction.

Surely she could not have heard right. The Earl of Ives was Drogo, Ninian's husband. In his satin and lace, he looked every inch the aristocratic gentleman, albeit he possessed an absentminded, scholarly air. He couldn't possibly be Aidan's father. The two men were nearly of an age.

That meant . . . Mora's eyes widened in horror. Drogo's father, the late earl, had clandestinely married Mr. Dougal's mother *before* Drogo was born, and the attorney thought the marriage legal. Which meant . . . Drogo and all his brothers would be disinherited.

The paper containing the ghostly warning crumpled in her grip.

If the court should declare Aidan earl, as his attorney advised, the family truly was in dire peril, but not in a way anyone would imagine.

Mora stared at the handwriting that had come from her hand, yet was not hers.

How had she channeled the messenger and how could she persuade him or her to tell her more so she might find a way out of this dreadful muddle?

Especially since it very much looked as if Aidan was the Ives catalyst causing the messages, and he would never in a hundred years believe her if she said so.

Aidan offered Harrowsby the manor's hospitality, but the chilly temperatures of earlier had transformed into the warmth of a sunny spring day, and the attorney was eager to take advantage of the good weather to start his journey home.

"Why the devil would my mother marry an Englishman, then hide it?" he demanded, attempting to come to terms with his mother's horrible secret.

"From what I understand," Harrowsby replied, checking his horse's cinch, "your mother was not one to hold her tongue when she saw an injustice. The English threatened her holdings in retaliation for her failure to support King George."

"Aye." That, he could understand. "She had no love of the Hanoverian king and would have hacked a soldier through with a claymore if he set foot on her land without permission. But to marry an English earl!"

"It seems the late Lord Ives was a charming rascal, cooling his heels in these parts after a romantic scandal in London. This is an Ives holding, is it not?" Harrowsby asked.

"It is now," Aidan agreed. And from what he knew of the late earl, he had not been one to accept banishment from civilization for long. Forbidden London, he would have headed straight to Edinburgh, where Mairead Dougal had reigned as queen of society in those days. "I know his lordship has bastards scattered aboot the countryside, but he was not much inclined to *marry* the wenches."

Aidan preferred not to imagine his irrepressible mother dallying with the earl, but she was all female, and Ives were all male. If he needed proof that Malcolm blood ran in her, he needn't look further than his father. Malcolm and Ives, with the attraction of iron and magnets. He wanted to pound his head against a tree as he considered all the ramifications of his possible conception and birth.

Of course, there was no real proof of his mother's theory that she might be in any way related to the Malcolms, only the sick realization that if his mother was searching for a Malcolm ancestor, then she was convinced that one existed.

"One assumes Lord Ives was a gallant fellow, or a drunken sot, or a bit of both," Harrowsby continued, bringing Aidan's thoughts to a merciful end. "If he declared they were wedded, that the land was already in English hands, he could have used his title to drive off the soldiers threatening your mother."

"My mother would have known better than to agree in front of witnesses!" But Aidan groaned, seeing how it could come about in the urgency of the moment.

At the time of his birth, both Scots and English law recognized clandestine marriages—a simple declaration of marriage before witnesses was binding, although frowned upon.

The cold chill of apprehension settled in his bones, but he refused to accept the facts. Drogo was the earl. Anything otherwise would be akin to turning the world on its axis. He'd never wanted the title or the responsibility. He'd only wanted family.

Harrowsby swung up on his horse. "I assume your mother would have used the future tense of a handfast that could have been easily voided or annulled. She would not think she was actually marrying the man, nor did the earl consider himself married, if we are to judge by his subsequent behavior. If he ever returned, I know naught of it. We must assume your mother never told him of your conception or that the marriage was made certain by your birth. I cannot say for the English court, but the union will hold up in a Scots court, which is enough to save your land."

"Even if I do not claim the title, I would be questioning the legitimacy of entire families. I cannot do that," Aidan argued back. "Not while there is any hope of another solution. You have your clerks looking over the family tree?"

He wasn't certain he was any more ready to accept that his mother was a Malcolm than that he was an earl. But if she wasn't, then he had nowhere else to turn. His heart felt squeezed by a vise.

"Aye, but the records are poor, scattered as they are. We are working from both your side of the family and from Lady Gabriel's. The closest female relation we have found is the viscountess's sister, but she died young and we know of no offspring. The family link Lady Gabriel is using to establish her claim goes back several generations."

"The entailment originates from 1600 or earlier. There are bound to be other descendants," Aidan insisted.

"Still alive?" Harrowsby asked with a lift of his heavy gray eyebrows. "I'll do what I can, but I fear it will not be enough. Do not count on having more than a fortnight to find another legitimate heir."

Aidan waved Harrowsby off, then turned back to the castle, determined to waste no more time in his search for his ancestors.

Mora stood in the entrance, a piece of paper in her hand. He had no right to court her while he was engaged in a war with his neighbor. Had she been any other woman, he could have brushed past without stopping, intent on his own business. But he could not ignore Mora in her old-fashioned gown, the sun glinting on her temptress hair, mysterious eyes regarding him with worry and concern.

"You will catch your death of cold," he scolded, taking her elbow and hauling her back inside, slamming the great oak doors behind them.

"And you won't?" she asked with a hint of irony.

If he didn't know better, he'd think she was criticizing him. But vicars' daughters didn't do that, did they?

"I'm a man. I'm used to cold. Now go upstairs and warm yourself at a fire." He left her at the foot of the grandiose stairs in the marble foyer, but she doggedly followed him through the drafty great hall.

"I think you ought to see something." She held out the paper on which she'd written the instructions.

"I haven't time to play. I've work to do. Have Ewen help you look for hiding places." He increased his pace through the echoing, enormous dining room.

She half ran so that she could rattle the paper in front of him. "The ghost said the *family* was in dire peril, did it not? I think it is trying to help you."

"There are no such things as ghosts." He brushed the paper away as he entered the library. He immediately began searching the shelves, methodically pulling out one book at a time, hoping for a miracle. "Christina stirs the air simply by existing."

"Messenger, then," she amended. "Spirit voice, if you will. Christina did not write this. *I* did."

He set a book back in its place, snatched the paper, and glanced at it just to be rid of her. Or to please her and send her away; his mind was too muddled to discern which.

"I told you . . ." He halted as his gaze found the last line in a bolder, blacker hand than the neat one preceding it. "This is what prompted you to search for a priest hole? Is it a joke?"

"I don't know. You made me leave before the message was complete. I really think he's trying to tell us something."

"*You* wrote this?" The penmanship looked much like the writing in Gaelic from earlier, but this was in clear English. "Why?"

"I did not *know* I wrote it," she said impatiently. "It was just there when I glanced down. Lady Leila says you might be a kind of catalyst. You were leaning right over me while I was writing."

"Aye, and it's all my fault of a certainty, then," he growled, returning the paper and pulling out the next lot of books, thinking one labeled *Malcolm Ancestry* would be convenient. "It's mind reading, I'm sure. I mentally told you to write it, and my overpowering strength of mind forced your hand across the paper." Not finding anything remotely useful, he started on the next shelf.

"I know it sounds silly." She didn't sound in the least hurt by his sarcasm. "I cannot explain it. But I have *never* done the like before. Someone or something must be desperately trying to communicate the answer to your problem. If we could find the priest hole—"

His *problem*? Aidan bit back a groan. However it came about, she was another one of *them*, persistent meddlers, stubbornly believing they had powers beyond the possible, and the ability to make everything right. Would he ever find a normal woman who would talk of cats and meals and homemaking?

"How do you know of my problems?" he roared with exasperation.

"Mind reading?" she suggested with a decidedly malicious glint in her eyes.

He didn't want to discuss his problems with anyone.

"It appears you are searching for a particular book," she said. "Did it occur to you that the index might aid your search and save you time?"

That bit of logic stopped him cold. Malcolm meddling sometimes produced surprising results, he had to admit. An index to the library could be useful in his search. And if by some strange circumstance the index was hidden in a priest hole, then by all that was holy, he would find it.

He snatched the paper from Mora's hand, grabbed her elbow again, and guided her toward the door. She dragged her feet until he said, "The ladies have naught better to do. We'll let them tell us about priest holes."

She ran eagerly to keep up with his strides.

"How can we search under the furniture as we must?" Lady Felicity was complaining when Aidan towed Mora into a rarely used upstairs salon where Felicity and Leila were searching.

"You call for help," Aidan grumbled, giving the message paper back to Mora and gripping the pilasters on one end of a cupboard. Carved of oak, it was nearly six feet long and three feet deep.

He scarcely seemed to notice the weight as he lifted the furniture and held it aloft, allowing the ladies to confirm that no book was hidden beneath it. Mora tried not to gape as his coat sleeves strained over the bulge of powerful muscles. She winced as she imagined what he was doing to his injured shoulder.

"Does the keep contain a priest hole?" he demanded while balancing the cupboard in his hands.

Leila signaled for him to lower the piece. "None that I am aware of, but Malcolms lost possession of the old keep to an Ives before Cromwell's time, I believe. It would be just like an Ives to hide priests, if only in spite. Why do you ask?"

Mr. Dougal sent Mora a baleful look. She assumed he was unwilling to speak of ghosts or spirit messengers—and certainly not the problem that had him scouring the library—and he wished her to clarify. He now classified her as the same sort of irritant as the ladies.

Swallowing her frustration, she held the paper out to Leila. "The invisible messenger has spoken again. I really think it is trying to tell us something important. It is possible the family is truly in peril, as the first spirit said."

She was grateful she did not have to say that Mr. Dougal was the danger.

While Mr. Dougal stalked about the room, raising furniture for Felicity to peer under, Leila studied the odd handwriting. Discreetly, Mora attempted to lift the heavy oak cupboard. She was sturdy and had often moved the vicarage's furniture to clean under it, but she couldn't budge this monstrous piece. The thing must have been built in place. No mortal man could lift it.

With her eyes, she followed Mr. Dougal's progress around the room. He might call himself Adonis, but Atlas was more accurate. No, Hercules, who was mortal and smarter by far. Mythological gods had more power than brains, not unlike some royalty she could name.

"If the message is urgent, we must persuade the spirit to write again," Leila said with concern, studying the paper. "We should experiment."

"Send for Dunstan." Felicity settled into a chair by the fire now that all the furniture had been searched. "He is more scientific about experimentation. You are apt to set the house on fire."

"I'll fetch him," Mr. Dougal said a little too eagerly.

Girding herself for a battle she didn't want, knowing it was for his own good, Mora stepped in front of the exit. "Mr. Dougal, you were with me when I wrote that. Mr. Ives was not. Doesn't experimentation require duplicating the events that caused the initial discovery and changing only one variable at a time to discern which variable created the effect?"

She was aware that the ladies were staring at her in fascination, but only Mr. Dougal held her attention. He'd crossed his arms over his broad chest and glared down at her as if she were a snake-haired Medusa. Or perhaps he thought of her as Cerberus, guarding his escape from hell.

"Do you, or do you not, wish to find the index that might list all the volumes of the Malcolm library and their contents?" she asked with feigned innocence. She didn't understand why he had been searching the library, but she knew he was no dilettante playing at games while his land was in jeopardy. He had an urgent reason of some sort, and she meant to help, whether he liked it or not.

"I did not touch your paper," he thundered.

"And you need not touch it now," she agreed. "We must simply return to the desk where I wrote it and assume the same positions to see if anything more is produced."

Aidan caught both her elbows in his hands, and lifted her from the exit and out of the way, just as Hercules had removed Cerberus from the gate.

Mora was breathless when he set her down again— not just from the surprise of being physically powerless, but from the glare that penetrated clear to her soul.

"I'll play your silly game until it is time to eat," he declared. "And then I will ask more sensible people where to find the priest hole."

He stalked toward the sitting room where they had first plotted the search for the index.

Mora had a distinct feeling the walls trembled with every step he took.

Eight

"The spirit hasn't moved her," Christina announced mournfully as Mora's quill refused to march across the paper as they'd hoped.

The attempt to duplicate the events that had produced spirit writing had been a complete failure.

"It is more likely that Aidan scared the spirit away with his scowl," Ninian said, patting Mora's hand.

The subject of her comment lay prone upon the floor, oblivious to them as he attempted to search for a priest hole in the darkened recesses under a dresser that even he could not lift.

Mora thought she might expire in wonder as Mr. Dougal propped up his breeches-clad knee to shove his upper body deeper under the furniture. His unfastened coat and vest had fallen back to reveal the placket of his breeches, and for the first time she was staring at a masculine bulge molded by tight doeskin. She did not know how he compared with other men, but the ridge revealed was truly worth her awe.

Mora wanted Mr. Dougal to be her catalyst, but she would be the first to admit that he was not looking upon her favorably at the moment. If his earlier regard had drawn the spirits, his antipathy now drove them away.

She *wanted* to draw spirits, she realized. The thought should terrify her, but the more Mr. Dougal disdained her spirit writing, the more she wanted to work on it. She didn't care if he might be an earl, and she only a lowly vicar's adopted daughter. She was tired of being invisible. Her tempestuous inner nature made her want to throw a tantrum to force him to take notice of her.

Her practical outer nature thought that being a witch or a medium might prove useful for a woman who must support herself.

Christina rose from the table and kicked Mr. Dougal's large boot sole. "You need not continue hiding under there. The gremlins have carried off all the dust bunnies and are having them for dinner. We'll have to solve the mystery on our own."

"You would think one of you would have located any priest hole over the years," he grumbled, squirming out of the crawl space.

"It's not as if any of us lives here by choice," Dunstan said in mild reproof. "Until Drogo came here a few years ago, none of us had set foot in Northumberland."

"Aye, ye London-bred milksops can't abide a little cold." Mr. Dougal stood and dusted himself off.

Knowing this strong man hid a horrible secret behind his aloofness, Mora understood his behavior with greater sympathy.

"The library is the first floor of the earl's tower, is it not?" she asked before she could submit to cowardice. When all gazes turned to her with interest, she continued. "I assume the tower is part of the original keep, with the thicker walls more suitable for hidden places. Is there a dungeon or cellar beneath it?"

"More like a barn for the cattle," Dunstan corrected. "The border lords were practical men. It's not been used for anything except storage in years."

"But it's a likely place for a priest hole." Ewen

recognized the direction of her thoughts and his eyes lit with interest.

"It's a likely place for spiders and snakes and cobwebs," Leila pointed out with distaste.

"If . . ." Mora hesitated over using given names, but saying *Mr. Ives* would not be very clear. She succumbed to the family's insistence on informality. "If Ewen and Dunstan could measure the ground floor of the tower, while Leila and Felicity measure the second-floor master suite . . . Aidan could measure the first-floor library while we experiment in there. That way we'd be seaching both scientifically and spiritually for the priest hole."

Aidan looked as if he'd rather sever his head and display it on a pike, but his stubbornness didn't impede his intellect. Mora knew she was offering him the opportunity to search the library while keeping the ladies happy. He was trapped.

He cast her a disgruntled glance, but merely crossed his arms and let the ladies flow excitedly past him to their assigned places.

"You would not like to read my mind right now," he murmured as he took Mora's arm and pulled her along behind the others.

She was aware of his strength and size as he strode beside her, and she was also aware that he didn't look at her. Another awareness rippled between them, a vibration under the skin that she could not name, which prevented her from resisting his need to drag her about.

"Men are very simple," she responded to his implied threat. "Your mind is an open book in some ways. So, yes, I know you would like to shove me up the chimney. I simply do not know why."

She thought he'd choke on muffled mirth. Well, at least he had a sense of humor, however perverted.

"Stuffing you up a chimney is not what I had in mind," he assured her as they descended the stairs to the great hall.

Mora cast him a suspicious glance, but his bland expression revealed nothing. Unaccustomed to exchanging witticisms with gentlemen, much less those who might or might not be earls, she wisely remained silent.

From the top of a ladder Aidan continued his pretense of measuring the library stacks. The light through the mullioned windows wasn't sufficient to read all the moldering titles up here, but most seemed to be agricultural or scientific tomes, along with Malcolm journals from the last century. None hinted at a genealogical subject.

He held out little hope that the ladies' experiment would reveal a priest hole, an index, or the miracle he needed, but for lack of any alternative, he doggedly continued his search. So far, both scientific and spiritual searches were coming up empty-handed.

Mora sat at the table beside Ewen's dragon, writing notes to her friends. He hoped she really didn't believe that she might channel the dead through the quill just because he was in the room with her.

"Let us try my mother's spell book," Mora suggested, confirming Aidan's suspicion that she was as insane as the other ladies. "If it is her that I am channeling, then the book might call her."

"I'll go fetch it." Christina started for the door.

Ninian rose from her chair, waving her cousin aside. "I need to check on the nursery and see if Felicity and Leila have finished their measurements. I'll find the book while I'm there."

Ninian's departure effectively left Aidan trapped with the foolish duchess and the alluring Vicar's

Daughter. He couldn't help but listen when Mora spoke in a confidential tone that captured a man's interest with just the timbre.

"The spell I am thinking of calls for candles, feathers, and salt," she explained. "Should we look for those while we're waiting?"

"A real spell!" Christina crowed. "We haven't tried one in ever so long. I'll get the ingredients."

Before Aidan grasped what Mora was doing, the library had cleared of all the women but her. Every fiber of his body pulled taut when he realized they were alone.

"Since I assume you are not really interested in the index or priest hole, if you would tell me what you are looking for, we could divide the room between us," she said.

"If I knew what I was looking for, I would have found it," he muttered, climbing down so he might move the ladder.

The scent of rosemary, mixed with the lilac pomander she must keep with her clothes, accompanied the rustle of her petticoat as she came to stand at the bottom of the ladder. "If you would enlist the aid of those who would help you, you might yet find it."

She spoke softly, with the modesty of a vicar's daughter, but Aidan heard a hint of mutiny underlying her complacence. Did she think this infernal *experimentation* was helping him? "You needn't play the mealymouthed spinster for me," he told her rudely, rather than respond to her implication.

"Mealymouthed?"

Her voice sounded so odd, he stole a glance over his shoulder to read her expression. Dark-lashed eyes the color of the sea at dusk laughed at him. So much for driving her away for her own good.

"Shall I be as rude as you?" she asked—with more interest than insolence.

Disrespectfully, he surveyed her prim figure from head to toe. She had a heart-shaped face that spoke of feminine delicacy, but there was something about the eyes and mouth that betrayed her stubborn nature. He let his gaze drop lower. Beneath the high-necked gray gown and petticoats, she hid full curves that begged for exploration. She didn't flinch at his stare, although her ears reddened beneath her lacy cap.

Remembering an earlier vow, Aidan snatched the cap from her burnished braids. "Caps are for old women."

To his delight, her dark arched eyebrows straightened in a scowl. "It was a gift from my foster mother. She wished me to look respectable."

"Your hair is too beautiful to be hidden." Rather than toss the cap in the fire where it belonged, he tucked it on a shelf she could not easily reach. He didn't wish to harm anything of value to her, even if he despised the cap.

"It is my mother's hair. Some say she was a witch, and the color reflected her sins." Defiance tinted her declaration.

He narrowed his eyes. "Some say the world is flat and the sun revolves around themselves," he answered, refusing to acknowledge her silly notion of witches. He pulled another useless book from the shelf to peruse.

"And some are so pigheaded that they believe the universe will collapse if they ask for help," she retorted.

He snorted in appreciation of her bluntness. "Not many dare call me pigheaded to my face."

"I am apparently saying it to your back since you

will not turn around. Surely, if I don't fear you, you have no reason to fear me."

"*Fear* you?" he asked incredulously, swinging to confront the damned woman. He didn't mind bluntness, but this insult bordered on the idiotic. He could break her in two, and well she knew it.

She clasped her hands decorously in her skirts and looked at him through eyes as wicked as the night. She'd provoked him deliberately.

"Was that retaliation for the cap?" he demanded. He donned his most intimidating expression and stepped closer, looming over her, casting her in shadow with his greater height.

She faced him with amusement. "Perhaps, a little. Mostly because it's true. You're afraid of me. You're afraid of all the Malcolm ladies and their bewildering ways. You're afraid of the inexplicable."

"*I am not afraid!*" he thundered so loudly that a book fell from the shelf.

"Goodness, I should think not," Christina said airily from the doorway as she rushed in carrying an assortment of feathers and saltcellars and other ingredients. "Spirits can't harm us. Ghosts can be a little mischievous, but I've seen no auras, so I don't think we're dealing with ghosts."

"I fear being nattered to death by senseless idiocy like that," he snapped, picking up the fallen book and slamming it back on the shelf.

His ill temper didn't deter his brave lady. He could sense her amusement warming his back.

"I see our Scots friend is being his usual charming self." Ewen entered bearing a paper he tossed on the library table amid his other sketches. "Aren't you finished measuring yet? Felicity has already drawn her diagram."

Relieved to have male company to balance the

overload of feminine sorcery, Aidan abandoned his search to examine the diagrams of cellar and master suite. "They're the same size," he said with disgust, throwing the papers back to the table.

"Where are your measurements?" Ewen asked.

"In my head. I dinnae need to scribble them."

Ewen's eyes widened. "You kept the numbers in your head? Even that alcove over there where the stairway descends on the other side?"

"And the chimney." Shrugging off Ewen's incredulity, Aidan picked up the cellar diagram again, making certain all lined up on paper as it did in his head.

"A human measuring stick! I should take you with me when I go surveying." Donning a pair of spectacles, Ewen examined his wife's drawing, then glanced around the room, measuring with his eyes. "They built their library as large as the barn." He shook his head in disbelief. "That's proof the place was built by Malcolm females."

"There was a Malcolm male somewhere back in time to give us the name," Ninian said, entering with Mora's book and handing it to Christina, who grabbed it eagerly.

A Malcolm male. Aidan swallowed hard and scanned the stacks as if the record of his lineage would leap from the shelf shouting, "Here I am, the line of male Malcolms who bred these witches!"

Mora waited expectantly, and when he still refused to ask for help, she left him to join Christina at the table.

With a gesture of defiance, she flipped open the book and pointed out a page. "Try the spell asking for aid in trouble. But I recommend it be done where there is nothing flammable about. We would not wish to disturb Mr. Dougal's opinion of magic by actually producing flames."

Nine

Sitting in the circle of women on the floor before the fireplace, Mora diligently prepared to record the results of their spell, hoping that Aidan might relax enough to come near as he had in the previous episodes of spirit writing. So far, he maintained his distance, scouring the upper shelves on the shadowy wall farthest from them.

It was rather like trying to tame a wild wolf, she decided, and just about as successful. Still, she suspected spirits occupied a different time and space from theirs, and it must take some powerful force to draw them here. Aidan was the most powerful force in the room.

"Why should we try the spell asking for aid in time of trouble?" Christina asked.

"I tried it at home on Valentine's Day, the day we discovered the hidden writing," Mora admitted. "I nearly caught the pot on fire. But it was also the day we found my father's handwriting."

"Valentine's Day?" Aidan asked, descending the ladder—apparently feeling safe since the children had just burst into the library to fetch the adults for supper.

Finding their elders conveniently on the floor, the little ones climbed into any available lap.

"I was desperate that day, but other than Christina,

no knight in shining armor rode to my rescue. . . ."
Not then, Mora suddenly realized. Holding Dunstan's
and Leila's oldest child, Verity, she looked up at
Aidan in shock. He pretended not to notice her regard. *He'd ridden to her rescue late.*

Did he understand that? Or was she imagining
things?

Christina's arrival could just as easily have been a
response to the spell. Why did she feel otherwise?
Why did she think Aidan looked guilty?

Mora jerked her attention back to the circle. "The
candle is starting to tilt." Ever mindful of the night of
terror that had ended her mother's life, she always
approached fire of any size with great caution.

Christina had used the decanter of malt on the library table to add the "spirit" required by the spell,
and Ninian had poured it into her teacup saucer.

Straightening the candle, Christina sat on the floor
with her skirts spread around her. "Alan, sit still. Hold
Verity's hand. Make a circle around me."

Mora settled Verity on the floor beside her and returned the lap desk to her knee.

"If she starts speaking in tongues, I'm leaving,"
Aidan muttered.

Mora's pen skittered across the paper at his unexpected closeness. She hadn't heard him approach.
Warily, she glanced over her shoulder.

Aidan had sprawled over a chair behind her so that
his boot toe nearly touched her skirt. Lifting mocking
dark eyebrows at her glance, he intertwined his hands
over his chest, and nudged her hip to show he'd noticed her. It made her feel peculiar to know this imposing man had fixed his attention on her. But then,
she supposed she was the only single woman available.

A cobweb adorned his coal black hair, and a
smudge of dust smeared his distinctive nose. But it

was the devilish gleam in his eyes that had her heart racing.

She turned back to the page she was writing. Nothing extraordinary had appeared with his touch or proximity, she noted with frustration.

"Spirits, grant us wisdom and guide us to what we seek," Christina intoned from inside her circle.

The children wiggled and giggled. Ninian sent them a calming smile that briefly restrained their energy.

"Spirits, rise, let your knowledge speak." Christina threw a handful of salt at the candle, and watched it sputter and smoke.

"Waste of good whisky," Aidan muttered. "If the spirit was Scots, he'd have drained the saucer by now."

The amber liquid reflected the candle's flame but no ghostly emanation arose from it. Instead of giving up, Christina handed the spell book to Mora. "Here, you try. It is your book, after all."

The lap desk slid one way and the book the other. Mora hastily caught the ancient tome. A large hand reached over to grab her desk and papers before they flew into the fire. By accident or not, Aidan leaned close enough to brush her nape with his breath as he returned the page.

"Spirits, grant us wisdom," he murmured laughingly near her ear, sending a shiver up her spine.

"Guide us to what we seek," she added wryly, torn between Christina's eagerness and Aidan's cynicism.

"The candle!" six-year-old Alan shrieked.

Mora jumped in startlement, distracted from her fascination with Aidan in time to see the candle tilt into the saucer of whisky and flame upward.

A draft from the chimney caught her paper and flung it at the flame. The children squealed and scattered as the paper caught fire.

Aidan leaped from his chair, planting his big boot on the burning sheet just as it fell onto Christina's skirt. "By Hades, woman, would you burn the place down around our heads?"

He ground his boot thoroughly on the scorched silk and paper while Christina wisely covered her mouth and sat still until the fire was out.

Only Mora noticed the sway of shadow and light rising from their scattered circle. Already scared half out of her wits by the fire and Aidan's sudden leap, she sat frozen, watching the cloud stretch across the darkened room to the settle. How was it possible to see shadow against shadow?

"Devil take it, Mora, don't just sit there like a—" Aidan stopped in midgrowl.

The children quieted with him as they all turned to stare at her.

She was whiter than a sheet, her dark-lashed eyes more green than blue as she stared past Aidan at a far corner of the room. Affirming that the fire was completely out, he cast a glance behind him to see what held her attention.

He saw nothing.

He glanced down at Christina, who appeared equally puzzled as she looked from Mora to him, to the dark corner of the library.

"Come along, children." Briskly sizing up the situation, Ninian rose, brushing off her skirts as if nothing untoward had happened. "Time to wash up for supper. We'll leave Christina and Mora to clean up our little mishap."

The countess's no-nonsense approach relieved their fear and sent the children laughing and scampering from the room.

Apparently jolted back from her trance by the noise, Mora flushed. She glanced around for the paper that had escaped, looking anywhere but at Aidan. Not finding the paper, she gathered up the writing desk. Her gaze encountered the ashes and the scorched saucer, and she hesitated.

Worried by her paleness and unusual silence, Aidan held out his hand. When she looked at his palm and refused to take it, he grew impatient.

"I thought you more courageous than that," he said scornfully, seizing her wrist and hauling her to her feet.

When she staggered at his roughness, he wanted to grab her waist, but she hastily righted herself. He hid his surprise at the way she clung to his hand.

"Well, I never liked this gown anyway," Christina said, examining the hole in the pink silk. "I told Harry I'm better off in breeches."

Aidan noticed Mora had no pragmatic comment to add. She wasn't the sort of woman who nattered incessantly, but she generally spoke when spoken to. He glanced over his shoulder at the dark alcove again. Was the shadow darker there?

"You want me to look in the alcove?" he asked, not at all certain why he asked.

Mora's eyes seemed to fill half her face at his suggestion. He couldn't have refused her if she had asked him to dance on the head of a pin. She nodded.

He didn't want to let her go. Her hand was small clasped in his great mitt. Her skin was work-roughened but far less so than his. When he squeezed her fingers lightly, she returned the pressure. Reassured, he handed her off to Christina.

Puzzled, Christina accepted her charge and, for once, held her tongue.

Wishing he had the candle so he might disperse Mora's fear along with the shadows, Aidan stalked over to the recess formed when the guard-tower stairs on the other side of the chimney had been walled in. More shelves had been built between the fireplace and the wall, and a built-in settle had been added beneath them.

At first, he thought that the children had opened the bench to play with the old pillows and draperies folded inside. The lid was ajar and a corner of one of the pillows had caught beneath it. But the settle was slanted at an odd angle to the chimney.

He caught the edge of the bench and tugged. It moved forward several inches.

He was aware the instant Mora appeared behind him. Perhaps it was the scent of rosemary or the rustle of petticoats, but he thought it more an impression of warmth sliding along his skin.

He wanted to warn her away, but that was foolish. The children had merely disturbed the old bench and jarred it loose. He tugged harder, and was rewarded by a rusty creak as it swung outward.

"A priest hole?" Christina whispered in anticipation.

The duchess wore more rustling petticoats than the Vicar's Daughter probably owned, but he hadn't sensed her presence as he had Mora's.

"We should have measured *outside* the library," he agreed obliquely, tugging the settle forward to reveal a black hole in the wall behind it.

Christina squealed in joy. "I'll light a candle. Just a moment, don't do anything without me." She ran back to the table for an unused taper.

Dubiously, Aidan measured the hole against his own size and concluded he couldn't crawl in there. "It had to have been one small priest."

"Or a woman," Mora said quietly.

Before he could stop her, she dropped to her knees and reached into the hole.

She emerged holding a dusty, cobweb-covered wooden box. "The hole extends upward to the underside of the stairs. Do the shelves move?"

"It's not a book," Christina said with disappointment, lifting the taper to study their prize.

"We haven't looked inside yet." Refusing to question how the immovable settle had moved or to admit that the woman he'd set his interest on might have magically caused the shift, Aidan took the candle from Christina to examine the shelves above the bench. They might pull outward, but they'd send books tumbling if the hinges were as rusted as those on the bench.

"We'll have to oil the door," Mora murmured beside him. "I daresay it hasn't been touched in a century. The lower door would have been the simplest way to slide in food and supplies. It's a very cramped space."

"The box won't open." Cleaning it off with her scorched skirt, Christina pushed at the latch without result.

Aidan slid the box his way, prepared to pry it open with force.

"I think we had best take it to the others so we are all witnesses to its opening," Mora suggested, covering his hand with hers to halt him.

Aidan didn't understand her reluctance, but he was perfectly willing to throw the damned thing in the laps of his half brothers. It was their property after all.

No, the devil whispered in his ear, *it's yours. You're the earl.*

Over his dead carcass. "Excellent, we'll have a little entertainment with our supper." Grabbing the heavy box, shoving it under his arm, he splayed his hand across the small of Mora's back and steered her toward the door.

He hadn't realized how proprietary his gesture was

until she sent him a considering look. Deciding against dropping his hand, he smirked and pushed her forward.

He loved the way her lips tilted in amusement as she lifted her skirt and obeyed his tactile command.

"Open it, open it!" Alan chanted, dancing about the small gateleg table in the upstairs salon where Aidan had set the elaborately carved box.

The smaller children joined his chant, tumbling over chairs and stools and the feet of adults to join the fun.

Superstitiously, Mora stepped in front of the box so the children could come to no harm from its contents. Catching Aidan's eyes, she saw he'd had the same thought. He'd crossed his massive arms and was guarding their prize with a scowl at the toddlers scrambling around his legs. They didn't seem particularly terrified.

"Do the lot of ye wish to open a box crawling with bugs and snakes?" he demanded, glaring at the imp who would be the future earl.

"Yes!" six-year-old Alan shouted with a grin.

"I think it would make your mama unhappy to pick bugs from your hair," Mora chided gently.

Laughing, Ninian tugged Alan away. "It's a box. I doubt a ghost will leap out of it."

"I don't wish to hear the cries of outrage if we dare open the box before Christina returns," Leila declared from her pillowed throne on the sofa. "But I shall perish of hunger if I do not eat soon."

Already nibbling from a plate Ewen had filled for her, delicate Felicity lifted her eyebrows at Dunstan, sending her bulky brother-in-law lumbering to his feet to fill a plate for his wife from the buffet.

"Henpecked," Aidan muttered for Mora's ears only.

"Gallant gentlemen who love their ladies and are grateful for their willingness to bear their children," Mora countered, more comfortable with this discussion than she was with the box behind them.

Christina swept into the room before Aidan could counter her argument. The duchess's cry of "Open it, open it," so echoed Alan's that her audience laughed aloud.

"Stand back," Aidan cautioned, continuing to block access.

Mora ignored his warning glare. "You know very well it's just the index and maybe a lot of dead bugs in there. You are making mock with this performance."

"How do you know the index is in there?" he shot back. "Did you wave your magic wand and will it so?"

"If you mean to argue about it . . ." One hand balancing his wife's plate, Dunstan circled around them, examined the fastening, then pounded the latch with his fist. The clasp popped open.

Christina skirted around Aidan and flipped open the lid. "It's a book!"

"Told you so." Returning Aidan's glare, Mora peered in.

The experience in the library had thoroughly unsettled her, but here in the normalcy of the family quarters, her confidence returned. She didn't know what she had seen or why the bench had moved, but she knew a moldering old book when she saw one.

Using a napkin Ewen handed her, she lifted the leather-bound volume from its container and laid it on the table.

Unable to resist a part of the Malcolm legend, the other ladies set aside their plates to crowd around. The children, disappointed that the box contained neither bugs nor jewels, lost interest and wandered back to the buffet.

"May I?" Felicity glanced at Mora.

Mora stepped away to make room for the younger, bespectacled woman. "It is your home and your book. I have nothing to do with it."

"On the contrary, I suspect you have everything to do with it," Felicity corrected quietly. Because of her ability to feel painful emotions left behind by others on objects they touched, she always wore gloves to shield her from the worst of any unanticipated distress she might encounter. With her gloved hand, she lifted the cover.

All eyes scanned the faded script that read *The Index of Malcolm Journals, Volume IX, Seventeenth Century.*

"Volume nine?" Aidan asked, appalled. "Is there one for each of the last nine *centuries*?"

"Our ancient ancestors preferred oral histories," Ninian answered as Felicity tested the page with her gloved fingers. "And one assumes there were not many written journals until the family began to proliferate in the Middle Ages. If the library was sorted by century, the first volume might have indexed several centuries at once. It's very likely that the original library contained scrolls from the time of the Romans."

"What became of the earlier indices?" Mora asked, unable to tear her stunned gaze away. She really had found the index. How? And how would it help Aidan, if that was what the spirit messenger intended?

Removing her gloves, Felicity turned the title page. "The other volumes could not fit in the box, so they were sold," she whispered, running her bare fingers over the old vellum. "The grief at their loss is so great that the pages still reek of it."

"The memories are still there?" Leila asked, watching her younger sister with some concern.

"Immense anguish." Felicity pulled her hand away

and retreated to Ewen, who wrapped an arm around her so she might lean back against his chest for comfort against the book's painful vibrations.

Watching the family gather around this most frail of their members, Mora instinctively stepped out of the family circle, into Aidan's presence. Caught up in the moment, he rested his hands on her shoulders. His strength seeped through her.

"It wasn't our many-times-great-grandmother who hid the index, but her maid, at our grandmother's behest," said Felicity. "The first Lady Ives and her daughter had already been banished from Wystan, from their home, and her husband had ordered the library sold off at the time this book was hidden. Look, and see if the entries don't stop by midcentury. Our ancestor must have been the Malcolm librarian of her generation. Her anguish reaches me even through the maid." Felicity choked back a sob and let Ewen lead her back to her seat.

Amazed and confounded, Mora could read only genuine acceptance in the faces of her companions. They believed Felicity had just described the emotions of a woman who'd been dead for a century or more.

Ten

After supper, unable to contain his frustration at the enforced confinement of four walls and far too many people, Aidan took his stallion out for a gallop through the familiar snow-laden woods.

As eager as his master for action, Gallant shook his ebony mane and sang his approval to the night. With the stallion's mighty flanks surging between his thighs, Aidan sought some power over his turbulent thoughts.

He wished he could run into the rogues who had attacked Mora so he might crack a few heads and release the tension that was tying him in knots. Flattening rogues had a simple basic appeal compared with his current predicament.

It wasn't *right* to steal Drogo's title. He knew that in his bones and with every particle of his body.

But it was also *wrong* to let the viscountess destroy the earth, drive out lifelong tenants, and steal land that had been in his mother's family for generations.

He would go mad if he found no alternative. Surely there had to be a legitimate heir somewhere back in time. Yet he'd searched every shelf in the library and found no useful title.

The index had not helped in the least. Everyone in the household over the age of eight had examined it and found no more than a convoluted list of titles and where they would be found on the shelves of a library that no longer existed. As Felicity had predicted, the index ended in 1631. He couldn't imagine why anyone had gone to the trouble of saving it.

He didn't know why he'd thought it might be the answer to his prayers.

Hours later, realizing he was scratching his nose with his leather glove, Aidan cursed and slowed Gallant to a walk. It was all bloody superstition, he concluded. Just because he'd fought a driving need to leave his home to follow an itch on Valentine's Day didn't mean he'd been bewitched by a vicar's damned daughter. It was coincidence that Mora had cast her silly charm asking for help on the same day.

His nose just itched, and there was an end on it. With his luck, he had a pernicious disease and the whole beak would fall off his face.

Still, years of habit had him turning his horse around and heading back to the castle where his half brothers slept with their ladies, and their children snuggled in dreamland. It was Mora his thoughts turned to.

If he could keep her firmly in his mind as the prim Vicar's Daughter with her fiery braids and courageous soul, he might settle the disquiet that had him riding the night. He could end up homeless, but he had the wherewithal to provide a fine house for a wife. A quiet, loyal bride might heal some of the wounds of failure.

But those blue green eyes with their hidden mysteries kept defying what he wanted to believe.

How had she seen the bench move when no one else had?

More superstitious silliness. At least she didn't attempt to make a production of it as the other ladies did. The children had probably dislodged the bench while playing. She'd simply noticed it in the flame of Christina's burning skirt.

Following his nose, he returned to the castle, his unease no more settled than when he'd left. A single flame flickered in the mullioned window of the library level of the tower.

He could stable his horse, then go in the kitchen entrance at the far side of the manor, and whoever was in the library would never hear him.

On the other hand, it could be Dunstan or Drogo in the library, sipping whisky and having a pleasant late-night conversation. He could use a bit of both right now.

He denied the twitching nose that told him he would not like what he found.

Do you believe in me now? her mother's voice taunted in the back of Mora's mind.

"No!" she cried to the empty room. "No, no, no! It is all in my head. I cannot *wish* myself to be what I am not."

Her mother didn't reply because Mora's mind could not summon a reply. Surely if she was sane, and her mother's spirit truly lingered, Brighid would prove her existence by countering her argument.

She'd seen a shadow open the settle. A spirit had led her to the index that the inexplicable writing had told her to find.

But the index hadn't *helped* anything. In despair, Mora ran her fingers over the brittle pages as she'd seen Felicity do, but the pages didn't speak to her of anything but dust and mold.

A tear slipped from the corner of her eye, slid down her nose, and blotted the page. If she had any magical talent at all, the tear should reveal the secrets she sought.

Instead, the tear merely smeared the already-faded ink.

Another tear threatened to follow the first, but she scrubbed it away with the back of her hand. She obviously didn't have enough to do if she could sit here crying over an old book.

At the very least she should have found something that would help Aidan and the family he must dispossess to save his land. Was that too much to ask?

Perhaps that was her problem—she wasn't useful anymore. The villagers would have their new vicar and his wife to help them. The Malcolm ladies were sufficient unto themselves, and she was an outsider. She wasn't used to being unnecessary. The ladies even made their own soaps and scents, the one practical trade she knew.

The Malcolms had endless talents and abilities that she could never hope to duplicate. She didn't know why she was here at all. Even her father didn't want her, if he really was her father. The viscount had never replied to her letter, and he'd had more than enough time to do so. So much for hoping she was a beloved and long-lost daughter.

Feeling as lonely and as inadequate as last month's newssheets, she flipped the page of the index in hopes of understanding why spirits might want her to find it, just in case she really had channeled the supernatural.

She was desperate to have a purpose.

She had slipped down here in her nightclothes after everyone else had retired. She would not have a better chance to explore without an audience to see her failure. Wiping her eyes, shoving her unbound hair out of her face, she applied her mind to examining each entry in the book. There must be something here she wasn't seeing that would help Aidan in his predicament.

Almost every entry began, *A Malcolm Journal of* . . . She could understand a filing system by date instead of title or author with a library like that.

A Journal of Fruits . . . of Midwifery . . . of Calling Spells—what exactly was a calling spell? And why would one need a book of them? The *Spelle for Trubble* had been filed under "calling spells," but it had been singularly useless—unless she counted Aidan's riding to her rescue weeks after the fact.

That he had come just in time to save her from kidnappers was merely a coincidence—wasn't it? And finding the index . . . ?

The hair on the back of her neck rose, and she realized she was no longer alone. Gulping down a lump in her throat, Mora glanced at the doorway.

If she believed in Satan, she could believe Old Nick stood there wrapped in a black cloak with his midnight hair windblown and falling loose of its confines. His dark eyes glittered with the fiery reflection of her candles. But she didn't believe Satan would suffer as this man did. She could feel his pain as well as her own.

"You've been crying." He crushed his gloves in his fist and strode into the circle of candlelight. Melted snow gleamed on his mud-streaked boots. He'd been outside at midnight.

"No, I haven't." She scrubbed at the telltale streaks on her face. Always speaking the truth was one of those lessons she hadn't found practical. "Are you a highwayman?"

His laugh was curt. "I no longer believe riches solve everything."

She nodded in understanding, and her unruly hair fell forward over her drab dressing gown. Realizing he'd caught her in complete dishabille, she hastily closed the gap in the blanket she had draped around her.

"Your hair is like the fiery coals that burn in my hearth," he murmured, catching a flaming strand between his bare fingers. "It bewitches me."

With another man, she might have been uncomfortable, afraid, or just irritated at his presumption. With Aidan, she felt safe and enraptured by his regard. Loneliness had obviously addled her mind. There was nothing safe about a man who could throw three others across a clearing.

"I always thought witches had black hair like yours."

He let loose a real laugh then and wrapped his hand in the strands crinkled by her braids. "Except for Leila, the Malcolms are blond witches. You have the hair of a temptress, rich and wavy."

"I do not feel like a temptress," she objected. "I feel like a fool caught reading this silly book at midnight." Although if he continued stroking her hair that way, she would not only feel like a fool, but act the part of one and touch him in return.

The scent of crisp night air embraced her as he leaned down to brush the slightest of kisses over her temple and catch the tear in the corner of her eye with a rough fingertip. She froze, not having any notion of how to deal with such intimacy.

"Shall I take you up to bed, then?" he whispered suggestively.

Double entendre or not, no man had ever spoken to her with such masculine assertiveness. She ought to be fearful, or at least modest, but for whatever reason, his intimacy reassured rather than intimidated.

"Last I looked, Verity was sleeping in my bed." She bit back a smile at his chuckle of understanding. Leila's three-year-old had a tendency to sleepwalk.

Casting his cloak over a chair, Aidan took the seat on the narrow sofa beside Mora as if he'd been invited. Propping his arm over the sofa back, he cupped her shoulder with his bare hand.

Mora thought she might spontaneously combust at his proximity. She burned at every point where they touched.

Aidan leaned over to turn a page of the index. "That should put you to sleep in no time," he said with disgust, recognizing the tome.

"It's fascinating in its own way, imagining all the ladies over the years penning their private thoughts and observations. Human nature has not changed much over the centuries."

Neither had the attraction between male and female. Aidan Dougal was exceedingly male, and next to his powerfully built frame, she felt feminine and protected. His whisker-stubbled jaw brushed her hair, and she drank in the raw scent of him. Men even smelled different from women—of evergreen, woodsmoke, and a musk that could be described only as masculine. If he placed his hand anywhere near her face, she would be forced to bite his finger to see if he tasted as delicious as he smelled.

"The ladies would have done better to lavish their interest on their husbands and households than to waste it on words no others but themselves would see," he said.

Aidan buried his long nose in the hair near her nape. Unsettled, Mora did not know whether to elbow him, leap from her seat to avoid his presumption, or pound him over the head with her book for his male narrow-mindedness.

"Are the husbands and household here hurting for the varied interests of the ladies?" she demanded. "You were looking for this book," she pointed out. "Some woman must have written something of importance to you. What is it?"

He explored her ear with his fingertip, not backing off an inch. "Sometimes, I have worms for brains," he suggested. "It is the only explanation I can think of right now. There is only one thing of interest associated with that book, and it's the woman holding it."

She might be unmarried and from an isolated village, but she had observed a great deal about life over her years of tending her neighbors. She wasn't a silly, unsophisticated miss bowled over by a few pretty words from a striking gentleman. Even if he did make her heart race.

You could seduce him as easily as he seduces you, a voice mused inside her head.

Startled by the concept as much as the voice, Mora jerked her head up so quickly that she nearly clipped Aidan's jaw. *Seduce him?* Was she mad, or just wicked?

He pulled back a little warily. "Did I offend you? I have not a gentleman's way with the ladies."

"Don't give me that trumpery country-boy cant." Angry at herself and him, and at the world in general for creating this ridiculously impossible situation, Mora turned the page and began reading the next list of titles. "You are about as unsophisticated as two dukes and three earls run together. I cannot believe no one sees through you."

Retrieving his roaming hand, he rubbed the stubbled jaw she'd nearly clipped and stared at her with fascination. "What makes you think that?"

"I grew up with country boys." She ran her finger over the page, determined to keep her wits about her with this unattainable man. "They are more likely to offer me a bushel of corn than to speak of my temptress hair. And they would expect to be smacked silly for touching my ear, and they do not ride stallions with the blood of Arabians in them. If they should luck upon one somehow, they'd sell it for two good plow horses and some cattle."

Before he could interrupt, she continued. "Nor do they rub shoulders with dukes and earls with the ease of a king. I know more about you than you wish. You might as well tell me all and make this easier for both of us."

"*This?*" he inquired cautiously, sitting even farther back.

"You, me, whatever is happening here." She waved her hand to encompass the candlelit setting. "I *saw* a spirit open that hidden door. And it is because *you* touched me. I cannot do these things on my own."

There, she'd said it. Let him make of it what he would.

"Because *I* touched you?" he asked with an incredulity bordering on anger. "What have I to do with it?"

"I don't know. I can't say." His anger fed hers. "I just know you are looking for something, and I am not, and the spirits are using me to help you look. Not the ladies, for they know even less than I do."

"They have known me longer than you have," he argued, pointlessly.

"They are caught up in their own lives, and I learned early to observe far more than I ought. I can tell you secrets even the ladies do not know, but I won't, for there is no purpose in revealing them. But if you cannot confide in me, there may come a time when I must reveal your secrets to ensure the safety of others."

"Ye cannae know anything of me," he protested.

"I overheard some of your conversation with the attorney. I know far more than you wish me to know," she declared, throwing all caution to the wind.

His resounding silence echoed in the old library,

and Mora wanted to weep. Instead she stiffened her spine and spoke out again. "It would be criminal if you lost your land because you cannot harm others by admitting your true birth."

He tensed, and she feared he would run off again.

Instead he clung to his scorn. "There is no magic in eavesdropping."

So he would not discuss the subject. She could understand the pain it must bring. But if she was to have a purpose, then it must be in helping him. Daringly, she provoked him again. "Fine. Prove we did not find the book together by helping me now to read through it."

"You are being more ridiculous than any Malcolm," he complained in a near shout.

"Hold my hand as I draw it down the page," she commanded. "Or do you not dare?"

"Hold your hand?" he asked, calming down.

She knew where his mind traveled, but she was equipped to deal with male fantasies. "Yes. Odd things seem to happen when we are close. Let's prove once and for all that it is merely coincidence."

"I can do that." Returning one brawny arm to rest behind her back, he folded her fingers in his other hand. The chill of the night was still on his skin, but it warmed quickly as he drew her hand down the page.

She was practically wrapped in his embrace. She could not get much closer unless she sat on his lap. Her cheeks flushed as that image rose in her mind. She'd seen Felicity sitting in Ewen's lap, teasing him with darting kisses. The picture had been such a happy, loving one—

When she nervously tried to turn the page, the book slid sideways off her lap.

"You are forever dropping things." Aidan grabbed

the heavy tome before it could slither down her blanket to the floor.

"It is only around you . . ." Her voice trailed off as her glance fell to the page that had opened when he'd grabbed it. ". . . that magic happens."

Her finger rested on a line that seemed to glow and jump off the page with dark light—*The Ancestry of the Descendants of Dunwoodie Mackenzie Malcolm and Erithea Malcolm Wystan.*

Eleven

Concentrating on moist ruby lips more tempting than all the treasures of India, Aidan saw in Mora's gasp an opportunity. Leaning closer, he tested his lips against hers.

Her mouth was as luscious as he'd suspected, soft and warm and tasting of strawberries. She struggled briefly, pushing a futile hand against his neckcloth. He pulled back a bit, giving her time to adjust, and when she did not slap him or flee in repulsion, he tightened his grasp on her shoulder, and tasted her again.

With a soft sigh, she returned his pressure. Her slender fingers curled in his linen over the place where his heart threatened to leap from his chest. Triumphant, he nibbled at her lower lip, kissing the sweet corners of her mouth, teasing her into opening for him.

And when she did . . . lightning flashed and thunder rumbled. Unsteadily, Aidan lowered his arm to her waist and tugged her closer, letting Mora twine her arms around his neck rather than remove his tongue from the welcoming haven of her mouth. He drank in her breath with her kisses, concentrating on this one sensation rather than the clamor of all his senses at once.

He could have spent hours learning all the ways he could kiss her. He had yet to taste her cherry cheeks or lick her cockleshell ear. But he gradually became aware that her hands pushed rather than clung, and that her breathing had become rapid pants. He was aware that his kisses were not that of a gentleman to a maiden. His head spun in delight that she'd allowed him so much.

Reluctantly, he closed her lips with a parting kiss, then sat back just enough to gaze down into her sea blue eyes. He caught a glimpse of panic behind the mysterious mists, but it was all right for a woman to be a little afraid of heady desire. He had enough confidence for both of them.

"You taste of strawberries," he murmured, trying to cool the rampaging need in his blood. He wanted to carry her up to his bed, but some semblance of sanity warned him there were reasons he should not. Life would be much simpler if he could just act instead of think.

"I . . ." She blinked rapidly, as if she was struggling to rein in the same forces that were engulfing him.

She touched her fingers to her puffy lips, and he feared he'd bruised them. Unable to stop himself, he planted a quick peck on her fingers and the corners of her mouth. "I did not mean to frighten you." Unrepentant, he stole another kiss.

This time, she touched her fingers to *his* mouth. He didn't mind. He wanted her to touch him, yearned for the tender caress of a feminine hand. He was having the devil of a time keeping his hands from roaming and frightening her more.

"You did it again," she finally whispered.

"I'll do it again and again now I know how sweet you are," he teased. He might never be steady again.

"No . . ." She reddened and ducked her head. "The book. Look at the book."

He wanted to look at her. With her hair spread in a fiery cloud over her shoulders, she appeared wonderfully mussed and ready for bed. He didn't want any other man enjoying this intimate sight. He gathered thick sheaves of mahogany in his hand to prevent his hand from straying elsewhere.

When she would not raise her fair face to him again, he cast a grudging glance at the damned book. Her shapely fingers rested on a line of text that stood out from all the rest. Why had he not seen it earlier?

"You think we made it appear?" he asked in exasperation.

At his tone, her lovely bruised lips tightened, but her reply lacked heat. "Did you have some need of a Malcolm genealogy?"

Aidan thought his heart had stopped beating altogether.

Slowly, he dropped his gaze to the page. This time, he read the highlighted words aloud. *"The Ancestry of the Descendants of Dunwoodie Mackenzie Malcolm and Erithea Malcolm Wystan."*

"Kissing cousins, perhaps?" she asked wryly. "Why do you need a Malcolm genealogy if you're an Ives?"

Withdrawing his arm from behind her, Aidan pulled the book into his lap. "I never said I was an Ives," he growled.

"Even your attorney says you're an Ives," she corrected. "I can keep your secrets, but if we are to solve this mystery, it would help if I knew for certain what you seek."

The truth of his ancestry was too raw a wound, and he had no intention of dealing with it now. He closed the volume, tucked it under his arm, and rose. "It amuses me to read family trees. Come along. It's late. I'll return Verity to her bed."

He held out his hand to her. She ignored it. Gathering up the blanket that had fallen from her shoulders, she picked up the skirt of her robe and stood up without his assistance. Chin high, she sailed out of the library ahead of him, with all the glory of Boudicca leading her troops to war.

Aidan chuckled. He'd found a warrior princess to warm his nights. Why had he ever thought he wanted a docile mouse?

"Where did the index go?" Felicity asked the next morning, sitting in the sunny upstairs salon and tossing aside the book she wasn't reading.

"Ask Mr. Dougal," Mora replied, looking up from the hem she was repairing on Verity's nightgown. The child had apparently ripped it in her night wandering.

"Aidan? Why would he have it? He scorns books."

"No, he scorns that which he doesn't understand. It's a common male trait." Mora bit off the thread and held up the lacy linen to examine it for further damage.

"Ewen studies what he can't understand until he figures it out," Felicity argued.

"Your husband is not a common male." Mora jabbed her needle into the pincushion.

"And I am, you imply?" Strolling into the salon with the book in question under his arm, Aidan snatched the scissors from Mora's worktable before she could stab him with them, and deposited them safely out of her reach.

One moment's rashness, and the arrogant man thought he knew her too well. He *did* know her too well. Her rebellious inner nature wanted to puncture his inflated arrogance.

He dropped the index on the sofa beside Felicity. "I've marked a page that may be of interest to you."

She had no right to question or argue, or stick him

like a pincushion, Mora reminded herself. Aidan Dougal and his stubborn narrow-mindedness were of no concern to her whatsoever.

Except he'd come when she'd been most troubled and kissed her until the stars spun in the sky. She wanted to kiss a man again. Not necessarily Aidan, she told herself.

Lie to others, if you must, her mother said, *but never lie to yourself.*

"Tell me something I don't know," Mora muttered back.

Both Aidan and Felicity turned to stare at her, and she reddened. "Tell Felicity how you discovered the title, if you dare," she retaliated to redirect their interest.

For a moment, dark mischief gleamed in Aidan's eyes and twitched on his wicked lips. "Aye, and that would be a pretty tale."

Mora reddened even more. Of course he couldn't tell everyone what they had done. She should have boxed his ears when she'd had the chance.

Apparently satisfied with her mutinous expression, he turned back to Felicity. "The book fell open to this page. Miss Abbott thinks the spirit is moving it."

Even Felicity heard the laughter in his voice and shot him a disapproving look. "You are doing just as Mora said, scorning something you don't understand." She studied the open page. "Which title? These all appear to be from the early seventeenth century."

Mora raised her eyebrows but said nothing. Couldn't Felicity see the bold title? Last night it had stood black and thick and almost radiated with life.

Aidan pointed at the page. "This one. Apparently Malcolms believed in marrying each other."

"Oh, that one." Felicity dismissed the title and closed the index. "Considering that the entire population of Scotland in the 1500s had to be less than five hundred thousand, and a very small percentage of those were substantial landholders, intermarrying among the wealthy was quite common. For a price, the church would offer a dispensation for cousins of a certain degree of separation. One must only look to our royal lineage to see how that works."

Mora choked back a smirk at Aidan's flummoxed expression. The genealogy was obviously important to him or he would never have come in here. And Felicity apparently recognized the title. Would he reveal his interest now? It would be amusing to watch His Arrogance squirm.

"You are familiar with the title?" he asked with feigned disinterest, pacing to the window and looking out.

"Why?" Felicity asked. "Do you think the spirit calls you to it?"

Mora couldn't prevent a giggle from escaping. The lady's mind worked the same as hers. She'd had little experience of that at home.

"That line of text was illumined last evening," Mora explained, knowing the stubborn idiot wouldn't admit it.

"Illumined?" Interest caught, Felicity flipped back to the marked page. "It looks the same as any other now," she reported in disappointment. She took off her glove and ran her fingers over the page. "No, I receive nothing more than I did before."

"Mr. Dougal does not believe he must touch the paper to make the magic happen."

"Mr. Dougal has touched the page and magic does *not* happen," he said mockingly, strolling back to the center of the room. "Does the name Wystan not intrigue you?"

Felicity gave a little shrug. "We've always known

this keep belonged to our ancestors. Dunwoodie Malcolm is legendary in our family, the last known Malcolm male, although we're none too certain that he was Malcolm by birth. We have no proof that he possessed any gift or talent. He acquired this keep when he married Erithea. I believe she was his third cousin and had what the Scots call second sight. They produced half a dozen children, and Wystan keep was given to their eldest daughter as dowry when she married an Ives. It has descended as an Ives holding ever since. I've glanced through this genealogy. It is a very small book, almost a pamphlet."

"You've seen this book?"

Mora thought Aidan might go through the roof in excitement or take Felicity by the throat and rattle more information out of her. He somehow managed to restrain himself, although the room almost shuddered with repressed tension. Or did she imagine that, too?

Felicity curled her bulk upon the sofa and wrapped her arms around a pillow. Apparently she enjoyed tormenting Aidan in her own quiet way. She cast Mora a laughing glance before following Aidan's impatient pacing. "It is part of your library in Scotland, one of the books your mother collected. It was tucked inside a portfolio of obscure references and drawings of Wystan Castle. No doubt some ancestor meant to write a history but ran out of time."

"My library," Aidan mumbled, pacing faster and rubbing his face.

Mora thought surely the floor shook with his every step. He was a big man, but this was a stone fortress. The floor should not shake.

Whether or not he was aware of the vibrations he caused, Aidan halted at the window. "The snow clears. I can ride home and be back within a week."

"You could spend another week fruitlessly search-ing that cavern you call a library and still not find it," Felicity argued. "Why are you in such a hurry to acquire it?"

He struggled inwardly, and Mora thought he would refuse to respond as was his wont. To her surprise, he gave a half answer. "A neighbor and I are having a dispute of sorts. There could be information of use in the pamphlet."

"In a *Malcolm* pamphlet?" Felicity asked, laughing, obviously rubbing in an old argument. "Our scribbling might be of use to you?"

He shot her a glare over his shoulder and refused to say more. Mora thought both parties to this silly teasing needed to be bopped over the head. However the ties were knotted, they were family, although Aidan seemed determined not to admit it.

Because he wanted it too much, she realized. He would never admit he needed anyone or anything—for fear of bringing harm in some way to those he cared about.

"You have a large library?" Mora asked, sympa-thetically diverting Aidan from his discomfort. A li-brary seemed unusual for a man who so obviously preferred physical activity.

"My mother collected it. Felicity has made some progress in organizing it. I don't see why I couldn't find the damned paper on my own." He leaned his broad hand against the icy windowpane, regarding the countryside with wistfulness.

"My foster father was an amateur genealogist," Mora confided. "I am familiar with the pamphlets that were favored at the turn of the last century. The rib-bons often come unbound and the pages are easily overlooked."

"If there is some importance attached to the book,

you should go with Aidan," Felicity said matter-of-factly. "But so far, I fail to see the significance."

"She cannot come with me. Don't be ridiculous." Aidan pushed away from the window.

He left the room without another word, leaving Mora deflated and empty, and just a little bit angry. How could he have said all those sweet words last night, kissed her as if she meant something to him, then walk away as if she did not exist? She knew better than to believe a man's pretty words, but was she really no more than a tedious spinster with whom he'd idled away a few entertaining moments? The thought tore a hole in her self-confidence. For that alone, she ought to smack him.

"He is a restless man," Felicity said, flipping through the index with her gloved fingers. "He never lingers, almost as if he's afraid of becoming attached to us."

Or afraid he would bring them harm.

He will die without your aid, her mother whispered inside Mora's head.

Who would die? Mora had thought the warning referred to her father, but if that were the case, why would the voice repeat itself now? Did the voice mean *Aidan* was in danger?

Perhaps His Arrogance deserved it, but she didn't want to believe a man as confident as Aidan could die—or that he must rely on the aid of someone as helpless as her for rescue. Certain it was her own need speaking, terrified she belonged in Bedlam, Mora tried to concentrate on her sewing.

Not until she heard the sound of Aidan's mighty steed galloping away did her heart crack open, and all the uncertainty and pain spill out.

She might never see him again. The one man in all her life who had awakened her senses, and he was leaving. Despite their heated kisses, she hadn't been able to hold his interest. Despite her cleverness, her experience, and the maddening voice in her head, she had not been able to help him.

If this was a test of her strength as a witch, she was failing.

She detested not knowing if she *was* a witch. One's place in life ought to be certain, but the peculiar clues she'd been offered came only when someone else was in the room, like Aidan. Uncertainty made her itchy.

She might be an unlovable spinster, but that didn't mean she couldn't be as strong as the Malcolm ladies.

Setting aside her needle, Mora stood. The obedient vicar's daughter that she had been trembled at her daring. Her mother's daughter that she wished to be whispered from her broken heart, cheering her into doing the outrageous.

"I must go after him," she said quietly.

Puzzled, Felicity watched Mora slip from the room as if she had said she would fetch some tea.

She glanced down at the index, then up at the window where Aidan's horse could no longer be seen.

Clumsily, she untangled her feet from her skirt and rose, steadying her ungainly body before setting off in search of her sisters and cousin.

By the time she found them, they were all in Mora's room, telling her what she should pack and sending servants to fetch horses and riders.

Twelve

The farther Aidan rode from Wystan, the more wrong he felt. He always rode toward trouble, not away, and this felt like running away.

Every ounce of logic and instinct in him insisted that he needed his mother's family tree to save his home. He *had* to find that genealogy. He could only hope that this was the one he needed, although why he should think so, he'd rather not contemplate.

The key lay in his own home, where he should have stayed in the first place.

But then he would never have met the Vicar's Daughter.

The witch who had called him from his home with her spells for trouble.

He desperately longed to believe she was the lovely, prim daughter of a vicar, an exceptionally learned one with whom he could easily converse while whiling away a winter's evening in front of a warm fire. A brave and bold one who didn't faint when the ground trembled and the walls shook. One whose kisses tasted like strawberries in winter.

It was pure wonder that the entire keep hadn't tumbled on their heads after that kiss. It still scorched his memory, keeping him warm as he rode northward.

He had tried to catch a few hours' sleep after their midnight encounter, but his mind could not get past the sensual woman in the library, the one who had drugged him with kisses and set his mind on fire with her odd combination of timidity and temerity. Rather than think about a musty old book with illuminated handwriting, he had sought refuge in trying to imagine the womanly form she had hidden beneath the folds of a blanket.

He wasn't a celibate priest. He'd had small, pert-breasted women in India, ones with lithe brown bodies scented with the exotic perfumes of brothels. He'd indulged in blowsy barmaids upon his return to England, women with a good heft to their hips and soft yielding flesh a man could sink his fingers into. He didn't have to fear harming women like that.

Physically, he'd enjoyed them all. They'd relieved his needs and given him pleasure. But over the years, he'd grown bored and sought something more elusive, a wit to match his own, perhaps, or a natural modesty not found in the type of woman who gave herself freely.

For a while, he'd thought his half brothers had discovered the cure for what ailed him. Their Malcolm women were refreshing, courageous, lovely, all those things he craved and more. He'd followed them about longingly, looking for the one who was meant for him—until he realized the daughters of wealthy aristocrats had manners and needs that did not suit the rough, isolated life he preferred. They wanted society and dancing and company, and created mischief when not otherwise occupied.

They were Malcolms, and more trouble than remedy.

And then Mora Abbott had appeared—like magic.

He let Gallant stop to drink at an icy burn while he tried to piece together the puzzle that was the Vicar's Daughter. He wanted her with every inch of his body, and that was a great lot of inches. Perhaps isolating himself in his castle without a woman all these long months had been a mistake, and the attraction was merely physical, but he didn't think so.

He admired everything about her—except her belief in superstitious hocus-pocus. Yet for a woman who possessed everything he wanted, he might even learn to tolerate that feminine whimsy.

He didn't know how she had produced the index or highlighted the title. He didn't have the patience to work it out, not when his mind and his heart were fixed on the battle for his home.

And that's where they must stay fixed until the viscountess was defeated. He couldn't afford to lose sight of his goal. No matter how wrong it felt to leave the keep and the fascinating Mora Abbott behind, he must proceed as logic dictated. It was not her battle to fight, although he prayed she kept her word and revealed naught of what she'd overheard. Should she say anything at all to Drogo . . .

As if the stress of his conflict afflicted the rocks below, the ground rumbled. He'd learned action worked better than thinking too hard. He spurred his stallion forward.

The ground beneath him surged in a rippling wave. Gallant threw back his mighty head and neighed his complaint. Easy in his seat, Aidan tugged the reins of his faithful companion reassuringly and ducked to ride under a low-hanging oak branch.

Without warning, the stallion reared up on his hind legs, flinging his rider's head backward, directly into the branch under which they'd just passed.

Despite the fur-lined, hooded mantle the ladies had provided, Mora's teeth chattered. She was certain the teeth of the two stableboys riding with her ought to do the same, but they were of heartier stock and yelled and laughed to each other as they rode through the winter wonderland.

It was easy enough to follow Aidan's path through the melting snow. No other had dared the isolated dirt road over such dangerous terrain. Beneath the slush were ruts of mud so thick the horses' hooves churned it into a sticky pudding that clung to their flanks and endangered life and limb.

She had never done anything so harebrained in her life as to follow him, but now that she had done it, she would not turn back. It felt amazingly right to be traveling this path. She had survived through stubbornness and determination, not by becoming a weeping, brokenhearted coward.

Once she had made it clear that she wished to go, the ladies had not told their spouses of her intentions, or she would now be leading an entire parade of protective Ives. The ladies had clucked and disapproved, but they had never once refused her request. The freedom of such a household still amazed her. Were she going anywhere else but after Mr. Dougal, she would regret leaving Wystan behind.

Felicity had drawn a detailed map, giving distances and noting inns. There were dismayingly few crossroads of civilization in this northern outpost of Northumberland, but there would be a few more when they reached the main highway into Edinburgh. She hoped to reach the highway before day's end.

She hoped she would reach Aidan.

She would not think on her madness. Perhaps being a witch meant one had to be half-mad, but it wasn't as if she had anyone or anything depending on her, so if she froze to death in her foolishness, it would be no great loss.

She didn't wish to die, though. She wished to live.

Apparently, taking chances on dying was part of living.

The ground rumbled, and her horse reared, shrieking in terror. Inexperienced at riding, Mora clung to the saddle for dear life. At the same time, the mare in front bucked and threw her young rider into a drift. The lad got up laughing and brushing himself off. Scarcely a cloud darkened the sun as the ground steadied again.

The vicar had never owned more than an aging carriage horse, and it had been a long time since childhood when Mora had practiced riding the poor creature. Biting her lip, she hung on to the reins and pommel while her mount settled. She had felt that rumbling ground before.

Aidan had to be near.

"Are you all right?" she called down to the boy.

"Aye, my lady. Just damp, I am." He grabbed the horse's reins and swung back into the saddle.

"Did you feel the earthquake?" she asked.

"Earthquake? Is that what that was?" He gave her a quizzical glance from beneath the knit muffler wrapped around his head. "Never felt the like before."

A little shaken, she steadied her mount and waited for the second boy to catch up with her. "Have you never felt the ground rumble before?" she demanded.

He squinted at her through the bright sunlight. "Not that I know of. Mayhap the snow melted too fast. I've seen the ice break and crash and rumble like that."

"The ground does not regularly quake?" As Aidan had said it did.

They looked at her as if she were peculiar, and she didn't ask again.

She had come north to lose her mind, she decided.

The duchess must have been humoring her when she said she'd seen the magic writing. Insane people probably thought they lived inside their dreams all the time. It was a lovely, pleasant world, thinking one had the power to change the path of one's life with a bit of heat or a circle of salt. A quite mad world where the voices of the dead spoke inside one's head. And she had imagined the ground surging and rippling to bring down an oak tree.

Had she imagined dragging Mr. Dougal to her workroom? What a wonderful imagination she must have to still remember the heat of his flesh when she'd dressed his wound, the redness of his blood as it had poured on the bandage, the size and hardness of his muscles when he'd held her in his arms.

And moved the earth with his kiss.

Well, it was certainly a more interesting world than sanity.

She tried to ignore the occasional rumble she continued to feel as they approached the brook—the burn—on Felicity's map. Her mare tossed its head restlessly, but she was a very well-trained animal. While the boys clambered down to explore, Mora let the horse drink and tried not to be too terrified of slipping into madness. Perhaps Christina would kindly wait until Mora was beyond knowing where she was before the duchess shut her up in an asylum.

The ground groaned and the bare path ahead rippled like water on a lake before a storm. Trees swayed and the wind whistled, although she could see perfectly well there wasn't a cloud in the sky. This wasn't ice floes crashing. Even the boys seemed puzzled.

An enormous black steed ran riderless down the hill ahead, tossing its mane and whinnying as it sensed the mares.

Mora didn't need the voice's warning to spur her terrified mare across the burn. She remembered the words all too clearly. *He may die without your aid.*

She no longer questioned who *he* was. Only one man could make the ground tremble. And only one man rode a steed that size.

Behind her, the boys shouted and scrambled to remount their horses, but she had no time to wait. Aidan was in trouble.

The huge stallion reared, screaming disapproval to the cloudless sky, as she approached. Then without a word or touch from her, it settled down, flicked its head, and allowed Mora to catch its reins. She was fanciful enough to believe the horse had granted her permission.

And now she was expected to follow the stallion's lead as it broke into a gentle canter that her smaller mare could manage.

Magic, she thought wildly. Having Aidan's stallion run to her for aid had to be magic. Terrified as she was for Aidan's safety, she still felt triumphant exhilaration. She really might be a witch!

It was a bit of a letdown when she finally came upon Mr. Dougal seated upon a snow-covered boulder, perfectly healthy, although scowling and sour. He nursed a bruise upon his jaw and had drops of snow in his queue, but his brawny shoulders rested nonchalantly against a large oak, warmly encased in his cloak. He wore his hat pulled down to reveal only his frown. Apparently bruised but unbroken, he sprawled his booted legs in front of him, crossing them at the ankles on a smaller rock. He looked for all the world like a king upon his throne, glowering upon his subjects. He could not help but see her from miles away, so barren was this hill. He had found the only tree upon it, and had not stirred from his seat to greet her.

"I trusted that horse," he growled as Mora brought their dancing mounts to a standstill before him. "And what does he do? Run after a pretty mare like every other damned fool male in the world."

"Is that what happened?" she asked in genuine curiosity.

"You have a better explanation?" he demanded, sliding off the boulder to come to his full towering height and stride toward her.

"Well, I thought perhaps the earthquake frightened him," she said tentatively, watching his face for any sign that he thought her mad. "Or your horse has better sense than you and came seeking my aid," she added pertly, for good measure.

He merely scowled more deeply and appropriated the reins. "What the devil are you doing out here all alone?"

"Saving you from walking home . . . and you are most welcome," she retorted, unreasonably irritated by his refusal to answer her question.

"The last time you walked out alone, you were beset by bandits."

"I had company—until the earth quaked." If she was mad, she'd revel in it. If she was a witch—well, she would revel in that, too. For all that mattered, she would rejoice in being in his company again, even if it also irritated her. She might as well learn to enjoy her perversity.

"Where is that company now?" He glanced back the way she had come.

"They're boys. They're fine. I don't know if they followed or turned back when I ran off without them."

"I'm in a hurry. I don't have time to dally for women and children. We'll wait until they catch up, and then you can go back with them."

Oh, that really baked the cake. Mora thought if she

truly was a witch, she'd burn a hole right through his fat head with her glare. "It is nearly sundown," she said frostily. "The inn is a few miles ahead. Unless you tell me that your injured shoulder is troubling you—which I'm perfectly well aware you wouldn't even if your arm had fallen off and was lying on the ground—I'm going on. You can stay here for the boys if you like."

Without waiting for him to utter another command, complaint, or idiocy, she spurred her mare into a walk. She had no clue where the road was beneath the snow because Aidan had yet to mark it, but she could tell north from south. She'd get there.

She heard Aidan's curses as loudly as she heard the pounding of his stallion's hooves. He didn't speak another word, simply pulled ahead of her and set the pace, leaving her to ride in the muck flung up by his mount's long strides.

She might be mad, but she wasn't so foolish as to race him. Dropping back slightly, she followed at a more sedate pace, forcing him to glance over his shoulder occasionally to be certain she was still there. She exulted in those glances, for they meant he hadn't forgotten her. She fully intended to be the itchy insect beneath his skin until the conceited coxcomb acknowledged not only her existence, but also the fact that she could hear voices he couldn't.

Oh, she liked that idea exceedingly well.

She liked it far better than being the vicar's obedient daughter.

She thought madness might become her.

Aidan brooded all the way to the inn, but the ground didn't tremble again. He refused to believe it was because the Vicar's Witch had caught up with him.

And he refused to believe it had trembled in the first place because he was angry about leaving her behind. If the damned earth shook every time he got angry, then it ought to be rocking like a cradle right now.

The women had simply scrambled his brain with their scents and laughter, that was all. Now that he was out in the clear air, all would be well. Life was far simpler when he traveled alone, undisturbed by riotous emotions.

Unfortunately, he wasn't alone.

Climbing down from the saddle, giving the hostler extra coins to feed the horses well, Aidan was forced to acknowledge the woman doggedly following him. Forced, not only to acknowledge, but to help her down from her horse since he damned well wasn't letting the hostler do it.

His great hands slipped beneath Mora's thick mantle, curving around her corseted waist in a perfect fit as he lowered her to the ground. Her gloves resting against his shoulders reminded him of softer embraces. Gazing down into her heart-shaped face beneath her fur-lined hood, encountering turquoise eyes not inches from his own, turned his innards upside down.

"It's a crude inn and no place for a lady," he grumbled.

"Felicity has stayed here." Removing her hands from his shoulders, she made a show of brushing out her skirt.

If he didn't know better, he'd say she had been as affected by his touch as he had by hers. He could still feel her hands on him. His nose was intoxicated by the scent of rosemary and lilac drifting upward with every brush of her skirt. He needed to taste her again.

"Or we could rest the horses and ride on," she continued while he stood there, tongue-tied. She met his gaze with bold defiance. "I'm sure your shoulder has magically healed and does not pain you at all."

That's what he had intended to do—ignore the knot on his head and all the bones he'd jarred in his fall and keep moving. But not with her along. He could tell she strained to keep her teeth from chattering, and there was an unhealthy pallor of blue beneath her fine skin. She was being as stupidly heedless as he was.

"I need food." Grasping her elbow, he dragged her into the tavern.

He was no stranger here. The innkeeper nodded and sent a girl to fetch supper when they took a table by the fire. The other regulars noted his companion and stayed where they were. He understood that traveling alone with a lady compromised her, but if she didn't care, he wouldn't either. Much.

"Why the devil did you follow me?" he growled, finally giving in to his curiosity.

"Because it's obvious you need me to find what you seek," she said simply, holding her gloved hands out to the fire.

"It's not obvious to me," he grumbled. "I'm perfectly capable of finding a pamphlet inside a history of Wystan."

She looked daunted for a moment, and a bit weary. Then she lifted her pointy little chin. She'd removed her mantle, and a curl shook loose from her coronet of braids. "You'll not know what to do with it when you find it. You are working with what you don't understand and refuse to accept."

"I'm working with madwomen who scribble all night and day, evidently for lack of anything better to do!" He tried not to shout, but he knew they were attracting attention.

"I'll not argue with you there," she answered, to his surprise.

He wanted her to argue. It was much simpler to hold her off if they were fighting, if he could slot her into the category of his brothers' meddling wives.

"You're here all alone. What if I want to kiss you again?" Aidan gave her his best glower.

The Vicar's Witch smiled with delight. "I think you should try," she dared him.

It was going to be a damned long night.

Thirteen

Traveling with Christina, a duchess, did not compare with traveling like a commoner, Mora decided as Aidan led her up to the inn's one private room. No maids preceded them to lay down clean linens, press gowns, or light fires. Or to act as chaperone.

She was nervously conscious of Aidan's closeness as they ascended the worn stairs. The hall was too narrow for both his broad shoulders and her, so he followed behind—watching the sway of her hips, she was certain. He even hummed a happy little tune.

She thought she might be obliged to slap him, except she welcomed his presence in the dark passage. And it gave her a shocking thrill to know he enjoyed watching her. She had never thought she would take such pleasure in the attention of any man. But Aidan was vastly more exciting than just *any* man.

Still, he had ridden away this morning without a second look back. She would do well to remember that.

"The lads will sleep in the stable," Aidan informed her as they reached the chamber door. The boys had shown up at the inn shortly after their arrival, apparently having chosen the adventure of trailing them over returning to Wystan. "They can escort you back in the morning."

Mora didn't waste time arguing. Aidan might be exciting, but he was still a stubborn mule. "Believe as you will, sir. Thank you for the excellent supper. Good night."

She entered and shut the door in his face, then stood there, holding her breath, waiting for the floor to crack wide open or the thin walls to tremble and collapse at her insolence.

Almost with disappointment, she studied the door when the room did not explode with the force of his fury. She had been quite certain he was the cause of the earth's tremors. And she'd thought she had the ability to stir him. That she did not now tore another shred of her confidence.

The door had the flimsiest of locks. She would need to set up a warning system before she could relax sufficiently to sleep. Not that she feared Aidan, but several of the men below appeared to be unsavory sorts. The attack by thieves had proved she wasn't in Sommersville any longer.

She turned to examine the contents of the room, seeking a means of blocking the door. Someone had already carried up her saddlebags. She dropped her mantle beside them on the bed and studied the problem.

She could push the chest across the doorway. That wouldn't stop determined thieves, but it would provide enough of an obstruction to wake her, and perhaps rouse the household, should someone try to get in.

She crossed the chamber to check the window. The sash opened easily enough, but the ground was a long way down. Throwing herself from the third floor to protect her virtue seemed a little drastic.

Nervously, she wondered how soundly Aidan slept. If she screamed, would he hear her?

Caution and rebellion did not sit happily with each

other. If she intended to pursue a course of doing what she shouldn't, she'd much rather be the impulsive sort who didn't consider the consequences of her rebellion.

She tensed at the sound of a scuffle outside the door. It stopped, and she breathed in relief.

There it was again. Swallowing a lump of fear, Mora grabbed the chest and began shoving it toward the door. That should be impulsively silly enough for her. She'd already determined the chest wouldn't stop a thief.

Halting, she glanced at her saddlebags. A hairbrush seemed an inadequate weapon.

The rustling stopped. She returned to moving the chest. And stopped again when she heard a restless thump outside.

She refused to live in fear. Grabbing her hairbrush, she cracked open the door with every intention of giving any unwanted intruder a thorough tongue-lashing.

And nearly tripped over a very large, lumpy log lying across the threshold.

"Watch your feet, woman," a disgruntled male voice protested from the dark floor. The blanket-clad log turned on its shoulder.

"Mr. Dougal!" So astonished she nearly fell to her knees in relief, Mora fought to maintain her composure. "What are you doing?"

"What does it look like I'm doing?" He plumped up the greatcoat he was using as a pillow. "Now go back inside. I wish to make an early start and need my sleep."

"You can't sleep there," she whispered. "Go find your bed."

He shot her an incredulous glance. "And leave you here alone? What do you take me for, a blackguard?

Just because I don't dress in silken finery doesn't mean I can't—"

"Oh, hush." Impatiently, she opened the door wider for the would-be gentleman. "At least sleep in here where the floor is not so drafty."

He studied her warily. "You don't fear me?"

"Why on earth should I fear you?" she asked. "You saved my life. I have no cruel or powerful father to hunt you down for compromising me and no place in society to uphold. I am a free and independent woman." Also, a lonely and unlovable one, but that wasn't relevant. She preferred his company to her own tonight.

Gathering his blanket, cloak, and coat, Aidan climbed to his feet. Mora suffered a twinge of doubt when he filled her doorway. He was twice her width, with muscles that could lift horses if he tried.

And he had kissed her like the most tender of lovers. She thought that might be more frightening than his size. He waited for her permission, not entering until he was certain of her invitation. How could she deny a man who was so considerate? Especially one with a large bump on his head that he'd previously concealed beneath his hat.

She stepped aside, and he crossed the threshold, glancing at the askew chest and snorting disrespectfully. He dropped his belongings on the floor and returned the chest to its proper place without comment.

"Someone should tend to that bruise," she informed him.

"Someone would be better served to keep her hands to herself."

Mora tucked her hands under her arms and refrained from touching him. "You'll have to turn your back until I'm in bed." She clenched her teeth to keep them from chattering at her own temerity.

The light of her candle didn't reveal his expression, but she heard the laughter in his voice.

"How many layers of wool and linen do you wear beneath that skirt and coat?" he asked. "It's not as if we'd see bare flesh until spring." Despite the contrariness of his comment, he knelt before the grate, turning his back on her to scrape up a fire in the coals.

Mora felt as if he filled half the room. She had never undressed in front of anyone except her foster mother, and that had been twenty years or more ago. Her fingers fumbled awkwardly at her coat fastenings.

"Here, let me."

She caught her breath as Aidan nimbly undid the frogs of her riding coat. Despite their size, his hands barely brushed her breasts as the coat parted. She wore a vest and linen beneath, but she still felt the heat of his touch all the way to her belly.

"Stop that," she hissed, tugging the fabric away. "You're supposed to keep your back turned."

"I did. You're slow." Aidan stepped away.

The wind rattled the panes in the window sash, blowing the curtains inward and lengthening the candle flame until it almost flickered out. The firelight cast shadows over the lady's fine figure.

Aidan wanted to light the lamps and see more of her—much more. But understanding that that shouldn't happen until he had proper time to court her, he returned to remaking his bed on this side of the door. If he kissed her now, it wouldn't end with a kiss. He refused to be as recklessly impulsive as his younger half brothers. He would treat his future wife with respect.

"You can't be comfortable there," she said worriedly. "Were all the beds full?"

"Didn't ask." He spread his cloak and settled on it, keeping his back on temptation. The warmth of the

fire had already improved his level of comfort, and he
stretched his weary muscles gratefully. "I'll sleep better this way."

"On the floor?" she asked incredulously.

"Near you. Are you going to natter all night? A
man needs his rest." Not that he planned on getting
much, knowing she was an arm's length away.

She remained blissfully silent. He relaxed and
smiled at that. He was an excellent judge of character.
She was a woman far superior to all others. She didn't
argue, fuss, or nag like his brothers' Malcolm wives.
She listened and accepted his commonsensical commands. She even had the wisdom to trust him.

Although he wasn't entirely certain he trusted himself. He was already lying there wishing she'd invite
him into that big bed. If there was any real magic in
the world, it happened when a man and woman shared
a mattress.

He frowned at the shuffle and thump behind his
back. What the devil was the woman wearing to sound
that substantial when she dropped it? The soft
scraping that followed almost had him breaking his
vow to keep his back turned.

A moment later, a heavy cloud flopped over him,
obliterating the light and nearly suffocating him beneath its weight. Aidan collapsed on his back and
flailed his arms and legs in an attempt to wrestle off
the unwieldy mass.

"The floor is colder than the bed." Mora's voice
was muted by the cloud. "The quilt on the bed boards
is goose down and quite comfortable."

Aidan fought with the feather mattress until he had
it off him and flattened on the floor. By the time he
could see again, the Vicar's Daughter was fully
wrapped in her blankets and fur mantle and no more
than a bulky silhouette upon the bare bed.

He would have spluttered, *You're mad!* except her smug silence warned she was waiting for it.

Two could play that game. Punching the mattress into place, failing to relieve his frustration with the blows, he made his bed and now tried to sleep in it.

Aidan was gone when Mora woke in the morning. He'd left the mattress neatly rolled out of her way. A fire burned in the grate and warm water filled the pitcher. The man was magic if only because he could move so quietly and grant her wishes before she thought of them.

She washed thoroughly, put on fresh linen, her riding clothes, and her mantle, and hurried downstairs to see if he'd escaped.

She found him leaning his wide shoulders against the wall beside the fire, sipping from a steaming mug, boots crossed at the ankles, for all the world as if he owned the place. His hair was neatly slicked back in a leather tie, but his boots were already wet and mud caked. His thick eyebrows lifted in greeting over the top of the mug when she appeared, but he made no other comment—a man of few words.

She would beg for a cup of tea but she didn't wish to give any excuse to be left behind. As much as she was enjoying the freedom of being an independent woman, she was discovering with some dismay that she preferred the comfort of his company.

"I am ready," she announced.

"Good. So are the lads. Your breakfast is waiting. I only lingered to bid you farewell."

She narrowed her eyes and studied his bland expression. "I did not come all this way to turn around now, and you know it. Unless you're keeping a wife and a mistress you wish to hide from me, I go with you."

"And if I have a wife and mistress?" he asked with interest.

"Then I shall travel a mile behind and give you time to hide them or explain me."

"I don't believe you are explainable," he muttered, his mouth twitching on a stifled smile.

"That's quite possible. I can hardly explain me to myself these days. Do I sit and breakfast or shall we go?" She stood stalwartly awaiting his verdict.

Not until he scowled and nodded at a table with steaming bowls of porridge waiting did Mora acknowledge how much hope she had placed on his agreement. She needed to be needed, and it seemed that against his better judgment, Aidan would not deny her.

They rode up to Aidan's ancient tower in the twilight of midafternoon. The keep sat high against the cloudy sky, as dark and mysterious as the hills around it. Square walls of stone reached out from either end of the tower as far as Mora's eye could see in the darkness. She thought she discerned the outline of another crumbling turret in the distance. No light welcomed them from any of the tall windows in front.

"Thank you, lads," Aidan called to the boys who had followed them. "Brush the horses down well. There's blankets and oats for them. Then go round to the kitchen and Margaret will feed you and give you beds."

Mora admired the way Aidan took care of the horses and children first, but she was drooping with weariness and anxious to enter the fortress that she assumed was his home. Wrapping her mantle tighter, she closed her eyes and waited for him to give her orders as he did all else.

She must have dozed in her saddle. She jerked awake when strong hands lifted her. She was becoming almost familiar with those hands, and the admirable physique of the man wielding them. She didn't even protest when Aidan cradled her in his arms and carried her up the stairs without letting her feet touch the ground.

"You will set your wound bleeding," she reminded him.

"The stone is icy," he explained as he banged his shoulder against the door and produced a pealing bell inside.

She longed to lean her head against his brawny shoulder and snuggle into the shelter of his arms, but that would make her seem needy, and she couldn't allow that. She held her head high. "I daresay the stones *are* icy, and it will be much more fun if we both slide down them together."

He chuckled and carried her across the threshold when the door creaked open. "Here ye are, Margaret, a lost waif to feed and tend." He dropped Mora to her feet.

"Aye, ye poor wee thing, and here the wind is blowing up a storm." Dressed in widow's black and half her employer's height, Margaret insisted on taking Mora's mantle before scurrying ahead of them through the towering dark hall. "The fire's warm in the kitchen," she said. "If the heedless beast would warn me of his coming, I'd have a room ready, but no, he comes and he goes without thought to any but himself."

Apparently unconcerned with his servant's scolding, Aidan slammed and bolted the entry door. "There are two lads who will carry in the bags in a while. I'll be in the library when the food's ready."

Mora instantly ground to a halt. Oblivious, Margaret hurried ahead, taking the lantern with her. Mora could see little of her surroundings except the tapestried walls ascending into shadows above her. Aidan almost walked into her when she stopped.

"I have as much right to look for the book as you do," she asserted, although why she said it, she couldn't fathom. The rebellious nature she had concealed all these years seemed particularly close to the surface in Aidan's presence.

"Aye, and you're frozen stiff as a statue and will make a pretty ornament for the mantel," he said with laughter. Hand at the small of her back, he nudged her after Margaret. "I'd thought to let you rest. Warm yourself first. If you do not fall asleep, we can search the shelves."

Since he stayed at her side, his enticing hand splayed across her back, Mora willingly hurried after Margaret. The great hall was as cold as the outdoors. And nearly as drafty. She would be grateful for a fire, though Aidan's bulk provided a warmth all its own.

After leaving the hall and traversing a windowless corridor, they emerged in a high-ceilinged kitchen lit by fire and lanterns. A kettle boiled on the grate, and a small roast turned on a spit. Mora's mouth watered even though she knew this must be Margaret's dinner.

"You have the look of a Gabriel about ye," the servant decided with a nod when Mora entered the light.

Mora froze where she was.

"Ye've had too much of the malt," Aidan protested, striding to the fire to check the pot. "Her hair's red, that's all. There must be millions of red-haired ladies in the world, and they aren't all related to the old goat."

Mora had tried to forget the memory of his cutting comment about Lord Gabriel that night in her workroom. She'd had no good opportunity to ask him about it without giving an explanation.

She had no proof, after all, that she was a Gabriel.

But here was a woman claiming she looked like one. And Mr. Dougal was scowling like a black dragon at the assumption.

With a sinking premonition, she wondered if the Gabriels were the neighbors who were threatening Aidan's land.

Fourteen

"Why do you dislike Lord Gabriel?"

Aidan glanced down from his library ladder to the woman ensconced in a chair by the fire. He had dumped an armload of histories beside the chair so she might stay warm while she read through them. Even with Ewen's amazing heating apparatus, the far corners of the old library remained chilly. Besides, the fire danced lovely lights against her wine red hair, and Aidan liked remembering how she had looked with that mass curling about her shoulders.

"You do not look like a Gabriel," he assured her, disregarding her question. "Margaret fancies herself a matchmaker and wants you to be Scots."

"All people with red hair must be Gabriels, as all large black-haired men must be Ives?" she inquired lightly, although a hint of something darker shadowed the question.

"I'm not an Ives. I'm a Dougal."

"Aye," she agreed, mimicking him, "and I've been an Abbott these last twenty years, but calling me by the name does not make me any less a Morgan. A jonquil may be called an Easter lily or a buttercup or a daffodil, but it's still a yellow trumpet flower that comes up in spring."

"Why were you called Abbott if you're a Morgan?" He'd heard bits of her story from his half brothers, but he'd like to hear it all from her. And he'd rather not answer her questions. She already knew enough to ruin his family.

" 'Twas easier to go by the name of my foster parents. The vicar had hoped it would help me fit in."

The faint trace of wistfulness in this disclosure stirred his protective instincts. "Some people are made to lead, not to follow." He repeated words his mother had often given him when he was an awkward lad and the others made fun of his size, his nose, or his stubbornness. "The majority are followers, so leaders aren't apt to fit in."

"I hadn't thought of it that way," she said with wonder.

She must have been more tired than he'd realized, for she didn't immediately follow with the obvious retort he remembered from childhood. Aidan waited for her brain to kick in.

"Who am I supposed to lead?" she finally asked.

He laughed. He'd often wished for this give-and-take with an equal of like mind. She would challenge him as no other but his brothers would.

For a brief moment, he felt the familiar ache of not growing up with a rowdy gang of brothers who could have ridden by his side across the hills and studied with him on long winter nights. He envied Drogo for his family, not his fortune. But he could never let his brothers know of their relationship. They'd done fine without him for these thirty years and more, and the knowledge would not aid them now. He was far more grateful than he'd let on at how easily they'd accepted his company.

"I daresay you're meant to lead some poor male by his nose," he replied. "I should think your foster parents were more than grateful to have such an industrious, intelligent child, although your tendency to meddle where you don't belong must have been a constant source of distress."

She flung a pillow at him, missing him by a mile, and him as broad a target as a barn. He grinned at her, and the warmth of understanding between them was stronger than the ache in his groin.

"I have found that sharing information is the best solution to problems," she replied stiffly, digging at him for not telling her more of his dilemma. "Why did your mother never tell you of your father?"

He shrugged. "Don't misunderstand. I adored my mother. I went to the ends of the earth to help her. But if you think I am the only one who does not share information, you never met Mairead. I come by the trait honestly."

"I should think it would be difficult for a mother to admit to her son that he does not have a father he can claim."

Aidan scowled at her. "Not admit I have a father or brothers or that I could stand to lose her land for not naming him? Much less the issue of her health, so that she died here alone, thinking I'd left her for good."

Mora eyed him with interest, and he knew he'd revealed far more than he ought.

"And why did you leave her if she needed help with this great crumbling pile of rocks?"

"Because it seemed safer that I do so!" he shouted, slamming another stack of books down beside her. "A man must make his own way in the world," he amended before she pounced on his first admission.

"And a woman must wait for a man to give her a place in the world," she said quietly, surprising him. "It is not quite fair, I think. Your mother may have clung to her home because it was hers, and she needed no man to give it to her."

"Particularly not a faithless English earl who was already betrothed to another." With a growl of exasperation, Aidan accepted his mother's choice. "She would have made a very poor countess, and I would have made a very bad earl. And if you repeat any of this to anyone, I will sever your tongue from your head."

"And thus I'll become as silent as Mairead, never sharing my information with anyone," she said, laughing at him.

"Isn't it time you went to bed?" he complained. "I will have to carry you to your room if you fall asleep here."

"These books are too fascinating to put down." She smoothed the journal in her hand. "My foster father's library was compiled of edifying sermons and textbooks. I wish I could have had these family histories to read."

"Do ye not know anything of your true family?"

She shrugged, but he thought he saw an element of despair in the action.

"My mother died when I was but nine. She's all the family I knew."

"I thought they said ye came to the north to search for your father?"

She looked as if she wanted to bite her tongue. Aidan would have questioned more, but she was faster.

"Growing up, if you did not know your Ives family, did you ever know the Dougal side of your family?"

"Aye, but only as a lad. My grandfather lived in the Highlands, and after he died, my mother preferred this Lowland home of my grandmother's family."

"Your grandmother Dougal?"

"My mother's mother was a Macleod. This is a Macleod holding."

She sat silent for a while, without a smart remark in reply, although he knew she wondered why he was searching for a Malcolm genealogy. He could hear the soft flipping of pages, the occasional crackle of old paper, and called himself three kinds of a fool for not confiding in her.

He wanted to know all about her. He knew she had no siblings, but she'd grown up in a village. Had she more companions to play with than he? Or had she always been a prim and serious scholar who hid the light of curiosity he'd seen in her eyes? Why would the genteel life of a vicarage give her a backbone of steel?

"I don't know my father either," she said quietly, whether hearing his thoughts or deciding to share. "I had always thought my mother remained unmarried. We lived in Wales and she called herself Morgan."

"It's a good Welsh name." He couldn't tolerate the distance from her forlorn figure framed against the fire, and he began climbing down. Paradoxically, he couldn't tolerate the closeness of the intimate conversation either. He was a cauldron of roiling conflict better left for another day when they were both well rested. "Your birth is not important. It's who you are now that matters."

"But I don't *know* who I am now," she cried, flinging down the unbound book she was holding so that papers flew every which way. "You'd think if my mother talks inside my head, she'd tell me something *useful*."

Her cry was so anguished that he wanted to scoop her up and tell her no one would ever hurt her again. He still felt the brand of all the places they'd touched when he'd held her earlier.

At the same time, the mention of a voice in her head had him freezing like a frightened stag. The papers blowing with the cold drafts of the floor offered an escape. He knelt to catch them before they blew into the fire.

"I'm so sorry," she murmured, dropping down beside him and hastily gathering sheaves of paper that rustled in the draft. "I don't know what came over me. I must be more tired than I thought after riding all day. I never say things like that."

He took the bundles she handed him and tried to even out their edges. "You have none other to talk to." He said it unquestioningly, relieved that she did not embellish upon the subject. "I am the same. Perhaps we could talk to each other."

She sighed and sat back on her heels, searching the moldering carpet for missing pages. "I've never had a friend with whom I dared share confidences."

She'd discovered the secret he hid from all else, but he'd never learned to share. She was right in that. If he couldn't talk to her, he wanted to hold her, but if he so much as touched Mora, he knew he would have her sprawled upon the floor beneath him. She had no one to protect her from scoundrels like him.

If he married her, she would have *him* to protect her. They would have each other. The notion warmed the deepest places of his heart.

"You may trust me," he declared brashly.

Her gaze was guarded as she studied him. "Why should I? You're lying to me and all the world."

He reeled from the blow of her bluntness. Angry at himself as much as her for forcing him to face facts, he rose, carrying the pages with him. "Does your *voice* tell you that?" he asked in retaliation.

"All the world knows you're an Ives. You're the one who won't admit it. What else are you denying?" Standing, she handed him an illustrated frontispiece she'd found beneath her skirt. "That's the *History of Wystan* you're mangling."

Staggered as much by the wild scent of crushed rosemary clinging to her as by her announcement, Aidan took a minute to register the significance of the book's title.

Then he looked at the scrambled mess in his hand and groaned. "The pages are all unsorted and unnumbered."

"And most likely contain the genealogy scattered in their midst." She eyed the wrinkled old paper with interest.

"It's my genealogy to search for. Go to bed and get some rest. I'll have to take you back to Wystan in the morning."

She raised incredulous eyebrows and grabbed half of the sheaf from his hands before he thought to stop her.

"If there is a Malcolm genealogy in here, I can't wait to see if you're on it." With that triumphant declaration, she began spreading her half of the book on the carpet to organize the pages.

Startled, he stared at her. Why had she said that? How could she understand what was on his mind?

He should have shoved her up that chimney days ago, when she'd suggested it.

But one didn't shove one's future wife up a chimney, especially one as dangerously perspicacious as this one.

And one did not question her abrupt and puzzling pronouncements unless one really wanted to know the answer.

Mora groaned at the stiffness in her neck and didn't open her eyes to the chilly darkness. She must have fallen asleep over a book again.

She had a vague memory of yawning and Aidan putting his arm around her sometime during the night, but she didn't recall going to bed.

Her bed seemed uncommonly lumpy.

Her bed snored.

She tried to go back to sleep and return to the delicious dream of being held in the arms of a large man who served as her pillow. The dream had been so real, she could almost feel his solid chest rise and fall beneath her. She reveled in the warmth of his breath against her ear.

She settled down in the bed and an arm tightened around her.

An arm. And a pillow that smelled of leather and horses and did not give when she tried to sink into it. A pillow that breathed and cuddled her.

Too embarrassed to admit she wasn't dreaming, she lay still a while longer. Maybe she would wake up and find herself . . . where? In the bed at the inn? She distinctly remembered leaving the inn.

She didn't remember going to bed in Mr. Dougal's home.

Mayhap she dreamed it all.

Her bed heaved, groaned, then chuckled. She squeezed her eyes tighter.

"As much as I regret not finding the genealogy within the book, I dinnae regret the search," a male voice rumbled near her ear.

He shifted her head to the floor, and a knee pinned her skirts. Mora stopped breathing while she adjusted to the force of energy surging over her. Aidan propped his weight on his elbows so he did not crush her, but it was akin to being enclosed in a snuggly cave, except for the part below her waist where they met. Even through the layers of clothing, there was nothing snuggly about his lower parts. *Impressive* and *alarming* came to mind. And frighteningly interesting.

"I'll kiss you unless you open your eyes," he threatened.

"That's a choice?" she muttered.

He laughed and brushed her forehead with a kiss that made the sun rise in the skies. Then he rolled off of her. "I knew my brave lassie was in there somewhere. Come along, we'll have something to warm us."

"How can you be so cheerful?" she demanded, her mortification fading when he was so matter-of-fact about their night together. Wouldn't another man be more concerned about their reputations or her expectations or some such? "We're frozen stiff as boards and still haven't found what you seek."

She finally opened her eyes to the spectacular sight of Aidan's muscular rump in tight leather breeches mere inches from her nose. She wanted to reach out and explore. She fisted her fingers to prevent such inappropriate behavior.

He was blowing on the coals to raise the fire, but the familiarity shocked her. Did people become this comfortable with each other after marriage? She couldn't imagine her foster mother admiring the sight of the vicar's rump.

Aidan was so blatantly physical, so comfortable within his own skin, that he did not seem to think himself any different from the trees or the grass. She was the one with the problem.

"I see you wake as cranky as you retire." He didn't sound displeased. "Will tea sweeten you?"

"I have decided to be a wicked witch and scowl all day." Mora sat up rather than watch any more of his intimate parts. She was cold where she had been warm

not minutes ago—in his embrace. Hugging her arms
around herself, she longed to go back to dreaming. It
had been lovely having someone hold and cherish her.

She would not dwell on that. Instead, she gazed
about the firelit room to determine where they'd left
off last evening.

The pages they'd begun organizing had scattered all
over again, victim of her skirts and their tossing and
turning during the night.

She gave an *oh* of dismay and hastily began tucking
the pages together again. "Do you think Felicity was
wrong about the genealogy?"

"If it's here, I'll find it," Aidan said with assurance,
prodding more coals into the grate before straightening.

Even kneeling, he was a powerful man, with muscular thighs as sturdy as a stallion's. Mora suffered a
craving to be in his arms, to ask for that kiss he'd
offered, but that was a path neither of them was prepared to take. He might be an earl, and she was not
the warm sort of person a man would wish for a wife.

His knee rested on her skirt, so she could not rise
until he did.

"There ye are!" The door swung open and Margaret entered bearing a tray of steaming pots and dishes.
"I'd thought to bring hot drinks to your rooms, but
ye were not there."

Mora thought the housekeeper's disapproval was
greater because they weren't where Margaret wanted
them than because they'd spent the night together.
Still, she tugged at her skirt to release it.

Aidan lifted his knee. She pulled her skirt free, and
a clump of papers flew out with it. They both reached
for the clump at once, but Mora pulled back so he
could claim it first. It was, after all, his book and his
library and his search.

"They're stuck together." He gently worked the top page free and handed it to her.

It was naught but a continuance of what they'd found last night, a lengthy, dry description of the architecture of Wystan Castle, complete with references to the estate tomes that recorded costs and materials.

Disappointed, she located the stack of related pages, added this one to it, and rose to claim a cup of the tea Margaret poured from a pot.

"I've water heating for a bath, if you wish it," Margaret said, chattering on without regard to her employer's silence. "And I've pressed out the gown in your bags. If there's aught else ye wish . . ."

Mora didn't hear the rest. Aidan's silence and rapt attention on the pages they'd slept on last night warned that he'd discovered something of interest.

Sipping her tea, she resisted kneeling beside him and breaking his concentration. She prayed he would let her see what he'd found, but she had no right to demand it. There had been nothing magical about this discovery, unless one believed sleeping on the pages had produced the book they wanted. That was a stretch of the imagination even for her.

There had been a great deal that was magical about sleeping in Aidan's arms, but that was human magic, the reason the world was populated.

He made a sound of disgust, rose, and tossed the papers on the table.

"It is an old genealogy, and nothing that will help me." He grabbed a cup and poured from a pot of coffee, swigging half the cup's boiling contents without seeming to notice the heat.

Suddenly chilled, Mora reached for the pages. Had she been wrong, then, about her voice and gift? Had she made an idiot of herself, thinking she could help him?

There were only six pages of lengthy, handwritten description. The loopy writing spilled over with dates of births and marriages and dowries and land grants, interspersed with the author's comments.

She read through quickly, tracing the descendants of the marriage in 1600 of Dunwoodie Mackenzie Malcolm to Erithea Malcolm Wystan. They produced half a dozen children, and each had his own page.

Her hand shook as she read of the marriage of their eldest son, Alistair Wystan Malcolm, to Brenna Abercrombie in 1625, producing a girl child—*Morwenna Malcolm*—in 1630.

She must have made a small noise because Aidan loomed over her shoulder to examine the page she held.

"It stops there," he said with disgust. "There's some rubbish about the keystone histories recorded in some scroll and hoping the infant Morwenna was the new keystone, but there's naught to trace any descendants beyond that. I don't know how the Traitor proves her ancestry."

Morwenna Gabriel—*our common ancestor* was the inscription on the book her mother had left her. How common was the name Morwenna? Could the infant have grown into a woman who had married an ancestor of her parents? "Who is this traitor you speak of?" Mora asked, just to keep him distracted while she tried to absorb what was laid out before her.

"The Viscountess Gabriel," he said impatiently, pouring more coffee. "Margaret, don't you have better things to do?"

Mora had forgotten the servant's presence. She only half heard the bickering as Margaret reprimanded him for his insult and Aidan responded in kind. *The Viscountess Gabriel?*

Rather than question, Mora quickly traced the descendants and marriages of the six Malcolm siblings. In 1610, the marriage of Dunwoodie and Erithea produced a Stella Wystan Malcolm, their eldest daughter, who married the Viscount Ives in 1625, at a foolishly young age. If she remembered the history of the Malcolm ladies, this was the pair who ripped the Malcolms and Ives asunder all those years ago. It was sometime after their marriage that the Malcolm library was destroyed and the index hidden.

The names of the other siblings and their spouses meant nothing to her. The infant Morwenna was the child of the eldest Malcolm son, Alistair. A Malcolm male. The ladies would be fascinated.

As far as anyone knew, there had been no males born to the Malcolm line to carry on the name since the rift with the Ives. Hence *Malcolm* had been added to the ladies' given names to keep the family name alive. Only with the recent marriages of Ives and Malcolms had male children been born to the line in centuries. . . .

As far as they knew.

Flipping the pages over to return to the first one, she discovered a more modern handwriting on the back of Alistair's page, noting the marriage of Morwenna Malcolm to a Gilbert Gabriel in 1655.

Excitement pulsed through Mora as she returned to Alistair's page and the enticing mention of Morwenna Malcolm. Was this the Morwenna who had written her mother's journal of spells?

Mora turned the other pages, but the genealogy ended with those six children, as if the journalist had lost interest before completing his task, or died.

If the modern writer's penciled notes were correct, Morwenna Malcolm's marriage to Gilbert Gabriel apparently produced twins, Fiona and Finella, and a boy, Angus. But the pencil drew a line only from the one

twin, Finella, and an Aodhagán Macleod to a Kate
Macleod, who married Ian Dougal in 1700.

"Did you not say that your maternal grandmother
was a Macleod?" she asked with fascination.

"Aye, but the hills are filled with Macleods," he
replied dourly.

"Kate Macleods?" she needled, knowing he was resisting the obvious.

"It's a popular name."

"It wouldn't also happen to be your grandmother's
name, would it?"

"That means naught!" he protested. "Everything on
the back is my mother's handwriting. I have no proof
that it is any more than wishful scribbling."

Presumably, Mairead knew of Kate's descendants
and siblings and had not bothered to write them down.
Did that mean they were deceased?

She traced her finger over the name *Morwenna*.
The Gilbert Gabriel mentioned here had probably
been dead for almost half a century. Could the writing
in her mother's spell book be that old? She knew
there were more questions to be asked, but she was
too confused and disappointed to worry over them.
For now, only one issue seemed important.

"I think this proves you're a Malcolm," she declared
with a hint of glee, hiding her own shaken reaction.

"Kate was a Macleod and a Gabriel! You have to
go back to the early 1600s to find a Malcolm," he
protested. "No doubt there were bastards aplenty
among them. As you say, a name does not a family
make."

"Your mother was trying to put together a family
history. Her writing says Kate's land is inherited only
through the maternal line, tracing back to Morwenna
Malcolm's dowry. In which case, since Morwenna and
Gilbert had two daughters, wouldn't both Finella and

Fiona Gabriel have inherited? How does this relate to your neighbor?''

Disgruntled, Aidan grabbed a bowl of oatmeal and began spooning it into his mouth. His long black hair had come undone, and his jaw was covered in dark stubble, but Mora still thought him the most striking man she'd ever known. Despite his frustration, he radiated self-confidence. Perhaps that was the attraction.

"The viscountess claims she is a descendant of Fiona," he explained, "making her and my mother second or third cousins or some such. Inbreeding explains much," he said with disgust. "She married a descendant of the male Gabriel line."

"The viscountess?" Mora asked faintly, finally questioning his earlier comment.

"Aye, according to my mother, Glyniss the Traitor married Gilbert even though he had been affianced to another when she seduced him. Mairead did not think highly of her many-times-removed cousin."

A creepy-crawly feeling crept under Mora's skin. She wanted to grab the papers and run away and study them until she had all the names memorized and calculated the dates. But pieces were still missing. She traced her fingers over the name *Morwenna* and wondered at the aged underlining of *keystone*. "To whom had the viscount been affianced, to your mother?"

Aidan laughed. "Hardly. She was years older than all of them and spent most of her childhood in the Highlands. When she returned here, she watched them mostly through gossip. She called him Gilbert the Baptist. It seems he was a rake and a drunkard in his younger years, but inheriting his father's estate at an early age cured him. I've always known him as a sanctimonious pinchpenny, but there are tales of how the Gabriels and the Morrigans once terrorized the village with their antics."

"Morgans?" Mora whispered, uncertain she'd heard right.

He shook his head. *"Morrigan.* It's an old name I've not heard elsewhere. Glyniss was a Morrigan. She had a sister and brother, and her father was said to be the spawn of Satan in his younger days, although he settled down eventually."

"Morrigan." So close . . . Mora shook her head, hoping to drive the thought out of it. "Morrigan was a Celtic faerie if I remember rightly."

Aidan laughed. "I would not call Glyniss a faerie. More like a wicked witch."

"Well, there are wicked faeries as well. What became of Lady Gabriel's sister and brother?"

He scraped the bottom of his bowl, finished his oatmeal, and reached for the coffeepot again. "Her older siblings all managed to get themselves killed. She's the last of the line."

No, she's not. The voice in Mora's head laughed. *Find the scrolls and you will see.*

Fifteen

With a heavy heart, Aidan returned the histories to their appointed shelf. Some tiny little part of him had hoped the Malcolms could brush him with their magic and save his land. Logically, he knew the foolishness of his hope, but it still twisted like a knife in his gut to know he had failed. He curled his fingers into a fist and slammed the sturdy bookshelves, rattling the walls with his despair.

He wasn't a complete dunce. If his mother's scribbling was correct, he understood that the Malcolms he knew were probably descendants of one of Morwenna Malcolm's siblings. Had he the time, he supposed he could attempt to trace all the descendants of Dunwoodie and Erithea, and research the land grants and property rights, in hopes that his mother was wrong about only Morwenna's descendants inheriting. But he hadn't the time. He couldn't even prove what his mother had written.

He didn't think Mora would mind a landless man, but it went against every principle he held to give up his mother's inheritance to a woman who had shown herself countless times to be shallow, greedy, and selfish. The blasting in the hills was already scattering the livestock, driving out wildlife, and cracking the foundations of ancient homes. What havoc would her mines wreak once they reached his property?

"What is a keystone?"

Startled, Aidan glanced over his shoulder at the delectable woman who unconsciously teased all his senses. She'd not taken time to repin her hair, and the coronet of braids was releasing her curls, haloing her head with flaming red and gold in the firelight. He had not even given her time to change from her riding clothes. They were rumpled and creased from their night on the floor.

He hadn't dreamed once while he'd held her in his arms. Nor had his nose itched. His restlessness had transformed into a peaceful calm. If he needed any more proof that she would be good for him, he had it.

"It's easier to show you a keystone than to explain." He needed to escape the inviting atmosphere of the library.

Using the keystone as an excuse to touch her, Aidan steered Mora into the great hall. The morning sun gleamed through the two-story Gothic cathedral windows of the keep's entrance. Added years after the castle had been transformed from a fortress to a residence, the windows were the crowning jewels of his home.

"There, see at the top of the window? The stone with the lion carved into the very center? That is the keystone that holds the arch in place. Without those center stones, the arches would collapse."

He could almost hear her brain process this information. If she were a Malcolm female, he would expect some type of nonsense attempting to tie together the word *keystone* in the genealogy to his windows. He waited to see what the Vicar's Daughter would think.

"How very odd," was her only comment.

Illogically, he wanted more. "You see how unreliable these old books are?" he demanded, pushing her to argue. "They're a waste of time. You should have stayed warm in Wystan as I told you."

She ignored his taunt and carried the pages of the genealogy to a sunny window to peruse them more fully. The sun lit her hair into a brilliant prism of color and added pink hues to her fair skin. It also clearly outlined the full curve of her bosom and waist. Aidan gallantly attempted not to think base thoughts, but the image of stripping all that heavy clothing from her fair form was too enticing to resist. He wanted to know that he could have her regardless of his landless status.

"The genealogy says the 'keystone maintains the scrolls in Wystan cave and keeps the Malcolm histories,'" she continued, unaware of his wandering thoughts. "Do you know anything of a cave?"

He gestured in disgust. "I know nothing of Malcolm nonsense. How can a keystone be responsible for anything except centering the balance of the other stones?"

"Well, the author seems quite concerned that the family is *out of balance* and has need of a keystone. I'd say this paragraph indicates that at the time this was written, the family was somehow disarranged and their prayers were resting on this poor infant who they hoped was the keystone."

Aidan grunted and, unable to resist her appeal, joined her at the window. But he was looking at her and not the book. "That sounds just like something a Malcolm would say. I'd say they're all unbalanced."

"That's because you're an Ives," she said in the same laughing tone that his brothers' wives used.

"Then if what I say makes me an Ives, your foolishness would label you as a Malcolm." Aidan forced himself to look up from her breasts, but her hair led him astray. He gave himself permission to capture a straying curl and tuck it behind her ear, enjoying the sensual slide of silk between his fingers.

She slapped the pages against his chest. "Your solicitor said your mother was legally married. You are the Earl of Ives, should you go to court and claim the title."

That abruptly shattered his fantasy. This time, he met her lovely sea-green eyes, and glared in outrage. "Is that what this is all about? You wish to be a countess?"

Startled, she backed away as if he'd just spoken in flames. "If that is what you think of me, then you are right. I should return to Wystan."

She turned on her heel and stalked toward the door, then hesitated, obviously realizing she had no clue where to find her bags or horse or even her mantle.

He'd just made an ass of himself and spoken his wish to make her his wife—his countess. And she had understood him, he was certain. Was it distaste at the idea of marrying him, or his insult, that sent her fleeing?

Aidan strode after her, grabbing her shoulders and shaking her a little to emphasize the importance of his point. "I am *not* an earl. An earl is raised to that position, taught from birth how to deal with family matters and estates and politics and all that rot. Drogo is the true Earl of Ives."

She met his gaze without flinching. To his relief, she spoke to his argument and not his unromantic and unplanned proposal. "I understand, and I agree. That is why we must find the caves in Wystan and see if the scrolls will help reveal another heir to the dower lands."

She agreed? Contrarily, he wondered if that meant she thought he would be a poor excuse for an earl. He swallowed his earlier lump of dismay and tried to work out what she meant. She didn't want him to be an earl. All he had to do was figure out what she *did* want from him, beyond a few kisses in the firelight.

Or if she wanted nothing at all from him and would rather see him in Hades. This courting business made an utter muddle of his mind.

"What chance is there of any scrolls in a cave having been seen, much less updated, in the last hundred years?" he asked, as annoyed with his thoughts as with her infuriating logic. "The Wystan caves have been owned by Ives for longer than that. I cannot imagine my mother or Glyniss crawling about English hills in search of scrolls to write in, and I would very much suspect the sanity of anyone who did. Scrolls will not hold up in court. I need legal documents."

"My voice says I must find the scroll." She said it with defiance, awaiting his reaction.

Aidan realized she was expecting him to be furious with her, that she repeated this twaddle to goad him into heaving her out the door. His only reaction to such boldness was to lean down and kiss her senseless.

To his utter gratitude, Mora flung her arms around his neck and hung there while their lips met in a conflagration of heat and desire and longing. He gripped her waist, lifting her to her toes so he could better explore the passion she offered so wildly. She parted her lips at the command of his tongue, and melted into his arms as he tasted deeply. The firm mounds of her breasts made an indelible impression against his chest, and holding her up with one arm, he daringly slid his free hand between them to explore her yielding fullness.

Her damned whalebones prevented a full appreciation of her generous curves. He found her coat fastenings while he sampled the sweet honey of her lips, playing tongue games that almost crippled him with desire. She clung to his nape and moaned, spurring him on. He almost had the fastenings parted. If his hand weren't so damned big, he could slide it between—

"The viscount's carriage is on the way up the drive." Margaret's voice intruded like the toll of a church bell.

Mora shoved away from his arms and fled to the shadows of the far corner of the echoing chamber to straighten her disarranged clothing. Driving his hands through his hair, Aidan gripped hanks of it to keep from yelling at his housekeeper.

"I'll put a bell on ye, Margaret!"

"You might wish to look more a laird and less a ruffian when ye greet them," Margaret replied without offense. "Old Paul saw you ride in and his flapping tongue has notified half Scotland of your arrival by now."

"Take Mora to her chamber so she might prepare to leave," he instructed, cursing the untimely interruption. "And call the boys to saddle up the horses. The Traitor can sniff around all she likes, but I have no need to deal with her."

When he turned around, Mora was gone.

Mora had every intention of returning to Wystan, with or without Aidan, but she would not leave without first glimpsing the viscount. She did not think it a coincidence that her mother had possessed a book with an inscription written by a Gilbert Gabriel and had named her daughter *Morwenna*.

Nor was it a coincidence that her voice had told her to come here. The voice had not been useless, no matter how much she tried to convince herself otherwise. It was leading her home.

She might have a home. And a real family. That

Aidan seemed to despise the Gabriels made no difference to her pounding excitement.

That he had kissed her even after she'd mentioned her voices had her shaky hopes rising. He had thought she wanted the title of countess. Did that mean he thought of her in terms of wife? The possibility staggered her. Marriage to a force of nature like Aidan? Surely she was embroidering fantasies based on a kiss that had transported her to another world.

She should not dwell on improbabilities.

Hiding in the shadows of the tattered tapestries of the old hall, she lingered as the great bell of the front door rang through the thick oak rafters overhead. She could see a rope threaded across the ceiling, no doubt attached to the bell in the kitchen. The morning sunlight pouring through the tall cathedral windows illuminated a massive fireplace and a medieval trestle table with stout carved Jacobean chairs at the head.

The man standing in a beam of sunlight belonged here, like a king of old commanding his castle. Aodhagán Dougal may as well have been wearing a knight's surcoat and carrying a lance as he waited to greet the invaders.

After his angry words, she thought he would leave, but he did not. He looked around, as if in search of her, and when he did not see her, he scratched his nose, crossed his arms, and glared at the door that Margaret opened.

Trying to prevent her heart from leaping from her chest, Mora watched with anticipation as two people entered. The man stood not much taller than his wife. To Mora's disappointment, he wore his hair powdered so she could not discern its color. His clothes were appropriately elegant, blue velvet with silver embroidery, and he carried a fashionable walking stick that

he actually seemed to use in entering the hall, as if
he could not quite see where to place his feet.

His wife walked in with the brisk buzz of an angry
wasp. She did not seem the type who could seduce a
man. Sting him, perhaps, but she did not look malleable enough for seduction.

Mora studied the lady whom Aidan called Traitor.
Lady Gabriel's eyes were her most distinguishing feature, much like Mora's except smaller and more blue.
She had a narrow chin and broad brow, but her hair
was a faded red gold, and her jaw possessed the sagging softness of a woman in her forties. Mora recognized the woman's tense stance. The viscountess knew
she did not belong here, but an iron will held her
in place.

Mora returned her wishful gaze to the viscount,
hoping to find some likeness to give her confidence
that he was her true father. But she could see nothing
in his cloudy blue eyes or square jaw to indicate that
they were related.

"I've nothing to say to ye," Aidan stated without a
word of hospitality.

Unable to resist, pushed by her own need to know
as well as the insistence of her inner voice, Mora
stepped from behind the tapestry into the sunlight. If
the viscount was her father, would he recognize her?
"Perhaps you should send Margaret for coffee?" she
suggested, earning a glare from her host. It was impossible to ignore Aidan, but she did her best while she
watched the visitors for their reactions.

The viscountess grew noticeably paler, gripping her
husband's arm for support.

Lord Gabriel squinted, apparently taking in Mora's
disheveled state with disapproval. "I do not think it
appropriate to introduce your doxy to my wife," he
said.

Aidan guffawed. That was the only word Mora could think to call it. She contemplated punching him to shut him up, but she merely smiled prettily as a vicar's daughter ought and waited to see how her host would introduce her. It gave her time to study the couple more thoroughly.

The viscount reddened with rage at Aidan's laughter. The lady's lips thinned as she looked Mora up and down, clearly not happy to see her.

"I would not insult Margaret by introducing her to doxies," Aidan said jovially, his good humor apparently restored by Mora's arrival. "This is a friend of my family's, Miss Mora Abbott. The Duke of Sommersville recommended her as an archivist for my mother's library."

Since she probably looked more like a bed-tossed doxy after having spent a night on the library floor, Mora couldn't blame the viscountess for her glare. She performed a proper curtsy to reassure them. "It is a pleasure to meet you, my lord, my lady. I understand Mr. Dougal is in some hurry to index his library, so I fear I stayed up all night and must look a sight. I apologize."

Suspicion did not leave the lady's eyes, but the viscount merely shrugged as if she was of little consequence to him. Had he not received her letter or the earl's? Her signature had identified her as Mora Abbott.

"It is our place to apologize. My eyes are not what they should be," the viscount said in a tone of dismissal. "And we arrived unannounced. But it is difficult to catch Mr. Dougal at home." Impatiently, he returned his attention to Aidan. "Have you a private place where we might talk?"

Arms crossed, Aidan grinned. "I've nothing to hide."

"Even that you are occupying land that does not belong to you?"

"So say you," Aidan said. "I have yet to see any legal evidence that you are related to my mother in any manner."

"The court has set the date for ten days hence," Lord Gabriel said impatiently. "Be assured we do not enter into this matter without all the necessary documents. I am offering once again to grant you the right to your home for your lifetime if you will sign a deed giving us the mineral rights now. It will save all of us a great deal of expense."

Mora watched in fascination as Aidan's expression transformed into one of supreme indifference. He still stood with arms crossed, legs spread, as if he dared his visitor to strike him. In crude leather vest and billowing shirtsleeves, his ebony hair falling loose upon his broad shoulders, he appeared a giant in a fairy tale, one far beyond caring about the cawing crows perched on his doorstep.

"The family fortune wanes?" he asked with arrogance. "Or the daughters need larger dowries? What need have you of more wealth from coal?"

Mora thought the lady's cheeks grew red with rage, but her thin lips remained bloodless and cold while she spoke. "You yourself know that these lands do not produce riches except for what minerals can be found. A large vein of coal can produce wealth for the comfort of all."

"Not for the tenants whose homes you undermine!"

The viscountess continued as if he had not spoken. "The entire property belongs to me and, eventually, to my daughters. You are never here to tend it, so the offer of the use of your home is a generous one. We can put the land to sheep and turn a profit. Why fight us on this?"

"You're offering me a falling-down castle in exchange for my mother's entire inheritance and the future of my tenants! Sheep will destroy their crops. Your bloody mine already threatens Old Paul's barn. His grandfather built a home for his sons to be proud of, and you would destroy it. And you tell me I have no interest in my tenants? Go away, old woman. I have all the proof I need to see you in court."

"A bastard cannot inherit!" the viscount insisted angrily. "You delay the mining for no reason. They are already at the border and ready to proceed. Time is money. We can offer a percentage of the profit, if that is what it takes."

Mora stared in astonishment as Aidan threw back his head and laughed, the echoes bouncing from the high ceiling and walls. She had thought this matter was tearing him in two, but he behaved as if he could snap his fingers and make his neighbors disappear.

The lady stamped her foot and tugged on her husband's arm to steer him toward the door. "You will be sorry about this, young man."

"I'm not the one in need of money," Aidan called cheerfully as she flung open the door, letting in another shaft of sunlight. "Too bad your daughters are too young for me, for I have no need of dowries."

Neither responded to the taunt. The viscount stumbled over the doorstep, but the lady swept out, leaving the formidable oaken door open behind them.

Mora was still trying to sort out how she felt about the viscount's having marriageable daughters who might be her relations, and Aidan's having no need of money, when Aidan turned his laughing gaze upon her.

"Well, what do you think of my charming neighbors?"

"If anyone is a witch, the lady is. I have seen her

sort before. There is nothing worse than a woman of frustrated ambition, especially if it is directed at her children."

"There is a great deal worse," he corrected her. "But you see why I must protect what is mine."

"I never doubted that you had good reason." Mora cast a longing look about the medieval great hall. "Your family has owned this home for centuries. Your entire history is here. This is where your children should grow up, learning the land of their forebears, growing strong in the security of their own home and family so that someday they might go boldly into the world. No amount of coin could be worth what you have here."

She spoke what she knew from her own heart. She would have given half her lifetime to have a home and family in a place like this.

The elegant man in powdered hair could be her father. His daughters might be her half sisters. Yet claiming either might alienate Aidan forever, and as a descendant of the paternal Gabriel line, she certainly couldn't help his predicament.

"This is but a crumbling old keep," Aidan protested, dashing her romantic observations.

But her heartfelt words had caught him off guard, and she saw the love and anguish in his expression before he remembered to assume his insolent pose.

"Perhaps," she said casually, "but even keeps can be homes. I am going to Wystan to seek the scrolls. Will you come with me?"

"I will see you safe at the inn tonight but no farther." He remained adamant. "As Gabriel says, time is short. I must go into the city and search for legal records there."

"And if you find none?" she asked.

He looked resigned. "Then I will consult Drogo regarding another solution."

She very much feared the only remaining solution would be for him to tell the Earl of Ives and Wystan that he and all his brothers were bastards, and the title belonged to Aidan. Mora bowed her head. She knew that the admission would kill him.

Exactly so, the voice whispered.

Sixteen

Halfway to the inn, they met the Earl of Ives galloping toward them, the capes of his greatcoat flying.

Aidan signaled the stableboys to stay behind and brought his own mount to a prancing, impatient halt. It seemed even Gallant felt his unease at letting Mora leave.

He had no other choice. He could not court her properly under these conditions. He had heard the love of hearth and home in her voice when she spoke of his crumbling keep. Would she despise him for losing it?

She seemed to disapprove of him more often than not, trying to scare him away with her talk of *voices*. He didn't scare easily, but he needed time to change her opinion of him.

He did not have time. He must take his mother's notes to his attorney and hope the names could be traced in a register somewhere, even if it meant admitting he was a wretched *Malcolm*.

"Have you come to claim your straying maiden?" Aidan called, challenging his half brother to an argument. A good rousing fight might make the parting easier.

The earl brought his winded steed to a halt and regarded him with his usual impassive expression.

Drogo was not one to wear his heart upon his sleeve, or his thoughts upon his noble face.

"Felicity has gone into labor, and the ladies insist that they need Miss Abbott's aid."

Aidan watched Mora grow pale, and firmly kept his mouth shut. He had wanted her to leave so he could fight for his home alone. Drogo had just sealed the matter.

"Is she not well?" Mora asked, letting her mare dance forward. "Lady Ives is a healer, not me. I had not thought I would be missed. . . ."

The earl gestured with the discomfort of one lost to understanding. "Ninian tells me that Felicity went into labor while she was reading one of their blasted journals. I had not thought her interested in architecture and cannot imagine how stones would affect childbirth, but they're all too frantic to make sense."

"Did they perchance mention *key*stones?" Aidan asked dryly.

Drogo narrowed his eyes and studied him. "They did. If you have some understanding of it all, then you had best come with us. In his anxiety Ewen has climbed the chimney and may not come down."

"Climbed up from the inside, no doubt," Aidan grumbled, knowing Ewen's penchant for inventing problems to solve when he was under stress.

He watched as Mora let her mare proceed to the earl's side. It wrung his heart to watch her go, but her place was with the ladies, while his was in his empty castle where he could rattle the rafters with his fury and perhaps disturb a few lawyers while he was at it.

Drogo offered a ghost of a smile. "I've tried to tear down the chimneys in my time. Be grateful you have never suffered the experience. Will you explain the meaning of keystones while we ride?"

"The lady understands better than I. I still have that

matter we discussed to deal with. The court date is only ten days away."

"My attorneys are still working on it. The Gabriels are a complicated clan. And Lady Gabriel's family does not appear to have believed in churches or their records." Drogo looked questioningly at Mora, as if expecting her to comment.

Aidan assumed the earl expected Mora to reveal what they were looking for.

When she held his confidence and remained silent, Drogo continued. "If you have found nothing of your own, have your man press for a delay."

Aidan shrugged. "I could spend a fortune buying the court and it would gain me little. The viscount is the nobility around here. He carries more weight with just his title than my coins could buy."

The title of earl would make the court grovel at his feet, he couldn't help thinking.

But the man beside Mora was the true earl, one who cared for and respected his vast family and holdings. Drogo had worked hard all his life to keep his estates and family together, doing without through the lean years, burning midnight oil to rebuild their fortunes. Even for the woman he would make his wife, Aidan could not take Drogo's title.

"I'll stand beside you when the time comes," Drogo said gravely.

Aidan nodded. "Thank you. You had best go on so you can make the inn before nightfall."

Mora turned her mare so he could see her great blue green eyes fill with tears, but she offered no farewell. With a nod, she tugged the animal's reins and set off down the road.

Aidan swore that the ground trembled in despair as she rode away. The next time he saw her, he might have lost his heritage. He did not think she would appreciate his sacrifice.

"Oh, thank goodness you are here!" Christina flew down the stairs at the sound of the front door opening. "Go up to Felicity. I'll send someone to bring you hot chocolate and biscuits."

Mora hid a weary sigh and surrendered her cloak to a maid.

Her legs ached from riding. Her heart ached with longing for what she could not have. But she'd known worse. At least she was needed here. Or someone thought she was needed.

"I am not a midwife," she murmured to Christina as they hurried up the stairs, leaving the earl below to send servants scurrying to obey his commands. Lord Ives had been all that Aidan was not—polite, respectful, and relaxing. He had hired a guard to sit outside her inn door while he slept in the innkeeper's bed for the few hours they'd rested. In his company, she had felt as if she were true gentry.

She would rather be arguing with Aidan.

"You needn't be," Christina assured her. "We all know what must be done. It is Felicity who has gone off her head. She's been in labor since yesterday, and she claims the babe refuses to come out unless the keystone is found. That blasted book she was reading has affected her mind."

Mora managed a weary smile. The ladies were all affected by the books they read, and half of everything they said would make a normal person believe them out of their minds. Felicity believed she could read the emotions of people long dead simply by *touching* things they had touched. Perhaps they needed to find an arch for her to hold.

As for herself, she would not argue with a woman in labor.

Mora quit smiling when she entered the maternity room. Felicity looked to be at death's door. Her lovely golden hair was drenched from sweat and lay limp across the pillowcase. Her frail face was white and pinched with pain. But her brilliant eyes lit with relief when Mora walked in.

"You're here, thank goodness. Now the child can come."

Mora's weariness dissolved with this welcome. She didn't deserve Felicity's friendship or trust, but she would return them with all the craving for family that was in her. Taking a chair beside the bed, she pressed the lady's frail hand between her sturdy ones and began to pray silently as she had been taught at the vicar's knee.

Only when Felicity emitted a groan that seemed to come from someplace deeper than a well did Mora remember that the lady was often painfully affected by people or objects she touched. Before Mora could drop her hand, Felicity wailed in agony and gripped tighter.

Mora held on and continued praying as the room erupted into action.

"Hot water and soap," Ninian commanded, gathering the bedcovers from the foot of the bed. "Someone help her to sit up."

"I'll fetch Ewen." Christina grabbed her skirts and ran.

Leila, her own figure unbalanced by pregnancy, leaned across the bed from Mora, sliding her arms beneath her sister to help Mora tilt her upward.

"Go to the children," Mora urged Leila, taking Felicity's weight in her arms. "They will hear the commotion and fret."

Leila nodded worriedly. She glanced down at her sister, touched her with affection, then departed in a swish of silk and a cloud of rose scent.

Mora shifted her position to the bed and gave Felicity an arm to grip as the contractions pressed down. Ninian took up a chant of soothing words that made little sense to Mora, but repeating them seemed to ease their patient.

Mora could hear the heavy feet of the men entering the outer chamber, could hear the maids chattering softly as they brought water and cloths and all the things Ninian demanded. But she concentrated on the woman in the bed crying out with the agony of bringing life into the world. She hummed a tune in accompaniment to Ninian's chant, and let her energy drain through her hands and arms to Felicity.

Within minutes, the frantic atmosphere changed to one of joy and excitement.

"The babe's almost here!" Ninian cried with such relief that tears slid down the cheeks of everyone listening.

Even Felicity began smiling through her weeping. "She's coming. Tell Ewen to hurry. We have to rename her."

No one seemed to think it strange that she called the baby a girl before it arrived. Mora continued rocking and humming until Ewen burst into the room. His thick dark hair looked as if it had gone through a windmill. He wore two days' growth of beard and appeared haggard and half-hungover. But given permission to enter, he rushed to Felicity's side, climbed up to sit ungracefully at the head of the bed, and dragged her into his arms, leaving Mora to return to the chair and hand-holding.

"We have another keystone," Felicity murmured in between pushing and panting.

"We have lots of keystones," Ewen assured her. "There's one in that window right over there. And the keep is full of them. I'll show you the grand one in the hall that supports half the tower."

Mora bit back a chuckle as Felicity sent him a look of frustration before bending in half and cursing with oaths that included half the goddesses in the Roman panoply.

"Call the babe Morwenna," Felicity gasped the second the contraction released her from its grip. "Promise."

"What if it's a boy?" Ewen asked.

Mora could tell by the way he smiled that he would even call a boy by that name if Felicity asked it of him, but he wished only to keep her talking and distracted as she struggled to bring his daughter into the world.

Morwenna. A family name, Mora now knew. She simply didn't know how *she* came to have it. These noble families of Malcolms and Ives seemed quite certain of their ancestry and did not appear to be aware that any of them was missing.

That could be because the branches started drifting apart 150 years ago. It would be a little encroaching to claim a relationship now.

"Why Morwenna?" Ewen asked when he received no reply to his earlier question.

"Because she's the keystone."

With that pronouncement, Felicity curled up with a cry of agony that pounded the old stone walls, at the end of which Ninian cried, "It's a girl!"

In delight, she eased the squalling infant into the world, holding up the red-faced, kicking, fair-haired babe for all to see.

In the jubilant confusion that followed, Mora

slipped from the happy family celebration to find her own lonely room, too weary and confused to be joyous.

"The birth records are all here, as much as I could gather, anyway." Harrowsby handed Aidan a packet of papers. "The Morrigans on the lady's paternal side aren't much on recording family matters in church, but the viscountess traces her maternal ancestry back to Fiona Gabriel. These are copies I've made from the kirk the family attended. The viscountess has a strong case."

With an icy wall building around his heart, Aidan flipped through the neatly scripted pages Harrowsby presented. Apparently the entailment descended through Sarah, Glyniss's mother—the daughter of Fiona Gabriel. The current viscount and viscountess were second cousins.

Aidan's mother claimed to be descended from *Finella* Gabriel, the other heiress. But Harrowsby had produced no records of the elusive lady.

Aidan handed the records back, restraining himself from flinging them to the floor and muddying them with his boots. "Have you made no progress in tracing Finella's children?"

Harrowsby shook his head mournfully. "Because of the lands, the families often intermarried. According to your record, Finella married Aodhagán Macleod, your namesake. I've checked the record of deeds, and the dower lands were divided between the twins. You have the Macleod half and the viscountess has the other, which runs along Lord Gabriel's lands. That seems to verify what your mother claims, but there the trail ends. The Macleods kept their own church and their own records. I do not even know how many children they had. I have been trying to trace the ministers who might have attended them, but you would have a better chance of that than I."

"The old church burned back in Aodhagán Macleod's time, and my mother's parents and sisters died young, leaving her unaware of any other relations. That is the reason my mother was forced to piece together her history." Aidan paced the library, trying to think while his brain shouted in rage at the unfairness.

"You've little more than a week left," Harrowsby warned. "I am doing what I can to postpone the date, but a judge will see the case as clear-cut. Unless you present your mother's marriage records, you are not of legitimate birth in the eyes of the court, and that negates the entailment. You are living here solely at the behest of the viscountess."

Holding his head high, gripping the library table, Aidan nodded and dismissed his attorney with a calm he did not feel.

If he was to claim his legitimacy, his rights to hold the land for any daughter he might have would be unquestionable. If Drogo were a different man, Aidan might consider claiming his birthright long enough to establish his claim, then cede the title back to Drogo.

But Drogo was above all a man of honor. He would never claim a title that belonged to another. The stubborn ass would not grasp that he had earned the right to that title.

The instant Harrowsby closed the door, Aidan flung the heavy walnut table at the wall.

Margaret appeared in answer to the crash. "It does no good to tear down the walls around ye," she remonstrated. "Ye'd do better to tramp the hills and explain to the tenants that they'll soon have a new master."

"It's not as if they don't already know." Aidan stalked out of the library toward the old door that led to the crumbling tower and church ruins. "I've quizzed them all for the family tales so many times that they are making them up to please me now. So far, they've raised my mother's sisters from the dead and given them three husbands and a dozen children, and now they've started on Glyniss's deceased siblings, as if they would help me any."

"Where do you go now?" Margaret called after him.

"The family crypt, where else? Perhaps I'll find an empty coffin and climb in."

Instead, as the walls around him shuddered and mortar drifted from the rafters, he climbed the stairs to the old Macleod watchtower.

His nose itched like the very devil as he climbed.

By the time he reached the roof, the tower was quaking in a wind that whipped at his shirtsleeves and sent birds screaming for the hills. Finding the hundred-pound mallet he'd left here the day Drogo had arrived, Aidan hefted it into his broad hands, glared at the sun hiding behind the miasma of clouds overhead, and swung.

He swung in a full circle, around and around, shouting his rage to the heavens, shoulders straining and building up power until he unleashed the mallet from his grip and sent it flying into the turret overhead.

Seventeen

"Caves?" Christina wrinkled her forehead at the question. "I used to explore a cave on the hillside when I was little. I'd forgotten that. Mama quit letting me roam when I almost fell through an abandoned well. Why do you wish to know about caves?"

Mora snuggled her one-day-old namesake over her shoulder, smoothing little Morwenna's tiny back, and drinking in her wonderful milky smell. "It is something I found in Mr. Dougal's history."

She turned to Felicity, who was looking much healthier as she sat up in bed, perusing a book. "Why did you ask about keystones? Who is this Morwenna for whom you named your daughter?" Mora had a dozen questions, but these were uppermost in her mind.

Felicity blinked back to the moment; then closing her book, she lifted her hands to take the sleeping infant. "I named her for you, of course. She refused to come until you arrived. Perhaps you channeled your spirit through our hands. In any event, you are a lifesaver."

Mora had to keep from rolling her eyes as Aidan would have done. She could understand his frustration in attempting to receive a reasonable reply from these imaginative women. She would like to believe she was dealing with higher powers, but she wasn't that arrogant. "I did nothing except show up. You should have named her Ninian. She is the one who knew what to do."

"She wished to be called Morwenna. That's all I know. Perhaps she wishes to be called after our many-times-removed great-aunt. According to the history that Ninian's grandmother kept, that Morwenna was the family keystone." Felicity pressed a finger to her daughter's pug nose and smiled softly as the infant twitched in her blankets.

Mora understood that pregnancy and childbirth often addled a woman's mind, so she resolved to be patient. "I repeat, what is a keystone?"

"The block that holds together both sides of an arch," Christina replied brightly. "Ewen has been going about showing them all to us."

"That is because during all the excitement, Jamie and Alan sneaked into the library to claim Jamie's dragon and carried it to the roof, where the wind smashed it into a chimney before Ewen could see if it would fly," Felicity explained with no attempt to hide her mirth. "He's most distraught but cannot blame Jamie, since the dragon was officially his birthday present, and not his father's toy. So he distracts himself with studying keystones."

Mora contemplated poking out her eyes or tearing her hair. Surely either would be less painful than persuading the ladies to answer a simple question. Before Christina and Felicity could indulge in a friendly competition over which child had the worse habits, she tried once more. "Keystone?" she asked, drawing on her best vicar's-daughter patience.

"I must say, I do not quite understand how a human keystone works," Felicity admitted. "Perhaps we could ask Mama or Aunt Stella. But according to the legend, the last Morwenna Malcolm in our records was born after the devastation wrought when our many-times-great-grandmother was banished from Wystan by her jealous Ives husband. The legend says the family—and I must assume that meant the children of Dunwoodie and Erithea—were all at arms."

Christina shuddered. "I am glad we are not at war. Those were dreadfully primitive times."

"England is at war with France as we speak," Mora argued. "Men are dying in the colonies and at sea every day."

"She means it would be terrible if Malcolms went to war with Ives," Felicity corrected gently. "As they did back then."

"Now we marry them and conquer them that way," Christina said with a laugh. "Nature versus science. But I prefer my Harry to your logical Ives husbands, who spend all their time competing. If they were not brothers, they would end up killing each other, I vow."

Horror struck Mora as she grasped what they were saying. The Ives brothers were all powerful, determined men who would fight for what was theirs. If Aidan should attempt to take it away . . .

There would be battles. He might die defending his right to the title and land.

"How could an infant halt a war?" she demanded.

"She didn't, of course, not until she was much older. Much blood was shed before then. One would think we lived in the Highlands with their clan warfare." Felicity laid her daughter upon the covers, where she could admire her slumbering features. "The book does not mention what gift she had. It merely says she restored balance, bringing the crumbling sides together and making them whole again."

"Ah, then *keystone* was merely a metaphor." Mora didn't know whether to experience relief or disappointment. She had feared it would take some supernatural power to save Aidan and find the scroll. She hated to see a gallant knight brought low—even by a dragon who might be her stepmother—and it was causing her agonizingly sleepless nights seeking a solution.

So why would the family need a keystone now? she wondered.

Perhaps it was because there was a good man out there who was both Malcolm and Ives and could make no claim on either, yet desperately needed the help of both. Mora hated for him to wait until baby Morwenna grew up to be delivered from his suffering.

She knew she must say nothing about Aidan's father, but he had not told her to keep his possible Malcolm heritage in confidence.

Before Mora could reveal the secret burning in her chest, Christina interrupted. "Oh, I meant to tell you. Drogo wrote to the Viscount Gabriel again. He fears the original letter may have gone astray."

"That was thoughtful of the earl," Mora said politely, although now that she'd met the dragon lady, she wasn't at all certain she wished to claim the viscount as family.

Better that she consider Aidan's immediate problem than hers. He had only a week before he lost his land. Since he had merely mentioned a dispute with his neighbor while he was here, she could not in all good conscience reveal his full dilemma, but these women knew of his search for the genealogy. It could not hurt to mention the result.

Clasping her hands in her lap, she crushed her fingers together and took this opening in the conversation to dare speak the impossible. "From notes we found on the pamphlet, I think Mr. Dougal may be a descendant of Morwenna Malcolm."

The room fell into such silence that the infant squirmed at the lack of soothing voices.

As if called by the sudden hush, Ninian and Leila

materialized in the doorway. Taking one look at the expressions of the room's occupants, they swept in and claimed the remaining chairs.

"What is wrong?" Leila demanded. "Has Morwenna already shown her skills?"

"Nothing is wrong," Ninian soothed her anxious cousin. "You'll bring on your babe too soon if you upset yourself like that." She scanned Mora's face with empathy. "You're the one who is torn in two. How can we help?"

Tears welled in Mora's eyes at this instant understanding. She could come to love these people—as she could come to love the fascinatingly complex man who had the power to destroy them.

She must tread a careful line between Aidan and his family. She was not one of them, and she would not hurt either side. "I just said that I think Mr. Dougal is a distant descendant of Morwenna Malcolm, although there is no real proof."

With the eager encouragement of her audience, Mora repeated what little she knew of Mairead Dougal's writings. She did not include the final lineage of Aidan's father and birth. It was only the Malcolm history that would matter to the ladies.

"A male Malcolm," Ninian breathed in wonder. "I had thought my Alan the first in a hundred years. How extraordinary."

"I kept telling you his aura contained a Malcolm rose," Christina said smugly. "I wonder if Aidan has a gift."

"If he does, it's for finding trouble." Ewen entered to admire the newest addition to his small family. He touched a finger to his daughter's curled fist as he leaned over to kiss his wife's head. "What are we gossiping about now?"

Mora let the others excitedly recite her findings

while she waited for an opportunity to ask—again—about the caves.

At last, after much discussion of possibilities they could not know and questions they could not answer, the ladies quieted enough for Mora to speak again.

"The pamphlet mentioned a cave here at Wystan containing scrolls the keystone must maintain. That is why I asked the meaning of *keystone*. Do you think I might explore and find these scrolls?"

"I remember reading about that." Felicity held her husband's hand as she frowned and tried to recall what she'd read. "It said the keystone was responsible for the scrolls. But as far as we know, there has been no other keystone since the first Morwenna."

"We wouldn't know one if we saw one," Leila said dryly. "Over the centuries the Malcolm blood has become diluted, and we've grown too far from the source of our gifts. Sadly, we're a dying breed."

"No, I don't think so," Felicity argued. "I think our children are stronger for having Ives blood in them. It is more a matter of finding the right mate. . . ."

Mora knew the argument could go on into the evening. Most times, she adored their lively discussions. Now she could see the clock ticking away the minutes until Aidan must give up his land or claim his title. The journey to his home took almost twelve hours. Horses needed resting, making it a two-day venture should she find the answer to his problem.

Find the scrolls or he might die. The command jolted Mora from her thoughts.

Had her mother said that? Or was that just her own mind screaming in panic?

She had to find the scrolls. It was all she knew to do. "I would like to look for the scrolls now, if someone would show me the caves," she finally said into the swirl of words.

"You can't go tramping around on that mountain at this time of year," Ewen argued. "The rocks are unsafe even in midsummer."

Mora donned the respectful smile she had worn when the vicar had told her there was no such thing as witchcraft. "That's a pity. Are the caves on this side of the mountain or are they more northerly? I suppose a northern exposure may have destroyed any contents."

"No, they're on this side, protected by a copse of trees, if I remember rightly," Christina said, unaware of Mora's ulterior motive in asking. "There are several caves, though. I cannot think which one could hide anything of significance. The larger one near the top of the hill might, I suppose."

"We'll have to ask Aidan to explore next summer after we've gone home," Felicity said with interest. "If he means to stay up north forever, it wouldn't hurt him to check on this one thing for us."

He wouldn't stay in the north if he lost his land. Mora wished she could tell them that, but that was Aidan's secret to confide. And there was little the ladies could do to help him. They certainly couldn't traipse about mountains.

Mora realized that Ninian had contributed nothing to the discussion. Not looking the countess in the eyes, Mora returned to the sewing in her lap. Lady Ives had grown up in this area. She doubtless knew precisely where the caves were located.

Mora just hoped the perspicacious lady did not interfere when she struck out on her own.

Aidan was quite right. The chance of ancient lost scrolls providing the current information he needed was precisely none.

Yet she had no choice. The voice said they must be found.

There was no sense in endangering anyone else in her search. She was the only one with no family who would care if she lived or died on a snow-covered hillside.

Aidan had almost leveled the dangerously crumbling watchtower to the base of the burned-out church.

He'd torn open his injured shoulder so many times that it might never knit again. He'd ripped holes in his hands and scraped the scabs off the holes. Margaret had retreated to her family's cottage back in the hills rather than live with the persistent thunder of falling stone, and he'd been living on whatever he'd scrounged from his meager larder ever since.

And now he was about to cut the nose off his face if it didn't stop itching.

"I cannae come after ye!" he yelled at the wall where his tower had once been. "I'm more dangerous than any trouble the lot of ye can find!"

His cry echoed against the hills and returned as a wail.

And still, his nose itched. It itched ferociously. And every time he thought of Mora, he wished to pound his well-scratched proboscis against a wall and end the irritation once and for all.

Studying the devastation around him, he let his shoulders slump in defeat. There was naught here to be accomplished. His attorney had found no further records. There had been no secrets hidden in the walls of the crumbling tower or church. In four days the court would rule that the lands weren't his. At least the blasting in the hills had temporarily halted. The miners must have reached the edge of his property.

Fleetingly, just to relieve the piercing anguish, Aidan stared at the sky and contemplated claiming his rightful name and title. If he thought his wealth and strength could aid his family, he would proudly step up and call all the Ives his brothers. He longed to take his rightful place as steward over the family celebrations, the births of the new children, the Christmas gatherings, the picnics, and even the parties.

No matter how much he protested their antics, he loved them all, each of them individually, even their addlepated wives.

And he could not have them. He would not improve his isolated life by claiming the title and destroying them. And if his crumbling castle was any indication, he did not dare linger in their company when his frustration ran so high, for fear of bringing great blocks of stone down upon their heads.

He rolled his eyes in self-mockery. When had he begun to believe he had a destructive power that could not be explained or understood?

He had *not*. Mora had him questioning whether up was down. She was as bad as the Malcolms—worse, because he kept wanting to believe her.

Striding past overturned stones as tall as his knees, Aidan aimed for the stable, following his nose for trouble, knowing it would lead him back to Wystan and whatever Mora's voices were trying to tell them.

Eighteen

The sheepherder who had promised to show Mora the caves strode more quickly up the hill than she could follow. She wore her old boots, sufficient for mucking through the lanes of Sommersville but ill equipped for the melting ice and deep snow still covering the Northumberland hillside. Her heavy skirt and woolen petticoat dragged the ground, soaked from her encounters with dripping trees and icy burns.

She'd found her scar-faced guide loitering at the kitchen door. Cook had handed him a heel of leftover bread and a bit of mutton. Mora had waited until Cook was gone to inquire about the caves.

"What's that you wear about your neck?" she called now, hoping to slow him down with a friendly inquiry. A circular stone with a hole through the middle swung from a leather string around his neck.

"Dobby stone," he answered in the same surly tone in which he'd agreed to guide her. "Ward against witches."

Well, *that* wasn't promising, but he was all she had. The stableboys and bootblacks and everyone else she'd approached had refused to let her climb the mountainside in winter. Not that it was much of a mountain. She'd always thought mountains were great ridges of cloud-covered trees and stone, going up as far as the eye could see. This was merely a higher ridge of snow-covered rock. Climbing it took determination more than skill. Determination was something she had in plenty.

That didn't mean her toes weren't frozen and her nose hadn't turned to an icicle. Or that she didn't wish for a warm horse to lean against. Or for a man's strong arms to hold her until she stopped shivering. But she wasn't to think of that.

"How much farther?" she called to the quickly disappearing back ahead of her. The man must have hooves like a goat to climb this narrow path so fast.

"Just ahead," was his faint reply.

Only when he disappeared from view, and the copse of barren saplings around her fell silent, did she begin to worry about her impulsiveness.

It had been in a lonely place much like this one where the brigands had attacked.

Aidan galloped Gallant as fast as the icy path allowed. The closer he came to Wystan, the more his nose itched.

The path, he had learned long ago, led along the base of the craggy, snow-covered hillside overlooking Wystan. Most of the trees in this part of the country had been felled, but the manor's servants had guarded their forest over the years, even in the absence of the rightful owners. It was on this path that he'd first heard Mora.

He didn't hear her now.

He prayed she was warm and safe in the manor among the earl's family and servants.

Yet his nose itched like the very devil.

He knew in his heart that she wasn't a woman to give up a goal until it was won—and she wanted the scrolls.

He didn't know why he had set his heart on an

interfering nuisance who was more accomplished in her defiance than any Malcolm had ever dreamed of being. The Vicar's Daughter looked so damned demure sitting in the parlor with her sewing in her lap and her cap pulled over her glorious hair, he could almost believe she truly was a ward of the church. And then she would raise those wicked eyes of hers, and the imp that lived behind them laughed back— making his heart melt.

She desperately wanted a home, and he couldn't offer one. Even if he bought a house for her, he didn't dare stay there for fear of destroying it.

It was becoming damned hard to deny his destructive tendencies.

If falling stones, trembling mountains, and a nose for trouble were evidence of his Malcolm heritage, then he cursed it. Not that he *really* believed such superstitious nonsense. He just needed someone to blame.

Torn by frustration, he stopped at a trickling stream to let Gallant drink while he took stock of the snow-covered woods. The rocky hillside loomed just beyond this stand of trees. If he craned his neck to look past the bare winter branches, he could see a glint of rock beneath the leaden clouds. His instinct for the land told him of the layers of softer, more permeable stone beneath the crust, which ones were soft and susceptible to centuries of water eating through to the interior. He could easily imagine caves hidden in crevasses behind those boulders.

A cloaked figure wearing skirts climbed into view from behind a patch of gorse, and his heart stopped in anticipation. Only one woman he knew would be brave enough—or stubborn enough—to be out on that hillside in this weather.

He watched as Mora halted, placed her gloved

hands on her hips, and glanced upward, as if searching for someone or something.

His nose was about to itch off his face.

He wanted to shout a warning, but he didn't know of what. His shout could cause an avalanche of melting snow, for all he knew.

With a curse, he looped Gallant's reins over a branch and searched for the best path upward. If the blamed woman had no mind to the dangers of climbing rocks in winter—in skirts yet!—she ought to remember their encounter with the brigands. Wasn't one adventure enough for her?

There were definitely disadvantages to fearless women. He needed to rethink that requirement in a wife.

Swearing under his breath, Aidan jumped over the burn, and began climbing upward. As he scoured the hill above him so he wouldn't lose sight of her, three male figures emerged from behind boulders below Mora. While she dug through a snowbank covering some low bushes, they furtively ascended the rock face. His temper jumped from mere irritation to uncontrollable fury and terror.

The ground beneath Aidan's feet trembled as he leaped from rock to rock in his haste to reach Mora first. He did not need his nose to tell him that the scuttling figures darting from bush to boulder were brigands intent on harming the Vicar's Daughter.

As Mora seemingly disappeared inside the mountain, the figures scrambled faster, and Aidan raised a roar of warning that might have shaken the heavens.

Instead, the mountain quaked and rocks began to slide.

An avalanche of pebbles against her hat startled Mora into looking up moments after she entered the

cave. She had brought candles with her, and the crevasse in the mountainside was quite cozy, out of the
wind . . . and out of sight. When the shepherd had
vanished, caution had directed her to do the same.
She didn't wish to encounter brigands again.

In any event, the cave looked like an excellent place
to begin her search. The candlelight flickered against
numerous ledges, barely penetrating the dark gloom.

More pebbles slithered along the wall. This time,
Mora felt the tilt and surge of the solid rock beneath
her boots. She threw a desperate glance to the intriguing hollows where a scroll might be hidden. She
vacillated, recalling the unruffled reaction of the stableboys the last time the earth's trembling had frightened her.

The image of a falling oak tree crushing Aidan into
the ground had her abandoning the search and hur-
rying toward the cave entrance.

With a rupture as violent as her sudden rush of fear,
a large rock dislodged from the cave's ceiling, missing
Mora by inches. She fell back in shock, then clung to
the side of the cave, watching the ceiling warily as she
edged toward the entrance.

She told herself she was in no danger. She had not
gone very far, and the opening was just ahead. Even
should her candle go out, she would be fine. She need
only take a few steps. . . .

A huge slab of rock splintered off from the cave
entrance, slamming to the ground between her and
freedom. Outside, a shocked howl sounding almost
like one of Aidan's rages erupted, followed by a piercing wail of grief, a lament as anguished as a bagpipe's
mournful cry. So powerful was the sound, she wanted
to hug herself in sorrow rather than consider her own
terror at being trapped alive in the cave.

The ground lifted and bucked like an ocean in a

storm beneath her feet—and the walls of the cave
threatened to tumble in on her. Somewhere beyond
the fallen rock, men shouted in alarm.

Mora threw down the candle and hastily hunted for
footholds in the layered obstacle blocking her escape.
She could still see a sliver of sky. If she could reach
the gap above her, she might slide through.

She didn't know what awaited on the other side.
Maybe she ought to stay right where she was.

She almost wanted to believe that the shaking was
a normal event that would end soon, leaving her safe
to hunt the scrolls undisturbed. But she did not need
her voice to tell her that this quaking seemed to happen when only one man was present.

Aidan.

Fine. Maybe she was being as foolish as the Malcolm ladies, explaining extraordinary events with
imaginative theories. She just desperately wanted to
believe Aidan was out there waiting for her, and that
he was not the one keening in grief.

If he'd seen her, he might think he'd caused her death
in this crashing cave. She couldn't let him think he'd
hurt her. It had been her own foolishness to come here.

Her boot slid on a jutting rock edge that broke
under her weight. She tightened her hold above and
shifted to the other foot, looking for a better purchase.

A cry of pain followed by a thump outside her rock
barrier had her hastily scrambling upward.

She reached the opening just as a wild wail shattered the frost-cold air and the rock she clung to
began to heave and roll. Biting back a scream, she
wrapped her arms over the top of the rock and
searched the hillside below—

Where Aidan lifted a shrieking man from the
ground by his shirt and pants' seat. She watched in
awe as he swung his victim in a wide arc, then, with

a thunderous roar, tossed the brigand down the hill-side after his fleeing companions.

Mora would have been relieved at his miraculous appearance had Aidan's increasing fury not shivered the mountain. A mass of snow and soil slid past her nose, straight toward him.

At a high-pitched cry of warning, Aidan swung to see a river of rock bearing down on him, tumbling past a glint of red braids and terrified eyes just yards above his head. Mora was alive! He hadn't killed her. Joy swelled his heart to bursting.

Instead of seeking cover from the debris, Aidan dived forward, hoping to reach that rocky opening and Mora before the entire hillside buried him. He grabbed the ledge as snow and rock cascaded past.

He'd been ready to die the moment the ledge had crashed over the opening where he'd last seen her. Imagining the boulder crushing her frail form into the ground, he'd keened his anguish and overset a damned mountain. If he needed proof he was a danger to the ones he loved, he had it now. But if she was still alive, he had to reach her.

Stones pummeled his arms and shoulders. His boots slid on snow and ice and gravel, seeking purchase in the fallen rock. Above him, Mora reached out for handholds, pulling and squirming past the barrier.

Rejoicing that she was alive, he wanted to curse and tell her to go back inside to safety, but if the boulder above her head fell, she might be entombed in there forever.

Heavy with the need to protect her from pain, and his desperate hope that he could keep her safe, he climbed the rock to catch her fingers. With a mighty pull, he hauled her out.

Before he could climb down to a safe ledge and

shelter her against his heart, the mountain gave a final rumble, and the rock to which they clung tilted. Grabbing tightly to each other, they tumbled head over heels off the ledge and down the hillside.

She screamed as they flew through the air. Aidan wrapped his arms around her and prayed his bulk would save her from the worst of the blows as the slide of rock and snow carried them forward.

Bouncing off the next outcrop, she went limp.

On the next rock shelf, Aidan's back hit a tree trunk with a shuddering thump that dislodged icicles and snow-laden branches. Halted by the force of the crash, they slid down through evergreen branches, breaking the soft wood and their fall as the mountainside continued to tumble downward without them.

Striking the ledge to which the tree clung, he hastily rolled beneath an outcropping of rock, carrying Mora with him, out of the path of trees and stone.

The ledge concealed a deeper fissure, and he dragged her inside.

"Mora," he murmured unthinkingly, tucking her into a bed of dirt and blocking the entrance so the dying cascade couldn't reach her. She didn't stir. Blood trickled from a cut above her hairline, and unskillfully, Aidan tried to stop the flow with the woolen muffler around his neck.

She was as cold as the icicles hanging from their barren shelter. He raised his bruised and aching body to cover her with his warmth. "Mora, dear heart," he whispered, brushing her cold cheek with kisses. "If I have killed you, I may as well die now," he whispered fervently.

He'd even pray to the Malcolm goddesses if she'd wake.

A trickle of icy water caught his ear, and he glanced around, finding a rivulet of melting snow coming through the rock. He tore off his gloves and wet his hands, then patted her face, hoping to wake her. She moaned and turned away.

At this sign that she lived, he brought her hand to his cheek and ripped off her glove with his teeth so he could press her icy fingers against his jaw and heat them. He thought he felt a pulse of life in her wrist.

"Wake, or I shall be forced to chew your fingers off." He nibbled on her pale thumb, drawing it into his mouth.

Did she move beneath him? Through the bulk of their clothes, it was hard to tell.

"I swear, if I lose you, I'll scour the mountain for those thrice-damned scrolls and burn them!" he shouted in rage and grief, remembering the outcome of his last cry only too late. He hastily rolled deeper into the fissure to avoid a shower of pebbles, pulling her on top of him.

"I'll come back from the dead to haunt you if you burn those scrolls," a caustic—if somewhat weak—voice squeaked.

Giving joyous thanks that his lady lived and retained some of her questionable senses, Aidan covered Mora's face with kisses, returning the pink to her cheeks before he claimed her mouth.

She didn't push him away but moaned and wrapped her arms around his neck.

In a heated passion of relief, he clasped her to him. "I thought I killed you," he muttered, running his hands through her hair and dispensing with the pins until he had a firm grip on the rich curls. "I thought I would never hear you scold me again."

"I don't scold," she protested as he carried his kisses across her jaw to her ear.

"Scold me now. Tell me I'm an idiot. Just keep talking so I know you're alive."

"If you're an idiot, what does that make me, I wonder?" she mused hoarsely, burrowing her ungloved fingers into his tousled hair.

With relief, he realized the cut on her forehead was just a messy scratch that seemed to have quit bleeding. He caressed it gently.

"A perfect match for me," he replied. He would chuckle, but he was still too terrified of losing her. "Have I broken all your bones?"

"I ache," she murmured, pulling his hand down to kiss it. "I ache so strangely. . . ."

"Where?" Panicking, he shifted to his side and laid her against his cloak so he might use both hands to tear at her mantle fastenings and the buttons on her jacket.

"Oh, there, touch me there, please," she moaned when his fingers discovered the open neck of her shirt and slid inside to her chemise.

"Here?" He slid his big hand to her ribs, trying desperately not to insult her by caressing the tempting softness of her curves.

"Higher, please." Instead of wincing with pain, she moved her mouth across his, begging for kisses.

Still taut with fear, Aidan succumbed to the temptation of her plea, needing this reassurance of life. Her tongue met his, and a red haze of desire obliterated further thought. His hand slid upward, cupping the full mound of her breast beneath the fine linen, and his kisses deepened to conquer the woman he would claim for his own.

As she had conquered him.

Nineteen

Mora's terror dissolved beneath the relief and joy of Aidan's impetuous ardor. He was a thrillingly physical man of vast complexity and intelligence. That her death would have mattered to him brought her to tears. Minutes ago, she would have thought there was none to mourn her if she died. His wail of grief had convinced her otherwise.

In elation, she ran her hands over the breadth of his shoulders, down his muscled arms, anywhere she could reach. She needed to know that he was real. That his concern was real. She feared he would back away, retreat to that aloofness he used as a shield, before she could grasp the wondrous feelings exploding inside her.

He cupped her breast so tenderly, explored her with such loving attention, that she did not startle at a man's hand where none had been before. She reveled in the sensation and craved more with such desperate desire that the mountain could be quaking again for all the difference she could tell.

"More," she whispered against his mouth when she sensed his hesitation. She did not care what she did any longer. The vicar's daughter had been lost in the rockslide, and the person she was meant to be struggled for release. Aidan was the key to her freedom.

He growled deep in his throat and kissed her with

an urgency that caused jubilation instead of fear. She wanted to free the passionate man hiding beneath his indifferent pose, as he was freeing her.

She cried out when Aidan's mouth abandoned hers, but he immediately lowered his head to press his kisses to her throat, and a flush heated her skin. She didn't recognize the changes in her breasts until his fingers rolled the pointed peaks, and a different kind of flush spread downward, to the apex of her thighs.

If she understood where this led, she did not give it any thought. The newly emerging woman inside her craved sensation, craved life, and all the longings bottled up inside her these long years burst loose. If there had been music, she would have laughed and sung and twirled in joy.

Instead, she arched upward with a cry of ecstasy as Aidan's kisses reached her breasts, and he suckled her through the linen. Need drove her on, requiring far more of these sensations now that she had tasted this little bit. She needed his flesh on hers.

"Touch me," she begged. "Let me touch you."

If it was cold, she didn't know it. She was on fire, and the source of the flames was the man looming beside her, protecting her from the dangers of the outside world.

He obliged by unfastening his coat and vest, guiding her hands to the heated muscle of his chest. Exulting in this very human contact, she slid her fingers beneath his shirt and crushed the soft hair there. Pushing upward on her elbows, she scraped her tongue and lips along the salty skin of his beard-roughened throat.

He moaned, and she felt the rumble like the quaking of her world. She was aware he kissed her as she explored. His kisses spread warmth from her ears down her throat and arms as he undressed her. She was too lost to her own explorations to fear what they were doing.

She tongued his nipples as he had hers, and was rewarded with his groan of pleasure and his hand pressing the back of her head to hold her there.

While she pleasured herself at his chest, his hand slid lower, cupping her buttocks through layers of wool to bring her hips closer. Excitement churned in her lower belly at contact with the ridge of masculinity beneath his breeches. She instantly turned her curiosity to that part of his anatomy that held great fascination for her.

"I take thee for wife," he murmured in her ear when she caressed the placket of his breeches and felt it swell. "I vow to love, honor, and take thee with equality, for so long as we both shall live, and beyond. You are mine now."

The low rumble of his voice comforted her, but Mora paid his meaning little heed since Aidan was drawing her skirts upward. She ought to be frightened by how swiftly everything was happening, but her earthy nature had overcome her civilized one. She needed this mating as flowers needed bees.

She almost shrieked in startlement as his callused man's hand covered her bare buttock and squeezed, but he recaptured her breast with his mouth and the two sensations combined in a lethal mixture to wipe out any second thoughts.

His hand was large and masterful and taught her all she needed to know about his desire. He plied her with kisses and explored parts of her that had been untouched by any hand except her own since infancy. He deepened his kiss until they breathed the same air, and the tug between her thighs seemed a natural extension of the tug upon her breast.

Laying her down upon the pillow of their clothing, Aidan caressed her sensitive inner thighs until she relaxed and opened them. Mora knew he held back his heavy weight so she had freedom to touch him as he did her, and she took full advantage. She could not see much with his bulk blocking the light of the low cave entrance, but she wanted to feel, not see.

With his gentle kisses robbing her of fear, he spread his fingers wider over her woman's place. She obligingly spread her legs to accommodate the width of his hand. He dipped his finger into the moistness there and growled with satisfaction.

"Fearless," he said. "Tell me I'm yours and you're mine. I need to hear the words."

Logically, she knew she could say no such thing. If she was thinking at all, she would realize these were the words of a practiced seducer. But her love-starved heart swallowed his promises hungrily.

"I'm anything you say," she answered. "Just don't stop. Please, I need to know you." She needed to understand the wonder that had eluded her—she craved the experience of love in any form.

Mora tugged at his shirt, freeing it from his breeches easily since his placket buttons seemed to have come undone. Had she undone them? She didn't know. Her hand gladly accepted the freedom to travel the narrow line of hair from his chest downward.

Aidan caught her fingers before they could reach the exposed part of him that most fascinated her.

"Let me show you pleasure first."

Her gaze flew upward at his serious tone. Until now, his gruff words had been loving music to her ears. She studied his dark eyes, searching for understanding, and saw the reflection of her own desperate desire. His jaw was tense with restraint, and she caressed the prickle of his beard to relax him. To learn from this marvelously heroic gentleman was far more than she could have ever hoped, no matter where this led.

His hand was still splayed between her thighs. She did not grasp what to expect next, but she trusted him to show her.

"I want to love you," she said simply, unable to explain how he had torn open the protective shield that guarded her heart. She touched his bandaged shoulder with tenderness, wishing she had the right to take care of him.

"It is enough that we have this to share." His finger slid deeper into the mysterious unplumbed depths that made her a woman, stirring shivers of expectation. "Know you will be taken care of no matter what else happens beyond this place."

Those weren't quite the words of love she would have liked, but physical passion was far more than she'd ever expected to share. She nodded her understanding, and he lowered his head and kissed her.

Mora cried out her surprise when Aidan increased the pressure between her legs with the heel of his hand. He dipped his finger deeper and rhythmically rode her until the building tension caused her to squirm, and retreat.

"No turning back now," he whispered, inserting a second finger until she gasped in a battle of ecstasy and distress at the strangeness.

Rather than remove his hand from his possessive claim, he ripped her chemise ribbon loose with his teeth and covered her bare breast with his hot mouth—driving his fingers deeper at the same time.

Mora instinctively thrust upward, succumbing to his suckling while bucking into his hand—until the world as she knew it surged and rippled as the mountain had, and she keened her release in his ear.

She wept when he withdrew his hand.

Aidan knew he should stop now, before he ruined her forever, but instinct held him too strongly. This was the woman he'd traveled the world in search of. She was the lady he craved, the fearless wife he needed, the intelligent companion he wanted, the soul mate romantic tales promised. No civilized rules of right and wrong could cause him to set her aside.

She would need all her courage and intelligence, because she wasn't experienced enough to understand what would happen next.

Terrified of the harm he could inflict, Aidan knelt between her legs, lowering his straining groin to brush against the place his fingers had just forsaken. Kissing her tearstained cheeks, he cuddled her against his warmth so she could learn the feel of his weight. "Be brave, my wife, and I will show you pleasure beyond this."

Holding himself up with his forearms, he eased his arousal between her thighs until she inhaled sharply. He knew he was excited to painful proportions, and her panic was perfectly understandable. He leaned down to cover her mouth with a kiss.

As soon as she relaxed into their kiss, he thrust his rutting thickness into the curls he'd moistened with his hand.

She struggled in shock beneath him, but he didn't relent. Couldn't. Nature had him firmly in her grip. He would not turn back now any more than he had let her retreat from their passion.

His knee parted hers wider. She grabbed his shoulders, but lost in the glory of her welcoming warmth, Aidan scarcely felt her nails digging into his flesh. He pressed deeper, past her wet curls, and lavished her with kisses. Rocking lightly in place, he prepared her.

"It's not possible," she gasped, transferring her grip to his arms and attempting to pry him free.

"You won't break, I promise," he soothed. He'd

always known he should never take a virgin for a bride. But if he stopped, he was terrified she would run away, and he'd never see her again. The thought of losing her was far greater than his fear of harming her. Besides, the very stillness of the hills around him said he'd chosen rightly. "Trust me," he whispered.

Then tensing, he focused all his patience and strength on the place where they were almost—but not quite—joined. With one mighty thrust, he pushed as deep as her narrow passage would allow.

She moaned when he tore into a barrier, shredding Aidan's heart along with her maidenhood. He stilled, allowing her to adjust, nearly weeping for her. But his tears were those of intense pleasure at the welcome friction of her inner muscles. Unable to restrain the hot flow of blood from his brain to his groin, Aidan gave in to the need to complete his claim.

He sank his engorged shaft fully inside her and gloried in his victory.

He would dry her tears and beg forgiveness later, but months of abstinence demanded their toll, and the soaring pleasure of claiming this marvelous woman as his own reduced his brain to rubble. He shifted his weight to caress the nub that had given her pleasure earlier, rejoicing when she shuddered in response.

"Wife," he said boldly, aware she had not fully comprehended his vows earlier. "We share this between us now."

"I can't," she claimed, clinging to his neck as he caressed and aroused her.

He chuckled when her hips arched to take him deeper in response to his stroking. "We can and we will."

As Aidan withdrew, then repeated his thrust, the ground moved and the heavens thundered, and Mora cried out in shock at both sensations.

The enormous male beast putting that . . . that thing . . . inside her surged and groaned with the mountain. The sensations he'd provoked earlier were nothing compared with this invasion of hot steel and velvet and pain that spiraled into pleasure. The moist scents of earth and moss mixed with the hot musk of their joining in a heady perfume that spun her back to a primeval plane.

As the pleasure-pain built pressure in her womb, she lost her fear and strained to match him thrust for thrust, searching for that release he had already taught her. He chuckled as she dug her fingers into his arms and arched upward.

The broad, strong muscles rippling under her hands brought comfort instead of fear. It was insane to believe he would do anything but kill her with his masculine demands, but the warmth and tension coiling in her middle spoke of pleasure to be had. Only half understanding what she did, Mora raised her legs to wrap around him.

It was his turn to cry out as she held him thus, deep within her. That she had the ability to make this great man shout in need gave her courage.

The tremor began then, shaking the ground, shuddering and coursing through their bodies. Aidan slid both his callused hands beneath her, lifting her from the quaking ground so he could drive deeper until he hit the swollen ache inside her. The tense coil exploded in spasms of pleasure that trembled and shook and grew more intense as he shouted his release. With the hot flood of his seed overflowing her womb, Mora collapsed in lethargic bliss.

A surge of warmth and peace followed, and the ground settled once more.

"The earth moved," she whispered in wonder when

he finally fell on top of her, smothering her in all that hard male flesh.

"Aye, it seems that way." He pressed a kiss to her cheek and stayed firmly embedded in her.

"It did. You move mountains," she insisted, if only to avoid thinking of the way their bodies had become one. He was *inside* her. It was incredible to believe. Her lower muscles rippled in a possessive dance of ecstasy.

He chuckled. "Thank you. I'm glad I did not harm you so badly that you could not enjoy the pleasure."

It was her first time, and he obviously knew more than she, but Mora was convinced that what had just happened was not a common occurrence. "No, you really are a Malcolm. Your gift is simply more masculine than the ones the ladies possess. You make the earth tremble."

The clouds must have parted, and without his shoulders blocking the light, she could actually see Aidan's slow, seductive smile. It was rather like watching a glorious sunrise after a stormy night. "We make it tremble together," he told her.

She thrilled at the sensuality of his smile, but at the same time, she wanted to smack reality into his thick male head. Glancing down at the spectacle of brawny chest and bare, muscled arms, she gaped in awe instead. His hair had long since come undone and swung over the bandage on his shoulder. She could see the bulge of muscle and vein in his arms preventing him from crushing her into dust. Her gaze traveled from the fine dark hair on his chest to the line narrowing downward to the place where his hips joined hers.

They had mated like animals in a burrow. He had planted his seed inside her.

A flush heated her cheeks and spread downward,

making her uncomfortably aware of the fullness of her unbound breasts and the way their crests grew taut and needy beneath his gaze. She had wanted to know physical love. Now she must live with what she had done.

"It is not the marriage bed I would have chosen for you," he admitted, seeing her redden. "But the bed I have will not be mine much longer. I will have to leave you here until I find a home for us."

"A home?" Mora didn't know whether to panic or weep from happiness. She was just learning to enjoy her freedom, and part of her was reluctant to let another man rule her again. But a home . . . she dearly wanted a home. And someone to love, and who loved her.

The two wants seemed mutually exclusive. Tears blurred her eyes, and she turned her head away.

Aidan caressed her breast and kissed her cheek. "Finding you is worth losing the old place. We can start anew, anywhere you like."

She was convinced she would make a very bad substitute for his home. Biting her bottom lip to keep from crying, she sought a means of releasing him from obligation.

Instead, her gaze fell upon a peculiarity in the cave wall that was not rock or mineral, and an odd sense of inevitability overshadowed all else. She pushed at Aidan's uninjured shoulder so she might better turn and look.

"What's that?" she asked, pointing to what appeared to be a bit of leather poking from a hole in the wall.

Aidan shifted reluctantly to follow her finger. "I see nothing."

Now that he'd moved from her, the icy wind of the outside hit her overheated flesh, and she shivered.

"We must get dressed. Hurry, and we'll be home by dark."

If she could help him get his home back, he would no longer need her. That was her goal, wasn't it? She must use her voice and what little talent she had to help people, even when they didn't believe her. And then she must walk away when they no longer needed her.

Mora clenched her fists and fought a knot in her throat as Aidan eased out of her. A gust of wind nearly froze her at his departure, a chilly reminder of all the cold nights ahead.

For a moment, she wanted to call him back and return to the hot, heathen woman she'd been with him.

Instead, she rolled up in the coat beneath her and reached for the pouch hidden in the recess of the stone wall.

Twenty

He would never understand women.

Reluctantly pulling on his breeches, wishing he'd not been so callous in introducing Mora to the pleasures of the marital bed, Aidan tried to tell himself it was merely maidenly modesty that had her hunting for those damned scrolls immediately after their lovemaking.

Perhaps she would have been more loving and relaxed in a silken boudoir. She would certainly have been enticed to dally longer in his arms if they had a fire and a downy bed.

He tried to help her rearrange the clothing he'd bunched about her waist, but she brushed him off. Her hands were trembling. He'd frightened her badly.

He'd known he would.

But she was as courageous as he'd hoped, and she did not flee him. Not exactly. Once she had covered herself, using the awkward contortions required by the low-ceilinged fissure in the rocks, she slid on her belly to the pouch.

He dragged on his shirt and coat while she cautiously peeled at the rotting leather protecting the scrolls. He thought it might be better to leave the leather intact until they were somewhere safe and warm, but he had a feeling that the hidden treasure was all that kept Mora from running as far and as fast as she could.

"It is bound by a necklace," she exclaimed, drawing the pouch completely from the crevice. "The chain is corroded. I cannot open it further without breaking it."

Aidan lay down beside her, no longer comfortable in his own clothes when he wanted only to have both of them naked again. Once had not been enough. He'd restrained himself for their first time. The ache in his lower belly demanded more than a stolen afternoon could satisfy.

To remind her of what they'd shared, he kissed her cheek before examining her discovery. Pride swelled when she did not back away from his proprietary tribute. Regaining the confidence that only this woman had the power to shake, he studied the strand of filigreed links wrapped around the package. "We had best take it back to the manor. I don't want to break the chain."

She didn't argue but silently accepted his assertion. Her gaze followed the pouch as he tucked it into his coat pocket. Aidan wanted her to look at him, not the blasted pouch. He'd just given her his marriage vows—stolen from the Malcolm ceremony, admittedly, but vows just the same—and he wanted her to acknowledge his claim.

"Can you walk?" he asked, more gruffly than he wished.

She flushed and nodded. "Do you think it is safe?"

"I think we dislodged all the snow on the hillside and sent it straight down to the valley," he said wryly.

She smiled a bit at that but still wouldn't look at him. "I saw you fighting with those men again. Were they the same ones as before?"

Ah, perhaps that was part of her fear, and not just what had happened between them. "I do not make a practice of studying the faces of men carrying knives. For all I know, the cave is their hiding place."

"Oh, I had not thought of that." She looked startled, then thoughtful. "I wonder if the shepherd who led me here knew that."

"What shepherd?" he said sharply.

She shrugged. "The one I asked to bring me when no one else would. Everyone knows about the cave, so it could not be a very good hiding place."

"Which is why your prize was hidden here instead of above. We would never have found it if it hadn't been for those scoundrels. I suppose we should thank them." He rolled out of the narrow aperture, then held out his hand for Mora.

She emerged into the daylight looking mussed and flushed and thoroughly ravished. Aidan smiled broadly and smoothed her thick hair, savoring the right to touch her as he wished. "You should wear your hair down. The curls make you look soft and lovely."

He thought he recognized a flicker of longing and uncertainty in her expression before she pressed her lips into a tight smile and stepped away. "I would not wish to fool people into thinking I am what I am not."

He snorted at this silliness. "You are a creamy pudding beneath that luscious crust. You may pretend as you wish for others, but not to me. You snap and argue with the intelligence of a man, yet you weep like a woman over troubles not your own. You hide behind demure caps and lowered lashes, but you respond to my loving with the passion of a goddess. I suspect it will take me a lifetime to learn all your facets, and I shall enjoy every minute of it."

He took her hand and would have started down the

hillside, except she dug in her heels and refused to follow. He waited patiently.

"You do not know me at all," she asserted. "You make rash claims and promises with the impulsiveness of a toddler."

He shrugged. "I've lived in this world long enough to know my own mind. My claims are not impulsive." He squeezed her hand and studied her. "And neither was my vow. I will renew it in a church as quickly as the weather allows."

He thought he saw fear in her eyes before her face froze, and she tore her hand free.

"You do not even know who I am," she declared frostily.

He didn't understand what she wanted of him. He'd spent enough time with his half brothers and their wives to know the minds of women did not follow the same paths as his own, but he thought women expected vows and promises after what they had just done. He'd thought she would be relieved. He had not expected gratitude, certainly, but he had thought they'd had an understanding, a companionship, and that she would like that he offered security.

"You are Mora Abbott, foster daughter of the late vicar of Sommersville, good friend and companion to some of the most incomprehensible women in the world, a lady of refinement, courage, and intellect. What more do I need to know?"

"That my full name is most likely Morwenna Morgan Gabriel and that my father may very well be Gilbert, Viscount Gabriel, your despised neighbor."

She could not have succeeded in shocking him more deeply had she immersed him in an icy snow bath. She could be the daughter of his worst enemy.

*   *   *

Mora contemplated jumping off a ledge and ending her misery right there rather than trudging down the hillside in this icy silence. The fact that they were already near the bottom and she could hope at most for a few broken bones dampened that desire.

She ached inside and out. Now that the first surprise had worn off, she felt every bruise of their muddy slide. Her head hurt where a stone had hit it. She tried not to think about the soreness between her legs, or she might die from sheer embarrassment.

She could not believe what she had done with this man who strode beside her as if she were a stranger. He *was* a stranger. She could not claim to really know him. She had no idea what went on in his head as he mulled over her declaration.

She could be carrying his child.

Another shocking thought. But her mother had raised her alone. She would manage. After all, she had the intelligence of a man, didn't she? That's what he'd said.

So, if she thought like a man, men must not think at all. That seemed to be the most comfortable way to go on. He was probably marching down the hillside without a thought in his wretched head.

She would be weeping again if she didn't stop thinking, proving she wasn't a man after all. He was already stewing over just the *possibility* that the viscount was her father. What would happen if he knew for certain? Or if she revealed that her mother talked inside her head?

Better that she should return to being the vicar's pragmatic daughter who never felt the highs and lows of her wanton nature.

With a sharp whistle when they reached the bottom of the hill, Aidan set out down the path through the woods surrounding the manor.

"He abandoned you?" he demanded.

Startled back to the moment, Mora had to retrace her thoughts to understand his question. Gabriel. He was still mulling over his neighbor. "I don't know what happened. I have no proof that I'm right. I have only an inscription in my mother's book." She quoted the phrases she had memorized, then finished, "It could be another Gabriel. But what if I'm not wrong?"

"*Gabriel* is a common enough name," he agreed grudgingly. "But not combined with *Morwenna*. That was his great-grandmother's name."

Since that was her thought also, she couldn't argue.

The gallop of horse's hooves followed them. Aidan stopped to greet his steed, patting him affectionately but not riding him as they continued along the forest path.

Mora thought it amazing that such a spirited steed had not kicked up its hooves and fled the trembling mountain, but Aidan didn't find the horse's behavior in the least unusual—as he didn't think trembling mountains unusual.

"It doesn't matter," he declared finally, returning to their interrupted conversation. He took her arm and steered her around a particularly muddy stretch. "Whatever happened in the past, you are mine now. Gabriel has no claim on you."

His arrogant possessiveness nearly knocked the breath from her.

Approaching an icy burn, Aidan swept her off her feet, completing her breathlessness. Gasping, Mora grabbed his neck. His raw strength overwhelmed and wrapped her in security. She longed to cling and never let go. It would be so much easier to give in and let him sweep her off her feet forever.

She had done that as a helpless nine-year-old, let the vicar carry her away from her home because it was so much simpler to let someone take care of her. As it had been simpler to ignore her inner nature and pretend to be the obedient child her foster family needed. She had spent twenty years being what others wanted.

She couldn't do that again. She couldn't spend the rest of her life pretending she was docile when she was not. She had to be brave and stand on her own. She struggled to be set down when he kept walking.

He glared at her through narrowed eyes. "You won't run if I put you down?"

"Have I run yet?" she demanded.

"In that head of yours, you're running as fast as you can."

He knew her frighteningly well, and she didn't appreciate it. As soon as she had her feet firmly under her, Mora propped her hands on her hips and refused to move. "I am not yours. I am myself. You are taking a great deal for granted."

He raised his great eyebrows, but said nothing, so she could not determine if he expressed surprise or puzzlement or amusement.

"What if there is some small chance that I am the heir you seek?" she asked, hoping to rattle him.

"It is Glyniss, not Gilbert, who inherits," he pointed out.

"You said that Gilbert is second cousin to his wife, Glyniss. If I'm related to him, I'm also related to her. It is even possible that my branch of the family shortened *Morrigan* to *Morgan*. And *Morwenna* is uncommon. What if I am heir and do not want to marry you?"

He grinned. "See, you're running inside your head again. Do you fear marriage to me? I thought ye braver than other women."

Irritated that she could not spike a hole in his arrogance, Mora picked up her skirts and started down the muddy path on her own. He'd shaken her out of her misery long enough to let her mind work again. And it was working frantically, remembering all the marvels of these past hours. She wanted him to be immortal. He wanted her to be clay. "Do you make mountains tremble with other women?"

"Don't be daft."

"Ha. I can tell by the way you refuse to say more that you're afraid I'm right. *You* made that mountain fall. It was because of you that we found the scrolls, not because of the thieves."

"The mountain didn't fall. It was just a wee rockslide."

"That you caused," she insisted. "Just as you made the earth move when we . . . when we . . ."

"Made love?" he asked, slanting her a look of interest. "We could try it again and see what happens."

She hit his muscle-bound arm with her gloved hand and winced when he did. They were both sore and bruised. With a sigh, she took his arm more gently and walked at his side. She could not despise this man, no matter how much easier it would make her choice to remain independent. "And bring the manor down upon us?"

"There is that. I will miss my castle. It crumbles anyway, and I would not mind the mess so much."

He said it with such wistful whimsy that she knew he was laughing at her. And hiding his despair. His upper arm squeezed her hand closer to his chest.

"The scrolls might give us the links you need to find another heir," she reminded him, ignoring the warmth his familiar gesture stirred. "All is not yet lost."

He shook his head. "It can list all the Malcolms back to the beginning of time and that will not change the entailment. The land was passed from Morwenna to her Gabriel daughters, and from her daughters to their daughters. Had my mother married, I could hold my half of the entailment for any daughters I might have, but without that legality, the land returns to the next descendant in line. The scrolls are so old, it's doubtful they even show the first Morwenna."

"Your mother was legally married," she said quietly. "I understand why you will not prove this, but justice must be served. I have to hope these scrolls will help. I have to believe my voice brought me here for a reason."

He fell silent, and the familiar despair crept back into the empty crannies of her soul. He would never accept the voice inside her head. And she could no longer go on pretending it wasn't there.

"This voice told you to come here?"

Aidan always spoke with such self-confidence that the unusual lack of certainty in this question stood out. They were nearing the manor, and she was hesitant to sever this connection between them by telling him what he didn't want to hear.

Better that she do it now, before her longing for what couldn't be overcame common sense. "The voice told me I must go when Christina offered to bring me here. It told me to look for the scrolls when you would not. It does not talk to me frequently and seldom with clarity of intention, but I think it is trying to help."

"Is it the same voice that writes messages?"

He still sounded doubtful and wary, but, encouraged that he did not call her mad and cast her off, Mora ignored the knots in her stomach and tried to explain. "I never wrote spirit messages until you came along. I sometimes think the message writer is you, and the voice might be my mother's."

"It is not me," he said flatly. "If it were me, I'd

simply say the scroll is in the cave and it won't help, so leave it there to rot."

She laughed. She couldn't help it. "Then I'll grant that you did not write the messages. But you may have given the spirit who works through me enough energy to cause the writing."

"That is almost as ridiculous as the things the Malcolm women say. At least they have the sense to leave me out of it."

"They claim their Ives husbands enhance their abilities," she reminded him. "And you are an Ives."

He cast her a questioning glance. "If your name is Morwenna, you think you could be a Malcolm also?"

She shrugged more casually than she felt. More than anything in the world, she longed to believe she belonged to that intriguing family. "According to my mother's book, I was named for a common ancestor of both my mother and father. If your mother's information is correct, it's very possible we're both Malcolms."

"If your ancestor was a Morwenna Gabriel, then you're a Malcolm," Aidan said firmly, waiting for a stableboy to lead off his horse before he escorted her up the front steps of the manor. "For all I know, all the world is Malcolm. Let us go inside where it's warm and find out."

Twenty-one

"**B**y the goddesses, where have you been?" Christina asked in shock.

Mora had hoped they would be able to return to their rooms to change without notice, but timing wasn't on their side. They passed the entrance to Felicity's suite just as the duchess emerged.

Christina took one look at their dripping, muddy clothes, discovered the rotting pouch protruding from Aidan's pocket, and shooed them into the salon.

"The wanderers have returned bearing tales of adventure," Christina announced with a hint of wryness as she ushered them toward the fire. "Although I'm not at all certain how they manage to always meet up in the woods instead of here."

"Shouldn't you at least let them change clothes?" Leila asked, looking up from her knitting and grimacing at their filthy attire. Even in her loose brocade sacque dress, she looked as elegant as a royal duchess, far more so than Christina in the apron and muslin morning gown she hadn't bothered changing all day.

"Aye, that's my thought." Aidan produced the pouch and laid it upon a table set with the evening's buffet. "But she'd not let us pass with this. Now may we be excused?"

Mora could have strangled him. She was dying to open the scroll, and he dropped it as if it were a pretty feather he'd brought for their entertainment. The man carried nonchalance too far.

"There is something odd about the two of you. . . ." Felicity looked up from the scroll to study them with speculation. Distracted by the cry of the infant in her arms, she didn't complete her thought.

"*Odd* isn't the word I'd choose," Christina said with an amusement that made Mora blush. The duchess was much too astute sometimes.

"Don't tease, Christina," Ninian admonished quietly. "If the two of you will trust us to guard your prize, we will wait until you've had time to find warm clothes."

"I'm sure the pouch belongs to your family," Mora protested. "You need not wait on us." She ought to bite her tongue, but Aidan nodded approval, grabbed her arm, and tried to drag her out.

"Oh, no, I'm quite certain you were meant to find it," Felicity called after them. "We will wait, but don't take too long!"

Mora had started to shake off Aidan's commanding hold, but embarrassed and a little frightened by how much she hoped Felicity was right, she let him steer her from the ladies' presence. Sometimes, it was not so bad having a strong man at her side.

"They know," she whispered as they hurried down the upper hall.

"They always pretend to know," he scoffed. "They are no different from any other meddling gossips except they're very good at acting omniscient."

"They know what we did, and they were being extremely polite by not mentioning it." Recovering from her chagrin, Mora halted at the door to her room to face him.

Aidan looked nothing short of gloriously in his element. Mud and twigs only enhanced his image as a colossus risen straight from the earth. Her susceptible heart cowered behind her vicar's-daughter shield, while the wanton thrilled at the way his gaze devoured her—before he stiffly dropped his hand and stepped away.

"Do you mind if they know what is between us?" he asked with that distancing poise he used to such good effect.

"If you didn't mind them knowing we are lovers, you would kiss me now," she said crossly, wishing he would do just that yet relieved he did not. "So don't pretend you are insulted. I am simply saying there are few secrets in this household, so don't do anything impulsive."

A hint of a smile crinkled his eyes. "I know what I want, but I'll give you time to realize I'm right." With that, he opened her door and, with a hand at the small of her back, gently pushed her in.

Arrogant, she thought resentfully as the door closed behind her.

For good reason, the voice said faintly inside her head.

Mora collapsed in a chair, buried her face in her hands, and prayed that if the voice was her mother's, she hadn't seen what she'd done today.

She prayed it wasn't laughter she heard ringing in her head. It was impossible to think clearly when her brain was littered with spirits besides her own.

A maid carried in hot water and, clucking sympathetically, carried off her filthy riding clothes to be cleaned.

Naked, Mora realized she smelled of earth and cold and Aidan. Rubbing the warm cloth over her skin returned vivid memories and shivers of desire. Touching herself where he'd touched her brought a rush of need as much as of shame. She was chafed and sore, but the emptiness within her craved filling again.

At least now she had a better understanding of why women through the ages had ruined themselves. She would be more sympathetic for the experience.

Rubbing her finger where he had done, she called forth the thrill and excitement, but a glimpse in the mirror over the washbowl frightened her into stopping.

She looked like a wild woman. Her uncontrollable hair had escaped its braids to form a halo of frizzy curls around her dirt-smeared face and a nest of leaves and twigs in back. She had a cut above her forehead where a stone had hit her. But it was the glow in her eyes that frightened her the most.

The woman in the mirror wasn't the plain, unassuming vicar's daughter. This vibrant woman was flushed with a luminous sensuality—as much of the earth as Aidan. Rosy cheeks, soft lips, and sparkling eyes were so distant from what she'd seen all her life that she almost terrified herself. How could any gentleman possibly want a wanton creature such as that?

Dunking her hair in the washbowl and scrubbing it as best as she could, Mora combed out the debris and pulled the wet tresses tight against her skull. No wonder the ladies had stared.

Focusing on the practical, eager to discover the contents of the scroll, she dressed hurriedly in her only dinner gown. She could not imagine how the scrolls might help Aidan, but so many wondrous things had happened lately that she had to hope.

Magical things had happened because she'd chased after a dream.

She opened her door to discover Aidan leaning against the far wall, his broad shoulders encased in a clean, if somewhat threadbare, jacket. He'd washed his thick dark hair, tugged it back in a civilized queue, and shaved his square jaw until it glistened. In the light from the oil sconce above him, he once again appeared king of all he surveyed.

Except she knew he waited for her so he needn't face the ladies alone. That this breathtakingly confident man relied on her at all filled her heart.

"It's a wonder you didn't scout up the gentlemen to join you." Regaining a modicum of assurance at understanding a little of this man, she let him appropriate her elbow.

"Food was present. They will have already joined the ladies. I wish you would wear your hair down."

He ran all that together in a way that required taking apart to ensure she heard it right, which gave her no time to react before he steered her into the cheery salon where everyone waited expectantly.

As Aidan had predicted, the earl and his brothers were already filling their plates. Felicity had returned the infant to her nursemaid and was picking at a plate of food while eyeing the leather pouch with fascination. Someone had removed the pouch to a table of its own, at a distance from the fire where the ladies sat, as if the pouch might explode—or be too valuable to risk near hazards.

"From what I can see, the parchment appears to be surprisingly well preserved," Felicity remarked as they entered the room.

"The leather was no doubt rubbed with oil to protect it from the elements." Artlessly dispensing with any notion that magic had preserved the parchment, Ewen used a knife to lift the darkened chain from the leather. In his other hand he held a chicken leg that he gnawed on while examining their find. "There's an old-fashioned catch on the chain. It should unfasten easily if dipped in a little oil."

"There should be enough grease on your fingers to do the job," Aidan observed wryly, seating Mora on a chair between the ladies and the table before retreating to a far wall to watch.

"If our surmise is correct, then the scrolls belong to the keystone," Felicity said. "Since the two of you found them after all these years, one of you must be the keystone." She folded her hands in her lap and looked at Mora expectantly. "Malcolms are almost always female."

"I am not a Malcolm," Mora reminded her gently, her breath catching as she realized how little conviction she voiced.

"You don't know that for certain." Propping her feet on the grate in an unladylike manner, Christina swung her fork for emphasis. "The inscription and the scroll suggest otherwise. *Morwenna* is a respected family name, and your aura has the same faint Malcolm rose as Aidan's."

Not a soul in the room appeared shocked or angry at the suggestion.

Mora swallowed the lump forming in her throat. Whatever followed, she would never forget how this family had accepted her, willingly, happily. Finally, she felt as if she belonged . . . almost.

Aidan watched her with a hunger that had naught to do with what had been said. She tore her gaze from his at the rush of warmth to places she'd discovered only hours ago.

"What the devil does this rotting log have to do with keystones?" Carrying his plate over to share with his wife, Dunstan took the sofa cushion beside Leila.

"We don't know," the ladies chimed in chorus.

Since it was obvious the stubborn man leaning against the wall had no intention of joining the family circle or coming near the pouch that he considered Malcolm—and thus feminine—territory, Mora rose to pluck at the latch Ewen held up with his knife.

It fell open without need of grease or force.

Aidan tried not to watch too eagerly. It was fairly easy not to think about his troubles when he could scarcely tear his gaze from the woman who was unrolling the old parchment. He would gladly trade all he owned for Mora in his bed for a lifetime. Mora needed naught but her firelit hair, luminous skin, and aquamarine eyes to dazzle like a treasure chest of jewels.

He wasn't a reflective sort of man. Normally, he decided what was right or wrong, what he wanted and what he didn't, and then acted on his decision. His was a simple life, unencumbered by anyone's preferences except his own.

He fully understood that was about to change. If he truly caused mountains to tremble, he might have killed Mora today. But he didn't want to believe that he was a danger to her. He didn't want to give her up.

Restless, he grabbed slices of the roasted chicken and stuffed them on a large roll with some smeary stuff that contained onions and pickles. The buffet table brought him closer to the group gathering around the parchment.

"The writing is very tiny and blurred," Christina complained.

"Not on all the pages." Mora delicately separated the top sheet from the others, placed it on the bottom, and revealed the next. "Look, this one is more yellowed, but the ink is quite clear. Someone hold a lamp closer, please?"

Aidan wanted to growl as the earl obliged, holding

up the brightest lamp in the salon while standing close to Mora, usurping Aidan's place beside the woman he'd claimed.

Stepping into the family circle, he shouldered his way past Ewen to take the position at Mora's right hand. He thought she swayed toward him, and satisfied, he finished his bread while she ran her finger over a family tree containing hundreds of tiny dates and names. Most of them looked like foreign gibberish.

"The writing is rather . . . eccentric," she complained.

"May I see?" Not rising from her lounging position, the new mother held out her hand. "I've had some experience in reading Old Latin."

Mora handed the top sheet to Ewen, who refused to hand the paper over until his wife donned her gloves. Aidan ignored the couple to study the next page. The dates were from before the Norman invasion. "Told you so," he said mockingly, for Mora's ears only.

"The names aren't even spelled the same," she said, running her fingers down the page, finding a familiar-sounding name here and there. "*Murvyn, Mildthryth, Morwanyg* . . . They never saw a name that couldn't use a *y*."

"Celtic origins," Felicity murmured as she examined her sheet. "Our family goes back far beyond the Dark Ages of Britain. You'll find many resemblances to words that have developed into Welsh and Gaelic."

With his bread finished, Aidan rubbed his fingers on his breeches, and flipped the sheets impatiently, looking for the most recent dates.

"The recent ones are the blurred ones," Mora said apologetically. "I have already looked."

"How recent?" he demanded. "Don't tell me these things have been touched in centuries."

"I thought I saw a date of 1600," she argued, flipping to the next-to-last page. "See?" She pointed out a name at the bottom. "There's the family from which Dunwoodie Mackenzie Malcolm was descended. It records his birth in 1579."

The writing on Dunwoodie's name was much like the large, loopy writing in the genealogy they had found. That didn't mean a thing except that the Malcolms had an ancestor who liked to write about family. Aidan flipped to the last page.

Mora gasped as she read it.

Christina poked her head past Drogo to see. "It's not blurry any longer!" she exclaimed in hushed awe.

Ninian rose to examine the page. Even Dunstan and Ewen gathered on the far side of the table to look.

"What does it say?" both Leila and Felicity demanded from their seats.

Aidan skimmed to the bottom of the page, and swallowed a large lump in his throat. Not daring to touch the blamed sheet, he stared at the damaging words drying into clarity.

If he chose to believe this pack of mysterious gibberish, then *Mora was both Malcolm and Gabriel, born of Brighid Morrigan and Gilbert Gabriel, distant cousins and direct descendants of Morwenna Malcolm.* And Mora's mother was older sister to Glyniss Gilbert, wife of Viscount Gabriel. The traitor was Mora's aunt.

And right in line with Mora's family was his own, descending from Morwenna Malcolm's other daughter, Finella. His name was listed along with his mother's. *And his father's.*

"Oh, my," Mora whispered, then hastily began rolling up the parchment before anyone else could read it through as he had.

To Aidan's horror, she suddenly went white, held a hand to her head, gasped, *"Keystone?"* and dropped like a stone.

Twenty-two

"Stand back, all of you," Mora heard Aidan growl at the people clustering around her. "Let Ninian look at her. Leave us alone."

Leave him alone, Mora translated, not opening her eyes until she had her bearings. She had a sudden sense of his panic filling her oddly empty head. Aidan was terrified he had caused her harm. She wanted to reach out and reassure the great, foolish man, but she felt so *strange*.

Her head felt like a newly cleaned cabinet, bare and waiting for contents, except for the places where tiny spiders of sensation raced about, attempting to rebuild what was lost. The emptiness terrified her, heart and soul.

For the first time in her life, she felt truly alone—while she was surrounded by people. Her family.

Aidan's family. Her family. The spiders raced faster, spinning their webs, stringing impressions and emotions across the vast emptiness. Her thoughts had to race to keep up with them.

Odd, she had always wanted to have a real family, and now that she had found them—now that she *knew*—she was frightened.

If she was frightened, Aidan must be in a state of near apoplexy. With her head empty, she better understood the strange energy rippling just beneath his surface—a fierce protective streak, coupled with a fear that his presence caused more harm than good. What a terrible conflict to live with. How amazing that she could understand so clearly now.

"She's fine," Ninian said somewhere beside her. "I think she overexerted herself."

"Overexerted?" one of the men asked incredulously. "She did nothing but turn a page."

A big hand tenderly brushed her hair, and Mora took strength from that touch. Aidan understood. At least he hadn't stormed from the room, never to be seen again.

"Go away, the lot of ye," he grumbled above her.

"It's my suite," Felicity pointed out from a distance.

"And I'm not going anywhere until I hear explanations," Drogo stated in a deeply emphatic tone.

Oh, dear, the fat was in the fire. Holding her head, Mora attempted to sit up.

Aidan was instantly there, wrapping his arm around her, supporting her, even though she'd just destroyed him by inadvertently revealing his parentage.

Perhaps it wasn't as bad as she imagined. Perhaps now that the truth was in the open, it would bring everyone together, and they would all go happily into whatever the future would bring.

Perhaps the sun would shine at nighttime, too.

Sitting up against the back of the sofa, leaning her head on Aidan's steady arm, Mora steeled herself and opened her eyes.

A blur of anxious faces surrounded her—her *family*. She had thought the world would be a brighter place if she ever found her position in it, but she hadn't realized that family came with a great deal of expectation and responsibility.

She wanted to close her eyes again and go back to

emptiness, but the man taking her hand wouldn't let her be a coward.

"My mother was the keystone," she stated flatly, repeating what she'd heard from the voice that she now knew had permanently left her, leaving her empty.

The women gasped. The men grumbled. Mora clearly comprehended both reactions. She understood far too many things and feared she would learn more if she examined the little she knew. It was as if her mother had occupied all of her mind until now, blocking out this extraordinary knowledge. For good reason.

"Is it too late for me to return to the village?" she asked wearily.

"Far too late," Christina replied. "First, tell us what you mean about your mother."

Aidan's grip on Mora's shoulder tightened. "She doesn't have to tell you anything," he said. "I'll take her away with me."

"You'll damned well not leave this room until I have explanations!" Drogo roared.

Mora winced, and Ninian left her side to hush her furious husband.

"My mother's voice told me to come here," she whispered.

"Of course," Christina agreed. "You said your mother's name was Brighid Morgan, but it is spelled *Morrigan* on here." She studied the incriminating last page of the scroll, the one Mora had tried to hide.

"*Morrigan* is the name of a Celtic faerie," Felicity intruded. "That is a very odd family name."

The idea that she was a descendant of a faerie made Mora smile faintly. If Aidan believed Felicity, he'd probably explode trying to comprehend the impossibility of feyness. But like all logical Ives men, he disregarded legends and stories.

At this moment, she was open to believing in anything.

Christina continued reading the names on the parchment she was holding. "Brighid was the daughter of Sarah and Rob Morrigan, elder sister of Glyniss Morrigan, descendants of Fiona Gabriel. You're a Malcolm, directly descended from Morwenna Malcolm Gabriel."

Mora didn't watch as Ewen and Dunstan leaned over Christina's shoulder, trying to follow this complicated path. The women simply accepted that she was family and waited for further enlightenment.

"She's gone now," Mora said as loudly as she could.

"Your mother?" Felicity supplied helpfully. "It says she died in 1737, when you were nine."

Mora smiled mirthlessly. "Her voice was with me for many years. For many years I tried to ignore her. I didn't want to be different. I didn't want a voice in my head, so I tried to shut out the gift I was given."

Aidan stirred restlessly. Mora lifted her face and stared right at him. His dark eyes reflected nothing, although she knew the conflict of his parentage was far greater than her problems, far greater than accepting that they were both fey Malcolms.

"As keystone, my mother was responsible for recording the Malcolm history," she said to him, repeating more of what her mother's voice had related in those last moments before it left Mora. "She abdicated that responsibility when she ran away from home. Or perhaps I could say she accepted the fact that she wasn't the kind of woman her husband wished her to be, so she left to protect her true self so that she could someday complete her task. Except her life was tragically interrupted."

"Gilbert Gabriel, just as we suspected," Christina

said triumphantly, finding the name on the family tree. "The way these names are entered, it doesn't record marriage so much as parentage. You would still need to produce legal documents."

"It's all a hoax," Aidan complained. "No one could have written all that nonsense there while the parchment was buried in the mountain."

"She didn't," Mora murmured, knowing he wouldn't believe her. "My mother didn't want us to know the answers to her cryptic clues until I found the scroll for her. She completed it just now, and then she went away."

Ninian patted her hand sympathetically when Aidan retreated. "She was the spirit who wrote to tell us where to find the index?"

"She said she channeled a friend for the writing." Brighid had called the friend Mairead, but Mora didn't think Aidan would appreciate knowing his mother had befriended a Malcolm keystone. But it made sense. They had been neighbors. No wonder Mairead had called the current viscountess Traitor. She had known the truth.

"Are you certain your mother's gone?" Ninian asked in concern.

Mora nodded. "She said she loved me and wished me well. It would be unfair to keep her on this plane forever."

Tears leaked down her cheeks. She didn't try to dry them. She'd cried secretly for months after her mother had died. She'd hidden her grief for the sake of the kindly vicar and his wife. For so many years, she'd hidden so much, it was a miracle there was anything left of her *self*.

She didn't have to hide anything anymore.

"I think we ought to put Mora to bed," Leila said. "She's suffered far too much for one day."

Just the fact that the men murmured agreement with this command warned Mora that she could do no such thing. The women hadn't quite grasped the fact that the men had. The women were thinking of Malcolms.

But the scroll showed Ives as well.

"I can carry her," Aidan argued.

"No." Mora didn't take his hand. "I may be a very distant cousin, but I think I'm also the missing link. You cannot settle this dispute without me." She said this in the firm voice she'd used with the villagers to convince them to take the medicine she gave them, or to break up fighting adolescents. She was used to setting her own needs aside to help others. There wasn't much point in forgetting that part of herself now.

"You are not an Ives," the earl said adamantly. "And the rest is an Ives matter."

Mora smiled at Ninian's irate exclamation, followed by Leila dragging her heavy belly from the sofa to snatch the document from Christina. Christina whispered to Felicity, no doubt explaining the problem. Within moments, the room fell into absolute silence except for the crackling of the fire in the grate.

All eyes turned to Aidan. Aodhagán Macleod Dougal *Ives*. Direct descendant of Morwenna Malcolm Gabriel through Finella Gabriel. Son of Mairead Dougal and Edward Henry Ives, fourth Earl of Ives and Wystan.

Aidan's secret was out. Because of her magical writing.

"You'll believe a blitherin' ghost?" Aidan demanded. "Have ye all maggots for brains?"

"That's why the new sheet was blurry when we opened it," Christina said in wonder, ignoring his protest to follow her own line of thought. "Until Mora touched it so her mother could pass the information into the parchment, it wasn't there."

"That's not possible," Ewen argued. "Mora didn't hold a pen."

Dunstan's laugh was heavy with irony. "You'll believe a spirit wrote the impossible, but you won't believe she couldn't do it without a pen?"

The earl's black silence was telling.

Examining the parchment, Leila stepped into the breach. "Mora's mother, Brighid Morrigan, was born in 1710. She was ten when Aidan was born. She could easily have known the circumstances of his birth."

"She's been dead for twenty years!" Aidan roared.

Mora knew even Aidan had to accept the truth eventually. The scroll showed that his father was the Earl of Ives. Only his solicitor knew that—and she. Oh, dear, again. She closed her eyes and waited for the inevitable. He wouldn't understand.

"You wrote this!" he shouted, leaping up from his place beside her. "You couldn't leave it alone, could you? I believed all your soft words, fool that I am! It's not enough to be the daughter of a damned bloody viscount, but you'd be the wife of an earl as well? Over my dead body!"

The entire castle quaked with the force of his fury.

As she feared, not only didn't Aidan understand; he sought to make sense of her actions by translating them into the only earthly logic he could find.

He stormed out, leaving horrified silence in his wake. The men recovered quickly and dashed out to follow him, while the old walls shook and trembled.

Mora bent her head wearily and let the tears fall.

Rage swept Aidan past the burn and the forest and the mountain where he had thought he'd discovered heaven. With Gallant beneath him, he rode more swiftly than the night wind, galloping northward on a path so familiar he needn't look for landmarks. The sky thundered and trees waved wildly beneath the moon. Gallant shook his mane in silent protest but followed his rider's command without hesitation, even when the ground beneath them surged and rolled like the sea.

Betrayed. How could she betray him like that?

How had she betrayed him like that? He'd held the scrolls until they'd returned to the manor. He'd left the scrolls in plain sight of his entire family.

His family. He snorted. So this was what it was like to have family. It didn't feel much different from before. He was still alone, outcast, and destroying everything within his path. He was like a hurricane as he swept through lives, shattering them into fragments.

As Gallant tired, Aidan let loose the reins so the stallion could carry him at an easy canter. He was bone weary with no place to go.

His nose was too frozen to itch. Not that he needed to be reminded of trouble. It was everywhere he looked. How could he have believed otherwise? All the wisdom and experience he'd gained over the years, and he'd still been betrayed by a pretty face. He just wished he understood how. And why.

He reached the inn in the early hours before dawn and reined in only because Gallant needed rest. If his half brothers followed, he didn't care. He would be out of their lives soon enough. Perhaps he'd go to the colonies this time. He'd heard of a vast wilderness beyond the settlements where a man could get lost forever.

He hadn't forgotten that he'd made love to Mora, nor was he bitter enough to believe she deserved whatever came of their encounter. She had forced him to realize what he should have known long ago—he was a danger to those he loved.

He would direct his man of business to see that any

child she might bear would not go hungry or homeless. Should he someday learn of a child, it would hurt like the devil, but he'd worry about the pain then. He hurt enough now without adding to it.

His shoulder throbbed, but he insisted on rubbing Gallant down, giving him oats, and stabling him without the aid of the sleeping stableboys, before dragging himself to the inn. The front door was locked for the night.

Shrugging, Aidan wandered back to the kitchen. He'd bought the place for his own convenience when the last owner had died, leaving no heir but his widow. The innkeeper was his employee and wouldn't throw him out, no matter what disturbance he caused. Given the howling of the wind rattling the shutters as he entered, that assurance was comforting.

At this hour of dawn, the kitchen was already astir. They stared at him as he trudged through, but didn't stand in his path.

He was hardly invisible as he traversed the back hallway toward the stairs to the public room. The men in the tavern didn't notice him. One of them snored mightily with his head lying on the table in a puddle of spilled ale. Two of them sipped and grumbled, barely holding their heads up, obviously having spent the night in their cups.

Not until he heard the name *Gabriel* did he halt.

The drunkards had their back to the doorway. Aidan leaned his sagging shoulders against the wall outside and tried to listen. He was so tired, he could barely hold his own head up. Even the wind seemed to die from sheer lack of energy. The shutters stopped rattling.

In the ensuing stillness, he could hear their drunken mutters clearly.

"Can't go back," the bulkier of the two said. "She'll throw us down the shaft."

The younger snorted. "Better the mine than through that again."

So long was the silence following that remark, Aidan thought they'd fallen asleep.

"It warn't natural," the elder finally agreed. "She's a witch, just like the lady said."

The other snorted again, as if articulation was beyond him. "No woman made a mountain shake. It war him."

Crossing his arms and closing his eyes, Aidan almost drifted off waiting for the reply. He didn't know why he listened. He just had a natural tendency to sense trouble in the making.

"Wonder if the Frenchies'll take us 'steada her."

The younger giggled. "Borrow Bessie's gowns and pretend we're her?"

"Reckon she's Gabriel's by-blow? Got that same hair. Kinda hard to match that."

The shutters began to rattle again. Aidan was fully awake now. Sometimes there were advantages to owning the only inn within a day's ride of anywhere.

"Powder it," the younger suggested with a yawn.

"Not natural," the other repeated. "Shoulda done away with her."

"Have to do away with him first," the younger reminded him. "Not worth my life. Take the coins she gave us and go to London, maybe."

Unable to tolerate this babble any longer, Aidan straightened from the wall and stepped in to fill the doorway. "I'll gladly arrange your journey to London, gentlemen," he said agreeably. "Or to hell, depending on how much you're willing to cooperate."

The ground rumbled, and a loose stone fell from the fireplace as the two terrified men faced the giant blocking their exit.

Twenty-three

"Might I have a word with you in my study before you retire?" Drogo, the fifth Earl of Ives and Wystan, murmured in a tone that brooked no refusal.

He had returned to report that Aidan had left the manor. Mora had refused to go to bed until she'd known what would happen among all the large, reckless Ives men. Apparently, they were satisfied in letting Aidan leave. For the moment.

Surrounded by the women who had insisted she eat while they scented the room with relaxing candles and offered possets to help her recover, Mora knew she had the strength to resist the earl's command. She also knew that morally she could not. He had every right to be concerned.

It had been a very long, strange day, but she had no intention of sleeping now that she knew Aidan had left. She had a decision to make, and perhaps the earl's reactions would help her choose.

With a brief curtsy, she followed Drogo up the tower stairs to his private study. She glanced around with curiosity, wishing she could examine the globe by the window, and the mathematical charts on the wall, but she knew why she was here, and it wasn't for a pleasant welcome-to-the-family chat.

"Please have a seat, Miss . . . Gabriel?" He gestured toward a cozy upholstered armchair beside the fire.

"I would not keep you from your rest if this were not important."

"I realize that, my lord." She didn't take the chair offered but helped him unroll the scroll he'd confiscated earlier; they used his inkpot and a leather volume to hold down the furled pages. "I wish I could answer your questions better, but I really know no more than I have told you."

He pointed to the damning writing at the bottom of the page. "This is my father, the fourth Earl of Ives and Wystan. I know that he has fathered almost a dozen children, most of them bastards, but I see only one listed on this chart. "Aidan was born a year before I was. His father is mine. I assume the birth was in Scotland. Was the birth legitimate? I cannot tell from this."

"I am very new to Malcolm legends," Mora answered without hesitation. "But from what little I've learned, Malcolms have little care for the civil niceties of written law. I cannot even say if *my* birth was legitimate. If you can accept that my mother's spirit wrote that line, you have to accept that she did not know or care if the birth was legal. All that mattered was that it happened."

He rubbed his forehead. "A male Malcolm by an Ives. This explains a great deal and nowhere near enough. Aidan told me that he'd lose his home because his birth wasn't legitimate. My father bred bastards enough, and I've always been told that I'm the legitimate heir to his title. But if my father actually married Mairead Dougal, Aidan's mother . . ." He sighed with deep foreboding.

"Aidan longs for family more than land or riches," she said quietly. "He does not want your title."

"He accused you of wishing to be the wife of an

earl. What did that mean?" Drogo met her gaze directly, as if he could see into her head.

She knew he could not. Thank goodness. "Men are prone to wild declarations when they are confused and angry. He wants to be an Ives, not a Malcolm. He does not understand how he can be what he calls *foolish creatures*. He is seeking logic where there is none."

Drogo shook his head. "The law works by logic. I must know more, and if my experience with my wife tells me anything, you will not give me what I seek. Thank you, Miss . . . Gabriel. And on behalf of our family, welcome."

She dipped a brief curtsy. She needed to leave before he understood all the implications of the page before him—namely, that she could claim Aidan's land, provided she could reach Scotland before the viscountess went to court. For as the daughter of Brighid, Glyniss's elder sister, Mora held a claim to Aidan's estate that superseded her aunt's. She could prove both inheritance through the female line *and* legitimacy.

Aidan might refuse to prove his own legitimacy, but she had the page from her mother's book proving hers. The scrolls weren't a legal document, but they would show the lineage, and under Scots law, the inscription on her mother's book, in her father's own hand, would stand up in court as proof of the legitimacy of their marriage. Mora was the rightful heir to both Aidan's land *and* the land that Glyniss had for years claimed as her own. Only her father's land, inherited through the male line, and the estate built upon it, could legally be said to belong to Gilbert. For now.

"Thank you, my lord," she murmured. "I have felt as if I've come home since arriving here. Now I have some understanding of why. I need time to contemplate the changes."

"I'm sure you do," Drogo answered. "And if you have any other revelations about these pages, would you kindly enlighten all of us?"

"Of course, my lord, but I doubt there is anything there that I can understand any better than anyone else. I think it would be best to devise a new container and return the scrolls to the caves, until the next Malcolm keystone can enter the new generation."

"I believe the ladies will wish to copy it first, but you are right. Good night, Miss Gabriel."

It took all her strength not to pick up her skirt and flee. With studied grace, she departed the room, quietly closing the door behind her. And then she ran down the stairs as if the hounds of hell were at her heels.

Fortunately, the entrance to Drogo's study was closer to her room than to the salon where the ladies chattered. She was able to slip down the corridor without notice. She had said her good-nights to the ladies earlier. They might send maids to scent her bedroom or bring her bedtime possets or new candles, but the maids had no reason to comment upon her absence.

Not until morning, at least.

After depositing the terrified brigands on a fishing boat sailing southward from Berwick, Aidan rode the long road from the sea back to the main highway into Edinburgh. He could have taken the bastards to Edinburgh and saved himself a great deal of trouble, but he needed to think. Besides, he expected company. His nose would be raw if he scratched it much more.

He settled on a boulder overlooking the muddy path that passed for a road in this lonely place. He'd wasted too much time. It was already late afternoon. Whoever was on his trail would have set out by dawn.

Drogo was not the sort of man to ignore what he did not wish to see. He had the Ives curiosity and stubbornness. Once he reached Edinburgh, he would discover the legitimacy of Aidan's birth if he dug deeply enough and located Harrowsby or the executors of his mother's estate. Aidan figured it was his tasks to prevent that digging until he could destroy the evidence of his parentage. Somehow, he would have to divert Drogo and his brothers until then.

In three days, he would lose his home. He may as well lose his family while he was at it. He could bring them nothing but destruction in any case. Perhaps someday he might even thank Mora for forcing him to acknowledge the obvious.

Chewing on the bread and cheese he'd brought with him, he leaned against a tree trunk and did his best to pretend he didn't have a brain in his head. If he didn't think, he wouldn't remember, and if he didn't remember, he wouldn't get angry. If he didn't get angry . . . trees might not tumble.

He leaned his shoulders against the broad tree trunk and let the wind unravel his hair as he waited patiently for an army of Ives men to gallop up the road. Dunstan would want to tar and feather him. Ewen would no doubt wish to dissect him to see what made him tick. Drogo would be unfailingly patient and understanding and hide his grief and wrath beneath a mathematical analysis of odds until he could locate official court documents and prove the appalling truth—they were all illegitimate except Aidan.

Aidan simply wanted to end it. He'd had an entertaining few years following his family about, learning their faults and foibles. He was a rambling man with no connections to tie him down. It had destroyed him to leave his home the first time, but he was used to it by now. The piercing loneliness only haunted his sleep. He knew how to fill his days. He could move on.

If it were not for one woman.

Aidan rubbed his eyes and hoped the image riding down the path was a figment of his imagination and would disappear if he blinked. She didn't.

She was alone, traveling through melting snow and mud bogs with naught but her skinny mare for company. He knew she'd be blue with cold, her teeth chattering, and her fingers numb. She wasn't even wearing the duchess's rich fur mantle but a woolen cloak that was as patched and mended as his own.

He'd known his half brothers would be furious, but he hadn't expected them to be cruel enough to send a woman to bring him back.

Which meant the damned woman was more devious than he imagined and had sent his logical brothers down another track while she came after him. He had to smile at her intrepid determination, which matched his own—with good reason, it seemed. Four generations ago, they'd shared a common Malcolm ancestor.

But he could not trust a traitor. Stubborn determination was dangerous in someone without a sense of justice and morality. The viscountess was a fine example of that. And according to the scroll, Morwenna Gabriel was her niece.

If Mora's parents were legally married, she was the heir that his mother had sought all these years. Mairead must have known of Brighid's child. And so had Brighid's sister, Glyniss Gabriel—which was why the viscountess had hired brigands to have Mora carted far, far away.

He was a practical man not inclined to philosophize on life's ironies, but this one hit him with the force of a broadsword—Mora could have his home. She could fight the viscountess on terms the lady understood.

And he could depart for the colonies immediately, leaving the title to Drogo, where it belonged. Perhaps she had done him a favor after all. He'd just have to learn to live with the aching misery of her absence.

He ignored the thunder and the swaying tree behind him as he watched Mora ride closer. She glanced around, apparently sensing the earth's trembling. Aidan had known from the first that Malcolm women were dangerously perceptive creatures, without the practical qualities he sought in a wife. Yet having Mora had been a dream more precious than gold. He would take the dream with him to warm his lonely nights, in hopes he might someday find another.

He rose and strode down the hill to greet her.

To her credit, she did not gallop wildly toward him and fling herself into his arms and beg forgiveness or any of that other sentimental rubbish women were inclined to do. She merely trotted her mare up and watched him warily.

"Has the earl sent messengers to his attorneys to scour the record halls of Scotland for proof of our father's misdeeds?" he asked jovially, catching the reins of her horse and whistling for Gallant.

"The scroll does not necessarily record legal marriages," she informed him.

Her icy tone should have frozen him. Catching Gallant's bridle as the stallion cantered to his side, Aidan swung into his saddle. "Drogo will not leave it at that. I'll have my attorney destroy his records, and I'll leave for the colonies so I need not lie to him or be a threat in any form."

"That's generous of you," she said coldly. "Now that your family knows you as their brother, you can run away before they make any annoying demands."

She kicked her mare into a walk. "Will you see me settled with my father's family before you go?"

He knew spite when he heard it, but he chose to ignore it. "Your charming aunt has been trying to have you shipped to France so her daughters might have my land for dowry. Will you feel at home with her?"

Mora lifted her riding crop and smacked his arm with it. Aidan almost fell off his horse in shock.

The strike didn't sting. He wore too many layers of cloak and coat, and she had no strength. He just hadn't thought of her as the type to lash out in anger. Of course, he hadn't thought of her as the type to betray his secrets either. Showed how much he knew.

"How can you tell me this so calmly!" she cried. "I have an *aunt*. I have never had an aunt before. How can you be so obtuse? I feel as if I have just lost my mother all over again, and you tell me her sister wishes me dead!"

Well, when put that way . . .

"I'm sorry, I did not think of it from your perspective. She did not wish you harmed," he pointed out, reasonably enough. "She merely wanted you removed from the country, since you did not have the courtesy to stay where you belonged."

"How do you know this?" she demanded.

"Aside from it being obvious that the rogues attacked you twice after two letters were sent to your father?" he asked, raising his eyebrows. Now that he knew to expect her anger, he rather enjoyed waiting for it.

To his delight, she shot him turquoise daggers. "So now you claim my father wishes me dead also?"

"Removed," he reminded her. "But no, I don't think your father knows of your existence. His eyes were injured in an accident in his misspent youth, and it is possible age has worsened the condition. The viscountess is likely reading his letters these days. It took a chat with the rogues who attempted to kidnap you for me to put two and two together. They mentioned only Lady Gabriel."

"Chat?" Icicles dripped from the question.

"Let us just say we have come to an understanding and those particular rogues will no longer seek your acquaintance," he assured her. "That does not mean more won't be hired unless you present yourself to all of Edinburgh and claim your place. The lady will have to admit defeat then."

"I know my place," she asserted frostily. "But it would be most interesting to hear where you think it should be."

That did not sound like a promising opening, but time was wasting. Before he had a chance to regret it, Aidan handed her the key to his heart.

"Your place is as heir to my home. You are the descendant for whom my mother searched. I can leave the lands safely in your hands."

Twenty-four

Mora debated smacking him for not acknowledging that they must go into this together, but she decided physical blows slid right off Aidan's back like snow off a hot boulder. Instead, she shook back her hood, freeing her hair from the cloak, letting the meager March sun strike the tresses she'd released from their braids.

The spring breeze caught a few strands, but a mere breeze couldn't lift the heavy mass falling to her waist. It felt wonderful to have the sun's warmth upon her head.

The sight held Aidan's attention. A shiver slid down her backbone at the intensity of his dark gaze, but she drew assurance from his focus. She wasn't an unwanted, unappreciated country miss. She had power over a man who was so intimidating that other men fled in fear of him. Now that she could be her real self, she was starting to take pleasure in her feminine influence.

"I don't want your land or your title," she informed him. She'd enjoyed expressing her anger earlier, but now it was time to deal with this knotty problem of their mutual families. She had the nagging feeling it was a lifetime knot, but at the moment, she preferred to revel in the illogical notion that she was the descendant of witches and faeries. She'd finally found her place in the world. If anyone could resolve their dilemma, she had to believe she could. "And if you run off to the colonies and leave me to deal with both our families, I'll hunt you down and torture you."

He chuckled. He actually chuckled! That hadn't been the reaction she'd hoped for. She gifted him with a frosty glare.

Aidan rode bareheaded, with the sun gleaming off his thick ebony hair and the formidable jut of his nose. As they rode, his cloak fell from his broad shoulders, revealing his shabby wool coat beneath. He could be wrapped in the plaid of the barbaric Highlands and still look like a knight of old in full gleaming armor.

"I can see you now, sharpening your hatchet, aiming for my scalp. You might need to fetch a ladder first." He grinned in appreciation of his jest. "But you'll have far better things to do than run after a worthless rogue like me. Margaret will berate you with all the promises I've neglected, and Old Paul will complain of the bandits thieving his cows, and you'll have to torture your aunt into keeping her blasting from the Smiths' bairns and from destroying the burn. No, there won't be time for me."

"You honestly believe that, don't you?" she asked in amazement. "You honestly believe that once you're out of sight, you're out of our minds. Just as you think you can continue pretending you're not a Malcolm, that you don't have the power to make mountains quake, and that you have no responsibility to anyone but yourself. Do you think your mother forgot your existence when you went to India? If so, you have a maggot for brains."

That snuffed his laughter. He shot her a black glare and pulled his stallion into the lead rather than continue the conversation.

She didn't have to follow in his footsteps any longer.

She knew precisely where she was going. She was tired and hungry and the horse needed rest. With her new-found freedom, Mora kicked her mare into catching up and passing him.

Not about to ride in her wake, Aidan urged his long-legged stallion into a canter.

In seconds, they were racing down the boggy road, mud flying from beneath the hooves of their steeds, their hair streaming in the wind like kites on an ocean beach.

Their mounts didn't have to be guided. Winded and hungry, the horses raced straight toward the nearby inn, where oats and a warm stable awaited them.

Mora's smaller steed didn't have the size or endurance of Aidan's larger mount, but the mare had spirit and determination. She rode into the stable yard only a few lengths behind.

Not waiting for Aidan to help her, Mora slid from the saddle, and hugged the mare's neck, resting against her for a moment. She had been exhausted before she started out in the wee hours of morning. She had gone far beyond exhaustion in the day since. And she still had to beat sense into the most obtuse man alive.

Without asking permission, Aidan handed the horses over to the stableboy, caught her waist, and practically carried her inside. Or maybe she was so tired that he needed to haul her because she couldn't move on her own.

"Send tea and coffee and whatever you have edible up to my room," Aidan called to the innkeeper, who appeared at their entrance. "Hot water, coals, and then no one is to disturb us."

Mora didn't bother to fight him as he swung her into his arms and carried her up. She remembered these stairs. They were too narrow for both of them to traverse side by side. She had no desire to race him up or follow in his path, so fine, she'd let him carry her as if she were the Queen of Sheba. If he thought he was the conquering hero, he'd learn differently soon enough.

"*Your* room?" she inquired as he ungallantly dumped her on the bed. It was just her good luck that she had chosen a man without a romantic bone in his body.

Of course, if she could admire a body like his, who cared if he was romantic?

Aidan flung off his cloak and didn't bother answering.

The room really was too small for him. He belonged in his great drafty castle with walls that towered to the sky. Mora watched him pace two steps and come up against the dresser, then pace two more steps and kick the coal scuttle on the hearth. He would be marching back down the stairs again if she didn't do something quickly.

It wasn't just Aidan's body that was large, but his mind and his heart as well. So much promise trapped by the narrow world in which they lived. All that passion stifled by fear of harming others.

She might conceivably stall him with words, but she was too tired to find them. She'd much rather *show* him that she'd made her choice. If he thought he could leave her so easily, she needed to make him think twice or three times. And her newly discovered femininity told her the best way to do that.

Rising from the bed, Mora dropped her cloak and deliberately began unfastening the frogs of her riding coat.

Pacing and waiting for the servants, Aidan pretended he didn't notice, but he didn't leave.

Mora shrugged out of the coat, folded it, and laid

it over the sturdy chair by the fire. She ran her fingers through her hair to loosen some of the worst snarls, then massaged the back of her neck to relieve the ache. The weight of her hair bent her backward slightly, which meant her breasts pushed forward against the thin linen of her shirt. Her breasts had been extra sensitive ever since he'd taught her how good they could feel beneath a man's hand. The crests furled into points at just the memory.

Aidan snarled and headed for the door.

The maid blocked his exit with a tray of food, and the innkeeper behind her barred the narrow stairs with his coal buckets. Aidan was trapped.

The stew smelled delicious, and the steaming pot of tea was perfect. Remembering he'd ordered hot water, Mora decided she might live another day. She was rather doubtful of Aidan's prolonged existence if he continued his obstinate denial of the attraction between them, or the family problem that awaited them.

"Thank you, this is just what we needed," she murmured, taking the last of her meager pennies from her pocket to give to the maid. She might be heiress to a viscount and a pretender to Aidan's lands, but she hadn't a silver coin to her name.

The maid dropped a curtsy, glanced at Aidan's scowl, and refused the coppers. Leaving the tray, she scurried from the small chamber so the innkeeper could add coal to the fire and the scuttle.

"It will be a wee bit before the water can heat," the man said into their silence. "You wish the tub?"

"Yes, please," Mora decided before Aidan could scare him off with a black glare.

The innkeeper bowed as if she were someone important, then departed with a quiet closing of the door.

"This inn is mine," Aidan stated. "You needn't pay

the maids. I'll take care of them. I'll leave the deed to the inn with my man of business when I go. If a child comes of what we did, Harrowsby will see that the child receives the income from this and my other properties.''

He was an eminently practical man. She should have known he would find some way of purchasing the only oasis of comfort on the road between his home and Drogo's. Heaven forbid that he should use his meager profits to purchase new clothes; instead he offered them to his future child. She would be grateful except she didn't mean to let him go that easily.

"Don't be such a great goosecap." Mora poured a cup of tea and sipped, letting the extravagant beverage soothe her throat and heat her blood. She enjoyed little luxuries like tea. But she didn't need them any more than he did. Before Aidan could recover his tongue and return her insult, she spread her skirt and sat down at the table.

Dining alone with a man was a new and interesting experience. Dining in dishabille was utterly reckless, but confidence surged through her with every motion.

She poured his coffee and served bowls of stew as if she didn't notice his gaze fastened on her shirt. She didn't think he was studying the neat tucks she'd sewn into the front. Her corset didn't adequately cover her but pushed her breasts up to rub against the thin linen of her chemise. If she could feel how the worn cloth felt against her aroused nipples, she knew he could see them.

Her teacup rattled as his confused anger grew. Mora set the cup on the saucer and studied it with interest. "Sit down. I'll not bite."

Aidan grabbed his cup of coffee from the table and returned to pacing. And brooding.

"I have my mother's book in my saddlebags," she

informed him, as if his behavior were common dinner-table etiquette, "the one with the inscription from my father to my mother. If I understand the rather eccentric laws of Scotland, just the statement that they are married, followed by his signature, can create a legal marriage, even if no formal lines can be found in the church. Am I correct?"

"You have written evidence of a marriage. Gilbert cannot deny that Brighid was Glyniss's eldest sister, and therefore heir to what Glyniss claims. There is no reason the court should not rule in your favor," he growled.

She set down her empty cup and watched the china rather than him. "If I take my book to court and the court agrees my mother and father were properly wedded, so that I may inherit your property rights, it will also make my aunt's marriage void and my half sisters illegitimate."

Her teacup shook as if it would shatter just from the angry energies battering it. Mora held her hand above the cup, and the rattling slowed.

"It is what the witch deserves!" he roared, swinging to face her.

Mora removed her hand and the cup burst into pieces. "Yes, I can see that," she said thoughtfully, but it wasn't her aunt she was talking about. "Do you think you might focus on something less breakable, like a hairbrush?"

He glowered and set his cup down. Hunger forced him to take the chair across from her, although he pushed it as far back from the table as his long legs allowed.

"I'd rather focus on you," he growled, then shoved stew into his mouth.

"I don't think you can rattle me," Mora informed him in that prim vicar's daughter's voice Aidan knew so well. Except now it sat oddly on her. With all that thick silken hair falling from the witch's peak on her forehead, she no longer looked the vicar's daughter, but like a Siren enticing him to rocky shoals. When she leaned forward, he could scarcely tear his gaze from the fullness of her lovely breasts. He wanted to see her naked in full sunshine. The dim light of the cave hadn't been sufficient for such glory.

"While shaking that overstuffed head of yours holds appeal, rattling you isn't high on my list of wishes," he retorted. Damn his perverse nature, but he wanted to take care of her, if she'd only have the sense to let him. He hadn't come to terms with her betrayal yet, but he couldn't change how his heart pounded when she was near, or halt the desire flooding him at just the scent of rosemary.

And those were just his physical reactions. If he stopped to admire her intelligence and fortitude—

"Humor me." She shoved the pewter bread plate in his direction. "Look at the plate and think of Lady Gabriel."

He helped himself to the bread and looked at her instead. "I do not wish to ruin the bread by thinking of that witch and what harm she could have done to you."

She lifted the bread plate on the tips of her fingers, balancing it between them. "What harm could she have done me?"

"She would have put you in the hands of soulless brigands!" he roared. "You would have been on a ship of men who think women are for pleasure only. I'd like to set *her* on a ship to the other side of the world!"

Aidan noticed that the bread plate danced in her hand but didn't fall. His irritating companion returned the plate to the table in front of her and leaned over it, nearly serving the perfect mounds of her breasts as a feast for his eyes. He couldn't resist focusing his gaze there.

"What about my father? Has he no fault in this? Do men who abandon their children not deserve some wrath?"

"Knowing the manipulative witches that make up your family, I suspect the poor man may not know what became of you!"

He knew he was handling this badly, but he couldn't look at her all soft and welcoming and perfect and not think what might have happened to her during those years her wealthy family had abandoned her. His fury was enough to shake the walls.

Except the walls stood steady. The bread plate danced below her breasts instead.

She sat back when he raised his eyes to meet hers. The bread plate quit vibrating.

"I knew you were an amazing man, but I had no idea how amazing," she said with such admiration that his anger dissipated as if blown by a stiff spring breeze.

"I didn't make the plate shake," he protested. "I was hitting the table with my foot and the table moved."

"Want to test it?" she taunted. "Think about Lady Gabriel and brigands and look at the bed."

"Don't be ridiculous." He spooned up his stew, but he couldn't help glancing at the bed. Since he used this room often, he'd made certain the bed was big and well padded. He wanted to share that bed with Mora.

But then he had to think of her betrayal. She was the only one who could have written those lines on the scroll. Better that he should just ride on and leave her here. He shouldn't let himself be distracted from his purpose. He had things to do if he was leaving for the colonies before Drogo caught up with him.

The bed shivered as if it had been hit by a wave.

"An earth tremor," he scoffed, hastily looking back to his stew. "They have them all the time in India."

"Around you, I daresay they did." She placidly returned to her stew.

She did not nag or berate the point. She sat there calmly eating as if the walls did not tremble around her. Not many people could ignore the effects of his presence.

Mora could. He had seen her sit in his library, thoroughly absorbed in his books without once noticing what he did.

He didn't rattle her.

Narrowing his eyes, Aidan stared at her bent head. She'd parted her hair in the middle. The rich tresses gleamed red and gold in the firelight.

It was getting too late to ride on. He couldn't leave her here alone. He wanted her. She wanted him. He'd provide for any result of their mating. In his mind, they were married. His conscience didn't bother him in the least.

Every utensil on the table began to vibrate.

Mora looked up and smiled into his eyes, and the world settled quietly into place again. Her smile grew wider.

"This is rather fun, but you'll sink any ship sailing to the colonies if you continue thinking whatever you're thinking. It's a miracle you traveled safely to and from India."

"They were stormy trips." He threw down his napkin and stood up, not daring to meet her knowing gaze.

"A keystone provides balance," she said thoughtfully. "But a keystone must rest between two opposing sides to work. I cannot quite grasp that part."

"Past and present, Malcolm and Ives, war and peace, they're all opposing forces." He didn't know why he said that. He shouldn't have a clue what she was talking about. But he did. He understood perfectly.

The floor shifted beneath his feet. He didn't want to understand. He wanted to be angry.

Before he could grow any more agitated, Mora stood before him, boldly searing his chest with her hands, tilting her head so he could see clearly into the changing blue green of her eyes. The floor settled again.

"Did your mother teach you how to control your emotions when all around you lost their heads?" she asked with interest.

"She taught me there was naught worth losing my head over," he agreed obliquely. "She was wrong."

"Not if a mountain tumbling crushed your head, but you may interpret her wishes as you like. Somehow, you have learned admirable restraint." Before he could argue, she held up her hand and continued. "I think we must speak with my father. If he truly does not know who I am, we do not have to tell him. We just need to find out what happened. I don't think a Malcolm keystone would leave her home and family without good cause."

"Malcolms are all the time running away," he scoffed.

"Not the keystones, I wager," she said softly, meaningfully. "The keystones are the center of the family."

"I am not a keystone!" he protested.

She rested her head against his chest, and without thinking, Aidan wrapped his arms around her. She hugged his waist and whispered so he could scarcely hear her.

"No, I think you're an opposing force, and I am the keystone who must keep you from destroying your family."

She was as insane as every Malcolm he'd ever heard.

And somewhere deep down inside of him, Aidan feared she was right.

Twenty-five

Mora could hear Aidan's heart beating as he sheltered her in the powerful lee of his arms after her admission that she might be the keystone. She no longer felt empty or alone. In his company, she felt strong and capable of learning what she must.

She couldn't hope he'd stay and help her. As obstinate as he was, he might ignore everything she said and sail off to the colonies tomorrow. But for right now, she needed Aidan as she might need a part of herself that had gone missing.

She stood on her toes and pressed a kiss to his bristly cheek. "Can you feel my heart beat as I do yours? They beat together, do they not? Is that usual?"

"Nothing about you is usual," he growled. But he bent and took her offered lips and his growl was a purr to her ears.

Her soul soared with this meeting of breath and tongue. He wasn't slow to touch her breasts this time. He squeezed her waist, then slid his big hands up the thin linen of her shirt until his thumbs rested exactly where she needed them. His kiss deepened when she pressed eagerly into him, and she almost swooned from the spinning sensation of desire.

A knock on the door jerked them back to the nondescript little room. There, for a moment, she had been returned to an exotic cave of light and shadow and magic.

"Your bath, sir," the innkeeper called.

Mora brushed her shirt down and turned her back to the door. She wasn't embarrassed so much as disoriented. At least she had the satisfaction of knowing Aidan was equally unsettled. He ran his hand through his hair and shook off the moment like a dog fresh from the river, before opening the door to admit the servants.

They carried off the empty dishes, leaving the platter of bread and cheese and a pitcher of ale at Aidan's request. The long tin tub they brought in must have been designed with Aidan in mind. It was enormous. After several trips, the bath was filled with steaming water. Mora thought she was almost too tired to undress and use it, but the steam looked so tempting.

"I'll leave you to bathe," he said awkwardly as she stared at the bath even after the servants had gone.

"I'll fall asleep if I climb in there. And then you'll run away, and I'll have to follow you all over again. Allow me a few hours' peaceful sleep, at least, will you?" she pleaded, searching for her skirt ties.

"I would not have it this way between us," he said with regret.

"And it wouldn't be, if you would simply let yourself believe what you cannot understand," she retorted. "You know perfectly well that it is not reasonable to believe I wrote on that scroll when no one was looking. You know I did not write your name on there. My mother wrote it. It was her duty. And now she's gone and we must deal with what she has left us."

"Your mother is dead," he said flatly.

Defiantly, Mora shrugged out of her shirt, dropping it beside the tub. Her skirt and petticoat fell faster, leaving her garbed in only a chemise, a corset, and stockings. "Her spirit is not dead. At least, I don't think it is. She's gone from my head, but not from my heart, so she still lives somewhere. So does your mother. Just not on this mortal plane."

"Spirits do not pick up pen and parchment."

"And the sun never shines at midnight." Really too tired to argue, Mora unfastened her garters and dropped her stockings. She preferred not to look at Aidan as she did so. The water in the tub was roiling like an angry sea. How could he possess all that raw power and fail to see it?

"Exactly," he said with satisfaction. "You cannot change the laws of nature."

"According to the vicar's books, the sun shines at midnight in summer in the far northern climes. You must know for yourself it shines well into the evening during a Highland summer. One need not experience everything to believe in it." She untied her corset and let it fall, then threw off her chemise. Naked, she stepped into the churning water.

She expected a geyser to shoot up at her reckless defiance. Instead, the water soothed and softened, and she leaned back against the tub with a sigh of gratification.

Only when she had relaxed every aching muscle did she dare lift her lashes and glance sideways at the man she'd set out to disturb.

He was sipping his ale and watching her with unabashed admiration. He had the audacity to lift his mug in salute when he saw her glance.

The gesture shivered her blood much as the water had roiled earlier.

Well, she'd asked for it. At least he'd quit vibrating the floors. She closed her eyes and leaned back again.

She was no longer young or virgin, and maidenly modesty had never suited her. In actuality, his blatant admiration of her nakedness stirred much baser urges—and greater defiance.

"You know, you might have the capacity to calm angry waters as well as stir them," she said as casually as if she were discussing the temperature of well-cooked beef.

She understood that she could not let her excitement at discovering their combined abilities influence his agitation. There had not been enough time to experiment or to know for certain if she could direct his gifts in any way, or if somehow she enhanced his abilities as the Malcolms said their spouses enhanced theirs. Perhaps all she did was distract or shatter his dangerous focus. She could live with that, if he would let her. But he didn't seem much inclined to let her.

So she allowed her excitement to bubble quietly inside. Her years of learning obedience had done her a service. Had she met Aidan as a tempestuous child, they would have battered each other with uncontrollable emotions, and neither would have survived. But now . . .

She had balance.

Most of the time, anyway. When Aidan was looking at her as he was doing now, balance was a relative term. She might start churning the waters herself. She didn't have to turn her head to know he was staring a hole through her. So much for distracting his focus.

"Do ye plan on staying there all night?" he inquired politely.

"I'm considering it." She wasn't certain she had strength enough for what she perfectly well knew was on his mind.

"Then I'll join you."

Before Mora could straighten and look around in alarm, Aidan stepped into the tub with her, fully, thoroughly, admirably *naked*.

And aroused.

Mora scooted backward and started to push out of the tub as he lowered himself on the other side. The water level that had only half filled the tub rose to slosh over the rim. There wasn't room for both of them. His great knees loomed on either side of her as he sank to the bottom. She only barely managed to move her feet out of the way in an attempt to escape.

Aidan leaned forward, wrapped his hands around her waist, and tugged her back down on the only available seat in the tub—across his hips.

Hastily, Mora lowered her knees so she was above the immense male appendage he would impale her with, but she could tell from the devil in his eyes that she wouldn't remain safe for long—didn't want to remain safe, not when temptation was a hair's breadth away.

He soaped his hands, then spread them across her breasts, massaging the soap across her nipples until she had to grab the sides of the tub to keep from sinking with the joyous arousal of his touch.

"I had thought to look for a dutiful wife," he murmured with a touch of disgust, shaking his head. "I wanted a woman who would be content to stay home and bake bannocks."

"I don't even know what bannocks are," she whispered as one of his hands slid lower and sought the place that ached to be filled. She shivered as he pushed a finger inside and gently soaped her.

"Aye, and ye're headstrong and rebellious as well. I cannae take ye with me to the colonies," he said with genuine regret. "The frontier is not the life for a lady who sets such store in her family as you do. But I would give ye something to remember me by."

Mora nearly cried when he removed his exploring fingers, but he shifted too swiftly for a sound to pass her lips. Circling her waist, Aidan pulled her down until she had no choice but to buckle her knees and sink on top of the hard shaft awaiting her.

She could not spread her knees wide enough to accommodate him. She squealed as he pushed the tip inside, tormenting sensitive tissues into arousal as he studied her.

With growing wonder, she stared at this powerful man who commanded her so easily, as if he had every right. Soap bubbles covered the hair on his massive chest. Water glistened on his broad brown shoulders. Firelight flickered shadows over the powerfully sculpted contours of his naked chest and upper arms, and she had to gulp at the sheer beauty of his masculinity.

He balanced her in his palms, cupping her buttocks to support her as she adjusted to the intrusion. With a wicked glint in his eyes, he rubbed soapy fingers between her buttocks until she almost rose out of the bath again. She couldn't read the expression hidden behind his dark lashes, but she could see the twitch of the muscle in his jaw as he restrained himself.

"I love looking at you," he said softly, admiring the swirls of soap across her breasts. "You were made to nurse a man's bairns."

She had never thought to have children. She wasn't thinking about them now, as he rinsed her with a cloth, every movement an exquisite madness.

Her inner muscles tightened with his caresses, and she felt him lose some of that commendable control. His fingers returned to her bottom, and his hips shifted upward, forcing him deeper. If she could just move her knees a little . . .

Aidan rose, dripping, from the tub, carrying her with him. Mora gasped as the movement brought her fully upon him. Carrying her to the rug before the fire, he knelt and lowered her without an ounce of effort, dislodging his connection while he positioned himself over her.

He hesitated, searching her face. When she reached her arms out for him, he bent over and seared her with his kiss.

She took his tongue and drew on it, showing him what she wanted. Grasping arms bulging with muscles and sinews, she lifted her hips. Without a word, he obliged, returning to his place and sliding deep within her without any obstruction.

There, in the firelight, they made *love*.

And magic.

Aidan couldn't deny the word any longer. Mora's touch seeped through his skin everywhere she rubbed her hands. She coursed through his blood, pounded in his heart and lungs, filled his head and his groin. She was more deeply inside of him than he was physically inside of her. Even as he thrust harder, taking what he had taken before, it was all new. Her narrow passage cradled him, gripping him more finely than the most luxurious glove. He knew only one goal, and he felt as if he would burst to achieve it.

Straining not to batter her into the floor, he tried to pleasure her breasts, to bring her to the full state of arousal that was shattering him. She grabbed his arms and lifted her head to cover his jaw with sultry kisses, denying the need for delay.

When she nipped at his chin and dug her fingernails into his skin, Aidan surrendered to raw animal need and drove up inside her. He wanted to make sweet love, but he *needed* the animal mating.

And she obliged, meeting him thrust for thrust, crying out, stabbing him with her nails, biting his shoulder when he took her hard. She thrashed in the throes of an ecstatic release, then rose into him, demanding more.

Given her blessing, finally freed from restraint for the first time in his life, Aidan unleashed the passion that had been pent up inside him for so long.

Raising Mora's legs above his shoulders, kneeling so he did not crush her, Aidan pierced her to the hilt, shuddering with the sheer joy of meeting his match. Mora's cries filled his ears as he loosed all the physical and emotional needs he'd harbored. Finding a woman at last who understood, accepted, and returned his need set free the wildness within him. When she quaked and cried out again, he shattered with her.

Aidan returned to his senses some time later, to realize he was crushing Mora, but he could not seem to find the presence of mind to move. She was warmer and softer than any mattress. Her body still held him, and he could feel the moisture of the seed he'd spilled between them. He imagined his child growing round and strong inside her, and an incredible longing almost crippled him.

Now was not the time to be weak.

"Are you killed yet?" he murmured against her ear, brushing the damp curls back from her forehead before rising on one arm to relieve her.

"I think so," she murmured back. "If this is heaven, I am ready to enter the pearly gates."

He chuckled, and the warmth he had learned at her hands filled him. He could not fault her for being a woman.

"You will not think the same when you are round with my babe as a result. I have heard the ladies complain of the effects often enough." With regret, Aidan pushed off of her. He tried to believe the coldness blowing between them was only their physical parting and not the effect of his words.

"That is why a man must stay at his woman's side," she muttered, rising up and shoving her wild hair from her face.

She looked like a goddess with fire crackling along the burnished strands that fell over her pale breasts and shoulders. Refusing to regret what they had done, Aidan cupped her breasts, playing with the nipples until they begged for plucking again.

"Perhaps I'll sail the sea and return once a year to give you another," he said wickedly. "Come along. We have your father to meet in the morning. You'll need your rest."

"I have all my life to rest," she complained, "if this is the only night you'll give me."

"Insatiable. I like that in a woman."

Lifting her from the rug, he carried her to the bed and slid her between the covers.

As he had expected, she fell asleep the instant her head hit the pillow.

Climbing in behind Mora, Aidan held her against him, watching her sleep, memorizing the feel of her curves against his angles, her softness against his hardness.

He could see no way to protect his brothers against the destruction his presence would wreak should he stay here. He would see the soldiers' reports in the attorney's office destroyed before he left, but Drogo would never be happy until he'd searched and found witnesses to bear proof of what their perfidious earl of a father had done—unless Aidan was gone and there was no other to bear the title. Drogo would have to accept the title and all its responsibilities or abandon them, which he would never do.

Aidan didn't want the title as Drogo did.

He wanted his castle, his land, and he wanted Mora. If he could choose only one, he would choose Mora.

Except to choose her, he would have to drag her with him into an unknown and possibly dangerous future.

Drogo was a sensible man. He would accept the earldom.

And the earl would protect Mora and her child as if they were his own. Aidan would be the only one to suffer, but it would be no more than he had suffered all his life.

Knowing there was one woman in the world made just for him would give his life new meaning. He would leave proudly, knowing he was doing what was best for her and his family.

As he had done for his mother, with disastrous results, an inner voice reminded him. After that he could not sleep.

Twenty-six

"**Y**ou will stay here and I will go to see your father alone," Aidan stated firmly, swallowing the last of his coffee before reaching for his neckcloth.

He'd eaten with his shirt untied and his leather vest unbuttoned. Mora had spent all of breakfast imagining every day beginning with such an awe-inspiring sight as his half-naked chest.

Of course, thinking of the things they had done the prior night—and this morning—wasn't conducive to high-minded intellectual pursuits. So sinful had she become that she actually considered seducing him again to prevent his leaving.

But his declaration reminded her of the many reasons she must use her head. She had a purpose to fulfill, and no guidance beyond instinct. One would think a keystone ought to have training.

"You may go on about your business," she countered, "but I intend to meet my family." She pushed in front of him to stand at the washbasin mirror so she might brush her hair into some semblance of order. As much as she feared meeting her father, it felt good to talk about *family*. She might have more aunts and cousins. She was no longer alone.

"You are safer here," he argued. Aidan checked the mirror over her shoulder to tug his neckcloth into place. He'd gone outside to shave, and Mora detected a small smudge of soap beneath his chin that she wanted to rub away.

"I will make it clear to the bastards that they have been found out," he continued. "That you are my wife, and under my protection."

She elbowed him out of her way rather than smell the exotic sandalwood of his soap. "I am not your wife, and you will only aggravate the situation by riding in and making threats. I have no more claim to the land than you do without disinheriting one family or another. This takes a woman's finesse, not roars and rattling walls."

"It is my place to protect you," he asserted, fastening his vest over his neckcloth. He'd already tied his hair back in a queue.

Laird Dougal looked all that was powerful and masterful, and Mora couldn't stop her smile at his dour Scots authority. She did not mean to bend to any authority other than her own from this day forward, but that didn't mean she couldn't appreciate his masculine insistence on taking care of her.

"Balderdash," she said simply. "If anything, you will need me to protect you. I go with or without you."

The walls started shaking before he even looked up. At least she would never have to guess when he was angry.

"The Traitor tried to have you kidnapped! I will not have another willful female killing herself to get what she wants!" he bellowed. "The land is not worth your life."

That was an interesting perspective. She would figure it out in a minute. "And you wish for me to accept a man who would kill himself for the same reason?" she yelled back. It felt good to let out all she would have once held inside.

Aidan shot her a black glare. "I'm bigger than you are."

"Probably not smarter, though," she said thought-fully, not meaning insult.

Putting down her brush, she finished buttoning his vest for him, stroking his brawny chest as she did so. She was rewarded with the walls returning to normal. "Is that what you think your mother did, killed herself trying to save her land?"

"There is no *thinking* to it. I know she did," he grumbled. "She took all the money I sent and bought *books* with it, looking for that bit of rubbish we found, I suppose, hoping your mother lived. Her lungs were weak. She needed warmth and medicine, not books."

"I am sorry you lost her that way," she said with sincere regret. "I would have liked to have known her. But she made her own choices, just as my mother made hers, and as I must make mine. I suppose I am too much a Malcolm to be any man's puppet." It gave her a thrill to understand where her oddities and strengths came from, and to recognize that those with whom she shared such traits had earned her liking and respect.

"And I cannot live with a woman who defies me, so it is a grand thing I am leaving as soon as I finish my business." Jerking away from her, he tugged on his coat.

Mora wanted to weep that he could talk so easily of leaving, but weeping would not change his mind, nor would it relieve her fears. She had learned long ago to be strong. If she must go on alone, so be it.

But she couldn't help mourning what could have been, if the lovely dream they had shared these last few hours was any measure.

The damned woman would drive him to an early grave.

Aidan watched Mora ride her mare to the brink of

a hill and eagerly scan the hills beyond. The ground was pockmarked with rocks and ice, and her mount could fracture a leg on any of them, pitching her off and breaking her fool neck. She ought to be at home knitting, where he need not worry about her safety.

But her presence eased something wild in his chest and expanded it with happiness.

No wonder his brothers were henpecked. Women were akin to a training bridle, punishing when men got out of hand. And the rewards for good behavior were so desirable that men had no other thought but to do whatever it took to gain them.

He ought to be glad that he was leaving before she dug her spurs in, but when he thought of being apart from her, the heaviness returned to his chest.

Mora threw back her head, letting her magnificent hair fall loose from her hood as she pointed out a hawk soaring high above the valley. He wanted to teach her falconry just so he could enjoy the sight again.

He wanted to take her home to his bed, and shower her with jewels and silk. She would look beautiful dressed in garnet velvet, standing next to the fire in his great hall, warming the cold stone with her beauty and laughter. In time, the castle would come alive again and ring with the shouts of children. He could invite his brothers, and Mora would make their wives welcome.

But the castle wasn't his, and he couldn't endanger Mora with his presence, or take her away from the family she so desperately desired. She was like a child in her eagerness to ride these rocky roads to find the people who had abandoned her.

He wanted to spare her the heartbreak, but she wouldn't listen.

She rode back to him, excitement dancing in her

eyes. "We're almost there. Should we go to your home and freshen up before we make our uninvited visit?"

"My home is your home," he said grumpily, "but it is best we get this over before dark. Gabriel's land is closer."

She hesitated, catching her hair in her gloved hand and regarding it doubtfully. "Perhaps I should put it up and look respectable."

"You look respectable. You are my wife, and I like your hair down."

"I am *not* your wife and your home is *not* mine," she reminded him.

"We are married in the eyes of God," he insisted. He wanted her to admit that there would never be another for her, as he knew there would never be another for him. He'd felt the melding of their souls in that cave, and he refused to deny the precious memory. It was the only sanity he was clinging to right now.

"We are not married in the eyes of the Church of England," she asserted. "That requires weeks of banns and a proper vicar and a church, and you're planning on running off before that can happen."

If there was disapproval in her voice, he couldn't tell it. "You're a druid and a faerie and you need no church to take your vows," he argued.

She cast him a laughing look. "So now that it pleases you, you will admit that Malcolms are witches?"

"Druids," he insisted. "Carriers of wisdom and knowledge. We can repeat our vows here, beneath the sky and trees, and they would be as sacred as any said before a vicar."

"Isn't that just like a man, anything to avoid the inside of a church," she teased, apparently not taking him seriously. "I don't remember agreeing to marry you."

"I don't remember asking," he retorted. "It's what people expect after what we have done. We're in Scotland now. You need only say yes before witnesses."

She halted and raised her eyebrows. "If I agree to marry you, will you admit you are a Malcolm with the power to tremble the hills?"

"I admit no such thing." He continued riding, setting his jaw. "But I will listen if you admit we are bound as one."

"Why bind yourself to me when you plan on leaving me behind? You would only complicate matters. Besides, I was raised under the laws of England and cannot accept heathen ceremonies. You must admit your abilities without my persuasion."

"You would believe in the supernatural but not accept the laws of nature over that of government?" he shouted at her perversity. "Do you get to pick and choose your own laws?"

"You are arguing for the sake of argument," she countered, undeterred by his shouts. "I may be the descendant of people who claim to be druids and faeries, but I have no supernatural talents. My mother is gone. I no longer hear her voice or write the secrets of spirits. All I can do is help you direct your anger, and that is singularly useless if you will not admit that you cause walls to shake."

"Who wants to admit that they wreak destruction wherever they go?" he cried in exasperation. "I would have to believe I can kill people with rolling boulders or walls of water. You could have died in that avalanche or in the forest beneath crashing trees! It is much better that I go far, far away where I have no chance to cause you harm."

There, he'd said it aloud, repeated his mother's foolish superstition, because the truth was, in her own way, his mother had been right. He was a walking, talking catastrophe waiting to happen. Twice, Mora's life had been endangered because of him. She might have been safer with the brigands. He waited to see how she would react to his revelation.

Instead of sympathizing, she cast him an angry glare. "That is your answer to everything, isn't it? You can claim kinship but no responsibility. Take a wife and ride away for her own good. Never settle in one place and help a community for fear you'll do harm—instead of staying and learning to work with what you have, as you can, as you demonstrated last night. Well, you may use those excuses with others, but they do not work with me."

She kicked her horse into a canter and rode off ahead of him.

Aidan wanted to roar and shake the countryside. Instead, he urged Gallant to race after her. "I am no coward!"

"Not in most things," she replied when he caught up to her.

Her calm agreement would have assuaged his anger except for the way she worded it. "I am not a coward in *anything*," he corrected. "Look at me and tell me you see a coward!"

"See that wee tree growing from those rocks?" She pointed at a sapling off the side of the road farther ahead of them. "See if you can shake it by just staring at it instead of waiting until you're angry."

"I'm already angry, and I refuse to play children's games."

Children's games, he thought suddenly—like Drogo's son, pushing his toys about the floor by no visible means.

She shrugged. "See, you're a coward when it comes to things you don't understand. You know no one else who can make mountains tremble; therefore such a thing cannot exist. And you're afraid to try, afraid to be different. I know the feeling well."

Aidan glared at the damned sapling. The wind whipped it until it bent and touched the ground. "There's too much wind up here. 'Tis a silly experiment."

"Look at my hair and tell me there's a wind," she said softly.

He cautiously glanced at her from the corner of his eyes. Her thick mane bounced with the mare's cadence, but nary a strand blew loose in the light breeze. He wanted it mussed and beckoning his touch as it had been this morning. In a fit of whimsy, he imagined the wine-colored glory lifting into his hands.

Thick tresses rose from her shoulders to stream outward, causing her to look up at him with surprise. Her turquoise eyes laughed when she saw the direction of his gaze.

"Do you wish to blow me off my horse?"

In the act of reaching for the strands blowing toward him, Aidan instantly dropped his hand and looked away. He was afraid to acknowledge what he'd done.

Afraid.

He didn't believe in fear. Only weak men were afraid. One faced the situation and did the best one could.

His heart pounded as if it would leap from his chest, and for a change, the wicked faerie next to him was not the cause. Sweat broke out upon his brow. His fingers clenched the reins so tightly that Gallant tossed his head in protest.

He had willed her hair to come to him.

Setting his jaw, Aidan held his head up to feel the icy breeze upon his face. It was March. The wind always blew.

He studied the sapling as they passed it. It danced in the breeze but did not bend in two.

He glanced askance at Mora, who seemed content to let him ponder this anomaly without comment.

They were nearing the road to Gabriel's home, and he was so shaken that the ground rumbled. He was in no fit state to deal with the damned viscount and his shrew of a wife.

Mora reached over to clasp her small, gloved hand over his great fist. "Do you think you might be able to put things back together with practice?" she asked with interest.

The ground settled with her touch. *He* settled with her touch.

He was a man of action, not a man who pondered the mysteries of the universe. Even his studious brothers might take a lifetime to ponder this mystery.

"I have yet to see an earthquake restore a house to one piece," he grumbled, "or a hurricane blow a ship to safety. You are playing with fire."

"That is my choice, isn't it? Perhaps I like fire. We seemed to have raised a bit of one the night we used the spell book. And it's very possible my Valentine's spell called you out of the frozen north to save me from my aunt's brigands. I'm sure, together and with practice, we could do more."

"There will be no such dangerous practice. Take the left up there. That's Gabriel's drive. Do ye have any idea what ye'll say to the man?"

"I will simply ask him if he knew my mother. After that, I cannot say. Perhaps you will vibrate his house until he speaks the truth. I don't know that we can plan things like this, can we?"

"Oh, aye, I could plan to pick him up by his coat and shake him until his teeth shiver. I could tell him what his gentle lady wife tried to do to you. I could flaunt his own writing at him from your book and ask if he really wants to take me to court. There are any number of things I might do," he said callously.

"Well, don't."

Twenty-seven

He had lifted her hair without touching it.

She was thoroughly shaken, but another small part of her thrilled in anticipation. She felt as if she'd finally come alive after a life of numbness. Energy flowed through her, and she wanted to dance and sing and celebrate.

Perhaps she ought to forget the viscount and his dangerous wife, forget Aidan's land, and follow him to the colonies. She would never be so alive as she was with him.

The gravel drive was rutted from carriage traffic and the snows of winter. She let her mare pick carefully over the holes while she watched for some sign of her father's house. It felt very odd to think of any man but the vicar as her father. She hadn't liked what she'd seen of the viscount earlier, but that had been a hostile encounter. Perhaps once they had some understanding . . .

A towering mansion of recent vintage rose above the next hill. Turrets and towers meant to mimic an old castle were built of a soft silver stone that gleamed in the light streaming through the clouds. Broad, evenly spaced windows glinted with shining glass. What would it have been like to have grown up there after her mother died, laughing with sisters, being loved by her natural father and her aunt?

As if he understood how close she was to tears, Aidan intruded upon her thoughts. "Gabriel uses the family's original keep for a barn and a home for his steward. From what Harrowsby tells me, the Gabriel land rights date back several centuries. They abut the Morrigan property that Glyniss inherited." Land that Mora's mother should have had, but he didn't say that. "So they've joined two great estates. My mother's land is over there." He gestured farther north.

"And the viscount has no sons to inherit? What becomes of the land then?"

Aidan shrugged. "All land in Scotland belongs to the Crown. We inherit the right to use it. It will depend on how the land right reads and if there are other male heirs, I assume."

"So the viscountess has a reason to be afraid for her daughters. Lord Gabriel has spent a vast sum of money building this magnificent house that his daughters may not inherit. That is sad."

"They could have built it on Morrigan property, since that descends through the female line," he said, "but I believe the last viscount began the construction. He had a son to pass it on to. They had no way of knowing that your father would have only daughters."

Her father. How very strange to think of him as that. She couldn't quite work her mind around knowing she was the daughter of a viscount. Even Aidan seemed to accept that the scroll was accurate, which was also odd.

"If you think I betrayed you by adding your name to the scroll, why do you believe I wrote the truth when I made myself the daughter of a viscount?" she asked in curiosity, and to keep her fear at bay as they rode into the courtyard.

"Because it suits me to believe it," he said with a shrug, climbing down from his stallion.

He was retreating into the aloof monster again, pretending he did not care but watched merely for his amusement. Now that she understood why he held himself from others, she wanted to cry rather than beat him over the head with a stout stick. Inside that powerfully built body was a man who craved love and closeness as much as she did.

A stableboy ran up to take the horses, and without permission, Aidan swung Mora down. For a moment, she rested her hands on his shoulders, absorbing his strength for the battle to come.

"I don't suppose I can wish my aunt a million miles away so I might speak with my father alone?" she whispered before pushing away.

"If wishes were horses, beggars would ride." Without sympathy, he took her arm and steered her toward the grand front stairs.

As Aidan lifted the door's brass knocker, Mora had a brief attack of wishing she'd plaited her hair and changed into a proper gown, but that was a remnant of the vicar's daughter returning. She needn't bow to the beliefs or expectations of anyone these days. She did not need another father who wanted her to be what she was not.

She simply wanted to settle this land dispute amicably.

A liveried footman answered the door and guided them into a dark parlor off the foyer. The house was so silent that Mora feared to speak.

Aidan prowled restlessly, swiping dust off shelves filled with gewgaws instead of books, picking up the bust of some dead statesman and hefting it as if he considered throwing it through the room's one window.

That would certainly set the conversation off on the wrong foot.

He strolled about the room as if he were master of

all he surveyed, but he did not belong in this civilized little room. He had the power of thunder, and like a storm, he belonged in the hills he loved. Perhaps the colonies had a land where he could roam, but Mora feared he would lose part of his soul so far from his home and the family he loved.

She did not doubt his love for his family. Why else would he give up what he wanted so badly except out of a misguided sense of loyalty?

A burst of giggles broke their separate reveries.

"Shhh," whispered a feminine voice in the distance. "Mama says he is as big as a mountain and just about as thick. We don't want to startle him."

Mora covered her mouth to hide a cough of laughter.

Aidan glared at her, but his mouth twitched in one corner.

"Mama exaggerates," another voice said with loftiness. "The maids say he is very handsome. A large man would be preferable to Twinkle-Toes."

Mora thought she might choke if she held in the gales of laughter threatening to surface. She had come here in fear of her father, and the unexpected encounter with what surely must be her half sisters left her giddy with relief.

"Ye don't think I have twinkle-toes?" Aidan murmured gruffly, leaning against the mantel and regarding the entrance with increasing interest.

"I cannot say," she returned quietly. "I have never seen you dance, but I should think a man who dances would be vastly preferable to a man as thick as a mountain."

He bit back a grin when the girls made their appearance.

They were twins. And they looked just like a younger, unformed version of Mora.

Aidan watched with fascination as the three women stared at one another. Mora remained the most composed, her striking cheekbones shadowing only the faintest twitch of tension as she studied her half sisters while allowing them to study her. With her wild curls spilling over her shoulders, she must look a regular hoyden to the girls.

The twins were about fifteen. They wore their silken straight hair unpowdered but neatly contained in soft rolls of red gold. Their eyes were a pale blue with just a hint of Mora's turbulent green. The cheekbones were softened by the roundness of youth. In time, they might be as striking as Mora, in a milder way.

When the silence stretched to awkwardness, Aidan gestured at Mora. "Ladies, this is my good friend and librarian, Miss Mora Abbott." He wanted to give her full name, but he abided by her wishes to keep her heritage secret. "We have come to see your father."

The girl dressed in blue faille bobbed a swift curtsy. "How do you do? I am Sarah Gabriel, named after my grandmother, and this is my twin, Fiona, named after our great-grandmother." The girl in pink bobbed at the introduction.

If he'd ever met the twins, Aidan had no memory of it. He didn't attend social events if he could avoid them, and the girls were so young they could have been presented to society only recently. He'd been vaguely aware that they existed as one knows a neighbor lives down the road.

"It is good to meet you, Sarah, Fiona," Mora murmured with practiced courtesy. "Have you met Mr. Dougal?"

He bowed his head but remained by the mantel, waiting to see how she would handle this unexpected event.

The girls bobbed wide-eyed curtsies, and then

Sarah, the more talkative of the two, couldn't contain her curiosity any longer. "You look so familiar," she exclaimed, studying Mora. "Have we met?"

"I have reason to believe my family is from this area. Perhaps I resemble someone you know," she said politely. "We have come to speak with your father. Is he home?"

"He's taken the dogs for a walk. He does that when he's pondering. Shall we call for tea?" Sarah asked, recovering her manners.

The girls appeared to hold no grudge against him, Aidan noted. They watched him with the surreptitious curiosity of all females but had apparently already dismissed him as too old for husband material. Their fascination was with Mora.

"I don't know if we have the time for tea." Mora cast a look over her shoulder, waiting for his opinion.

"I can look for the viscount while you warm yourself by the fire," he suggested, removing his shoulder from the heavy carved oak, eager to be out and doing something useful.

"Papa always goes toward the spring in the druid grove," Fiona said shyly, studying the carpet instead of him.

"Druid grove?" he asked. "I know of only one spring and grove of trees hereabouts." And that was on the far end of *his* property. . . . Although, if he sketched out a map of the three properties in his head, he could see that the trees might stretch across the eastern point where all three came together. "I never heard it called a druid grove."

"That's what our nanny used to call it," Sarah admitted. "We had a playhouse in the old ruins and liked to pretend we were faeries when we were very young."

Aidan snorted. That must have been about two

weeks ago. They were still very young. Before he could say anything of the sort, Mora quietly intruded.

"Aidan, if you know the direction, I believe I will go with you. Is it far out of our way?"

"We must go north anyway. The grove is halfway between here and home, but farther east of the road. It's not more than a mile or two out of the way—a pleasant ride but a rather long walk."

"Papa used to ride it, but his eyes are not what they used to be, so he prefers to let the dogs guide him." Sarah looked at them expectantly. "Mother has taken the carriage to the mine and should return soon. Perhaps you could have tea and wait for her?"

He'd rather blow up the mine and the viscountess with it than take tea with the Traitor.

As if the heavens had heard his thoughts, an explosion rattled a glass display case on the wall.

Aidan froze and shot a wary glance to Mora. She frowned and shook her head slightly at him. She hadn't felt the earth quake, then. He sighed with relief. It wasn't him but blasting at the damned mine.

"I thought they sent the miners home," Sarah said in puzzlement as another blast shook the walls. "Didn't Mama say they could go no further until . . . ?" She covered her mouth with her fingers and sent Aidan a nervous look.

He grasped the meaning of that look swiftly enough. "Is she destroying my property?" he shouted, and this time the walls did shake. The minute he'd left home, the viscountess had schemed behind his back.

A dog's anguished howl raised the hair on the back of his neck. That wasn't a hound's hunting cry.

A second dog took up the howl, yipping and crying in the distance as if to warn that the day of judgment had arrived.

The twins went white.

"That's Pepper and Salt," Sarah whispered. Without further explanation, she and her twin lifted their skirts and ran for the exit.

"Your father's dogs?" Mora cried, running after them, following the pair down the front hall.

"Papa didn't know they were blasting today," Fiona called, tears breaking her voice. "He was afraid the blasts would harm the druid ruins, and he went to inspect them."

The look of horror on Mora's face was all Aidan needed to spur him on. She might lose her father before she could speak with him. The howls of the dogs echoed against the hills as he raced for the stable.

"I'm going with you," Mora shouted after him.

But Gallant could reach her father faster than the mare. Without arguing, Aidan swung into the saddle and kneed his mount into a gallop.

He knew she had no way of finding the ruin without him. As much as he wanted her with him, he hoped she would be far safer at the house than back in those hills where the blasting was cracking open the earth.

Twenty-eight

Swallowing her terror, Mora hugged the neck of her trembling mare as the stableboy checked her girth.

Without you, he may die, her mother had said weeks ago, before Mora had ever known of Aidan. Or her father. Mora had thought she'd resolved the question of identity, but now she wasn't so certain.

Sarah brought two frisky geldings running from the field with just a call. Mora didn't think that an easy trick, but no one else seemed to think it extraordinary.

Fiona called for saddles. Mora knew she could not find her father without the twins. She understood why Aidan had left her behind, but neither would she let him act alone.

"One of you must ride to the mine, find your mother, and halt the blasting," she told the twins as they shed their petticoats in a stall and girded up their expensive silks as if they did this all the time. "The other can show me the way to the druid grove."

The dogs howling in the distance raised goose bumps on her arms, but she had to think clearly and keep the twins calm. They'd been on the verge of hysteria until she'd started giving them orders.

"The mine isn't far from the grove," Sarah told her, knotting her skirt into place. "I can find Mother."

"Excellent idea. I'm sure your father is fine, but a

tree or stone may have fallen on one of the dogs." She lied. She knew she lied. But the twins looked braver.

"Pepper likes to dig under the ruins. I bet he hurt his paw," Fiona said, trying to keep her lip from trembling. "I can make it better. I'll go with you."

Mora didn't question the girl's declaration. Fiona's twin seemed to accept it without argument, and they were old enough to know what they were doing. She let the stableboy assist her into the saddle and waited for the girls, although impatience tore at her. Anything could happen in the space of a few minutes.

Fiona tucked what appeared to be a sack of medicinal supplies in her bag before she used a mounting stone to climb onto her horse. "I'm ready," she said.

With Sarah riding across country toward the mine, Mora followed the quieter twin down the drive and toward the road.

Once clear of the house, Fiona kicked her mount into a gallop. Relieved, Mora did the same. Swallowing her terror, she concentrated on not falling off while the horse stretched its powerful muscles.

He *may* die. Not *will*, but *may*. There was a difference. They could be just fine. The dogs could be howling after a rabbit.

Another blast shook the ground they rode. How long would it take to find the viscountess and stop the blasts? *Could* they stop the blasts? Mora knew nothing of mining.

Fiona guided her horse off the road and down a crumbling hill of gravel. Icy patches remained in the shade of gorse and heather. Mora wanted to close her eyes, but she was too terrified she'd be plunged headlong over the horse's head.

"It's a shortcut," Fiona shouted. "The carriage cannot take it."

That was stating the obvious. Mora wasn't at all certain her horse could either. The mare slipped and slid on the unstable stones, finding footholds that she would never have noticed.

She was frozen in terror by the time they arrived at the bottom.

"That's Pepper's cry of greeting," Fiona called as Mora caught up with her. "Mr. Dougal must have reached him."

Mora nodded, too terrified to speak. Aidan was there without her. He could be heaving stones and rattling ruins any moment now. Should they ever survive this calamity, she would never leave his side again.

That thought didn't shock her as it ought. He was right. Whatever had happened between them had been meant to happen. He was the only man in existence who could appreciate that she was not a docile female, even if he did have a tendency to overprotect her. All the Ives men were overprotective of their wives, she'd noticed. No doubt it had taken time for them to work out their differences, and it would be the same for her and Aidan.

And he needed her. She understood that somewhere deep inside herself, where instinct trumped logic. A man with Aidan's physical prowess and intelligence would never admit to needing anyone. He was all male and must behave as such. But she was the feminine part he was missing, the part that could soften his stubbornness and guide him into understanding, as he was teaching her independence.

If she understood anything at all of what her mother had tried to tell her, she had to provide the balance between Aidan and the rest of the world, to prevent one from destroying the other. He needed her, and she was glad of it. Being totally independent was far too lonely.

"Ahead," Fiona shouted. "That's Salt coming toward us."

A white spaniel with black markings, long ears, and silky curls raced toward them, yapping frantically. She raced in impatient circles until they caught up with her. Then she charged toward a large grove of trees spreading along what appeared to be a creek bank.

Another blast shook the hills, and the trees shuddered.

"It's nearly the same distance to the mine as to here," Fiona called. "Sarah will be there soon."

Mora hoped that meant Sarah knew exactly where her mother was and it wouldn't take long to halt the blasting. She could hear the skitter of gravel on the hillside behind them and gave thanks to the heavens that a blast hadn't gone off as the horses had climbed down it.

They reached Gallant grazing on a patch of grass sheltered in the lee of a standing stone. He pranced sideways at the arrival of her mare and Fiona's gelding. Grasping the saddle pommel, Mora slid off her horse and followed Fiona, who raced down a path between the winter-bare trees.

In summer, this would no doubt be a magical place of whispering leaves and babbling brook. But it was not quite April and the path was slippery with melting snow, and the trees provided no protection against a brisk breeze.

A second dog ran down the path, greeting Fiona with yips. This one was the same breed, except more black than white. Mud stained his paws. He'd been digging, as Fiona had said.

But even Fiona had to understand that the dogs were fine—which meant her father might not be.

"Papa!" Fiona cried, reaching a clearing where a jumble of large stones lay scattered across the mud among brown stalks of broom grass.

Mora couldn't see the viscount. Nor could she see Aidan, and Aidan was difficult to miss.

As they neared what appeared to be the arch of an ancient stone temple, Mora had the heart-tripping feeling that she knew why they couldn't see either man.

A raw fracture in the earth had widened from the temple back into the trees. Saplings and old oaks alike tilted on a precipice of mud and forest debris. An evergreen had completely toppled, forming a bridge over a narrow passage of the fissure. Had the earth opened and claimed her father and Aidan? She was practically gasping with terror when Fiona daringly ran to the steps of the old temple.

"Stay back, Fiona," Mora shouted. "The blasts may widen that crack."

"Papa!" the girl cried, halting on the flat stones that formed the floor of the temple. Heedless of her expensive gown, she got down on hands and knees to peer into the dark crevasse reaching beneath the temple foundation.

The ground rumbled without the sound of a blast. With absurd relief, Mora grabbed the back of her sister's bodice and dragged her from the edge. Aidan must be alive if he could still make the ground rumble, but it would be best to keep from upsetting him further. "I'm here," she called, trying to keep her voice steady. "Tell us what to do."

Fiona looked up at her as if she were mad, but Mora prayed that Aidan was close enough to hear and understand that he need not shout.

She didn't know how he could fit into that narrow aperture in the temple foundation. It looked as if the ground had opened to swallow the viscount, and the mud had slid in after him. There was still an opening, but not much of one.

"You recall how you dragged me through the forest when we first met?" Aidan's voice seemed to come from under them.

Startled, Mora studied the moss- and lichen-covered stones they knelt upon. Did the stones cover a cavern? He was asking for a litter. She hoped that meant the viscount lived. "I'm wearing my cloak. How can I get it to you?"

"Drop it down the hole and poke it through with a stick, toward the altar." His voice echoed slightly off the stones.

A druidic altar, of course. The basin over there would have a bubbling spring, if the blasting had not diverted the stream.

Fiona offered her fur-lined mantle, but Mora shook her head. She wore her old woolen cloak. It was tough and the loss would be no great one. Unfastening the ties, she lowered the cloth over the edge of the stones, into the gaping crack. Fiona brought her a stout branch and, between them, they poked the cloak down the tunnel under the altar.

"I see it," Aidan called softly. "Can you bring Gallant close enough to lower his reins down the hole?"

Mora was trembling and Fiona was white-faced with dread. No sound from the viscount meant he was at very best unconscious. Fortunately, the girl did not give in to hysterics. Mora instructed her on how to detach the reins of all their mounts, and offered to go with her, but Fiona assured her that she could handle the stallion.

Mora had her doubts, but she wanted the girl out

of hearing before she could ask the questions that needed asking. "Is he alive?" she said into the crumbling hole after Fiona had left.

"He's breathing," Aidan replied curtly.

"We've brought bandages and the like. Do you need them?"

"I can't tell. We're not too far down a tunnel that leads to a room beneath the temple. We'll haul him out first."

And there was the question she feared to ask. "You cannot haul him on your own?" she asked carefully.

Silence. Just as she thought she might have to go down the hole and strangle him, he finally answered.

"The blasting has loosened the timbers holding the temple floor. His leg is caught under one of them. I will have to hold it up while Gallant pulls him out. I want both of you off the stones before then."

Mora swallowed a large lump in her throat and wished she could go down there with him. Frantically, she tried to think of some way of lifting the stones before they toppled into the hole on top of Aidan, but she knew she had no chance of so much as digging her fingers beneath one.

"Mora?" he asked warily when she did not immediately reply.

"I'm thinking," she croaked out.

"Don't think," he said with what might have been amusement. "Just do as you're told for a change."

"I want you to come out alive," she murmured, not certain if he could hear.

"I'm thinking I'd like the same."

If he was uncertain of the likelihood, she couldn't tell it from his voice. She desperately wished to see him, to see how bad it was under there, but she heeded his wisdom in this.

Fiona arrived with the reins and leading Gallant.

The stallion seemed to understand her urgency, just as he had the day Mora had used him as a packhorse. The horse was as magical as his owner.

"Gallant cannot stand in the crack, so we must pull from the side." Mora gestured to indicate the plan she'd conceived while waiting. "We can lower the loose reins under the altar and see if they reach."

Fiona understood at once, and between them, they began securing knots to hold the leather together. Mora wished she could have known of her sisters sooner, but she was thrilled that they seemed bright, capable girls, ones she would be proud to claim as family. She didn't want their meeting to be forever marred by the death of their father. Surely, she had been sent here to save him.

A moan echoed from beneath the floor, and their gazes met. Mora shook her head warningly. "Do you have him on the cloak?" she asked softly.

Aidan muttered with what sounded like a grunt of effort. "I need four hands to manage it all."

That could be arranged. Without stopping to think of what she did, Mora dropped into the crevasse and crawled down the fissure beneath the altar.

Aidan cursed his loose tongue the instant the crack of light filled with a dark shadow. He traveled alone for many good reasons, and this was one of them. He would not have the blood of innocents on his hands.

"Go back," he urged. "There is not enough room down here."

"There seems to be a great deal of room down here," Mora replied, squirming through the collapsed tunnel to kneel beside him. Ignoring his warning, she leaned over the man sprawled beneath the fallen beam. "Lord Gabriel?" she murmured, resting her hand against the viscount's chest.

The viscount twitched and groaned lightly. Aidan wanted to moan with him, but he had to get the fool woman out of here. Bracing one of the remaining log supports above them with his hand while she checked on the viscount, he prayed the blasting wouldn't begin again. He didn't think he could hold up the entire roof. "Did you bring the reins? Can you knot the leather around the ends of the cloak?"

"Miss Abbott?" Fiona's faint voice called from above. "How is he?"

"It's too dark to see much," she called back. "We will have to pull him out, just as Mr. Dougal says."

Aidan bit his tongue on a *told you so*. The faster they got out, the safer they would all be. "When I lift the log, see if you can slide the rest of the cloak beneath him."

"I have candles and flints in my supply bag," Fiona called. "I will drop the bag down there if that will help."

He could see Mora look to him for that decision. His instinct was to get the hell out as quickly as possible, but the viscount would be the one to suffer for his impulsiveness. "It can't hurt," he agreed.

Mora crawled back to the entrance to retrieve the leather bag Fiona lowered. In the light at the hole, she pawed through the bag's contents until she'd secured both candle and flint.

Still holding the ceiling brace, Aidan rested while she lit several candles and found places for them on rock shelves lining the walls. This was no accidental crack. Someone had built this tunnel to a vault beneath the temple.

The man on the floor began to writhe and moan.

"That's enough," Aidan whispered harshly. "I'll lift this end of him if you can slide the cloak beneath his head and shoulders as far as it will go."

She worked swiftly, lifting her father's head and shoulders and smoothing the cloak down as far as possible. Once she had Gabriel arranged, Aidan dropped to his knees, praying the ceiling held long enough to get Mora out. He crawled under the fallen timber and propped his back against it, raising the timber enough so that he could free Gabriel's leg.

"There, that has it. Now, can you tie the reins to the cloth?"

"I've almost got it. Fiona, do you have your end secure?"

"We're ready," the girl cried from more of a distance than earlier. "I have Gallant's head. Tell us when."

Mora glanced to him for reassurance. Aidan wanted to kiss her for making this so much easier, and he wanted to shake her for endangering her damned life.

He nodded.

"We're ready—"

A blast shook the crumbling walls, drowning out Mora's cry.

With an ominous rumble, the slabs of slate that formed the ceiling splintered. Dust trickled through the rapidly zigzagging cracks.

And the fissure in the earth beneath them widened.

Twenty-nine

"N̲o-o-o-o-ooo!" Aidan howled, flinging himself forward to reach Mora before the slabs of ceiling could crush her into the ground.

His cry shuddered the walls and shifted the earth beneath them. Small rocks and mortar pounded his back, and the overhead slab shifted sideways, just missing them. He had Mora safely beneath him—until the earthen floor became a landslide, unceremoniously dumping them into the vault at the bottom of the tunnel.

Gravel dust filled his lungs. He coughed and choked, but the sweet music of Mora's coughs worked miracles. He held his breath, and wrapped his fists in the folds of petticoats all around him until he could feel the solidity of her legs and hips. Working his way upward, he found her waist and pulled her against him.

"Tell me you're alive," he murmured in the vicinity of her ear, although her ragged cough spoke without words. He just needed to hear her voice.

"My father?" She squirmed back against him in a way that reassured him that all her parts were whole and functioning, and so were his.

Her reminder of the other occupant of this cellar swiftly doused his rising ardor. "I don't want to move until the dust settles, and we have some hope of seeing. He should be nearby."

He felt her nod against his chest, and he took a

moment to squeeze her waist and give a prayer to whatever gods watched over them. If he even stopped to consider what life would be like without her . . .

Fiona's panicked cries penetrated the ceiling above, but they came from a greater distance than before. "Can you make her hear?" he whispered. "I fear I will shake the walls." That he could feel Mora nod relieved him more than he could measure.

"Fiona?" she called.

"Are you there?" The child was obviously weeping and terrified.

An odd peace stole over Aidan, a need to reassure rather than express frustration or anger. He spoke gently so as to calm the girl. "We're fine," he called, although he had no idea of the truth of that. "Fetch the miners and their equipment. They will have to lift the stones."

"Are you sure?" she sobbed. "I don't want to leave you."

"Go, Fiona," a rough voice rasped from farther down the hole. "Hurry."

Mora jerked abruptly from Aidan's arms. The man who had agreed to the mining and had thus brought all this down on them was still alive. Aidan supposed he ought to be grateful, but he'd like to slam Gabriel's head against the stones for allowing the blasting in the first place.

At least they were in the vault now, and he didn't have to prop up the tunnel ceiling any longer. Leaving Mora to look after the viscount, Aidan located one of the candles still flickering on a shelf.

Using the light to find the medical bag, he rummaged inside until he produced an assortment of old tallow stubs and set them about the walls of the chamber, giving him a sense of the space where they were trapped.

The narrow tunnel entrance had collapsed, but the

back of the tunnel had fallen open into the small stone vault several feet below. Aidan glanced back at the timber he'd been propping up and shuddered. It was now the only thing holding up the remainder of the tunnel. The shifting earth had formed a slide that had tumbled them downward, away from the falling rocks. Otherwise they would have been crushed beneath the timber and stone in the entrance.

Ordinarily, he would have raged at the vile viscount, but Mora's safety took precedence. So he tested the security of the old stone walls while Mora bent over the man on the floor.

"Brighid?" the viscount whispered.

Aidan halted what he was doing. Mora stiffened. "I'm Morwenna," she replied carefully. "Mora Abbott, remember?" When he did not respond, she continued. "I fear your leg may be broken." She folded the cloak under his head now that it was impossible to drag him through the tunnel on it.

"Mora is short for Morwenna?" Gabriel leaned into the cushion of wool and closed his eyes. A slight smile tilted his lips. "I knew a Morwenna once. She had the laugh of a nightingale and ran through the heather like a fawn."

Aidan squeezed Mora's shoulder and nudged the medical pouch toward her. She cast him a grateful glance and sorted through the contents, but he caught the stain of a tear running down her dirty cheek.

"My head feels as if it's broken," the viscount muttered suddenly, returning from his reverie. "What the devil happened?"

"The blasting opened a crack in the ground. I do not know how you ended up under the temple." Mora produced a jar from the bag and held the label near a candle to read it.

"I was checking the foundation for damage," the

viscount murmured in a tone of irony. "Some of my happiest memories are of this place."

Just as he knew how Mora's heart was breaking, Aidan knew what she was looking for when she glanced around without replying. He nodded toward the trickle of a stream that should have been running through the basin above.

She found a tin cup in the bag and handed it to him. Taking one of the candle stubs, he crawled to the back of the cellar, filled the cup with water, and carried it back to her.

As naturally as if they did this every day, she kissed his cheek with warm lips lightly salted with tears. "Thank you."

Her kiss impaled him.

They were trapped no telling how many feet underground. Their air could be running out with every word spoken. The ceiling could cave in on them at any moment. And Aidan felt as if he'd just been given a glimpse of heaven.

She was right. He was a great goosecap. A mushy-headed, softhearted goosecap. He didn't know how she'd touched his heart and brought him to life. He wasn't much interested in questioning, if only she would always be there with him to take care of the damned soft heart she'd exposed. If only he could keep disaster from occurring everywhere he went . . .

He didn't have any idea how he could bring about the impossible, but Mora seemed to know. If they survived being trapped here, he had to try.

Aidan settled behind Mora, giving her his chest to rest against and his back as a bulwark against any falling stones. And his support as she dealt with her father. These were things he knew how to do.

She mixed the powder in the jar with the water he'd given her and leaned over to help the viscount lift his head. "This will ease some of the pain. Your leg does not seem to be bleeding, so you may have only cracked the bone. I don't wish to chance disturbing it until it's time to move you."

No sense in putting the old codger into any more pain until they knew whether they could be rescued, Aidan translated. While she worked, he studied the stone arches overhead.

"I wanted to honor our ancestors and call her Erithea," the viscount murmured. "But Brighid said it was an ugly name, and she wanted our daughter to know only beauty."

"You should rest your head." Mora set aside the cup and leaned over to smooth a strand of the viscount's graying hair from his brow.

Her patient turned his pale gaze to Aidan. "I lost her. I lost both of them. If you have ever lost the loves of your life, you would understand why I will do anything for those left to me. You do nothing with that great pile of rocks in which you sit and brood. You have no woman to defend, no daughters counting on you to give them happiness. What difference can that land mean to you when you do nothing for it?"

"His mind is wandering," Mora whispered for Aidan's ears alone. "Do not argue with him."

Aidan thought the man knew exactly what he was saying, and Gabriel was growing more agitated by the minute. In the interest of peace for Mora's sake, Aidan tucked a rebellious curl behind her ear and turned her face to the candle so the viscount could see her plainly despite his poor vision. "How did you lose them?"

The viscount stared greedily, his gaze never leaving Mora. "Stupidity. Negligence. Obstinacy. All the usual human sins. And then they were gone, and I could not make it up to them."

He choked on what sounded like a sob. Shaken,

Mora leaned forward to offer him another sip of the medicated water.

"Gone?" Aidan asked.

Mora jabbed her elbow into Aidan's chest to shut him up. She was terrified the viscount might be talking of her and her mother, and she didn't want to hear more. And yet she wanted to hear everything. Her heart was cracking in two.

"Gone," the viscount agreed, turning his head away. "My father was alive then. He thought I was a rake and a fool to have anything to do with the Morrigans. He called them witches and heathens."

Mora bit her lip to keep from crying out. He spoke of her mother. She knew it.

"He was right," the viscount whispered. "She bewitched me. We exchanged betrothal vows, and I never strayed again. I was never happier, and if that is witchery, then the world needs more of it. Too bad I was too blind to see that then."

Tears streamed from Mora's eyes. She wiped at them hastily, feeling the grit of dirt on her hands.

"They're a bewitching clan," Aidan spoke from behind her, rubbing her arms reassuringly. "Since I have found the love of my life, I know what you mean. I would do anything for her."

Before Mora could contemplate Aidan's declaration, the viscount swung his gaze sharply back to them.

The mist in his eyes transformed to angry clarity. "She is not Morwenna, so do not try to deceive me into giving you what isn't yours. Morwenna died when she was just a toddler learning to chase butterflies in the field. She died in a bloody fire because her witch of a mother insisted on practicing spells from that thrice-damned book I gave her. I must live with that guilt for the rest of my days, but I will not let you destroy my daughters for it."

Stunned by his vehemence, Mora couldn't speak.

"Did you see your daughter die?" Aidan asked. "Did you bury her wee body with your bare hands? Or do bloody viscounts not do that?"

Gabriel rose up with a roar, but his elbow crumpled under him, and he fell back to his makeshift pillow again. Covering his eyes with his hand, he cursed until the pain subsided. "I would that I could have, but I was not there when it happened. I was an only son. It would have broken my father's heart to know of our marriage, so I hid my wife and child in the hills with a crofter's widow, while I stayed home, hoping to persuade my father into accepting her."

"My mother did not like that much, did she?" Mora asked softly, hoping to draw him out and keep Aidan from antagonizing him.

Her father rubbed his eyes. "She was like a shooting star, so far out of my reach that I could never hope to hold her. I gave her the book in hopes that would keep her happy until I could make peace with my father. When I told her he was dying, that she need only wait until I could bring her home with me, she wouldn't listen. I tried to explain to her that with my father's death, I would have a title and responsibility and could not go on pretending we were what we were not, but she did not listen to that either."

"She told you she was a faerie?" Mora suggested.

He uncovered his eyes to glare at her. "That's a very fine game you play. Morrigans are Gypsies, nothing more. We grew up on the legends and tried the spells, but she had no more magic than I did. I wanted her to be a proper wife and honor the home and position my father built."

"And she insisted that she would go nowhere with a man who wouldn't believe in her faerie power," Mora prompted, hearing her own anxiety echoed in her mother's story.

He covered his eyes again. "Not that it's any concern of yours, but she claimed to hear voices of ghosts. It was all immature silliness she would have grown out of. I'm just explaining why I won't give up what rightfully belongs to my daughters."

"You argued with her," she persisted. "What happened then?"

"I left her and my wee daughter in a croft just beyond this hill," he finished angrily. "And they burned to death there in my absence. There were no remains left to bury." He choked the last out with angry terseness, then wept into his hand. His whole body shook with the force of his grief.

"Leave him be, Aidan," Mora murmured as she sensed his rising discomfort. "Until the age of nine, my mother was my life, and I loved her dearly. That does not mean I was blind. She was a willful, strong-minded woman, much like me."

"Not precisely like you," Aidan replied, kissing her temple. "I did not know your mother, but I know you put the needs of others before your own. If you are willful, it is for the benefit of all and not just yourself. You had the advantage of your adopted parents' teaching. I do not see that as a flaw."

She wept, but the tears were those of gladness that she had found a man who understood her heart. She missed the kindness of the vicar and his wife. For so long she had tried to please them. Aidan's words gave her hope that she had not turned out as badly as she feared.

"I love you," she whispered through her tears, because she could not die in this place without him knowing how she felt. "You are the most wonderful, caring, understanding man in the world, despite all your other faults.''

He chuckled. "My faults are legion, I know. But I will hold you to those words when we get out of here. I don't plan to die yet.''

"It would simplify everything if we did," she said pragmatically. "The twins would inherit it all. The Malcolms and Ives would go on as before. All our problems would be solved. That must have been what my mother thought when she faked our deaths here and ran away to Wales.''

He wrapped his arms around her waist, circled his legs around hers, and pulled her snugly against his chest. "What will be, will be, as they say in France. But I do not think we've come this far for no purpose." He nodded his chin against the top of her head and directed her attention to the arches above them. "Look up there. The keystone holds.''

Rubbing furiously at his eyes, Gabriel returned his attention to them. "Don't give me any more of that bloody painkiller. It's making an ass of me.''

Mora poked Aidan with her elbow before he could make the obvious reply. "My mother was the family keystone. Her name was Brighid. I have her book.''

Gabriel whitened and stared. The cellar grew so quiet she could hear the trickle of water on the back wall and the sift of crumbling mortar from the ceiling overhead. "That's not possible," he said.

"I sent you a letter. Did you not receive it? It was franked by the Earl of Ives.''

"I do not know the Earl of Ives," he responded stiffly. "Do not try to fool me because I'm half-blind and currently lame. My mind still works.''

"Ask your wife about the letter," Aidan said coldly. "I wager she read it.''

Mora hastened to intrude before he explained his

theory that the viscountess had tried to have her kid-napped. She wanted her mother's story told first. "I was too young to remember, but I suspect my mother set your croft on fire and ran away. The keystone has a serious obligation to her family, and by telling her to forget who she was, you were asking her to dishonor her duty and kill her soul. We lived in Wales, but she died in a different fire without fulfilling her obligations. So you are not wrong about her willfulness, and maybe you are not wrong about the book causing the fire. But the book survived, and so did I, thanks to the kindness of strangers."

"The book?" the viscount repeated warily, staring as if she were a ghost risen from the grave.

"*A Journal of Lessons* by Morwenna Gabriel," Mora replied.

"Impossible." Pinching the bridge of his nose to remove any trace of his earlier distress, Gabriel spoke strongly. "No one could read the inscription. I don't know how that heedless bastard who put you up to this learned so much, but you cannot trick me into cheating my daughters of their dowry."

Quietly, Mora repeated the inscription that had been engraved upon her heart since its discovery. "To Brighid Gabriel upon the birth of our daughter, Morwenna, named after our common ancestor. With love and adoration, your husband, Gilbert."

Her father stared at her through haunted eyes, searching her face until she was tempted to turn and bury it against Aidan's shoulder and pretend she'd never come here at all.

"*Morwenna?*" the viscount croaked in disbelief.

The galloping of horses, creak of carriage wheels, and shouts of men above them destroyed the moment.

Thirty

"She can't be Morwenna," the viscount muttered a Aidan rose to examine the ceiling above them.

If Aidan's surmise was correct, the arched stone supports held the slabs of slate that marked the floo of the temple above, and dated this cellar to Roma times. He hadn't thought the Romans had come thi far north, but perhaps escaped soldiers or slaves had found their way past Hadrian's Wall at some point.

Or his ancestors had learned the art of building arches from the Romans. There was no doubt a Mal colm journal somewhere that would explain. His ow fascination with rocks and gems and mountains could stem from some great-great-grandfather who had worked underground.

"She is Morwenna, without any doubt," Aidan as sured his injured enemy. He poked at a solid slab ove his head and was rewarded with a trickle of dust.

He could hear voices in the distance. One of them was shrill and commanding—the viscountess. Aida waited for someone more sensible to approach.

"Mora has proof of her birth and parentage," h continued. He'd been thinking about this, desperat for any way to solve their mutual dilemma. He coul see no way out of his problem, but he would do wha he could to solve Mora's. "She is your legitimat daughter. And I assume you already know the illegality of your current marriage to your wife's sister."

"It is not illegal," Gabriel shouted. "Brighid and I did not say our vows in church. She died. I was free to marry as I wished."

Aidan snorted. "Any way you look at it, your second marriage is illegal. Under the laws of Scotland and the church, your vow to Brighid was made permanent when you had a child by her. The inscription in the book gives evidence of your marriage under civil law. The commissary court will not accept a marriage to your wife's sister, no matter when you married her, and neither will the church. It's within the first level of affinity and forbidden. By right, Mora is the only legitimate child and heiress to both my land *and* her aunt's. You are mining Mora's property."

"That cannot be," Gabriel argued angrily. "Miss *Abbott*," he addressed Mora, emphasizing the name, "you said your mother died when you were nine. In what year was that?"

"She died in 1737. I was born in 1728. I am Morwenna, but I do not wish to harm your daughters," she said quietly.

"Even if you were wedded after your first wife's death, you are guilty of marrying your sister-in-law," Aidan emphasized. "All I have to do is take it to court, and I can have Mora's legitimacy recognized and your second marriage annulled. That's no more than you intended to do to me. And since your bloody wife tried to have Mora kidnapped and shipped to France, I'm not much inclined to offer mercy."

An astounded silence followed. Mora continued trying to make her father comfortable, but she sent Aidan a look he couldn't attempt to fathom. The viscount grew very still as he pondered the horrible possibility of Aidan's accusation.

The scrape of a shovel in the tunnel entrance broke the silence.

"The tunnel is collapsed," Aidan called to the outside world, hoping they could hear.

The shoveling halted.

"You will need to lift the floor of the temple. If you pull the wrong stone, it will bring the whole ceiling down." Aidan hated saying that where Mora could hear, but he'd examined the situation thoroughly and saw no alternative. He prayed the twins were out of earshot.

"Is there a *right* stone?" a male voice asked overhead. "Is it even safe to walk on the temple floor?"

Not if he grew agitated, but Aidan wouldn't say that aloud either. Mora understood and didn't seem to fear him. He took comfort in that.

"It is for now. The supports are secure. I am no engineer, but I think if you begin with this stone"— he pounded on an octagonal slab of lime at the far edge of the room—"the main support should hold the stone next to it. Should the stones around it fall, we'll be far enough away. Remove too many, and the whole structure will collapse."

Even so, the whole structure might cave in with the removal of the one stone. He could not see how the whole held together. He just knew it would be days before they could open the tunnel, and the result could easily be the same. He favored instant death over suffering if that was the way it must be.

"You think we're going to die here," Gabriel said harshly.

Mora said nothing. She merely looked at Aidan with a calm assurance that made him feel as if he were a superhuman god instead of a mortal man. For her sake, he wished he were that god.

"We won't die," she said. "Aidan has the instincts

of a Malcolm and the technical knowledge of an Ives. But I suggest that you not anger him. The result is sometimes unpredictable."

"I'm thinking we can reach a compromise," Aidan offered to the dazed viscount. "I'm an extremely wealthy man."

Both Mora and the viscount had the same raised-eyebrow look at that bold declaration. Given the way he dressed and lived, Aidan supposed he deserved their disbelief. "I have a knack for finding gems. Mine owners in India rewarded me well."

Neither of his listeners looked convinced. At least he needn't worry that Mora wanted him for his money. He hid a grin at that.

"I want to marry Mora," he continued. "The only dowry I'll ask of you is the rights to my land. I'm sure with your connections, you can persuade the lord advocate to amend the original deeds to allow a direct female descendant to inherit without proof of legitimacy."

"This is blackmail," Gabriel argued. "First you tell me my wife is a kidnapper, and now you blackmail me."

"I have written statements from the kidnappers," Aidan assured him. "And half a dozen earls and duchesses and various relations to give evidence. I could have your wife arrested. If you wish to call that blackmail, then so be it."

The earl grew more pale. "Glyniss is somewhat irrational on the subject of her sister. She believes witches are the tools of the devil."

"Then she had best not look too closely at your daughters," Mora said quietly. "I have only just met them, but already I see an unusual talent with animals and a healer's touch. They are Malcolms, whatever she wishes to believe."

The viscount abruptly turned his head away and wiped at his eyes again. Aidan was almost starting to feel sorry for the man. A man couldn't be weak and deal successfully with women like these. He was developing some understanding of why the Malcolm women insisted on writing down all they knew and banding together to help one another. Without education and support, Mora's family had not fared as well as the other ladies.

"How would you have me explain this to my wife and daughters?" Gabriel finally asked, less belligerently than before. "The twins are counting on dowries to find them good husbands. I cannot simply hand away a fortune in land without explanation."

"You have *three* daughters," Aidan reminded him coldly. "And you owe one a debt greater than you can ever repay."

Mora rose from her father's side to lay her hands on Aidan's chest. He liked it when she did that. It recalled the moments when her hands had touched him in bed, and he wanted to imagine a lifetime of nights like that. That promise might be the only reason the stones over their heads weren't rattling with his anger.

"The viscount and I are nothing to each other," she said soothingly. "I would not claim his acknowledgment at the cost of pain to my sisters."

Aidan wrapped this amazing woman in his arms, and she laid her head against his shoulder. Her action allayed his fury, but not his determination.

Over her head, he glared at the man on the floor. "My land as dowry for your daughter," he insisted. "And because Mora is worth more than silver and gold, I will pay you the worth of the land so you have wealth enough to provide for her sisters."

The viscount looked sorrowfully at his daughter's

back. "You will have the better of the bargain," he agreed. "For the sake of the twins, I cannot acknowledge Morwenna. Silver and gold cannot replace her, but I will speak to my wife. Perhaps, in time, we can learn to be good neighbors."

That's what Aidan wanted for Mora's sake. He kissed the top of her head and hoped his heart didn't break before he could get them out of here. "My wedding gift to you," he whispered.

She met his eyes, and he could see the sea's passion in their stormy aqua. He wanted this woman with all his heart and soul. He would die for her. But he didn't want to hear what she was thinking right now. She knew him far too well. Thank the heavens that she'd learned better control of her thoughts and words than most. She was right. She was the balance he needed, and his heart pounded unsteadily with hope and fear.

They could hear murmured voices and scraping at the far end of the ceiling. Aidan knew the time was closing in on them. He wished he could have her alone for a little while. Defiantly, he bent his head to kiss her in front of her father.

Mora drank in the welcome bliss of Aidan's kiss, reveled in the strength of the man who held her—not just his physical strength, but his ability to do what must be done despite the tremendous pressures confining them. He was her match in so many ways—

Hurry it up, lass, a voice interrupted from inside her head. The nagging rumble had been there for some minutes, except she hadn't understood the rumble as words until now. Startled, pushing away from Aidan's embrace, she tilted her head to listen.

The voice spoke in halting Latin, she realized now that she heard more clearly. *We have work to do,* she translated.

Hope filled her heart. At Aidan's frown, Mora

rubbed her fingers over his clenched jaw. Instead of pulling the walls down around them, he patiently waited to see what she would do next.

She would not let him die as he was so obviously prepared to do. She would make him believe her, as her mother had never made her father believe.

"I take you in sickness and health, richer or poorer," she murmured against Aidan's lips. She knew only the Church of England service and not the words he'd used to make his vows earlier. "I take thee, Aodhagán Dougal Ives, for husband."

"You vow to love, honor, and take her in equality," the viscount prompted from the floor.

"I do," Aidan agreed, covering her face with kisses.

"In equality?" Mora asked in surprise. "I like that."

"I now pronounce you man and wife and stand witness to the marriage under Scots common law," her father said with a hint of irony. "And if you wish the ceremony to be legal, you must get me out of here alive."

Eyes wet, Mora laughed quietly into Aidan's shoulder while his arms clasped her more tightly. They were well and truly married, tied together for eternity in a crumbling cellar with none about them but a man who had not known of her existence until minutes ago.

And a voice in her head, grumbling impatiently.

"I love you," she murmured into Aidan's shirt. He kissed her nape, so she knew he heard.

When he did not respond in kind, she wiped her eyes and straightened. "Now, let me do what I was brought here to do."

"I believe you came in hopes of rescuing us," he said in forced amusement. "That didn't work so well, did it?"

She stood on her toes and pressed a hasty kiss to

his lips. "In equality, remember? I am a Malcolm, too. My mother left me her heritage. I do not fully understand it yet, and neither did she, but if I read enough of your library, someday, I may be more useful."

Aidan tried to pull her back in his arms, but Mora danced away, tilting her head and listening. "I do not have your strength and experience," she continued after a moment, catching his gaze with seriousness, "but I can support you, and balance you with my own abilities and knowledge."

"I'm sure you can," he said patiently. "But you had best stay away from the stone where they are working."

"No, he says you must place the timber here and hold it." She stood directly under the stone that was being dug out above them and pointed upward. Mortar and dirt crumbled down on her, but she didn't blink.

"He?" Aidan asked cautiously.

"Your engineering ancestor." She didn't try to explain, just met his gaze, defying him to argue with her.

"What timber?" he asked, intelligently not questioning her reply.

The one in the tunnel, the foreign voice rumbled. *The great oaf ought to be able to support it.*

"He says removing the stone will cause no harm if you use the timber in the tunnel." Mora prayed she was hearing correctly. She had never channeled a stranger's voice before, and certainly not one who spoke a halting form of Latin with which she wasn't quite familiar.

If she was crazy, they would all die. But so far— with Aidan's aid—her voices had brought her a family and a man beyond any she could have imagined. She wouldn't deny them now. Her mother may have passed on, but she had left a legacy that Mora would learn to use.

She knew her father stared at her as if she were crazed, but he had given up his own heritage too long ago to remember how it must be. Or perhaps he had never known. Perhaps most men did not inherit the Malcolm instinct, or let it atrophy as she had. But Aidan still possessed his, to the credit of his mother, she suspected. She watched her new husband with confidence.

Her husband. She had just handed Aidan her life and freedom. She loved him enough that she believed she had not done so foolishly. In any case, there would never be another man for her, so she did not regret it.

Giving the ceiling a second look, Aidan nodded and crawled up the pile of debris to pry loose the timber that had prevented the entrance from falling earlier. The last blast had finally knocked it loose of its supports, but dirt and rock slid down into the cellar when he pried it from the rubble. Dust filled the cave again.

"It's all right," Mora assured him through the choking miasma. "The keystone holds the main supports to the ceiling, not the tunnel."

"The engineer tells you this?" Aidan inquired, appearing through the dust like a ghost, carrying the enormous timber.

"No, I think that is you I hear," she said, searching the place in her head where the words appeared. "But the engineer does not disagree."

"She's mad, just like her mother," Gabriel whispered from his place on the floor. "You are trusting our lives to a madwoman."

Mora froze. Those were the words she had feared since childhood. They were the reason she'd kept her rebellious inner self hidden all these years. She had so much wanted to be understood, but she had known she would only be despised. Aidan was enough of a logical Ives to listen. She stared at him in fear.

And realized with relief that he was enough of a man to chart his own course.

He grinned down at her. Dirt blackened his face and dulled his glossy black hair, but Mora could see the white gleam of his teeth, and her heart pattered faster in joy. Nothing could drive the perverse giant more fully into her camp than to have her father call her mad. She grinned back, understanding him quite well.

"Just think how much more fun you would have had if you'd trusted your life to your mad wife," Aidan countered, not looking away from her. "Sharing your knowledge, making decisions together, learning how a woman thinks, are adventures I have just paid good money to take."

Mora laughed. "You have not paid it yet, my love. You could still die a wealthy man if you don't hold that timber steady beneath those stones."

"I'd not leave my wealth to my lazy brothers," he scoffed. "Let's get out of here and spend it ourselves. I have in mind seeing you in wine-colored velvet. Show me which stones you wish me to hold."

The square ones between the wall and the keystone, the voice supplied in answer.

Translating the Latin inside her head, Mora pointed to the stones indicated. Aidan ran his fingers over them, and nodded his approval.

"Ahoy up there," he called, without an ounce of anger to tremble the walls. "Do you have support timbers ready?"

After a brief hesitation, a familiar voice replied, "They're hauling the logs now."

Mora's eyes widened. *Drogo.*

"Your voices didn't warn you about him, did they?" Aidan asked, the laughter dying from his eyes, replaced by apprehension.

She glanced at the ornate square block in the center of the vaulted ceiling. Enough dust had cleared for the candlelight to dance upon its carvings. The Roman numerals were too faded to read, but the magical griffin engraved on it seemed to nod approvingly. Her ancestors and Aidan's had planted that block there to last centuries.

Those same centuries had created her, and she understood her purpose. Being a human keystone would require a great deal of inner strength. She had spent her lifetime practicing caution, studying sermons, and learning languages. Her knowledge would help her use the voices.

She would need all she had learned to keep Drogo from destroying Aidan, or vice versa. The question of an earldom remained unanswered.

She took a deep breath. "One task at a time."

"Aye, I'll agree to that." With resignation, Aidan lifted the ancient timber above his head, propping its length directly beneath the stones she'd indicated. He braced his legs, strained his back upward, and, with muscled arms bulging, held the heavy beam in place.

Take out the octagonal, the voice instructed.

"Have them remove the octagonal stone, please," Mora called. Silently, she prayed to the only god she knew. Then facing Aidan, she lifted her arms to join his. She couldn't quite reach the ceiling or the timber, but she rested her hands on his forearms and hoped she knew what she was doing as their arms formed an arch beneath the timber.

The octagonal stone overhead lifted slowly. Mortar sifted down. Light appeared in the ceiling, casting a beam on Aidan's filthy face.

"I love you," Mora whispered, meeting his gaze as 1e ceiling rose above them and the ancient stones roaned.

"I love you and will be with you until the end of me," he returned fervently.

Her heart soared dizzily at his smile as much as his ow. The octagonal stone was gently pried free, llowing the fading rays of sunset to bathe them.

The connecting stones supported by Aidan's tim-er held.

Thirty-one

Mora clung to Aidan, feeding him her support an[d] energy and balance until new braces were [in] place, and it was safe for him to release the timb[er] holding up the ceiling. He groaned in relief when m[en] swung down to prop up log supports in place of h[is] tired arms so they could safely lift Lord Gabriel o[ut] of the cellar. He ordered the men to haul her o[ut] before he let go, just as a precaution.

She cast him a look so admiring, so full of love an[d] longing, that he could have died happy on the spo[t]. He had no idea how he would extricate them fro[m] the predicament waiting overhead, but the joy [of] knowing he would live to have the chance carried hi[m] through the next moments.

Once Mora was safely aboveground, Aidan release[d] the timber. The stones sagged on their crude suppor[t] but they held. Rather than trust his weight tugging [at] the ceiling, he had the miners stack stones so he cou[ld] climb out. Hands reached down to pull him up whe[n] he reached the top.

"He weighs as much as a mountain," Dunsta[n] grumbled, using his size to bear the brunt of th[e] burden.

"All the better to crush you with," Aidan taunte[d,] stepping hurriedly off the temple floor before it cou[ld] give way beneath the combined weight of him and his brothers.

"You saved him, you saved him!" twin voices cried from out of the twilight. Before Aidan could sort out shadows from the crowd in the clearing, the twins threw themselves at him, and he was inundated in silks and red hair and perfume.

"Thank you, thank you." Kisses rained on his cheeks as he instinctively lifted the pair to keep them from knocking him over.

"Hero worship is a dangerous thing," a delightfully wry contralto murmured from behind.

Aidan thought his smile would crack his face. He knew his heart would pry its way out of his chest if he did not hold his wife soon. Setting the twins firmly back on the ground, he gave them stern looks. "Never, ever enter this clearing alone again, do you understand? It's riddled with tunnels and extremely dangerous."

"Yes, sir," they agreed hastily, nodding their promises. "We will come find you when we wish to visit."

Mora chuckled. Even though he needed to correct the twins' assumption that he would ever let them near the temple again, his brothers waited. His fate was sealed, but Aidan couldn't resist turning to gather Mora into his arms. He buried his face in her cloud of hair and simply absorbed the wonder of her.

"Yes," she laughed breathlessly. "I feel that way, too."

He wanted to glare at her, but Drogo was making his presence known, and there was still a crowd of people staring at them. "You have some explaining to do about these strange voices," Aidan said in a low tone only she could hear.

"I know. I'm just gathering my wits. Give me time." She took a deep breath and pushed away from him.

Aidan followed Mora's glance to where several people were creating a litter to carry her father back to
the house. Mora had said something about the twins
being Malcolms, and Aidan didn't doubt the truth of
that. Only a Malcolm miss would be calmly applying
splints to her father's swollen leg as Fiona was doing
now. She had the makings of a healer. And the bolder
twin was apparently handling his restive stallion and
several other horses with mere whispers.

He shook his head in wonder and returned his attention to Drogo. His half brother looked deadly serious. The fat was in the fire now.

"I'm glad you're all here," Mora announced unex-
pectedly to the assembly, intruding on Aidan's anxious
thoughts. "Lord Gabriel has just witnessed our marriage, but I would like the members of Aidan's family
to do the same. It is very strange for me to have any
family at all, much less one so large and diverse."

Drogo strode forward so he could speak without
being overheard. Aidan placed his hands on Mora's
shoulders, needing the physical contact to steady his
roiling emotion.

"You have shown yourself worthy of any family you
would claim," Drogo said solemnly. "And I would be
proud to call the two of you Earl and Countess of
Ives and Wystan."

"No, I don't think so," Mora said impertinently.
"After all is said and done, I am still the vicar's daughter, and Aidan is far more engineer than earl. We are
not at all suited to be earl and countess. I think if you
will ask the viscount, he will be perfectly willing to
tell you that Aidan's birth is as illegitimate as mine."

That was only a partial falsehood, Aidan realized.
Gabriel would certainly lie and deny Mora's legitimacy if doing so would protect his daughters. He
might also lie about Aidan's birth, but there were still

the documents in Harrowsby's keeping proving otherwise. He assumed Mora was lying to buy them a few stolen moments together before he must leave or accept the title.

Drogo nodded. "You don't mind if I verify his birth for myself?"

"It would be foolish of me to think you would do anything else," she agreed. "But keep in mind with whom you are dealing before you make any decisions. Do not hastily conclude that Aidan is earl based on some piece of paper. We have only just discovered that we are Malcolms, and we have yet to learn our limits. Should Aidan take his seat in the Lords, and they should make some foolish change in a law of Scotland, his outrage might possibly shiver the walls of Parliament. Do you really want that?"

Aidan grinned as Drogo raised his damned questioning eyebrows in his direction. "You heard the lady. I rattle walls. I also make mountains slide, and it's possible I might make rivers roar."

"But you will learn to put things back together again if you continue your studies," Mora said serenely. "After all, you were the one who just held the ceiling together."

He shot her a startled look that had Drogo chuckling.

As if to confirm her statement, a piece of the temple floor crashed into the cellar below.

The clearing grew quiet while dust drifted upward from the hole.

He had been the one holding the stones together? Not the supports? As with most Malcolm idiocies, he had no proof.

"She's the worst witch of them all," Aidan declared with a sigh of resignation. "Would you like to stay the night with Gabriel or with us? I'm telling you now, it will be morning before I wish to speak to anyone again."

"I think that's understandable." Drogo stepped back. "Shall we bring a man of the cloth with us in the morning? I'm a little tired of these vague Scots marriages and would see your union tied tight under English law and Christian ceremony."

"Bring the entire kirk, if you like. Bring in the family and set the ladies to decorating the halls of Wystan. We'll have the knot tied again in England for the doubters among ye. I'm grateful for your aid, but it's been a damned long day, and I'm a new groom. So do not take it wrong when I say I'll be glad to see your back for a while."

Mora laughed as if all was right with their world. Aidan wished it could be so, but for now, he would settle for a few hours of enjoying her laughter in the privacy of their own chamber.

Wearing an elaborately embroidered lawn nightshift she had discovered laid over the bed to which Aidan had brought her, Mora turned eagerly as her husband entered the room.

She'd not paid much attention to the walls of her new home except to ascertain that they stood sturdy against her husband's tempestuous temperament. The fire heated the bedchamber delightfully, and the hand-carved tester bed was built for kings, with its bed-curtains and covers made of heavy velvets and brocades in midnight and royal blues with accents of gold. If the mattress was as sturdy and well stuffed as the one at the inn, they would sleep well, when they were ready to sleep.

From the look in Aidan's eye, that would not be soon. Wearing only shirt and breeches, hair still damp from his bath, he carried a leather pouch that he tossed aside at the sight of her.

She thrilled to the heat coursing through her at his admiring gaze and knew she would be thoroughly ravished by this powerful man before the night ended. It thrilled her equally that she knew she was his match. But first, she must give him the explanations his Ives mind required.

Before he could reach for her, she picked up the book she had waiting at hand. "We can start here," she said. "Or with any of the other books in your library."

Warily he eyed her mother's spell book. "I know how I wish this evening to end, without need of a book to tell me."

She smiled at that. "I'm sure we both do. But even though, between us, we have a great deal of knowledge of human nature and practical matters, neither of us has the learning the Malcolms have provided in their marvelous library. They have left us the means to be what we must be."

"And that is?" He stalked closer, until the book alone separated them.

"We were destined to find each other. You have the power I do not. I have the control you lack. We provide balance for each other. And once we gather the library under one roof, we can learn together how to use that balance to teach others, like my sisters."

"You wish me to learn witchcraft?"

She heard the laughter in his voice. He was a man, and she must appeal to his mind. "And science. Had you studied the science of rocks, instead of relying on your Malcolm instincts, you could have prevented the damage the mine has done. I think, in time, we can accumulate the knowledge to tutor the next generation in both science and intuition. The Malcolms and Ives—and Gabriels—will work together to create a better world, a world where science saves lives, and education brings understanding."

Gently, Aidan set the book aside. Mora did not resist when he engulfed her in his embrace. She buried her face against his broad shoulder and inhaled the scent of masculine musk and sandalwood as she wrapped her arms around his waist.

"You stayed Drogo with your bold words, but he is like a dog with a new bone. He will not be satisfied until he's chewed it through and declares me earl. I fear the relationship between us and our families will not be as pleasant as you foresee."

Tell Aidan I love him dearly and it is thrilled I am that he has chosen his wife so well. Brighid said you would be his match.

Mora snuggled closer and kissed the V of flesh revealed by Aidan's open shirt. "Your mother sends her best wishes on our marriage. She and my mother have been conspiring together to help us find each other."

Aidan's arms tightened around her, and he growled deep in his chest, a veritable purr against her ear. Mora nipped his shoulder, and the vibrations building inside the volcano that was her husband settled.

Tell the great lug that I wouldnae marry an English earl, no matter how pretty, even should my life depend upon it. Tell him what I told you about the witnesses lying to protect me and the land. The earl was a masterful lover, and a faithless man. He was already on his way home to his betrothed when the soldiers came.

"Mairead says she wouldn't marry an English earl, no matter how pretty, if her life depended upon it," she repeated obediently.

"You are talking to my mother?" Aidan demanded with as much outrage as disbelief.

"Aye." She mocked his lilt. "And she says the witnesses cited on your lawyer's document—the ones who sent the soldiers away—lied. My father was but a lad at the time, in the company of his own father, but they all lied for the soldiers' report. That is why I suggested Drogo consult with my father. He and the last viscount gave the soldiers your father's name, but the Earl of Ives never made a claim of marriage. He was not even there by then."

"Not there?" he rumbled in disbelief.

"Except as the seed he planted growing within your mother," she said mischievously. "They were most concerned with protecting the lady's name as well as the land. I think Lord Gabriel will be quite happy to bear witness that you are a bastard, don't you agree?"

Aidan roared his delight and swung her onto the huge tester bed. "You, my wife, shall be a pleasure to keep around for more reasons than I ever thought to imagine."

Mora hastily knelt when he fell down beside her, shaking the great stacks of feathered mattresses with his weight. "Now that I have solved your problem, how do you really mean to solve mine? I fear my father is stubborn enough to break his promise if you cannot provide dowries for the twins. Shall you give him the inn?"

Propping his head up on his hand and studying the way the light behind her silhouetted her ripe curves through the thin lawn, Aidan lifted the leather pouch he'd carried in earlier. With a flick of his fingers, he dumped an array of gleaming gems across the covers. "Did you nae believe my wealth?" he asked, feigning astonishment. "A few of these should convince both of you, should they not?"

Mora stared at the glittering jewels, recognizing diamonds, rubies, and emeralds but not knowing the names of the other glorious colors. "You were not jesting when you said you found wealth in India. Why do you go about looking as if you're a ha'penny from bankruptcy?"

He shrugged. "I'd no reason to do otherwise. The wealth was to save the castle and my mother's health, but she died. I'm a simple man. I saw no reason to pose as someone I was not."

Shaking her head in incredulity at his utter disregard for himself, Mora returned the gems to the pouch. "In that case, we can use your wealth to find the rest of the library," she said wickedly. "And to restore your home and improve the lot of your tenants."

Aidan took up the better portion of the bed, but she dodged his long reach when he growled and sought to bring her down. She had to avoid falling for the heat in his dark eyes and the beauty of his raw masculinity until she'd settled all matters between them. They were married for all eternity, and she had to make her point clear so they started off on the right foot.

"First, you must admit I'm a Malcolm and can talk to our ancestors," she said firmly, holding off his hungry grasp with her hand.

"Oh, aye, I'll agree to that if the ghosts keep saying things I wish to hear." He tugged her down on top of him and spread kisses across her face so she could scarce think.

"And you will admit that you are Malcolm and can tumble mountains?" she asked in a muffled voice as his mouth found hers.

"Call yourself mountain, and I will tumble you," he agreed with great enthusiasm, rolling over on top of her.

There was no further discussion between them for a long, long while. Yet their communication was intimate, thorough, and most satisfying.

Epilogue

"Did ye mean it about keeping this ragged old place for our home?"

Mora heard the uncertainty in her husband's voice. Leaning back against his sturdy strength, folding her arms over the brawny ones clasping her waist, she gazed upward at the outer wall of the keep where he'd single-handedly torn down the old tower. "It is a wonderful home. I could not ask for better. Why did you tear this section down?"

" 'Twas the old Macleod watchtower, built so far back none have any recollection of it. The mortar had weathered out, the chapel burned, the blasting loosened what was left, so it wasn't fit even for cattle. I'd hoped my mother's Malcolm ancestors might have hidden our chapel records among the stones, but it had to come down even if the records were lost."

"Besides, it gave you something to destroy," she said with a smile. "We should do something with the stones to commemorate those who built it."

Aidan gazed up at the three-story wall of the keep. "I thought to put windows where the old doors into the tower used to be. They will add light to the halls inside."

With her head pillowed against his shoulder, Mora studied the old oak doors now bereft of the stairs that had once occupied the tower, and realized they framed the end of the keep's gloomy corridors. "That will be lovely," she exclaimed happily. "They will catch the south sun all day." She turned her head to look up at him. "Are you certain mending the castle is what you wish? Or would you rather continue your travels?"

He crushed her close and kissed her until her head spun and she'd forgotten the question. They'd had only two days to celebrate their vows, and she was quite willing to keep celebrating. Except the sound of carriages traveling down the road reminded her of the event scheduled for this evening.

"If you can teach me to mend instead of destroy, I would stay here and be the laird my mother wished me to be," he admitted.

"You've already started, inside your head." Pulling from his arms, she stood on tiptoe to kiss his newly shaved jaw. *Love* was not a strong enough word for how she felt at having the wifely right to touch her hero anytime she wished, in any way she wished. "You did not destroy your home, only the part that was too dangerous to remain. You have already thought of ways of improving it. You need to write down what you learn of engineering as you go, to aid any other Malcolm with your difficult gift. Our sons and grand-daughters might be miners or bridge builders or architects someday."

He chuckled. "You are planning the future of our future already. I will write that keystones are great plotters." He bent to whisper against her ear. "The vicar and our wedding guests are arriving. It's too late for you to escape."

Mora stiffened and instinctively brushed down the beautiful garnet velvet gown Aidan had given her for this occasion. Margaret had said His Arrogance had ordered it for her days ago. If she could love Aidan more than she already did, she would for the thoughtfulness of the gift alone. It was the most splendid gown she'd ever owned.

Of course, the bodice was cut so daringly low that she knew where her husband's thoughts traveled when he looked at her, and it wasn't to the elaborate necklace of garnets and pearls that had accompanied the gown.

"It's too much," she whispered fearfully, touching the necklace and her unbound hair. "They will call me uncouth and above myself."

"They will call you beautiful and opinionated, and will stay until I must throw them all out," he declared with great confidence. "You would make the ideal countess."

Mora laughed. "I think the family has enough outrageous nobility. I do not mind being the eccentric librarian."

She sobered as she recognized the carriage stopping at the drive. "I had hoped Drogo would come first."

"He has been in Edinburgh with your father, solidifying our agreements with the court so that no one can take our home away. With my money and their titles to smooth the way, our children will be saddled with this monstrosity into eternity. It is too late to run off to the colonies now," he said with a wry chuckle.

They watched as a footman assisted the Viscountess Gabriel from the carriage.

"I think your aunt intended to arrive before the guests," Aidan said thoughtfully. "She has much to account for if we are to be neighbors."

"She is an unhappy woman," Mora acknowledged warily.

Gathering the poise she'd learned in dealing with the vicar's parishioners, Mora followed the overgrown stone path to the drive. She had plans for a lovely garden along here to soften the old stone walls, with perhaps a low edging of the ancient stone Aidan had scattered across the grounds. She hoped she would learn to soothe his temper so he never felt the need to destroy again.

"Lady Gabriel," she said with a nod of her head but no respectful curtsy or welcome as she reached the carriage. They would meet as equals this time.

"I believe your tenants refer to you as Lady Dougal," the older woman said stiffly, sending the carriage and her servants away with a wave of her hand. She watched Aidan with caution.

" 'Morwenna Dougal' is good enough for me. It is the person and not the title that matters. We will try to act as a good laird and lady."

For someone wearing an expensive brocade gown and bejeweled wig that declared her wealth and status, the viscountess looked oddly uncertain. "I thought you might have questions about your mother."

Mora's heart nearly split in two, and with gratitude, she grabbed the arm Aidan offered. With a calm she didn't feel, she gestured for her aunt to enter the castle.

An army of people had spent the previous day cleaning the great hall until every crystal lamp glittered, and the ancient trestle table gleamed. A fire roared in the enormous fireplace, heating the hall as it hadn't been heated in decades. Torches flamed in every corner, dispelling the gloom and illuminating the spectacular tapestries in their rich colors.

For the first time in years, the castle had come to life. It was a fitting setting in which to bring together families long parted and soon to be joined in the eyes of church and state.

Aidan offered the viscountess a carved, high-backed chair and called to one of the maids for refreshment. Most of the new maids were wide-eyed country girls who had never served more than their own families, but they had jumped eagerly at the opportunity to work in the castle now that the laird had a wife. They were too timid to step forward now, though.

Margaret brought hot mugs of mulled cider to the fire, then shooed the girls back to setting the table.

"I knew my mother well," Mora said into the awkward silence. "I was very young when she died, but her memory stayed with me." She did not explain her mother's *voice* to a woman who refused to believe in her gifts. "I really only have one question."

Lady Gabriel stared into her cider. "Yes, I knew she ran away," she replied before Mora could ask. "I helped her. I brought her coins and jewelry and the means to escape. I did it selfishly, because I loved Gilbert more than she did. Once Brighid learned of my love, she regretted her reckless vows."

Aidan squeezed Mora's shoulders, kissed her temple, and left her with her aunt while he went in search of chairs. She was grateful that he stayed silent and did not shatter the walls or dishes in fury at this admission that Mora's aunt had conspired to send her niece away from the only home she knew—then never looked for her again.

"Thank you. I think I understand now. She never loved my father, did she?"

The viscountess stared at her in amazement. "How can you know that? You are young and in love and must think I'm a dreadful old witch."

"Oh, all that, too," Mora said cheerfully, settling into the chair Aidan produced for her. "But we are not weak women, and we do what we must. I resent that you thought I would be foolish enough to stay in France after your churls kidnapped me, but you had no reason to know me."

"You are your mother all over again. I can see now

that you would never have stayed where you did not wish to be." The viscountess scowled. "We were all wild and invincible when we were young. Only Gilbert and I could see where the wildness would lead. But he thought he could tame Brighid."

Mora knew her aunt would never admit to the source of the "wildness," but her mother's memory told her that without family or education to guide them, they had experimented with their gifts and magic as if they were games. Mora had learned that she couldn't know what powers she possessed until she tried them, but she'd also concluded that testing those powers was best done under the supervision of someone with experience and knowledge—which was why the Malcolm library was so valuable.

"Lord Gabriel was the wrong man for my mother," Mora replied. "His desire for wealth and title unbalanced her."

Lady Gabriel frowned at this description of herself as well as her husband and continued what she had come to say. "In their wildness, your mother was foolish enough to get with child, and Gilbert did what was right. If she had just agreed to be the lady he needed, all would have been fine."

Mora shook her head. "No, it would not have, but we cannot prove either argument now. I believe she was moderately happy in her new home. How did you know when she died?"

The viscountess looked visibly shocked, and stuttered over a reply until she recovered. With resignation, she clasped her hands in her lap and watched the fire. "I knew when she was gone. She told me."

Standing behind Mora's chair, Aidan said, "You are like Mora, then? You hear the voices?"

He almost chuckled at the irritated glance the she-devil sent him, but he refrained. He really wanted to snap the lady's neck for not coming for Mora and taking her home. Or perhaps— He glanced down at his wife's head and did not speak his words aloud.

Perhaps Brighid had deliberately not told her sister where to find Mora, preferring that she learn the lessons the vicar could teach her. He smiled. He was learning.

"I never heard any voice except Brighid's," the viscountess snapped, proving that he'd best hold his thoughts. "She was the witch among us."

"I would like to be friends," Mora said, rising as the bell at the door echoed through the towering chamber. "And I should like to get to know my half sisters . . . cousins," she amended hastily at the lady's disapproving look. The viscount and his wife could not admit Mora's paternity without branding the twins illegitimate, but there was no shame in admitting that the viscountess was her aunt. "There is much we could do to improve this land if we work together."

The viscountess rose, clasping her bag in her hand. "We cannot mine further without your permission. Now that the twins' dowry is assured"—she cast Aidan an almost approving glance—"perhaps we can level the hill for pasture, if there is someone here capable of preventing his tenants from stealing our sheep."

Balance, Aidan thought, deciding not to throttle the lady. Mora would be good for his tenants and his family. And hers, if he understood the gleam in her eyes as she again assured her aunt that they meant to be good landlords. Mora meant to teach her sisters about their heritage and open the Malcolm library to them, despite their parents' disapproval. Balancing the scales of justice could make the future quite entertaining.

Drogo and the viscount entered, handing over hats and cloaks to a maid.

Carrying a package of legal documents in his left

hand, Drogo extended his right to Aidan. "You did not give me time earlier to welcome you to the family, brother. It gives me great pride to do so. I hope we can live up to your expectations."

Mora thought she saw the glint of tears in her new husband's eyes, but bear of a man that he was, he would not acknowledge them. Instead, Aidan ignored the distinguished earl's hand to wrap him in a crushing hug that had Drogo staggering.

Released, the earl righted himself and laughed. "I'm reintroducing the concept of fostering our children to others. You're nominated as the one to scare sense into their heads when they grow older and rebellious."

Aidan roared, and the stone chamber echoed with the sound of his joy.

More carriages rattled up the rocky drive, and the bell rang continually as guests poured through the ancient oak doors.

Christina arrived, directing the duke's footmen to carry a cooing, fluttering covered crate to a far corner of the great hall. Ninian entered with her, ushering in a trio of servants carrying a live rowan tree in a barrel.

Aidan hugged them all, introducing Mora to Christina's mother, Hermione, the marchioness, and to Duke Harry, Christina's husband, and the various other guests filling his hall.

"The timing is perfect," Christina cried, hugging Mora. "Harry brought Mama with him from London. Leila just had a baby boy. She sent a perfume she made specially for you. They're carrying in the gifts now. Felicity sent books filled only with happiness. You'll love them! The illustrations are exquisite."

Duke Harry gestured to a large package being hauled into the hall. "I had to bring that with me or

I would have been skinned alive. Lucinda seems to have known of the wedding before anyone else."

Lucinda was the Malcolm cousin with a propensity for painting pictures of events long before they occured. As servants stripped back the wrappings, Aidan tried not to gape at the magnificent oil painting revealed, featuring his home standing tall and solid against the hills, with a ray of sun illuminating windows he hadn't yet installed.

Beside him, Mora gasped as she crouched down to stroke laughing figures running through shrubbery that she had only just imagined planting. "The boy looks like Aidan," she said with wonder and a tear in her voice.

"And the girl looks like you," Duke Harry agreed. "But Lucinda knows you, so I'm sure she simply painted what she knew. See, she's even painted the other children. There's Dougie playing doctor with Jamie's bruised knee." He lovingly pointed out his son and nephew—as they would look in a few years.

No one bothered to mention that Lucinda was half a world away, in her husband's adopted home in the Caribbean, and couldn't possibly know about the wedding.

Aidan stared in awe at the future in store for him. He had great difficulty accepting the mysterious Malcolm gifts, even his own. But this painting made a believer of him. He didn't think his heart could hold much more joy without bursting.

"Alan and Verity wanted to come," Christina chattered blithely, "but we told them they had to wait until they were old enough to read, so they're studying their books."

Tears of happiness in her eyes, Ninian admired the painting, kissed Mora's cheek, then gestured to chase

Christina away. "Come along, it's time we prepared the altar."

Keeping Mora at his side, Aidan greeted a small jovial man in a clerical collar who stepped up next, followed by Harrowsby, who beamed when Aidan passed him the papers confirming ownership of the estate.

Gradually, the ancient hall filled with Aidan's tenants and their families, so that wool and leather mixed comfortably with silks and satins. Musicians set up their lutes and flutes and even an illegal bagpipe, forbidden after the '45. If her spirit lingered, Mairead would dance in delight this night.

Aidan was ecstatic at the acceptance of his family and tenants, and awed by the world of the unknown that Mora had opened for him. But for the moment, Mora was his entire world. Her laughter filled his ears. Her claret hair gleamed in the firelight just as he'd imagined. Her gown glowed with the richness and warmth he wanted for her. The old stone fireplace had always seemed cold until she stood next to it, supplying the fire that no log could.

Eventually, the bell stopped ringing, and the vicar called the company to attention. Standing before the fire, with all his friends and family in attendance, Aidan took Mora's hands in his, and together they repeated the vows of the church in accordance with Malcolm ceremony. As he slid a band of gold and diamonds on Mora's finger, her eyes lit with the love and acceptance he'd thought never to know for himself.

Released from their crate, a flock of doves flew to the old rafters, creating their usual merry havoc among the guests. The musicians struck up an old hymn, the ladies broke into song, and one of the children climbed the rowan tree and overturned it. Mora's laughter rang like crystal chimes when a dove landed on Aidan's shoulder.

Finally, Aidan understood why his brothers were willing to make asses of themselves for their ladies: The ceremony wasn't foolish; it was sacred. His eyes misted when Mora came into his arms, and he held her for all the world to acknowledge that they were man and wife, together for eternity.

The musicians allowed only a moment for Aidan to kiss his bride before they broke into a tempo that sounded more march than dance. Aidan didn't care. Recognizing the excitement and delight lighting his lady's eyes, he took her into his arms, kissed her soundly again to a round of cheers and applause, then swung his new bride through the crowd in the first steps of a reel.

Mora's untamed hair flew with her skirts in the circle he spun her in, and her joyous laughter painted his old walls with pleasure, promising happiness for future generations.

With luck, he could swing her up the steps once the guests were sufficiently occupied, into the bed where they'd create the little lad and lassie, and the future Lucinda had painted for them.

DUNWOODIE MACKENZIE MALCOLM (m. 1600) ERITHEA MALCOLM WYSTAN

(b. 1579)

Alistair Wystan Malcolm (b. 1605)
m. 1625
Brenna Abercrombie

Stella Wystan Malcolm (b. 1610)
m. 1625
Earl of Ives

(four younger siblings)

Morwenna Malcolm (b. 1630)
m. 1655

Gilbert A. Gabriel (b. 1625)

Finella Gabriel (b. 1665)
m. 1680
Aodhagán Macleod

Angus Gabriel (b. 1660)
m. 1680
Unknown Female

Fiona Gabriel (b. 1665)
m. 1681
Mitchell Crichton

Kate Malcolm Macleod (b. 1680)
m. 1700
Ian Dougal

Gilbert Gabriel Sr. (b. 1681)
m. 1700
Unknown Female

Sarah Crichton (b. 1682)
m. 1710
Rob Morrigan

Mairead Dougal (b. 1700)
m. 1719
Edward Henry, 4th Earl of Ives

*Gilbert Gabriel Jr. (b. 1708) m. 1728 + Brighid (b. 1710)
(d. 1737)

Glyniss (b. 1715)
m. 1737
*Gilbert Gabriel Jr.

Aodhagán Dougal (Ives) (b. 1720)

Morwenna Gabriel (b. 1728)

Sarah & Fiona (b. 1742)

Merely Magic: Drogo and Ninian
Must Be Magic: Dunstan and Leila
The Trouble with Magic: Ewen and Felicity

This Magic Moment: Christina and Duke Harry
Much Ado About Magic: Lucinda and Sir Trevelyan
Magic Man: Mora and Aidan

Read on for a sneak peek at
Patricia Rice's
next contemporary romance

Sweet Home Carolina

Coming in February 2007 from
Ballantine Books.

Amy yanked the stuffed mushroom caps from the dead microwave and shoved the pan in the oven with the warming chickens. "Fine, tough toadstools it will be."

"Tough toadstools is the story of our life," Amy's sister Joella, half owner of the Stardust, said philosophically, tying on her *Star of the Stardust Café* apron over her flashy red hostess gown. "You'd think someday one of those toadstools would have a fairy and a pot of gold under it."

As tall, blond, and gorgeous as Amy was petite, dark, and striking, Joella studied the pots and pans simmering on the stove, and clucked in disapproval. "No wonder you're frying appliances. You're working on overdrive again. I know it's Saturday, but how many customers do you realistically think we'll have?"

Amy slammed a lid on the pot of creamed peas. "Not as many as you need to make a profit. Even I can see the writing on the wall."

Jo tsked sympathetically. "Evan didn't send the support payments yet?"

"Evan deserted the kids again this weekend. I hate being a cliché." Amy reached for an onion and whacked it with her butcher knife. Onions used to give her an excuse for tears, but she was beyond crying now. She just wanted to whack things.

Amy had always been the responsible member o
their irresponsible family. The sensible one who'
slaved to earn a scholarship and worked herself ha
to death putting herself through school. She'd felt re
warded for her efforts when she married an amazin
man who worked as hard as she did—and she worke
harder still helping him up the ladder to success. Fa
lot of good that had done. He'd left her for another
more *glamorous* woman who could aid his career eve
more. She slammed a lid on the steamer of broccoli

Jo filled glasses from her flask and shoved one int
Amy's hand, hiding it from their customers. "Unti
Flint persuades the town to go wet, this will have t
do. It's just lemonade with a little extra," she sai
when Amy hesitated. "Call it an intervention. Yo
need a break. Your pot is about to boil over."

Grabbing the pot of peas from the stove, Amy se
it to one side, then sipped Jo's weird cocktail. She wa
perfectly aware that Jo wasn't referring exclusively t
the peas.

"If we could get the mill back in production b
Christmas, there would be reason for caroling," Am
declared fervently, returning to the original subject. A
real job would solve half her problems, although sh
figured it wouldn't save her house unless she was of
fered a bonus up front just for existing—when and i
the town acquired the mill.

Her one prayer of staying here, where she grew up
rode on the town's acquiring the mill property. No
only could running the mill provide her with a decen
job, but part of its assets included a vacant, run-dow
Craftsman cottage that had once housed the mill'
managers. She had high hopes of persuading the com
mittee to sell her the cottage for a price she coul
afford.

The house wouldn't do her any good without a job. She couldn't restore a single floor tile without money. Besides, she couldn't *fix* anything, she reminded herself, to prevent riding too high into la-la land.

"Tourist business is dead after this weekend." Amy slid the browned mushrooms from the oven and tried not to think of the stack of bills at home on her desk. "If we don't get year-round employment soon, this whole town will shut down."

"Yeah, we're worried, too." Flint, Joella's husband and the other owner of the café, leaned against the counter. "We can pay you to stay on, but we may have to go back to being a coffee shop instead of a restaurant."

"Only if you want to hand out free soup," Amy predicted gloomily.

Flint grabbed a hot mushroom. Throwing it from hand to hand, he retreated toward his office. "We'll do what we have to do," he called over his shoulder before he disappeared back into his world.

Amy whacked a bell pepper.

"If you don't watch out, you're going to cut off a finger." Jo grabbed the knife and nudged Amy back to the stove with her hip. "Is this about losing the house?"

Flipping off a burner, Amy lifted the heavy frying pan and poured the gravy into a waiting gravy boat. "I can't look for a new house until I know where I'll be working."

"You're working here," Jo said firmly. "We can't replace you."

Amy slammed the pan back on the burner, put her hands on her hips, and glared at her younger—taller—sister. "That's what I'm trying to tell you. You cannot pay me on what this restaurant is making. I'm giving away meals instead of earning tips, not that anyone here believes in tipping. *I'm* facing facts. You and Flint are the ones with your heads in the clouds."

As if on cue, the cordless phone Flint had installed by the counter rang. Amy snatched the receiver before Jo could. "Stardust."

"Amy, this is Mayor Blodgett."

Amy took another swig of Jo's spiked lemonade to calm her suddenly shaky nerves. "Is there a problem?"

"That depends on how you look at it." The mayor enunciated slowly. "Another interested party has asked to look at the mill. As I understand it, the company is European and cash-heavy. It could be just the investment we're hoping for."

"A foreign company won't want to hire our workers," Amy warned the mayor, wishing she could reach through the phone and throttle some sense into him. "The whole point of our buying the mill is to keep Northfork residents employed."

"You don't think they'd bring in illegal immigrants, do you?" Bill asked in alarm.

Amy rolled her eyes, handed the receiver to Jo, and opened the bottom oven to check the rolls. If she were Queen of the World, men would be relegated to hard labor. They were obviously not meant to think. Parallel parking, maybe—they could do that. Make them chauffeurs. Hole diggers. Bricklayers. But not politicians responsible for the lives and welfare of entire communities.

While Jo chitchatted and applied her charm to the mayor, Amy removed the rolls and began buttering their tops. She glanced at the clock, remembered it wasn't working, and checked the mullioned windows to see if the sunlight had faded. After the first of September, the sun dipped behind the mountain around five. It should be almost time for the early dinner arrivals.

While she watched, a sexy yellow sports car rolled to a stop, parking half on the sidewalk in front of the café. The narrow mountain highway barely had room for sidewalks. The low-slung front end halted inches from the snout of Myrtle, the concrete purple pig. Blocking pedestrian traffic obviously meant nothing to the wealthy owner. The shiny hood with its space-age angles would end up as tinsel if a semi came around the curve going too fast.

No one in town owned a car like that. Had ever *seen* a car like that. Which meant it was European. After the mayor's call, Amy had a very, very bad feeling about that car.

She turned from the window and tossed back the cup of spiked lemonade, superstitiously deciding if she didn't look, the car might go away.

Jo hung up and turned to see what had Amy tossing back alcohol. "Oh, my. That's a *Lamborghini*," she said with a reverence reserved for gods and teachers.

"That will soon be a flattened Lamborghini," Amy replied. The liquor gave her just enough buzz to feel in control. Maybe she ought to drink more often.

Jo's exclamation and the low rumble of another powerful vehicle forced her to glance out the window again. A shiny black Hummer sporting satellite antennas drew up behind the sports car. They could play bumper cars when the next semi came around the bend, Amy mused. How far would a Lamborghini travel after being slammed into by a Hummer propelled by a semi?

Deciding bad news could wait, she checked the simmering pots on the stove and missed seeing how the Lamborghini owner squeezed out of the front seat into traffic. Jo's chuckles as she exchanged observations with the locals sipping coffee at the counter were sufficient commentary for amusement.

The café's red door swung open. Amy unconsciously waited for a biting *What a dump!* from the owner of a car that cost more than the entire town.

"Catarina, look!" a smoky baritone with an accent Amy couldn't quite place called to someone outside. "Did you see the pig?"

She couldn't resist. Like everyone else, she checked out the new arrivals.

The speaker was a lean, elegantly dressed gentleman propping open the door to let in an entourage of characters as strange and out of place as their vehicles.

"My, isn't he the prettiest thing?" Jo whispered admiringly.

At that instant, the object of their fascination whipped off his designer shades and winked in their direction. Amy felt every cell in her body light up like one of the appliances she'd exploded. The elegant stranger really *looked* at her, igniting her hormones like neglected hand grenades.

The longer she stared, the more his eyes appeared to deepen, revealing hidden depths behind the flash and charm, like a one-way mirror hiding the real man. No wonder he wore sunglasses.

He was more than pretty. She could swear he'd just walked off the pages of a fashion ad, one of those where the male models had six-pack abs and deliberately mussed hairstyles that cost a fortune to achieve. Straight-cut brown hair brushed his nape and fell Hugh Grant–style across his wide brow. A black ribbed polo shirt was pulled taut over his admirable chest, and the camel sports jacket topping it was probably Armani, and was tailored to emphasize his square shoulders and lean hips.

She'd be panting shortly. Better to fasten on the

decisive set of chiseled lips and a jaw that was firm and more than a little stubborn despite his easygoing smile. And behind the twinkle of his eyes was a polished steel that spoke of power and the ability to wield it.

The likes of Hugh Grant didn't appear around here without reason, and after the mayor's call, she had a sinking feeling that she knew the reason.

"Are we too early for dinner, *ma petite*?" the stranger asked in a seductive accent that was as rich and as elegant as the man who spoke it—and just a shade phony.

Good. Suspicion was good. If he was the competition who'd come to outbid her on the mill, she would rather despise than admire him.

It took Jo's elbow in her ribs before Amy realized the stranger was talking to her and not to her beautiful, blond baby sister.

"Dinner's on," she agreed with assumed nonchalance. "Take seats anywhere."

The gentleman sauntered—Amy swore that was the only word that could describe the way he caught his hand in his pocket and gracefully dodged tables and chairs without looking at them—to the counter.

"Would you like coffee, tea?" Amy lifted the coffee carafe.

"Tea, if you would be so kind." He smiled in delight, and his eyes crinkled in the corners. He looked at Amy with a thousand-watt smile and extended his hand. "Hello, I am Jean-Jacques Aristide Saint Etienne, and I have come to look at your antique mill."

All your favorite romance writers are
coming together.

SIGNET ECLIPSE

Whispers of the Night
by Lydia Joyce
0-451-21897-3

New York Times Bestselling Author
Jo Beverley

THE ROGUE'S RETURN	0-451-21788-8
A MOST UNSUITABLE MAN	0-451-21423-4
THREE HEROES	0-451-21200-2
IRRESISTIBLE FORCES	0-451-21724-1
SKYLARK	0-451-21183-9
WINTER FIRE	0-451-21065-4
SECRETS OF THE NIGHT	0-451-21158-8
DARK CHAMPION	0-451-20766-1
ST. RAVEN	0-451-20807-2
LORD OF MY HEART	0-451-20642-8
MY LADY NOTORIOUS	0-451-20644-4
HAZARD	0-451-20580-4
THE DEVIL'S HEIRESS	0-451-20254-6
THE DRAGON'S BRIDE	0-451-20358-5
DEVILISH	0-451-19997-9
SOMETHING WICKED	0-451-21378-5
LORD OF MIDNIGHT	0-451-40801-2
FORBIDDEN MAGIC	0-451-40802-0

Available wherever books are sold or at penguin.com

All your favorite romance writers are
coming together.

SIGNET ECLIPSE